i

LONG WALK TO
CHERRY GARDENS

ANDRENE BONNER

New York

i

Published by

Sisal Publishing
www.sisalpublishing.com

Publisher's Disclaimer

Long Walk to Gardens is a work of fiction. Names, characters, places, business establishments, organizations, and incidents are the product of the author's imagination or are used fictitiously. The author's use of names of actual persons, places, and characters are incidental to the plot, and are not intended to change the entirely fictional character of the work.

Long Walk to Cherry Gardens: a novel/Andrene Bonner/Publication

Cover Design by Mirjana Krasojevic
Author's Photograph by Yvonne Taylor [From Author's Personal Archives]
Series Book Developer: Faith P. Nelson, Watercourse LLC

978-1-7363635-1-5

The use of Claude McKay's *If We Must Die* is now permissible in the public domain.

Printed in the United States of America
Set in Garamond Font

Copying Legal Notice

Also By
Andrene Bonner

No Life In Olympic Gardens

Teaching Guide: No Life In Olympic Gardens

Stories to Heal Your Life So You Can Help Your Child
Succeed

Stories to Heal Your Life So You Can Help Your Child
Succeed Workbook
Daily Affirmations and Exercises for Self-Care

I Got This
Affirmation for Teens to Relieve Stress and Create an
Awesome School Year

Room One Eighty
The Forgotten Students of Outerbrook High
A Play in Two Acts

The Dolphy Code
A Pastor's Legacy

For All Children

Literacy is a human right.

Advanced Praise for
Long Walk to Cherry Gardens

Masterfully written. Through her words and his eyes I see every young windshield wiper at a stoplight in Jamaica and every lost boy throughout time; but I also see every triumph of marginalized youth who push through to rise above their circumstances.

Judith Falloon-Reid
Author, Filmmaker & Host of Shelf Life

Bonner skillfully takes us on a roller coaster ride where the reader experiences the highest emotional highs and deepest emotional depths and back up again. One minute you are elated by the strength and determination of an abused and victimized child to dream big despite life's most debilitating circumstances. Next, hopes are dashed and dreams snuffed out when hit with the excruciating pain of child abuse by an evil aunt and the horrors of life on the streets – a life which no child should ever be allowed to experience...This book is sure to lift your spirit.

Dr. Judith A. Duncker Ph.D.

The Griot/The Storyteller tradition in the west is a very important African retention for many of us who embrace our Afro-centricity and Andrene Bonner keeps this in the forefront of our minds. Thanks Andrene. The transformation of a community from "middle-class" to "inner-city, ghetto, poverty," call it what you will, allows the Griot to remind us of our Ancestors' greatness and determination. The author's characters do that through her ease with the gift of the "tale well told." A trained dramatist herself and an avowed "Miss Lou" (Louise Bennett-Coverley) pickni, the art of storytelling lives on in Andrene Bonner. It may be "A Long Walk To Cherry Gardens," however, let this author get you there in fine Jamaican literary style. One Love.

Steve Golding, Musician

As a raconteur, author Andrene Bonner is sound, her multilayered message oozes with subliminal resonance that is markedly detailed and rich in imagery. The sociological underbelly of her work surfaces at every turn. In fact, the tale of Roderick is told against the wanton abuse of Rastafari. Bonner captures the existential severity of Roderick's condition without surrendering his innocence and joie de vivre. We can only anticipate a denouement befitting this astute and indomitable lad. No doubt, 'Long Walk to Cherry Gardens' brims with sheer inspiration and proves a monumental triumph for Bonner.

Dr. Glenville Ashby, Ph.D.

v

Contents

The Fire And The Flood

Some children will lose their way.

Roderick's first ritual bath was in a Yabba pot of secrets that scalded his very soul. He never understood the sudden change, and no one gave him a straight answer. A lanky, brown-skinned, sandy-haired, light eyed boy, he wore pale threadbare clothes. His high-water pants rode above his ankles, told how much taller he had grown. Slit crepe sole uppers made room for his growing feet.

Roderick squeezed his ears against the sweat-drenched seats, snuggled up to Ellen and listened to her Kingston accent whisper to Lillian amidst the chatter of holiday shoppers on a crowded Number 8 bus.

"He's a good boy, Lillian. Roderick deserves better treatment than what he's getting now. He should be in school already."

The muscles on the side of his mouth crunched. He blinked his eyes rapidly as a smile formed on his face. *I am a good boy.* His smile got wider and revealed his white teeth. Then he quickly covered his mouth with both palms. *She right. A should in school long, long time so a can learn to read better. A want to get good, good, good with mi stone art so a can make plenty money and help meself.*

"What you suggest we do, Ellen?"

"Exactly what we are doing; give him a good time as often as we can."

At the thought, Roderick tapped Lillian three times on her soft spongy arm in knock-knock fashion, "Scuse me, Aunty. A can say something to you?"

"Sure."

"A can't wait to show Aunt Hope mi new clothes and gift them that you and Miss Ellen buy for me." He pulled his cheeks and made a big turned up smiley face. "She going be happy. Aunt Hope know a did really need some good clothes and shoes, don't it Aunt Lillian?"

"Yes, Roderick. She knows you need good clothes and shoes. You have outgrown what you are wearing. I am sure she will be happy for you."

"Mi glad Christmus time come at last. The year did long and it look like the holiday would never reach."

"For many folks, 1968 seems that way but it is still a good year. It just needs some more joy in it."

"When mi tell Aunty you and Grandma Tata want me to come spend Christmus and New Year till school start, you think she really going to let me come?"

"Definitely. You will get a break from the shop and she won't have to worry about you for a little while."

"O Aunt Lillian. A feel so glad. A will get to spend some time with Grandma Tata, La la."

"Tata is longing to see you. I told her you are coming and she couldn't stop laughing. She loves you very much."

"That nice. Me love her plenty."

Please let Aunty send me. Please.

The bus pulled into the Three Miles terminal, where it sat for a while. Folks came on and off the bus in near equal numbers. It was hot except for a cross current of cool air that flowed through half-open windows. A gentleman with a briefcase unbuttoned his shirt, held the collar and placket, and flapped it robustly up and in, cooling off. The evening newspaper boy hopped on the bus, peddled the day's happenings, and told funny stories. Roderick smiled. A woman selling grater cakes and toffees fussed with a passenger who accused her of charging too much during the holidays.

"You see that Aunty?"

"Shhhh," Lillian put her finger on Roderick's lips.

"Stop her. Stop!" an elderly woman yelled out to the bus driver as a girl in a mushroom hat and sunglasses grabbed another woman's purse while she paid for her toffee. The girl bored her way swiftly through the passengers.

"Who…stop who?" The driver stood up and looked in the cabin's direction.

"The girl in the hat."

By now, other passengers secured their bags. Loud chatter filled the cabin. The girl threw the handbag to a boy who was standing in the stairwell, holding the door open.

"Is two of them," a man hollered, wearing thick lens glasses. He rolled his newspaper into a ball and tossed it at the girl. Folks tumbled on top of each other, cursing and shoving. The bus driver had to choose between squishing the girl caught between the power doors, one foot in and one foot out. Instead, he pulled the lever, released her and she ran. Roderick's ears perked up as some passengers quarreled with the driver and blamed him for not moving swiftly enough. Others talked about the lawlessness of these young hooligans.

"You have to look out for these pickpockets on crowded buses, especially during the holidays."

"That not right, Aunty. That not right." Roderick got up from his seat so Ellen could get off the bus. "Bye Miss Ellen. Be careful."

"Bye Roderick." She patted him on the head. "See you soon."

"She nice eee, Aunty."

"Yes, she is very nice. Ellen is my best friend since primary school."

"Where she live?"

"A long way from here. She is going to transfer to the Number 7 bus so she can get another bus to go to Cherry Gardens."

"That sound far."

"Far enough. Her car is at the mechanic's shop or we wouldn't have to take the bus. My friend Ellen would not miss spending time with us today. But I am sure one day you will visit her or she will come and visit you."

"That would nice me, Aunty. Me like her. Look how much things she buy for me."

Lillian nodded her head and pinched his cheek. "You tired? It was a long day."

"A tired little bit."

"We have quite a few more stops before we reach to your house."

Roderick heard the roaring engine of the bus as it rolled along over the newly asphalted street. He could smell the sharpness of the tar. Now and then, the tires made a slight bump along the roadway, forcing him to stay awake. His eyes wandered in swift motion as the houses and cars seem to move away from view like wisps of dried sugarcane in the brisk autumn breeze. Trees changed to black while the blue sky peeped in sporadic clumps. The sun was setting. Roderick rested his left elbow on his knee, cupped his face and smiled. *Kiss mi neck. Outside here look like one a aunty pretty dress eee!*

Every stop the bus made, it became emptier closer to home. Just before the bus got to his stop, Roderick stretched his neck and he could see over the heads of the few people left on the bus. Some slept, mouths open, sweat rolled down their faces. Others read the evening news or tended to children. *Is not me one look tired, them look tired, too.* He steadied himself as the bus came to a full stop. Jumping off the bus, his parcels in hand, he skipped ahead of Lillian, singing,

> Gran Market O,
> Gran Market O,
> Christmas mawnin
> A coming O o o.
> Gran Market O

"Eh Em!" Lillian cleared her throat. It was her signal for him to slow down and keep pace with her.

Two bright eyes shone in the stillness of the shadows among the dandelion bush that grew along the sidewalk. As the pair got closer to the apparition, the eyes moved forward and a lonely black cat, heavy with kittens in her stomach, lumbered across their path.

"Mama say if a black cat cross in front of you it bring bad luck you know Aunty."

"That's an old saying. It is not true."

A knot formed and pressed deep in his stomach; he felt a cool breeze tickle his face. *Bad luck tonight. What Aunty a talk bout 'old saying'.*

Moments later, Aunt Hope emerged from the darkness. To Roderick, she looked tired, glowered intently as if she lost something precious. Roderick's heart thumped and raced, threading the moments like wild, bitter lemon herb. *When Aunt Hope put her hand on her hip them, wide out her eye them, and frill up her nose like donkey a bray, she in a rotten mood. She bound to rough me up bad, bad, cause me come home when it dark.* He felt deep down that it was time to take it easy. Leave the blame on Aunt Lillian and Miss Ellen. After all, they kept him late at Grand Market. *Maybe she will feel a little better and don't cuff me.*

Roderick imbibed his line of reason, shuffled the tingling bottom of his feet in his new white crepe soles Aunt Lillian bought him earlier that day. He pouted his lips, took three deep breaths just like old man Suraj taught him,

"Heeuuuuu, heeuuuu, in-and-out, in-and-out, in-and out," slowing his heart."

He watched as Lillian approached Hope and listened closely to their conversation. His stomach thumped as if his heart drifted there.

Why mi heart beating so hard? Mi foot them want to drop off. Why Aunty out here in the dark?

"See a bring back the young man safely, Hopie. We had a great time at Grand Market."

"What a way him load up with things, Lillian."

"We had fun today, didn't we, Roderick?"

"Yes Aunty."

Roderick relaxed his soft face, but could see the serious face on Hope staring at him through the shadows. He cozied up to Lillian every move as she walked through the gate. Roderick and Lillian followed behind.

"Let Roderick stay with me until New Year's so he can get some rest before school starts next month. Mama Tata says to bring him."

"This is the best time of the year and I will need the boy to keep my shop door opened and food on my table for me and my children."

"Roderick needs to go to school like your children; the poor child has been working in the shop since he got here. No schooling. Him tired, Hopie."

"Don't bring my children into this at all."

"Right is right, Hopie."

Roderick saw this as his signal to pull himself from Lillian's embrace and walk away.

That look on Aunt Hope face not good. She upset. A better leave.

"Scuse me, please," he whispered, shook his head, stepped away, and crouched behind the door.

"Why it so hard for Aunt Hope to give me a break for the holiday?"

Listening to the two women argue about him, Roderick understood how hard it was for Aunt Hope to take care of her two sons, Stephen and Nelton, on the money she made from her grocery and knick-knack shop. Now he was a recent addition, and it made her fuss a lot.

A wonder why Aunty make sure Stephen and Nelton go a school every day but won't make me go. She always say she want my cousin them to 'get a good work with the government.' So what happen to me?

The cussing got louder and louder. Roderick curled in his toes so his aunts would not see his feet and know he was there listening.

"No wonder our darling mother, Tata, says every Monday morning you wake up from some strange bed with a new baby in your belly. She warned you, life would be tough, Hopie."

"Go on with your tough belly."

"What wrong with Aunty belly?" Roderick couldn't believe what he heard. He put two and two together and figured something went wrong. That's why his Aunt Hope had not taken him or his cousins to see Tata. Hope took her mother's words to heart.

Must be why she stay to herself. She believes that if she wants things done right; she have to do it herself.

Yet, a little help was more than welcome and Roderick fit perfectly into the plan and her "good-for-nothing sister," that's what she called Lillian would not derail her life like the Kendal Railroad Crash.

"You was always miss rightie-rightie. The boy head tough, him can't learn a thing. School is not for everybody. You know how long it took him to figure out how to write up the grocery list for me to take to the market?"

"But that's not his job. Why you can't do that or make one of your boys do that for you? They have more schooling."

"A say to leave my children out of this. If him was so bright, what make him mother send him come give me?"

Yes, why mi mother send me come live with her. Mi would love to know.

"You are asking a lot of questions. Our dear sister Mara'Belle has her reason. Heaven knows what it is, but Roderick deserves better than this."

"How you mean, this?"

Hope flung her hands in the air and stomped her feet on the concrete. Lillian waved her hands in front of Hope's face. Roderick shuddered at their anger and sat on his parcel to peep around the corner. *Them a go fight! La la.*

Hope said, "Him have a place to sleep and food to eat—"

"And plenty dirty clothes to wash, starch and iron for your lazy boys."

"A say to leave mi children out of this."

"You can make them do something around here, you know. Just look at how they keep their room messy. You spoil them."

Roderick felt Lillian was really on his side. After all, he did not have the guts to chide with Aunt Hope, although he knew deep down in his heart that she did not treat him well.

"You know what, you are taking this too far now. Get out of my place, Lillian Holy Righteous Flowers."

Lillian dropped her packages on the ground. She pointed to Hope's face and pressed her finger below her nose.

"No, you can't dismiss me. I leave when I am good and ready. You will listen to me. I am taking this to Canon if you don't straighten up your act. The boy needs to go to school and he should at least be sleeping in better quarters than the old moldy storage room in the back. Why him couldn't sleep in the boys' room?"

"None of your business." Hope turned to walk away and Lillian grabbed Hope's apron.

"O yes, it is my business. He is my nephew, too. He deserves every opportunity to succeed in life. What the one Mara'Belle have a burn her in her chest is no excuse for you to add to it. Is like putting salt into old wounds. We have Roderick now and so we need to care for him."

"We, which we you talking bout?"

"We—me and you. The whole neighborhood, for that matter. He is our responsibility; he is in our care, Hopie."

"Nay … ba … hood! Me don't mix-up-mix-up with people around here. I offer a service with this shop and that's that. No naybahood not into my business."

Lillian picked up her package and hissed her teeth. "You are so ungrateful. Look how Mr. Goodman and Chloe make the boy feel welcome. They have been helping him to read so that he can write your stupid grocery list."

"Oh, so Goodman gets the praise for this now?"

"Yes. If it was for you that boy would see him name on a bulla cake and don't even know it because he can't read. You are pitiful, Hopie, and heaven balk at your attitude."

"I have heard enough of your cuss-cuss tonight. The boy wouldn't last a day chasing fowl and sweeping your dirty yard in Waterhouse. His life is right here in this shop."

"Don't make fun. Waterhouse has been good to you and all of us. That is where we learned to be somebody. Obviously, you learned nothing. You are just bitter because the little good part of your heart washed away down Sandy Gully Bridge."

Heart wash away down a bridge. What she mean by?

"Leave that alone and get out nowwwwwww!" she screamed, and pointed her to the door.

Lillian turned around to leave. "You are a very selfish woman. Your children will suffer for this."

"Get out I say!"

"I will leave, but remember, Tata always say, 'hog ask him mother how him mouth so long and mother hog replied: by and by you will know.' It's the same lesson for you, Hopie. By and by you will understand when life hits you real hard in your gut." Lillian hissed between clenched teeth.

"Don't put no curse on my children," Hope shrieked, pounded the wooden gate with her fist. She pushed Lillian against the wall.

Lillian grabbed the gate to break her fall. She raised her fist to clobber Hope. Her left foot lifted off the ground, she swung at her sister and lost her balance. "You evil woman, you." As she steadied herself, she stumbled right into Roderick, who sat curled up in the corner. Lillian bent over and wiped the sweat from his brow. She sighed really loud and bit down on her bottom lip.

Aunt Lillian lost the fight tonight. Roderick looked up at Lillian, who reached out her hand to him and pulled him gently to his feet. Roderick felt that this big quarrel between his two aunts was his fault.

If me didn't come a town come live, them would happy with them one another for it sound to me like them grow up good.

"You were hearing all of this?"

"Yes, Aunty." His face was wet with sweat and tears.

"I am going to make it better for you, but I will need some time." She wiped his face with the end of his shirt.

"You can't even take care of your damn self." Hope swished her skirt in disgust and went into the living room.

Roderick gazed into Lillian's eyes, held onto her arm. "Please take me. Don't leave me. Please Aunty. Mi don't want to live like this."

"Give me some time, Roderick. Here. Take this. It is your present from your Grandma Tata. She wanted to give it to you herself tomorrow, on Christmas day. I may as well give it to you now. I guess you won't be coming to see Tata for Christmas." Lillian hugged him close to her heart and whispered, "Merry Christmas," and pulled away.

You mean to tell me when Aunt Lillian was buying this present today, is Tata ask her to buy it for me? La la. "Aunty. Please tell Grandma Tata thanks for the present. Tell her a love her. Tell her a see her soon." He cried from the bottom of his belly, squeezed out quick breaths through snorty nostrils. "Christmus, Auntyyyyyyyy ye ye ye ye ye ye." His hands reached for her, tears flooded his face like a broken levee and clouded any signs of hope. Roderick could feel his blue-green watering and the lids swelling, yet he could see that his sadness touched Lillian's heart.

"It is a lot of responsibility to care for a growing boy like you, Roderick." Lillian made a swift about turn and closed the gate to a dull foreboding echo. She stepped out into the dark night towards the bus stop.

Roderick picked up his two oversized bags of gifts, dragged his feet to his damp and dismal quarters, put his bags on the old trunk. He made a backstroke dive on his cot and looked up at the ceiling; it was as if goblins danced between the cavernous wrinkles in the tiles, grimacing at his thoughts.

One day, a will know why me mother send me away. One day, a will find mi father. One day mama will take me back so me can play a bush with mi brodda and sista them. He sighed, leaped onto his feet, opened one bag, pulled out his school uniform and tried it on. Roderick ran his hands up and down the leg of his pants, gently pinched the woven fabric along the waist, and shoved his hands in his pockets. He tilted his head to the side in a photo pose, opened his arms like propeller blades on a windmill, spun around and laughed.

"I am going to school next month. Me not no shop boy."

2

Gifts and Barefoot

Christmas morning.

Roderick woke up before the rooster sounded his first alarm. He planned his early morning chores. Then he dragged his feet to the standpipe in the backyard, washed his face, cupped his palms and filled them with water. After that, he poured the water in his mouth, swished it around, gargled and spat it out. On tiptoes, he approached the chicken coop. Six hens were fast asleep on the lower level. Scoping them out for the fattest, he reached in and grabbed one under its warm wings, pulled her out and closed the door. This startled the others, who flapped around in protest. Roderick tied the hen's left leg with a string and wrapped the other end of the string to a post on the coop.

"Now you just stay right there so a get the other one. Aunty going cook you for her Christmus dinner."

So far, he caught only one. The sun was creeping slowly over the horizon and he could see much clearer. The hens were restless.

"How me going to get the other one eee?" Roderick built his courage and took a stick to separate one hen, but the others began picking at his arm.

"Stop it! Is one of you this morning, not me."
After much pushing, shoving and blowing away dried poop and feathers from his face, he captured another hen and tied her to another post. Then he helped himself to nearly a dozen warm brown freckled eggs, which he placed in an enamel basin. He went back into the house, placed the eggs on the

kitchen table. On his way to his quarters, he heard Aunt Hope offering her morning prayers. She spoke real loud in unknown tongues.

Is who trouble her this bright Christmus mawnin eee?
Roderick returned to his quarters and took an inventory of his gifts, again. It made his eyes water. He could not get the quarrel between his two aunts out of his head. "This is no way to celebrate the holidays," Roderick said, with his palms against his cheeks. After all, it was Christmas morning, and he thought of nothing more than to give his friend, Chloe, the Viewmaster he bought for her. She could enjoy reels of slide shows of faraway places and exotic animals. Roderick imagined the tricky twinkle in the eyes of his old friend Suraj when he hands him the sombrero he got for him. "This is my Christmus," he blurted, not mindful if anyone was listening. Roderick knew that amid the cuss-cuss, he would have to create his own reality of a fun holiday. Although there was a feeling of sadness about the way Lillian parted company with him, touching the gifts made him feel alive as he sang and danced a little jig:

> So much shirt, and khaki too
> Red suspender, cardigan, roun toe shoes,
> Socks, sandals, wash rags, towels
> colonie water, underarm rub rub,
> toothbrush, cap, pen and pencil
> La la la la so much things.

Flinging them in the air, catching them, smelling his leather sandals, rubbing the furry sweater against his cheeks, he closed his eyes and breathed deeply. Roderick reached for his khaki school shirt and held it up to his chest, and then he spread it out on the bed and used his hand like an iron to smooth out the creases. Slowly, he strung the leather cowboy belt through the loops of his new trousers.

"O Aunt Lillian, you mean a going to school for real?" Roderick dived on the cot and was rolling around in his pile of clothes when his Aunt Hope barged into his quarters.

"Is which school you think you going with them khaki clothes? Make a see the big ole bag of things Lillian and them get you. You never plan to show me what you get?"

"Yes, Aunty."

"Lay them out better on the bed." Hope inspected the gifts.

"But this shirt is not too big for you?"

"Aunt Lillian say a can grow into it."

"Nelton would look really nice in it." She put it aside and opened the box with his skillfully crafted leather sandals.

"Nice sandals."

"A know, Aunty." His broad smile filled the room.

"My sister Lillian did always have good taste."

"Is not she buy it for me. Is Aunt Ellen."

"Aunt Ellen noh. She not your aunt." She rolled her eyes at him. "Stephen did always want a good pair of sandals. It looks a little small for him but I will make him try it on when him wake up."

Dread rose from the bottom of Roderick's stomach. "You going to give away mi sandals, Aunty?"

"After you don't know how to wear nothing good like this. You have to share around here. Your mother never drop you off with nothing good."

Roderick felt an electric current ricochet through the side of his head. It became numb. He could not imagine in his wildest dreams that his aunt would give away his clothes to her horrible boys, especially since he had been wearing hand-me-downs for two years.

Why Aunt Lillian never just keep them at her house for me?

When Aunt Hope was through sharing up his gifts, she left him a cardigan, a shirt, a pair of pants, the little red Viewmaster and the hat.

Roderick yelled. "You lef me barefoot. Me want mi shoes. Give me mi shoes back!"

"You are a selfish boy. Who you talking to like that, anyway? How come you want so much things and my boy them mustn't get nothing?"

"But is my things—"

The words hardly left his mouth. Hope slapped him across his face with a flourish; once to the left cheek with her palm and a rapid return to the other cheek with the back of her hand.

Roderick's head rocked left and right faster than a chicken spotted a mongoose. "Lawd God Almity!" Roderick threw himself on the floor and stretched out in a cold sweat. "Help, Help, Help! Yuh beat me for mi own a things!"

"Stop di cow bawling in the place. You live here for free. Stop going on like somebody for you just dead."

Roderick could hear Nelton and Stephen as they scurried down the hall to see what was going on. Nelton snapped his fingers in rapid succession, mimicking lashes to great delight.

"Eee hih now, Spanish town, yuh madda going to beat yu wid di doodu stick."

"Shut up and move from here, Nelton," his brother
Stephen chided. He covered his ears and turned to his mom.

"All right now Mama. Enough of that now!"

"Roderick, you see how you call down crowd on me.
If you keep this up, your head is going to roll inside here!"

"Mama!" Stephen insisted.

Roderick screamed, "You is a wicked woman. You
wicked!" His eyes burned like pepper burst in them, sweat
rolled down his face and arms like he had just emerged from
a baptism in the river. He breathed heavily and his heart sped
as he tossed himself from one end of his quarters to the other
like he caught the fit.

"So you are in a temper now. You see my dying
trial."

The more Hope chided, the more Roderick heaved
and stomped.

"Get out of my sight, you ungrateful creature," she
said, picked up a whistle and turned to leave.

Still shaken, Roderick could see through the miasma
of nose, snort and tears, Hope's face distorted by scorn. One
side of her face looked like a donkey and the other like a
wretched duppy. For a moment, this haunting specter was
real. Aunt Hope had transformed into a vile animal. Roderick
had come face to face with a brute. Undaunted, he stared
down at the ghoul and, in his mind, declared,

Mi not your boy to beat like mule. "Look how Aunt
Lillian and Miss Ellen treat me nice yesterday, eee. Like
everything just dark in here all of a sudden with this miserable
woman." He got up slowly and sat on the edge of his cot, his
body hurt. "Perhaps Aunt Hope was not a real person."

Yesterday, while Roderick, Lillian and Ellen took a rest from shopping on King Street, the women ate sugar cane and talked. Roderick tried to make sense of a conversation the women had as they competed with tooting car horns, chiming bicycle bells and pedestrians bustling to catch the last hours of Grand Market bargains.

"No wonder she sent Felix away to Portland. Imagine, Ellen, he is her firstborn. She dash away the boy like old clothes." Lillian peeled the thick stalk of sugar cane with her teeth, sucked on the sweet juice.

"But she was only fifteen, Lills."

"It doesn't matter. Tata loved that boy and wanted to keep him so Hopie could go to commercial school to learn shorthand, typewriting, and better herself. She could have gotten a job as a court reporter right across the street from where are we sitting at Supreme Court. Big job. But she sent him away, telling nobody and before you know it, she had a big belly again for the Justice of the Peace for the area."

"But the Justice of the Peace is married with children."

"Yes. But whatever Hopie wants, she gets."

"You sure is whatever Hopie wants? She was only fifteen, and he was a big man to her."

Roderick was a little puzzled at what he was hearing. Aunt Hope never talked about Felix and he never saw the Justice of the Peace man come to the shop. *Why she didn't want to go to school to make her life better? It looked like she never liked school.*

"That girl treats poor Felix like he was something she picked up off the rubbish heap."

"Lillian, I keep telling you, Hope was so young."

"Drop that young thing. That has nothing to do with
it. She claimed is John's child, but she passed him off on
Kentish. Hopie never knew who the father was."

"You serious!" Ellen quickly covered Lillian's mouth
with one hand to remind her of Roderick's presence.

"Chuuuuups." Lillian hissed through her teeth,
brushed away Ellen's hand from her face. "Don't cover my
mouth. Look here, Roderick is a big boy. Him can hear for
me don't care. Don't worry. See God give her two more boys
she treats like baby powder puff."

"O yes. And that out-of-order one, Nelton," Ellen
added, "is going to be the death of her. He has no manners."

Roderick shook his head to get rid of the chatting in
his mind and raised his right arm to wipe the sweat from his
brow. He looked at the remaining clothes scattered on the
bed and sighed. Reaching out to fold them, he gasped at the
sight of a blue-red welt rising on the soft flesh at the crease of
his elbow. The flogging had left his body broken and in pain.
Wincing, he closed his eyes as if to shut out the memory of
the women's conversation taking up space in his head and
Aunt Hope's cruelty. Staying in his quarters afforded him
some quiet time with new thoughts. Food was not enticing.
When he gathered a modicum of strength, Roderick wrapped
the gifts he bought for his friends: a viewmaster for Chloe
and the sombrero for Maas Suraj. Every fold of the gift paper
pinched a little spot in his heart. He couldn't tell if he was
happy or sad. All he knew was that it felt strange and fun at
the same time.

Today, memories of Christmas in rural St. Ann of his
early childhood were nothing like the one he was
experiencing now. He wiped the sweat from his nose.

"How mi going to look in Suraj and Chloe face? Mi feel so shame. Mi whole body like somebody knead me like flour dumpling. Lawd God."

Walking down the corridor, he heard Stephen playing Christmas carols on his record changer, while Nelton added his discordant notes on his metal toy drum. Roderick's groin felt weak, as if to conspire against his already wobbly knees. Every step stung the soles of his sweaty feet and his insteps, like suction cups, tried to keep traction on the concrete floor. Looking through the kitchen window, he saw the Christmas pepper-lights flickering in Chloe's front room window.

"Red on—yellow on—green on, all a dem on," he played with the blinking lights repeatedly until his happiness rose above his pain. "A better get to work in the shop. It soon start full up with people." He cleaned the countertop and packed the Betty Milk on the shelf.

"Top of the morning to you, young fellow." Roderick's heart leapt with delight as he sprung up from below the counter, dropped the scrub cloth on the floor, raised the bridge of the counter and ran into Maas Suraj's arms. He could feel the old man's frail body that was still firm enough to support a growing boy.

"Mi—gla—gla—glad fi see you, Maas Suraj. Mi glad fi si you!"

"Happy to see you, too."

"Wait right here. A soon come back, Maas Suraj."

"I am not stopping for long. Just sell me a Ferrol."

"One second. A soon come."

"If you insist. Counting—one, two!"

Roderick made a hasty retreat toward his quarters; he could feel his thoughts speeding through his head faster than his feet could take him. His emotions pricked every nerve in his body as he burst through the door. He picked up the gifts and ran back to the shop.

"What going on out there, boy?"

"Nothing Aunty." With all that noise Nelton dem making she have to hear me. He handed Suraj the present. "A buy this for your Christmus, Maas Suraj." He stepped aside and studied the old man's facial expressions.

"What do you have wrapped here, Roderick?"

"Open it…open it…open it noh!"

Suraj delicately opened each layer of paper to reveal a straw sombrero. "O Roderick. Thank you, but you shouldn't have."

"Me have though. Me did have to give you something nice for yuh Christmus."

Suraj put the sombrero on his head. "I bet I must look sagacious in this."

"What you mean by?"

"Mean you want me to look like a wise man."

"Oh is so you mean. You wise, Maas Suraj. You wise plenty."

"One day, you too will become wise, soldier."

"Souljah… me? Souljah Maas Suraj?" Roderick chuckled way down in his belly and clasped his hands on top of his head. "You a the souljah."

"You were always a soldier. You just need to find the real soldier inside of you."

"What you mean by?"

"Just look around you and observe. You are not like the other boys around here. Pretty soon, you will realize that you are a disciplined soldier."

"But souljah a fighta, doh."

"Yes, soldiers are fighters against injustice. If you must fight against the unjust—it is fair."

"You always a talk things what me don't understand."

"One day, young fellow. One day. I must go now."

"Ba bye. Merry Christmus, Maas Suraj."

"Merry Christmas to you, son."

Roderick could see Suraj press the top of the sombrero to secure it on his head. The old man looked over his shoulder at him, raised his chin with the back of his hand and mouthed, "Chin up!" He smiled and stepped lively along the sidewalk.

About an hour later, Roderick picked up Chloe's present, looked at it, stroked it gently and smiled. He was no wastrel. Roderick had saved enough money from the sale of his stone art, coins he picked up off the ground, on the sidewalks and those customers who said, "Keep the change." Roderick bought the perfect gift for his friend.

The air was fresh; the wind raked his tender flesh, but he wasted no time to walk next door to give Chloe her present.

"Chloe, Chloe. Come quick, quick," he yelled across her gate. She was reading on her veranda. Roderick picked up his pace a little and hurried to her. She threw down the book and hugged him.

Ouch. If she did know how mi body a hurt me she wouldn't hug me. Lawks.

"Hey Roderick. Merry Christmas."

"Merry Christmus. What you reading?"

"A Nancy Drew detective story."

"What it name?"

"The Secret in the Old Attic."

"Tell me bout it?"

"It going to take long."

"Just tell me anyway."

"Nancy Drew is on a quest to help a man and his granddaughter out of money worries. It looks like she is going to find the answers in some dead man's letters. O Roderick, it is scary fun."

"Whoooooo. Niceeeee. When you finish, a want to read it." He pushed out his chest like a peacock.

"No problem. I was looking out for you from morning but no sign of you. Where were you and how come your face is so red?"

"A don't know, Chloe."

"Your eyes are red, too. Were you crying?"

"Make you ask so much question?"

"Nobody cries on Christmas. What's wrong with you?"

"Mi say nothing no wrong with me. A bring something nice for you."

"What you bring?"

Roderick's hands began to shake as he presented her with the gift.

"Awewee. Thanks, my friend." A big smile bounced across her face as she caressed the small parcel wrapped in pretty paper with a ribbon around it.

"Open it—open it—open it!"

"Is bad luck if I open it outside. Why you never give me last night?"

"You want the something or you don't want it?"

"Of course, I am just telling you how we do Christmas around here. The night before, Santa Claus comes down the chimney and puts it under the Christmas tree."

"After you don't have no chimney. Me lef Santa downtown inna the store a give out a whole heap a present to the children dem. How him did fi reach a your yard before me and drop this off?"

"You don't understand this thing, Roderick."

"You right. I don't understand this Santa thing. I saw Santa with my two eyes and he—"

"Truly?"

"Yes. He had a big cardboard with a lot of balloon on it, some big, some small. He pull one and give to me. I blow it up. By the time I reach to the bus stop, breeze blow it away."

"O Roderick, that still nice."

"That is why I don't understand how come I leave Santa downtown and him reach your house before me. A confuse bout this thing, Chloe, me confuse."

"I opened my presents early this morning with daddy."

"So you not going open it with me?"

"Yes, I am going to put it under the tree first and then open it. All right."

"That is foolinish, Chloe."

"No, that is not foolishness—it is a custom, my dear Roderick."

"Hm. Awright then." Roderick turned to leave, grumbling. "Foolinish, so-so foolinish. Me did want fi see her gladness when she open it. Foolinish, so-so foolinish." He hissed his teeth.

"You not upset with me?"

"Upset? Me not upset with you. Is chance me take and come over here. I have serious things to go deal with."

"What serious thing you talking about?"

"Serious things. Mi mother always say, 'Is not everything good to eat good to talk.'"

"Sounds like a secret to me, Roderick."

"A just going to go study my brain how to get back mi things this wicked woman give away."

"What? She took away your things."

"Yes. My Christmus things. See God there!" He pointed to the sky in oath. "One way or the other, somebody have to give me back mi things or else—"

"Or else what?"

"You don't worry your head about that."

"You need to calm down before you go over to the house."

Roderick turned again to leave, unbuttoned his shirt and wiped his face with the hem. He pressed down hard on the ball of his right foot, raised it and it vibrated up and down, faster and faster.

"Chloe. It hot out here. You holding me up you know," he continued, desperate to get back to his post. "It not fair to bad up people and take away them things. It wrong, wrong, wrong. Is my things and nobody going to bad me up, Chloe. Nobody."

"Just be careful."

"Me don't know about careful right now. A gone."

3

A Table Before Me

Later that morning, Roderick was sprinkling the side of
the yard outside the old porch from a bucket of water he
used to keep the dust down. "Is Miss Dillon slippers sound
so pretty a slap on the concrete? O gosh. A promise to help
her set up the stall. Let me go help her bring in the crocus
bag of food and toys." He ran to get to her fast. "A can't wait
to see what she bring today. Last time she bring feefee
whistles, firecrackers, balloons, dollies for the girls.
Everything. Good morning, Miss Dillon."

"Good morning, Roderick."

"Let me help you," he said and began to unpack the
poinsettia flowers, sorrel buds, ginger, green gungo peas,
bananas, yams, cocoa, dasheen, potatoes and vegetables.

"Thank you, Roderick. How are you today?"

"Fine and not so fine but a happy to see you."

"Let us stick with fine. It's Christmas day."

"Yes, Miss Dillon. No problem." He watched as
church ladies in magnificent hats and dresses with tinges of
red and white applique swung hands with their children along
Olympic Way on their way to church. Men in suits, bright
colored ties and shiny shoes stepped righteously on the
graveled sidewalk. Two little ones tried to keep up as their
parents rushed to catch the approaching bus.

"Mawnin Miss Dillon. Merry Christmas little boy!"

"Merry Christmas children. Merry Christmas Mazie."

Waving and smiling, he looked over at Miss Dillon,
who was putting fresh roots of ginger in a paper bag. She

said. "Here, give this to your aunty for her ginger beer and sorrel."

"Yes, Miss Dillon. Is me grater the ginger last time soh me know she going to want me do it again this time." He ran into the kitchen, picked up the grater, a small stool, sat opposite Miss Dillon and got to work.

"You are a good boy, Roderick. You are so willing. Better than the two boys she has inside there. Them don't do nothing."

"She beat me so bad soon this morning. Give away mi clothes, shoes and sandals Aunt Lillian and Ellen them buy for me at Grand Market. That noh right, Miss Dillon. That noh right."

"Shhhhhh. Careful. She might hear you. No, that is not right."

Roderick looked over his shoulders, closed his eyes, opened them, took a deep breath and sighed. "She didn't hear anything."

Moments later, Roderick cried out, "Whoooooooooi. Whooooi. Whoooi!" The perforated steel grater ripped the soft skin on the outside of his right pinky finger. The white flesh showed. Screaming, he flung away the piece of ginger and dropped the bowl on the ground. Blood oozed like a fire hose and the ginger seeped into his raw flesh. Roderick sprung to his feet and ran to the standpipe, hippity hoppity like something was more wrong with his feet than with his finger. Holding his finger under the cold water did not stop the blood from flowing. His tears kept streaming down his face.

A few minutes later, he presented his finger like a sacrifice on Miss Dillon's altar of compassion. She cut a leaf

off a Single Bible plant, put some of the gel on the wound
and tied the finger with a piece of cloth to stop the bleeding.

"Roderick! Roderick! Where that boy, eh?"

"A out here Aunty."

"Him cut him finger on the grater, Miss Hopie. A
here dressing it for him."

"The boy just clumsy and careless, Dillon."

"Don't say so, Hopie. It can happen to anybody."

"Him never did want to grater the ginger from
morning. The boy spiteful yah." She grabbed him by the
wounded arm. "Come inside and finish di something. Mi
church sister them coming for dinner this evening."
Miss Dillon shook her head and grumbled, "She going to kill
that little boy one day. I don't know why she so cross. Why
she bother read her Bible, anyway? She has no mercy."

Roderick returned to his chore, tears in his eyes, and
cautiously grated the remaining ginger roots. He spent the
next two hours chopping cabbage, picking the weevil out of
the flour, scrubbing the cooking pans shine, just like he knew
he should.

"Isn't it nice that we have a maid again this
Christmas, Stephen?" Roderick overheard Nelton yelling out
to Stephen through the blaring music.

"A maid? Me is nobody maid. All a want is my things
my aunty take give you. One way or the other me going to get
them back." Roderick ground his teeth, frayed his nostrils
and squinted. With clenched his fists, he set his eyes on the
room where the offending boys were enjoying each other's
company on Christmas morning.

"I am going in that room and them better not stand
in my way or I am going to break somebody hand today."

Roderick made an about turn and walked toward the boys'
room when there came a loud knocking on the gate.

"Roderick!"

"Yes, Aunty."

"Go see who at the gate."

"Yes, Aunty."

Roderick pointed his fist at the door one more time,
twisted it in half circles like a baseball bat. "You won't get
away with this, Nelton and Stephen." Then he turned around,
walked to the gate, and opened it. A woman and a little girl
were standing there.

"Good morning. Hope inside?"

"Yes miss. Aunty, somebody come to you."

"Is who?"

"Is me, Daphne."

*What a way the woman eye them dark. Her eyelash them so
long eee? She must be a spirit.*

The woman wore a straw hat with silk flowers tacked
to the crown. Her dress was pale. She carried a bundle of
fresh callaloo in one hand and held the child by the other.
Roderick's mouth opened as if to say something, but nothing
came out. He stared at the little girl. Her freckles glowed in
the sunshine. Roderick remembered his little sister Esther;
she was about the same size as the little girl when his mother
pulled him away from her just before shipping him off to
Kingston. Tears filled his eyes.

"You all right, little boy?" asked Miss Daphne.

Not a word came out of his mouth. Over his
shoulders, he sensed Aunt Hope's presence, and he shook
inside.

"Kiss mi neck! Daphne. A you that?"

Roderick emerged from his mesmeric gaze and scurried to his work area at the sound of Aunt Hope's voice, his ears pinned to every word.

When the lady gone, a going straight back in them boy room and get mi things.

"Mawnin Hopie."

"Mawnin Daphne. Mawnin Little Miss Petal. What a way you grow big. How old are you?"

"I am five." She spread her five fingers, stretched her arm, and touched Hope's apron.

"All of five." Hope rubbed Petal's nose. "You are pretty, like your mother."

"Say thank you, Petal," Daphne said.

"Thank you, miss," Petal ruffled her little skirt.

"Which breeze blow you round here this mawnin, Daphne? Me couldn't tell when last me see you in these parts."

"Is the season to be jolly, girl."

"Work business me into or me and my boys will dead from hunger."

"Me don't have no work but me still jolly."

"Seriously, Daphne. Which mule you ride on come here today? Me never know you remember this address."

"Lord. Why you so suspicious? A come to give you a helping hand."

"You right. One of mi hand just rip up the grater on the ginger."

"You so silly. You don't change one bit. You mean somebody rip them hand on the grater. Who?"

"That same little boy that just answer the gate. Him so spiteful."

Spiteful? Is my hand get cut and burn up with the ginger. What a wicked woman. Roderick shook his head.

"Well, I am getting ready for my yearly holiday dinner, so you are right on time."

"Great. I will make myself useful, just like old times." Daphne eased her way into Hope's kitchen and shelled the gungo peas.

"Gwaan go bathe, little boy. I will finish wash down the kitchen floor. When dinner is ready, I will call you."

"Yes, miss. I just have to finish polish and shine them boy shoes to wear to the dinner." Roderick watched as Daphne parted the curtains, rolled their ends in a knot, pushed open the windows to let in fresh air and sunlight. *So why Aunty never used to open the kitchen window? Look how the table top and the stove pretty. I don't know. My aunty strange.*

Hope called out to Daphne, "You staying for dinner… right?"

"Thanks, but I planned to do that anyway."

"You don't change one bit." Hope laughed so loudly Roderick could not believe she knew how to laugh.

She so happy since her friend come.

The pungent smell of Hope's lavished menu of traditional black rum cake, sorrel, rum punch, ginger-beer, gungo rice and peas, roast duck, oxtail and curried goat made Roderick's mouth water. He remembered growing up in the country with his mother, sister, brother and step-father and he dropped his chin to his chest.

"O no. A won't ever see my sister and brother again. A won't see mama and Missa Cupidon. Everybody for me just gone." He cried. Seeing Aunt Hope put out her finest crochet patterned linen table cloth, bone china dinnerware her cousin Tulip sent her from London, reminded him of his own mother."O my goodness, mama have the same pretty green drinking glass them. She and mama must did buy them same time," he mused as he put the finishing shine on the last pair of shoes. Then, he went to the standpipe, bathed, returned to his quarters and changed into clean clothes.

Around four o'clock in the afternoon, the hypnotic sounds of music drew Roderick out front. Wanting to feel happy, at least for a while, he edged closer to his older cousin Stephen and watched his every move. Stephen delicately wiped old 78s and 45s with a soft chamois towel, flipped each record from side to side and placed the needle ever so cautiously on the records to produce the best sounding music. Stephen played from traditional Christmas carols to the blues. Roderick nodded his head and hummed along.

"You all right, Roderick?"

"Yeh man. Mi awright."

"Like the music?"

"Yeh man. Mi like how you work the thing."

"You mean the record changer?"

"Yes. The changer." Roderick smiled, revealing his pearly white teeth. *Man, Stephen kind of cooler than Nelton. But me still mad with them and Aunty fi take away mi nice clothes.*

"You want to wipe off this record for me, Roderick?"

Cautiously, Roderick took the chamois and the 45 rpm record from Stephen. Holding it now with great care, Roderick wiped off the dust with pride the same way he did dress shoes. By now, he was making more effort to read and became curious about the inscriptions on the record. "Nat King Cole, Jim Reeves and Mahalia Jackson."

The cool breeze rustled the laced curtains as Hope's friends from the Ladies Group started filing in one by one. Roderick's attention shifted from the music as he became absorbed by the colorful spectacle. Colors made Roderick giddy with joyfulness. After all, he saw his world come alive through the magic of paint on stones or any surface that allowed his imagination free rein. Roderick leaned against a wall near the entrance to the living room. No one noticed him, but he noticed everyone. He transformed into a Fashion Show Commentator, whispered in his cupped fist to his absent mother, his imaginary audience of one.

"La la. Look Mama. Sister Pennicook in her pretty frock and frill hat. So much green in the frock she look like a green lizard. Except for her silver purse and silver shoes, she still look mighty stylish out of her milk factory uniform today. It don't look like there is one piece of silk left in Maas Suraj, Punjab because Deaconess Rose a wear all a it. Me love her pillbox hat with the veil though. She reminds me of Mother Porteous, who work miracles right there where you are in Paradise Glen. La la. Mama, Sister Beecham from the Usher Board. Kiss mi neck, she still wearing her gloves from the last supper. La la. Mama, you should see Aunt Hope. She look just like you in her white linen hobble-skirt suit with a big ole green button on the blouse. Me like how she hang the pretty, pretty pearls round her collar bone. La la. Mama, if you ever see her red and white broad hat, she can hardly get through the door it so wide. A wish you were here. She must be really vex with Aunt Lillian and Miss Ellen because she didn't invite them this year."

"SteeeeeeVen darlingggg!"

"That's Aunt Hope with her cranky voice. I am signing off now, mama. Dinner is ready and Aunty calling us to the table."

"SteeeeeeVen darlingggg, put on my favorite Naaaaaaaat King Cole's Christmas song for me deaaareee. You know which one and come sit down at the table. Tell Nelton dinner ready. Is time to eeeeeat," and she turned on the pepper lights.

"Daphneeeee," fix a plate for Roderick and set him up in the kitchen. Pull up the little stool give him."

"No problem, Hopie."

Roderick saw Daphne shake her head and he could hear her grumbling to herself.

"That's why Lillian encouraged me to come help out. I never believed her, but now I see it with my own two eyes. Hope really treats the little boy poorly."

Oh. So Miss Daphne catch on. If Aunt Hope find out that Aunt Lillian and Miss Daphne was into any tricky business to help me out, she would dash Miss Daphne and the little girl out the house like a bucket a dirty water. He looked at Daphne in disbelief, then at the plate of food in front of him. "So why me couldn't sit down at the table with everybody?" Roderick did not care if Aunt Hope heard what he was saying this time. "Look how me burn off my hand a grater the ginger, me wash the pretty pretty plate and glass them. Me not somebody, too? After them not better than me. Bad to bad my mother always make me sit down at the table with the rest of the family. One day me will go back home. One day, Miss Hope. One day." Roderick shoved the food aside, pushed the chair outward with his bottom, kicked the leg of the table, got up, and walked swiftly to his cousin's room. He turned the doorknob, but it jammed. "Strange. Them never lock door before. Is what so?" Enlisting the hem of his shirt, Roderick put more muscle into turning the lock, but no luck.

"I am getting inside this room if it kill me."

Roderick kicked the door three times, but it pouted as obstinate as a mule. A door squeaked down the hallway. He stood still. No one emerged except a cool puff of wind.

Roderick ran outside, looked up at the window and it was ajar. He climbed onto the water pipe that ran along the base of the wall, held on tightly to the windowsill with one arm and stretched the other and held onto the side jamb. He pushed his body through the opening and into the room. Rummaging through the clutter of toys and sundry gifts on their bed, he yanked his new sandals, a pair of brown school shoes, and clothes his aunt stole from him. He stuffed them under his arm and climbed out the window. He looked over the wall and saw Chloe outside, looking straight at him.

"You think I was joking, Chloe? Is my things." Roderick walked triumphantly to his quarters.

While putting his shoes and sandals under the cot, he felt something hard in the way. He lay on the floor, looked under the cot, and saw a square object. He reached for it with both hands. "This thing heavy, a wonder is what." He eased his body under the dark cot. Grabbing a hold of it, he pulled until it came to full view.

"A old radio. Imagine that. A radio. La la. You work radio?" He picked, pulled, turned and squeezed buttons. Nothing. If a plug it in maybe it will work.

Chhhhhhhhhhhhhh. Chhhhhhhhh!

Roderick jumped back at the hissing sound. "It work!" He took an old rag and wiped the dust from the radio.

Right away, Lij crossed his mind, a young Rastaman he met when he first came to Olympic Gardens. "A wonder if Lij can make it work good for me? Then me can listen to music all night," he slapped the rag on the floor. "Yes, yes, yes. But me can't make Aunty know a thing." He patted the radio. "You stay right there so." Kneeling down to make sure his sandals and shoes were out of sight, he pushed them further under the cot. "If my cousin them think me a joke this time. Is my something them. Make them come get them back if them bad. All I want now is to put my things together for school next term."

4

Window What You Know

Olympic Gardens spread out like an anole lizard soaking up the mid-afternoon sun. The town was changing color, just like the reptile. Roderick had a front-row seat to see boys and girls who skull school every day, make mischief in the neighborhood. The Petgraves were becoming teenagers; all four were a year apart and springing up tall like papaw trees. The Browns had saved enough to buy a house Mr. Goodman owned on De Lisser Avenue. Miss Mack's eldest son had joined the rude boys and moved away. Heaven knows where he ended up—maybe like the unknowns in the morgue. Roderick wanted more.

"When I go to school, a will get out of the miserable shop with this wicked aunty of mine. A won't have all this shop work and yard work to do. When a go to school, a will get to have plenty friend and walk home with them just like the ones them that pass here every day. Them so happy and noisy. A will get to play with them. A will get to turn out good, good, good like Chloe for she so bright. Look how she talk good. All them big word. Sometimes is hell fi me understand her but me like how she talk."

Roderick spotted Mr. Goodman, Chloe's father, walking towards the shop. He came down from the wall and ran inside to serve him, but Aunt Hope was already sitting on her high stool at the counter reading her Bible. She often told Roderick that the Bible is the true word of God, and children who do not obey their parents will not live to old age.

38

Roderick listened to the adults as he stacked the cans of bully beef and tin mackerel on the shelf.

"Happy New Year, Hope. This is for you."

"Thank you. Happy New Year." She unwrapped the gift. "A bottle of wine!"

"Yes. Rice wine I made. It's velvety and the perfect way to start the New Year."

"You know I only drink wine during communion, Goodman."

"Come on. 'Eat thy bread with joy, and drink thy wine with a merry heart.'"

"Ecclesiastes 9 verse 7. You know your Bible, man!"

"You thought I was a heathen?"

"I know better than that."

Aunty smiling. She don't smile for nobody. She always so cross.

"Roderick ready for school on Tuesday?" Goodman said in a near whisper.

"I need him in the shop, Goodman. The Chiney man pickney them help in them shop so why him can't help, too? I don't see what school will do for that boy. Him savage. Him ungrateful."

Roderick got this strange sensation in his gut that he would have to work in the shop for the rest of his life.

Me. Savage. Wonder what she mean by though eee. Mr. Goodman mus a say something bad to Aunty bout school or something like that why she blurt out.

"O no, Miss Hope. Don't say that. I find him to be very polite. I know he is useful in the shop, but you should really consider sending him to school when it opens for the Easter term, five days from now. It will be good for him."

A wide smile formed on Roderick's face. He pinched his thigh. *Me a go a school. Thank you puppa Jeezas.*

"You know what, people like you, Goodman, don't understand. You have everything you need in life. I have to work ten times as hard for what I need for my children. Roderick born to do this kind of work. Him not school material. You are wasting precious time."

Crash! Cans of bully beef tumbled off the shelf.

"You see what I am talking about, Goodman? The boy is spiteful. Is do him don't want to do what I tell him to do. He is disobedient and going straight to hell."

"He's a little boy, and the shelf is high for him. Don't you think?"

"Think! You see him face, full of the devil. The government would have to build a special school just for him alone."

"The government is doing its best. Two years ago, around this time, they talked about expanding educational programs. There is enough money for teachers and students in the primary schools. Roderick will benefit."

"I need money and workers to run my business."

Poor Missa Goodman, him really trying to get Aunty to send me to school but she want me to be her shop boy. That's all. Shop boy. A devil.

Picking up the cans one at a time, he carefully placed them on the shelf, recalled it was his mother who first taught him about the devil in Sabbath school. She taught him that God kicked the devil out of heaven because he was out of order and he was no longer allowed back in there with the rest of the angels.

"So how come me is the devil?" He mumbled.

"My daughter told me Roderick still has difficulty reading and that he yearns to go to school. She entreated me to continue to give him private lessons in reading and arithmetic. That's why I am here to see if you could free him up on Sunday afternoons. He ought to be in school. What you say?"

"I say your daughter needs to read her books and don't worry about him. He's not worthy to shine her shoes. They are not the same."

"What you mean, they are not the same. They are children."

"You really would equal up your good-good daughter with that devil of a boy. Whoiee, mi belly o." She laughed so hard her head tie fell to the ground, displaying her four unkempt, graying Bantu knots and pencil behind her right ear.

Something slammed like a door inside Roderick's brain and he jolted into a memory of his mother saying to anybody who would listen. 'The devil is in that boy. No wonder him can't learn.' It look like the same devil crosses follow me come to Kingston. Roderick looked over at Mr. Goodman, who reached in his pocket for money. The cool polish of Mr. Goodman's face was becoming Otaheite apple red. Sweat formed across his furrowed brow, his eyes narrowed. He avoided looking at Hope and instead made eye-contact with Roderick. He surmised the referee felt rejected. Roderick sat on a milk carton, his elbows on his knees, and covered his eyes with both palms. He could not believe how calm Mr. Goodman was, but remembered his mother telling him, 'It is better to please a fool than to vex him.' *It didn't*

*make sense for Missa Goodman to make Aunty mad anymore because
she would take it out on me.*

"Very well, Miss Hope. It is really your decision to
make. I have some things to which I must attend." Mr.
Goodman paid her for the shaving powder and coconut
drops. "Have a good evening, madam."

"Poor Missa Goodman. Him try him best." He
watched Mr. Goodman push through his front gate,
scratched his right temple and shook his head. Aunt Hope
put the money in the bin, hissed her teeth in disgust at the
thought that a neighbor was so bumptious to come up in her
face to meddle in her business.

"I always respected that man!" With that, she flung
her skirt above her head in utter contempt and yelled,
"Roderick Brissett. Come here, boy!"

Roderick got that funny bubble in his belly. He
trembled, passed the loudest gas like his butt would explode.

"Yes, Aunty." His eyes burrowed the floor.

"Listen here, boy; don't bring down crowd pan me.
Look at me! You will not be going to school any time soon.
Put. That. Out. Your. Head."

Roderick did not respond.

"You hear me?"

No response.

*I am going to school even if I have to live in the chicken coob or
in the outhouse. I am going to school. Nobody going to stop me. A going
to find a way.*

"Answer me."

"Yes, Aunty."

"A say, put that nonsense out of your thick skull.
You will keep this shop and this yard tidy. Your mother did

not want you. Only me did want you to begin with or you would have to live in the bush. Now go and wash your dirty feet and go to your room."

Live in the bush? After me never live into no bush. We live in a good good house. Me did have a good good room for me and my little brother and sister not some stinky quarters. We have all kind a tree in the yard: mango, orange, June plum, guinep, grapes, pear. Uncle plant yam and banana and dasheen in the small farm. We have a big tank of water. Plenty fowl, goat and cow. Me don't come from no bush. Roderick kicked the air as he made his way slowly towards the back door.

Stephen was helping Nelton to wrap his school books with brown paper. His sympathetic expression showed he'd heard his mother lambasting Roderick. He looked away.

"Look at rotten Nelton. I know him don't really care to learn, him skull from school all the time with him bad friend them. That is why Aunty force poor Stephen to help him study and them things there. What about what I want to do? Why I don't get the same help? Since Aunty not going to help me, I am going to help me. Watch me."

It was the earliest his aunt had ever sent him to bed. She kept the shop opened for business although it was bright outside. Everything around him was clean except his quarters. He had grown tired of hearing the rats gnaw at flour sacks, the wretched darkness and the dampness. After all, the New Year was here, and he fancied becoming a schoolboy again, but his aunt had other plans. Deep down, he knew that his happiness connected to the quality of his quarters.

"If a clean up this place and turn it into something good, a real, real room, maybe a will feel better." Sitting crouched over with both elbows on his knees, his palms propping his chin, Roderick imagined the room he would like to live in, a room where he could read lots of books and study for exams just like his cousins.

"A going to school one day. A will find a way and nobody is going to stop me." Then he shot up and took his pencil and drawing paper and sketched the layout of the room he would enjoy. In the far corner, he drew a desk with an electric lamp, much like the one in his cousin's room. Next to his bed would be a side table with a basin on top. "Light go out so often in Kingston, me might as well have a kerosene lamp, too." He drew that next to the basin. "My shoes, my shoes. Okay." There was a place for his shoes and an enormous wardrobe for his clothes. At the southwest corner, he sketched a shelf for his paint set and art supplies Chloe had given to him when he first moved into Olympic Gardens. Roderick wanted two walls to be cleared so he could fill them with his drawings and paintings, the way Aunt Hope fills her dark living room walls with photographs of her family, good looking picture of Jesus by himself showing his bloody hands, and one with him and his disciples eating and laughing.

"But me bright eee. If Aunty did catch me a sneak into her cave, mm hm. Her cave yes, for it dark like what, she would a strangle me like duppy. My room must have plenty sun a come inside." He drew a big, bright golden sun.

"How a get rid of them flour bag, this old vanity with all them drawers and heavy handle?" Roderick put his sketch pad down and wiped the sweat from his face. Then he tackled the vanity, which was the heaviest and awkwardly out of place for his new design. He patiently emptied the vanity—one shoe polish at a time. In one drawer, he found a pile of exercise books with a pretty lady in a crown with 'On Her Majesty's Service' written on the cover. He opened one of them, and, in it, someone had written the names of customers who had taken groceries without paying, some ten years earlier. "They hoped to pay back Aunt Hope it look like, much like the one she keep in the shop. So much money them owe!"

Now the vanity, without the drawers, was much easier to push to the other side of the room. He pushed with all his might—inch by inch for nearly fifteen minutes. He was getting tired and so he sat on the floor. Through his weary eyes, he saw something behind that vanity. "Is wha dis?" A section of the wall was all boarded up with two strips of plywood that formed an x. "Is why mek Aunty board up the place soh?" Questions ran through his mind, but he had no answers. Overcome by tiredness, he dozed off on the floor.

Crash! A rapid succession of thunder growled outside as if to burst through the walls and rip the roof off the house. Startled but not afraid, Roderick sprang to his feet and he saw the lightning flashing through the crevice of the boarded scar on the wall. Roderick laughed like he was watching a picture show.

"You know what this remind me of… in the country when Teacher did hang up the white sheet over the blackboard at school and point a light on it. Yes. I remember how the picture them move. She was teaching us the story of Noah and the ark. La la. Suppose the rain fall so hard tonight that it reach up to the window? After me don't have no ark like Noah. La la. This is fun to think about!" It felt much like those stormy days he would climb up into Uncle's bed to watch the rain walk mightily across the cane field. Every blade of cane grass bowed and bounced up and down through the misty haze like the lithe necks of a hundred giraffes. Roderick touched the ragged lump of scarred wall, rubbed his palm across its coarse splintery surface. "Ouch!" He quickly attended to his nipped finger. The stripes on the pieces of wood made crisscross patterns. He smiled. "This is a pretty drawing inside the wood."

Relieved that he had no shop duties for the rest of the evening, he turned his attention to more pressing matters. Without delay, he tried to break off the wooden barrier, but it was too difficult for him—he needed some help. "Mi nah call nobody fi help me. Me a do dis myself. A going use this old rusty sad-iron nobody seem to be using anymore to iron their clothes around here. It is heavy enough." He hammered away until the termite infested, worn wood crumbled to the ground. Roderick shuffled backwards, brushed the dust from his hands and face. "A don't believe this. A window deh here soh. You mean to tell me Aunty board up the window and paint out the sun—not even little fresh air? No wonder the room soh dark and frowsy." Roderick tackled the crudely painted panes of glass. He reached for one drinks bottle stopper from the pile he was saving to decorate his wooden skate. Like a carpenter preparing to repaint, Roderick scraped the paint from the window panes. At first, the stopper was not doing the job fast enough. "This likkle bokkle cover a goh tek a whole year. Mi cyaa use that. Mek a see. If mi use di can top off a the bully beef…no that not going to work eedah. Mek a si…mek a si. Awright. Seeit yah!" Roderick reached for the drinks bottle from the crate, broke it and used its sharp edge to scrape the paint from the window—one pane at a time—until he could see the luminescent sun of evening making its way through rain clouds. "Too sweet! Now a can climb through this window and take off down the road any time me want and Aunty will never know me leave the house. Yes, yes, yes, A free! Hold on Roderick. Not so fast. Think again." *If Aunty find out you leave the house, she won't let you go to school. Try don't get her mad with you.* Roderick pressed his hand over his mouth should such thoughts escape and reveal his secret. *Maybe I can open it and air out the smelly room.* Knowing that Aunt Hope can hear a pin drop and see the smallest star in the darkest night, Roderick was extra cautious. *A have to be careful. Aunty have eyes all around her head like fruit fly. If she catch me, dog eat mi supper.* "You know what, a can't worry about Aunty all the time. A need fresh air. So what if she find out? What?"

The coconut trees in the backyard lowered their heads against the bluest sky as soft gray and white clouds embroidered red, purple and orange ribbons of light—the sun was setting. Before retiring to bed, Roderick went outside to the standpipe and washed the dust from his hands and face. Upon his return, he lay on his cot, made a pillow with both hands and smiled at the moon—half of its face beamed from the setting sun and the other half in the shadows. Whispering ever so softly, "This window deh here so long, Aunt Hope must did see so much something around here. A figure is right here Aunty was standing the night when she did see Dextan and him friend them hold up the peanut man and take weh him Bulova wrist watch. Aunty tell that story all the time bout the tiefing rude boy them from Pelican Parade. It makes me scratch my head to figure out if she did blame the window for every bad thing that happen in the area? That's why she shut the window eye. Whoiee. A tired.

Seriously though, a curious to know what my aunty hiding from the window? Same way she keep her room dark."

Next day, Roderick woke up to fragmented rays from the sun peeping through the crudely scraped paint on the windowpanes. He remembered Maas Suraj telling him how he used turpentine to melt the paint on the old ships when he was in the army.

"Where a going get turpentine? Maybe Maas Suraj know." Roderick tried to open the window. Something obscured the nail head, fastened. He enlisted the old rusty hammer he found in a drawer and used the hook end to pull out the nails. "Anything you can't find in the house is in this dingy hole Aunty dump it." Roderick could not believe how strong he had gotten to tackle those old nails. "Thank goodness some of the wood a rotten. It little easier fi hook the nail them."

Nothing would stop him from getting the window opened. Roderick toiled for close to an hour until he removed the last nail. He tried to push the window open. It squeaked at the hinges. He heard footsteps coming down the hallway. Muscles in his back tightened, sweat seeped salty in his eyes and he wiped them. *Please don't let Aunty catch me, please!* Roderick tried to stay calm, but his breathing became more labored. He listened closely. Dust filled his nostrils, and he made a loud sneeze. Peeping under the door, he saw a shadow, so he stayed still. Another sneeze was coming.

O no! Roderick squeezed his nose to stifle the sound and stop himself from sneezing. Then he recalled the children telling him if you stop a sneeze, it can blow up your brain. Well, is my brain or a whipping tonight.

The footsteps faded. A door slammed. Silence.

"Wow, that was close." He sighed. One more big push and the window opened. Puff. A cool breeze floated into the room, bathing his sweaty face. The little scare was worth it. What a surprise when Chloe's bedroom window came into full view. All the worry from Aunt Hope's meanness disappeared. The window had now opened a new panoramic view of Olympic Gardens grist for his ever questioning mind. Roderick pressed his navel on the wooden sill and swung his upper body through the window. The blood rushed to his head as he panned the ground below. From his vantage point, the window was a little high above the ground. He saw a thick mound of green shrubs of every color, yellow dandelions, orange and pink gerberas, red and white poinsettias like a plush carpet, rich from rainwater that ran down the gutter from the roof. Roderick somersaulted out the window and landed among the foliage that almost swallowed his slender body. He waded in the grassy swamp until he bumped his head on a wooden barrier that blocked off the garden from the backyard.

"Ouch! Why Aunt Hope close this off from the rest of the house? You know what, a going to weed up the place. This is a nice little spot where I can hide from everybody. Yes, yes, yes. O my goodness, look at them big butterfly wings, yellow, brown, black. Woooo hooooo!"

Roderick could not believe his eyes. Bees danced among the petals and birds fed off the sweet nectar. "So much color, like my painting set. Jeewiz. The flowers them pretty eee. Look like a big flowers garden round here so. Then is how Aunty leave it up so? I never hear Nelton and Stephen around here. A check say them don't even know it around here so." He touched the soft petals of the flowers. "Maybe I can pick some of them flowers here to pretty up my quarters."

Roderick set to root up the wild weeds when he found a pile of stones. "A can get these for my stone art. A can paint pretty things on them. Wheeeeeeeeeee." Not knowing what to do with himself from the tingling in his belly, he embraced the joy. As he kept clearing, he noticed something like a giant rock emerging. "A bench. A stone bench." Roderick looked up at the window to see if anyone heard his excitement. "Nobody must know about this spot here." Finding the garden made him smile so much that the dreariness of the shop paled. "This is my hiding place from now on."

Hush your mouth, boy. Chicken merry, hawk deh near. It was as if he could hear Uncle's voice warning him to be careful.

"Maybe me and Chloe can sit down around here, read wi book and study wi lesson. Nobody will find wi. A can do this. A can do anything a want around here." He waved a bunch of flowers in the air that he picked to pretty up his lodging, looked up at the window, "Everybody! A going to the school down the street next term. One, two, three, four days from now," he counted on one hand. "Watch me."

5

Black Power

A whole month had slipped away and Roderick's aunt had not sent him to school. At least he could carve time in the evenings to tend to his little stone art enterprise, which he enjoyed. Every splash of paint on stone became beautiful paintings of birds, trees, flowers, fruits and whatever the muses inspired. He could make an oval stone transform into what looked like a real apple with stem and all. The only thing that would add a little flavor to his art sessions was some music, especially at night. His aunt had such a hold on him he didn't even have time to have his radio fixed. Roderick would always find a way.

It was early evening and freedom shone for Roderick like the mirage along The Way. Roderick followed its effulgent path on a leisurely stroll to visit his Rastaman friend, Lij. He lugged with the old radio on his shoulder, winced at the sizzling asphalt under his barefoot.

"A hope Lij can fix the radio for me. A feel so lonely when night come. Me want to hear the news and nice music coming all the way from America."

The house sprawled in a tranquil whisper on a small incline, sun-bathing its fresh coat of salmon paint on concrete walls with rust colors that accentuated the window frames. Roderick took a deep breath, held on to one of two towering Greek columns. He sniffed the sweet fragrance of the gardenias and oriental lilies that grew along the outskirts of the carriageway.

"Pssssst."

What Chloe doing so far up here? Only she psssst me. He turned around. A man stood by a breadfruit tree at the edge of Lij's yard, beckoned him.

"Come here, youth."

"A can't stop. This thing here heavy," Roderick replied.

"Just rest it down on the ground. Need to talk to you," the man said, revealing his two buffed gold-capped incisors at the front of his mouth that looked like he stole them from a rich rabbit.

What him want with me today? "A can't stop!"

"Big man say you must stop. Seen."

Roderick's heart skipped a beat, his hands became weighted down by the radio, and he stopped.

"Tell the youtman in the house that big man say to link with him first thing in the morning."

"Yes, sir." Roderick picked up the radio and moved swiftly up the carriageway. He stumbled on a welcome mat that tossed him onto the door, which made a loud thud; a dog barked. Roderick knocked on the door and waited.

"Who's there?" A thunderous voice came from within.

"Is me. Roderick. Mr. Lij at home?"

"You mean Lionel. Hold on. Lionel! Someone is here to see you. That, that… name!"

A forget Lionel is him real, real name. Them don't like the Rasta name him give himself.

Moments later, Lij came to the door. A tall young man, his face shone like bronze showing off his dark eyes and heavy lashes. He wore plaid shorts, a black t-shirt with a picture of Malcolm X etched on the front. A red-green and gold band tied his locks together like a groomed stallion's mane. Leather sandals cradled his delicate feet. He smelled like sweet oil. Roderick greeted him with a smile.

"Good evening."

"What a gwaan youtman?" Lij reached out and touched his shoulder."

"Nothing. A come to ask if you can please fix my radio for me."

"How you know I can fix radio?"

"My aunty say you went to school for it."

"She knows a lot about school and yet she won't send you. She forgot to tell you that if you know how to fix radios, you can make plenty of money instead of working in that shop every day. Give it to me. Let me see what I can do."

Roderick handed him the radio, flashed his hands from relief.

"You mean if I go to school I can learn to fix radio and make money?"

"O yes, but is not every school teach you how to do things like this so you can make money. Come inside and sit down."

"That sound good. That's why Aunty don't want me to go school. She don't want me to make money. What a wicked woman."

Lij directed him to the couch but Roderick preferred to stand, his eyes panning the house like a cameraman.

"Your house so big and pretty."

"Thank you. Is so my parents rest. Babylon System."

Roderick rubbed his bare feet on the shiny tile floor and raised his hand to his mouth. *The floor look like is marble make it. Aweee. The same kind Uncle told me he used to fix up the rich people them house in Covent Grove when him used to live in England.* The tile felt cool beneath his clammy feet. Looking down, he saw his thin elongated shadow moving; he swayed and played with it. He ran his little hand over the arm of the couch and squeezed against the firmness of the wood.

"Blue Mahoe," Lij shared. "Our National Tree. But is so them cut down the trees… destroying the earth… rob we of the oxygen we need to breathe."

Roderick shrugged and squinted. "Oksajen? Where me hear that word before?"

"When you take a deep breath, you inhale oxygen into your lungs. You need oxygen to grow and stay alive. Cutting down the trees to make furniture is pure vanity. We soon can't breathe good air."

"O. Then is why Nelton say me take up di oksajen in the place?"

"He is just rude. You need oxygen. We all need it to live."

Roderick made a one-eighty and smiled. "Is so my aunty house big, too, but the shop part take up most of the front room them and the porch. That is why me squeeze up in the back part."

Gently stroking the surface of the three bookcases that stood side by side, he closed his eyes and sniffed the smell of furniture polish. It was an old smell he remembered from his time in the country when his mother would clean the living room on a Sunday morning. *A wish me could see mama and mi brother and sister again.* He was quiet for a minute when

Lij interrupted his pensive mood. "You like to read youtman?"

"Yes." Still fingering the bookshelf, he read the spines of books: "Can-ter-bury Tales. En-cy-clo-pe-dia."

"Big words. Excellent."

"I just getting better at sounding out words." Roderick smiled and leaned his head towards his right shoulder. "My friend Chloe say I just need more book so a can read better."

"She is a good friend. Black man needs to read, for in books are wisdom and evils of the world. Which one you reading now?"

"Hardy Boys Missing Chums. Mi just finish it two days ago."

"Tell me about the book."

Roderick widened his eyes, stretched out his arms like wings. "Tell the whole story?"

"Not the whole thing, just a little gist of it."

"Awright. Them is best friend. Chet and Biff. Three bad man come up and want to cause ruption. Ahmm. Ahmm," Roderick paused trying to remember what's next.

"So what happened?"

"Hold on, hold on. Make a show you." Roderick leaped into action, struck a pose with his hands flung wide. With an opened chest, he acted out a nuanced moment. "A big storm lik them a sea. Them boat nearly capsize. You know what them boat name?"

"No. You tell me."

"Envoy. Man, the Envoy nearly sink, but that never stop them from ride it out. Them brave you see, Lij. Them brave, man. But them get missing. Some bad man capture them. Yes." Roderick was now fully in the middle of the storm; he rocked from side to side, forward and backwards and around in circles.

"Did they escape?"

"The friend them get save and the bad man them weh capture them get lock up inna jail." His storytelling picked up speed like the police car in hot pursuit.

"So what you learn from that story?"

"Hooooo." He exhaled loudly. "What you mean? I just tell you what a learn."

"Let me put it another way. If you were one of the bad boys in the story and your little brother wanted to join with the bad boys, what would you tell him about the police?"

Roderick did not answer, but thought about his own little brother he left in the country three years ago. *After me never tell Lij about my brodder. Me miss him bad bad bad.* Roderick rubbed his sweating hands on his trousers; tears welled up in his eyes. "A would tell him police beat bad boy. Don't bad."

"Anything else?"

"Don't rat out your friends them. Stick together."

"Sounds good to me."

"Mi never tell you this part, them did have a Aunt Gertrude, but she never beat up the boy them like my aunty."

"I man like the story, youtman. I used to read those books when I was a youtman, too. Yes, I. Well, you can come here and read anytime."

"Not anytime me want. Me have to do it when Aunty not here. Like this evening so, she gone to bible study."

"All right, I will give you one book at a time. Promise you will read it and tell me what you learned. Promise?"

"Promise."

Lij held Roderick's hand and led him to the far end of the bookshelf, and took out a book. The cover, wrapped in brown paper. He placed the book gently in Roderick's hands.

"You read this book, for in it there is much knowledge about our people."

Roderick ran his right thumb across the edges, ruffled the pages and blinked his eyes at the cool air they made. *The book smell like old cigar, the kind Uncle smoke.* "Thanks Mr. Lij. A will bring it back."

"Take your time. It is quite a lot to read."

"Awright then. Thank you, Mr. Lij. A can't stay any longer."

"No Mr. Lij. Ras Lij. Blessed love, youtman."

Roderick turned to leave, but quickly swung around. "A forgot was to tell you that a saw a man at your gate and him give me a message to give you."

"What message?"

"Him say to tell the youtman in the house that big man say to link with him first thing in the morning."

"Big Man," came the thunderous voice he heard earlier.

Is Lij father. O goodness. Him tall eee.

"What does this man look like, little fellow?" Lij's father asked.

"Him was on a bicycle, sir."

"You know about this Big Man, Lionel?"

"No dad. He is just one of those politicians I hear walking around recruiting young people."

"Politician? How you know he is a politician?"

Look like Lij fraid of him father. Him just draw up in the corner against the wall. What a man face serious. A wonder if Lij get beating, too? But him have manners to him father.

"Dad, let me see the little boy to the door and I will discuss it with you."

"O. So you have something to discuss with me."

"Please dad. Babylon System."

"That's what you call it, Babylon System."

"Is awright, Lij," Roderick said.

"His name is Lionel. That's the name I gave him. Lionel."

Roderick gasped. Coiled. *O boy, him rough, too. I better get out of here now.*

"Goodbye, Lionel. Goodbye, sir."

A wonder who is Big Man? Him must be somebody important. Hmm.

It was the very day that Michael Manley took over the leadership of the People's National Party, 9 February 1969. Knowledge of this filled the young people on the island with euphoria. It was about a new way of thinking and governance. Lij could not care less about politics.

The sunlight was so brilliant it washed the front yard and bounced intense rays off the iron trimmed gate. Roderick narrowed his eyes at the glare, put the book under his arm, leaned slightly to his right and walked with a bounce. He made a quick dash across the street.

Roderick returned home to see Nelton locking the big gate with the padlock.

"Open the gate, Nelton."

"You stay outside till mama come and let her see say you left the yard gone about your business."

"So what happen, me can't leave this yard when me want? You do it every day. Open the gate a say." Roderick kicked the gate. "Open it a say." He banged on the gate harder with a stone he retrieved from the pile that encircled the base of the mango tree. "Stephen, talk to your brother. Tell him to open the gate or a going to break it down," Roderick yelled across the gate.

Look like this bwoy not going to let me in tonight. It getting dark and Aunt Hope soon come and find me out here. Hmm. Mek a think. He cuddled the book; put it to his right temple. *Hmm. I can walk around the back and go through my secret window, but a can't let them know the window is there. What a going to do? Mek a think some more.* Roderick sat on the wall, his blood boiling, seeing no way out of this rabbit hole that was getting darker by the minute.

"A can't believe Stephen on Nelton's side." A swift decision had to come sooner than later. An assing tonight was not in his plan. Roderick looked up and down The Way to see if his aunt was coming. The peenie wallies were glowing exceptionally bright against the darkness creeping across The Way. Tonight their firefly dance made him happy for a moment as one fell in his lap, blinked its yellow light and flew away.

Squeak!

Roderick quivered, turned around to see Stephen opening the gate. He jumped down from the wall, ran towards the gate. Nelton blocked the entrance. Roderick pushed Nelton into his chest. "Move out my way."

Nelton thumped him on his shoulder. "A going to tell on you and make mama give you a backsiding."

Roderick pitched Nelton to the ground, "You think you bad? A not afraid of you chicken foot."

"Chicken foot under yu mumma bed, bwoy."

"Stop it, the two of you." Stephen pulled them apart.

"Go inside. Both of you. Now. You acting like hooligans. People turning down their lamp already. Go inside!"

Back in his quarters, Roderick began to peel the paper wrapper off the book. Its dog-eared, food-stained cover told its weary years. He read out loud syllable by syllable: Sto-kely Car-mi-chael…Char-les V. Ham-il-ton. Black Power The Po-li-tics of Lib-er-a-tion in A-me-rica. Roderick repeated the title in chunks three times.

"Black Power. Black Power. Black Power," until he could feel the words fill his belly as he attempted to predict what the book might be about. "Lib-er-a-tion. A wonder what this word mean?"

Roderick played this game over and over in his mind. Closed the book. "Black Power. Liberation. Goodnight Stockley Carmichael." He placed the book under the cot. A cool breeze played on his neck. He looked up at the window; the moon was out.

"O man, a forgot to ask Lij when a can pick up the radio. So much things going on."

6

The Trunk And The Key

Roderick had cleared the clutter from three corners of his quarters and now he had to tackle the fourth to make the place look pretty. He had staked it out for a good two weeks as the perfect spot for the big leather trunk that stood unmoved at the foot of the cot ever since he came to live with Aunt Hope. The trunk had served as a place for him to sit on and just relax. Now he wanted to make the trunk a proper home for his artwork.

"Look how Lij house nice and pretty. I can make mine pretty, too."

Rolling out an old merino, Roderick got down on his knees and cleaned the trunk. Soon its rich army green color burst through all the grime. There were a few craters from cigarette burns. On the top was a destination label with the picture of a ship on a solid steel crest: American Railways, First Class, Sailing Date: 25 July 1959. Sailing From: New York. Thick tacks fastened the label. The moon cast a weary light on the iron lock. He tried to open it, but rust sealed the lock. "A wonder what Aunty have in here make it so heavy? I will find a way to open it. I will find a way."

An old pair of trousers hung conspicuously on a long nail. A soft, round, green wool felt beret hung on the nail over the top of the pants. Roderick climbed on the trunk and yanked down the trousers and the hat. So much dust emanated from the hat, he sneezed. The hat looked a lot like those worn by sailors, with a black visor and a crest on the front. Roderick rubbed his hand over the uneven surface of the metal crest.

"What a big bird, look like a John Crow to me. La La. Maybe a sailor-man used to wear this hat." As dusty as the hat was, something inside Roderick made him place it gently on the trunk. Then he examined the trousers. They clearly belonged to a tall man. Roderick had never seen a man visit for any length of time with his aunty. He quickly dismissed the idea that it belonged to her husband or even her brother.

"Perhaps somebody did live in here. Nahhh. Not with all them rat and cockroach. Aunty must be just dump them in here."

He rummaged through one pocket and found a dead spider. He flung it to the other end of the room with all his might.

"Roderick Brissett, when since you fraid a spider and a dead one at that?" He couldn't stop laughing. Then he went through the other pocket and found a small bundle with a knotted rope, a silver anchor, three keys and a metal tag with JBB written on it.

"A wonder what these keys open? It would be dandy if one of them can open this giant trunk. Hmm. Let me see for it lock up so tight."

The first one was too big; then the second just didn't fit. There was one more opportunity to see if the last one worked. Roderick twiddled the key in the trunk's hole and although it was a little rusty, it fit perfectly. "A don't believe it. Look like this one going to open it." He looked at the ceiling. Roderick crossed his middle finger over the first finger on his left hand. "Is me and you now!"
I always wanted to know what was inside the trunk.

He jiggled the lock. It burst open.

Blup!

Roderick jumped back, his heart raced like horses. He coughed from the cloud of dust.

"Sound like a motor bike backfire from bad gas. Shhh." He looked up at the door. Had anyone heard and was coming to see what just happened? "Them boys must hear this noise and thinking what going on inside here. A better cover up this trunk quick, quick, quick."

He rested his head on the trunk for a while and when he thought no one noticed and would come barging in; he continued to open the lid of the truck. "Man it heavy. What a heap a noise it make." The smell emitting from the truck was an old smell of aged crumbling books and clothes that were not worn in years. Seeping through was the clashing smells of cologne and camphor balls. Everything neatly folded and placed in some kind of order and Roderick was hesitant to disrupt the order, but wanted to know what else was in it.

"The somebody what own this trunk was very neat. Is so me like to see things neat, too." He examined the clothes. "Man clothes. Clean white shirts. Merinos. White underpants. A wonder if them can fit me." He found a pair of goulashes and a black dress boot, still shiny. He held on to the lid of the trunk to steady himself. Roderick tried on the shoes, but they were just a little too big for him.

Mi can soon grow into this. He placed it back in the trunk. Roderick unwrapped sheets of newspaper and discovered a brass lantern, studied it carefully. "This must be what the sailor them use on the ship. A like this. It will look nice on my little table over there."

He walked over to the table and placed it gently on top of it. Leaning back, he tilted his head to the right, then to the left. It really look nice fi true. But Roderick, suppose Aunty catch you with it? She will take it away. Maybe is something she want to keep for herself.

Some books were in a compartment on the cover of the trunk. In another, a bundle of papers and envelopes held together with a piece of sisal cord.

"Then is why this somebody save all them letter here? A going to find out." Untying the cord that held the letters together, he thought about his mother, how she never wrote him a letter since she sent him away to Kingston.

"Mama could give it to my step-father to mail it to me since he work at the post office." He looked at the trunk; something moved in his belly. "A want to know what's going on in this trunk but if Aunty catch me, is my bum bum in hot water. You know what, mama always say, 'If you peep inna people yard, duppy will jook out your eye.' A better put them back now."

"Roderick!"

She catch me now. Mercy. It done. His hands trembled, his nose tickled, and his heart pounded. He quickly put the letters in the trunk and closed it.

"Roderick Brissett!"

"Coming Aunty."

Afraid that his aunty would find out that he had gone into the trunk and discovered perhaps what he shouldn't, like old folks would say: Big people's things, Roderick temporarily abandoned his expedition. He would clean the dust from the surface of the trunk but dared not open it again. Some days, he would sit and think about what mysteries they buried inside those letters. There was just something about the trunk that made him want to understand things.

Dinner time had morphed into supper time and no one had called out to him to come and eat. The Blackie mangoes Roderick got from Miss Dillon two days earlier were quite ripe. Nothing pleased him more than the juice from a ripe mango. Roderick ate the first one to his heart's content, but he was still hungry. Making even soft steps, he tiptoed down the corridor and into the kitchen, where his dinner, now cold, covered with a small kitchen towel in his enamel bowl. Hurriedly, he picked it up and scampered back to his room, where he ate the scrumptious stewed peas and rice with spinners, his favorite. One more mango made a perfectly sweet dessert. Roderick stretched and yawned, took the bowl and spoon back to the kitchen, washed and dried them. Then he placed them in the cupboard and hastened to his quarters.

It was getting dark as night enveloped the house. Roderick reached for the matches and lit the kerosene lamp. In a matter of minutes, the flame settled from a blazing red and orange with smoke to a cool blue, illuminating the Home Sweet Home lampshade which he placed carefully on the dresser. The first book he opened, which he retrieved from the trunk, was Sonnets From The Portuguese, love poems written by Elizabeth Browning. On opening it, a photograph with corrugated edges fell from the book onto his lap.

"Pretty girls like Chloe!"

Upon closer scrutiny, he discovered that there were three girls and one man in a sailor's uniform in the middle. One could hardly see the sailor's face, partially covered with the visor from his hat. Turning to the back of the photo,

Roderick read the cursive ink, slightly fading: "Lillian, Hope, me, Belle. Myrtle Bank Hotel. Kingston. 1962. Lillian, that's Aunt Lillian. O my gosh! She was so young." He flipped over the photo again. "Is Aunt Hope that? Why she look so cross?" Her two long dropped curls on either side of her head rested on her chest. She stood tall and rigid. "Aunt Hope body look strong but her face mean."
Roderick flipped the picture yet again to inspect Belle. "Who is Belle?" He was a little puzzled. Then he recognized the mole on her right cheek. "That's my mama, Mara'Belle."

His mama's smooth skin tone matched her wide smile; she raised her head, revealing a deep cleft in her chin. It was as if her cheerful slanting eyes wanted Roderick to know how much she loved the man next to her in the picture whose hand she held–the tall handsome sailor-man. Tears swelled up in his eyes. This old picture of his mother and aunts told a different story of a distant past when the Flowers' children were happier.

"But who is this sailor-man in the middle? This must be his trunk. A wonder what else a will find out?"
He placed the photograph smoothly into the book, closed it, and returned it to the slot in the truck. With a full stomach, Roderick played, "one letter, two letter, three letter, four, five letter, six letter, seven letter more. La la!"
His first finger landed on a little bundle of airmail envelopes with blue and red edges tied neatly together with a satin ribbon. Roderick cautiously untied the ribbon and chose the first letter.

"What a hell if Aunt Hope catch me a read them letter here?" He crumpled up an old newspaper, formed a wedge, jammed the door and read away.

My Dearest Hope,

I must go out to sea next Thursday. My heart can barely stand to leave you and Roderick behind. Yes, I know you preferred the name Felix, but I always wanted to name him Roderick after my great-grandfather. That's the name his mother gave him when he was born in Germany. Alas. You won like you always do and it broke my heart on the banks of the Sandy Gully. I don't know when our ship will set sail again for Kingston Harbour. Till then, enjoy the secret garden outside your window, my love. May our love blossom like the red poinsettias that bloom in the autumn. I will be sure to write. Sweet kisses, my love.

With all my heart,
JBB

"Felix should a name Roderick, my name. A wah this? Who this somebody who sign him name JBB? Secret garden outside the window. Hmm. A wonder! A wonder if the garden under my window is the same one in this letter. Hmmm? This JBB somebody must be special to Aunt Hope. A better put this back right now before she find out me all into her business."

Lying on the cot, he reminisced about the wonders of the day. He felt chilly and then he felt hot. "What's going on with me? Wonder what else a going to find in this trunk. This picture with mama and my aunty them, the sailor-man. Who

Felix?" Roderick put the letter in his Stokely Carmichael book. "Nobody will find it. I can't wait to show Chloe."

Olympic Gardens was a rather unusual neighborhood in Kingston. Imagine an area named after a festival that honors the ancient Greek god Zeus. There was nothing Greek or ancient about this neighborhood. What was strikingly noteworthy was that they named some streets after Jamaicans who competed in the Olympic Games. It was a sleepy community of young working people, some elderly who still hustled. The sidewalks often filled with children who played competitive sports with crude bats, balls, stone markers, marbles, and pushcarts. Makes you wonder if they were dreaming of the Olympics. Yet, Roderick spent most of his day on chores. At least they allowed the other children to play and get strong in the sun. He had a friend in Chloe and could hardly wait for her to return from school.

Roderick had finished his morning chores, having cleaned the chicken coop and swept the back yard. He stepped onto the piazza where Miss Dillon sold her produce, greeted her, sat on the landing and stared into space. Olympic Way was breathing a balmy air. The blinding silver sun pinned itself tightly against a cloudless blue sky. A row of houses across from the shop stood persnickety behind pink and white periwinkles and red hibiscus flower-hedged yards. The neighbors painted their houses in two or more colors of the rainbow and wore personalities that murmured minds of their own. Laced curtains, plaid curtains, cotton curtains escaped the heat through opened windows; their bellies rose high like duppy umbrellas, surrendered to an occasional swell of wind, then retreated to their sills, becoming still again.

Roderick watched as Gladstone and Chiquita knocked on gates, called out to shadows of persons in opened windows, looking for a day's work to weed anybody's yard, wash and iron dirty clothes. The pair had been traversing the town for more than a decade so they could feed their six children, one of whom had the fit. The sidewalks knew the rhythm of their feet; their feet knew every scab and puddle of pus that fought against their will to survive. Everyone along The Way knew Gladdy and Chicky. Yet, today, no one wished to know them. No one offered them work.

"Life hard ee!" Roderick searched the thoughtful chambers in his heart as he wiped the sweat that trapped a few strands of soft hair on his forehead.

Roderick imagined the grandmas, grandpas behind those sweating cement walls sipping Blue Mountain coffee and smoking Craven-A cigarettes, ears glued to their radios, listening to the prodigious love story of Doctor Paul; others read Bibles and offered midday prayers against the backdrop of secrets and lies and the courage of a beautiful woman on the radio serial, Portia Faces Life.

He watched people get off a bus. "Miss Dillon, Miss Dillon. Who tha lady just come off the bus?"

"Who, you mean Mona?"

"Is so she name. O Miss Dillon she pretty eee?"

"She is a pretty lady. Live on DeLisser Avenue."

"You know her good good?"

"She a good lady. Grow up right here in Olympic Gardens. Mind her own business. Don't trouble no one."

"O my, she pretty for real."

"Little boy, don't let your head worry you about them pretty woman there."

"Me not worry. Me did just asking for me don't have no friend round here, except Chloe. Of late, every couple of weeks she spend her weekends uptown in Beverly Hills."

"You need friends your own age."

"Chloe tell me personally that she love going up a Beverly Hills because she get fi swim and play tennis with her cousin them at her uncle and him wife big house."
Roderick became quiet for a while, thinking about Chloe's kindness since he moved into town.
It hard to live without her when she go away. My two cousin them don't even bother with me. I can tell Chloe anything. She can keep a secret. A hope she hurry up and come, me have so much to tell her.

"Miss Dillon, you think Mr. Goodman going to send Chloe go live with her aunty in Beverly Hills?"

"I don't know, dear. The way things going around here these days, it wouldn't surprise me at all."

"How me going to live without her?"

"Who says she is going anywhere?"

"Is just something me been feeling inside me belly. She going away so often. When she not gone to London and Miami, she gone to Beverly Hills."

"Then you must ask her if that is so. This way, you can stop worrying your head about that."

"You don't understand, Miss Dillon. Apart from you and Mr. Goodman, Chloe is all I have in Olympic Gardens."

"You have Nelton, Stephen and Miss Hope."

"I never check you would say so, Miss Dillon. You see for yourself how them treat me bad around here."

"You right. But Miss Hope is still in charge of you."

"Me in charge of me, Miss Dillon. My aunty don't want me. She use me fi care her shop."

"Never mind, boy. One day you will grow big and can help yourself."

"Don't look like me going to grow big for aunty brutalize me so much. Mi don't think me going to live long."

"Don't say that. God will take care of you."

"I hope so. For Aunt Hope don't look like she care." The afternoon wore on and Roderick became more concerned that Chloe was late coming home. A bus pulled up at the stop, down the street from the shop. Roderick watched as the school children and adults got off. He stared at groups disbursing: some going across the street, others going up or down Olympic Way. The street was abuzz with laughter and conversations that spilled over from their bus ride. There was no sign of Chloe.

"A wonder what happen to Chloe. She didn't come off the bus, Miss Dillon."

"Maybe she on another one."

"But that going get her home too late."

"No. Be patient. The buses run every thirty minutes. One will soon be here. Take this little bunch of guineps. They are very sweet and will make you feel better."

"Thank you, Miss Dillon. You notice is you feed me all day. First you give me that bowl of green banana, sweet cassava, okra and salt fish for lunch. You so nice to me. A like to talk to you."

"I am a mother and I love other people's children, too."

Soon, another bus arrived, and Chloe was the first to alight. Roderick smiled, and she walked towards him.

"You reach!"

"Yes. I have arrived in one piece."

Chloe dropped her bag on the ground and Roderick opened his arms wide and hugged her. His heart raced, and he pulled away quickly.

A wonder if them can hear mi heart a beat hard? Roderick took a deep breath.

"A have so much to tell you, Chloe."

"Really."

"Yes. You wouldn't believe some things me buck upon this weekend."

"When you coming over so you can tell me everything?"

"Tomorrow."

"Great!"

Roderick turned to Miss Dillon, "Excuse me, please, a going to walk Chloe to her gate."

He whispered in Chloe's ear. "A can't let anyone hear these things."

"Sounds like some serious business, Roderick."

"Serious fi true."

He took her in for a moment and noticed her hair looked different. It was long and straight, like Indian girls who live on Booby Drive.

"Why your hair look like Rapunzel?"

"Rapunzel? Very funny. Her hair is not real. Besides, it is gold."

"All the curls them gone. What them do to your hair?"

"My aunty cream it so it got straight."

"Cream it? How cream make your hair straight. Don't is something you eat pon cone?"
Chloe burst out in laughter, flung her head back, and circled it to the side. Her lacquered mane whipped the air stylishly.

"Is a thing like hair oil them put in your hair and straighten it just like when people press hair with the hot comb."

"You mean it smell stink like when Aunt Hope friend come over and straighten her hair with the hot comb in the fire?"

"Yes, it smells funny, but not like the straightening comb."

"After me don't know about them things there. But it make you look different."

"It looks good, Roderick?"

"Me never say it look good. Me say it look different. Me did like it when it curly."

"Lord, Roderick, you need to get out more often," she chided in an uptown inflection, altissimo.

"A check so. Can I come with you the next time you going to visit your aunty? I want to know Beverly Hills, too."

"I have to ask my father."

"Me miss you when you go away on weekends. Me don't have nobody to play with."

"You know your aunty is not letting you out of the cage."

"Me soon let out myself. Trust me. Me tired of her wickedness."

"So, what you have to tell me?"

"Look here." He pulled out the letter from the book. "A find this letter in the trunk. Me read it and some strange things go on in my family. A so confused right now. We can't talk about it outside here. A have a little spot we can go tomorrow and nobody will know we around there."

"That sound creepy."

"No. Is our hiding place and we can read the letter. Is more letter me find too. Going to take me a whole year to read them."

"You not afraid your aunty catches you."

"Of course me fraid but wi little hiding place safe, she can't catch we there."

"I don't know, Roderick. You brave. We will finish up tomorrow. Right? I have to do my homework and Daddy soon comes home."

"Awright. See you tomorrow. Remember to ask your father if a can come over on Sunday to get some reading lessons."

"Yes. I will. I am sure he will say yes, but that cantankerous aunty of yours will be so upset with him again."

"She don't matter to me right now. Is not she going to school, is me. Just ask him for I."

"For I, Roderick? It's for me, not for I."

"For me. For I. Is the same somebody."

The two children scrutinized each other's faces for a moment, and locked pinky fingers, a sign of devotion to their sacrosanct friendship.

7

Who Am I

Roderick was the first to get to the secret garden outside his window. He planned to meet Chloe there just as the sun was sinking behind the breadfruit tree. The chickens were still shuffling around, trying to settle down in their coop. An occasional dog barked in the distance. Silver frogs croaked in the big puddle that formed near the outhouse after the heavy rains and sounded much like a flock of chirping red breasted robins. Roderick sat still, looked out as the evening shadows painted abstract shapes on the walls. Trees danced a Rocksteady to the gentle breeze. He couldn't help but wonder about his life in Kingston, how far he had come, his hope as bright as the sunset.

"This trunk thing have me a think bout plenty things. Look pon mi finger them how them crack up crack up." Looked in the mirror. "Jeepaz. Mi want a trim. Aunty treat me so bad like she pick me up out a rubbish pan. At least Chloe have her father. Lij have him father. It look like me is the only one weh don't have nobody." He took a deep breath. Closed his eyes and opened them again.

"Okay Roderick. You have Suraj. Poor Suraj him can hardly help himself." He threw a pebble in the puddle and smiled as it rippled in tiny circles. "One, two, three, four-five, six-seven. Look how one stone make so much circle. Awright. Don't worry about a thing."

"Pssssst!"

Roderick looked up to see Chloe climbing over the fence to meet him. "Shhhh. Careful." He cupped his hands so he could help her down the wall.

"What took you so long, Chloe?"

"Practicing my part to sing in the choir when the Archbishop of Canterbury comes to visit Jamaica."

"You mean Canterbury like the Canterbury tales story book?"

"Yes."

"When him coming?"

Counting her fingers. "Thursday, Friday, Saturday. Three more days. First Sunday in March. Since Perennial Primary is an Anglican school, we are holding a special sing-along to honor him."

"That good, Chloe. That good."

"Your father know you here?"

"No. I told Miss Peaches to look out for me. Only she knows. Dad went to the Kiwanis Club meeting. We have a little time."

"I don't see Miss Peaches that often. One time she wave to me."

"She is really nice. She will keep my secret."

"All right then. Come sit down on the bench with me."

He watched as she ran her hands along the sides of her pink and white polka dot dress, sat on the skirt, pressed her arms on the bench, stretched her spine tall, looked around the garden, and smiled. Although weeds filled the garden, the patches of dandelions, like yellow broaches, glowed from the last rays of evening sun. Roderick took out the bundle of letters and gave them to Chloe.

She turned it over and read: "Air mail."

Sensing her curiosity rising like a kite, he pointed to the letter he had read earlier that week. She opened it and read to herself.

"No, Chloe. Read it loud mek me hear it."

"Shhh. Somebody might hear us."

"No. You read it out loud."

"All right. I will pick up where I left off."

"Yes, I know you preferred the name Felix, but I always wanted to name him Roderick after my great-grandfather." Chloe paused. "You mean Aunt Hope has a son named Felix and his dad wanted to name him Roderick?"

"It look so."

"What a prekkeh!"

"That's what me talking about. Something strange bout that, Chloe. Something strange. Go on read more."

"Till then, enjoy the secret garden outside your window, my love. May our love blossom like the red poinsettias that bloom in autumn. I will be sure to write. Sweet kisses, my love. With all my heart, JBB."

Silence. They looked into each other's eyes. No one said a word for a good ten seconds.

"So what you make of it, Roderick?" Chloe was whispering even softer.

"I think Felix should be me and me should be Felix. I don't know, Chloe. It don't make any sense to me."

"What I know is that this JBB loved your Aunt Hope."

"And it look as if is right here where we sitting them used to come and spend time. Lord, if is so it go and Aunt Hope find out we out here I won't have a bottom to sit on."

The evening sun disappeared behind the trees. The chickens became still. A cool breeze rustled the mango tree. Roderick looked over at Chloe; she was still reading letters and postcards by the street lamp that came on down the lane.

"Quiet. I hear a car pull up at the gate, Chloe. I think your father come home."

"So soon. No. Your mind playing tricks on you."

"Shhhh. Hold down your head. I hear footsteps." Roderick tossed the bundle of letters in the shrubs to hide them. The footsteps got closer. Roderick knew he was going to get the whipping of his life tonight. Slowly, he raised his head to see Miss Peaches, peering over the fence beckoning to Chloe that it's time to come over.

"I have to go over now, Roderick."

"Awright. We can read some more again."

"Bye." She placed both palms by the side of her mouth like a bullhorn but whispered, "try to find out what JBB stands for."

"Big detective on it, my friend." He winked at her, pushed out his chest. "Bye."

Roderick helped her over the fence, picked up the letters, climbed up on the water pipe and made his way through the window. As the evening wore on, he became restless and wanted to know more, so he jammed the door, lit the kerosene lamp and curled up on the floor with the pile of letters. So much going through his mind, but these letters drove his desire to read on. Five letters in Roderick felt exhausted, yet had not figured out what JBB stands for.

"I guess is a code between him and Aunty. Maybe them don't want nobody to know. A wonder why? The only thing left to ponder from a postcard is that JBB is a real somebody and Grandma Tata likes him."

> Hopie, I miss visiting with your mama, Tata. She is such a jovial woman. Tata makes me feel really special, like a son. Last time was not so good. She scolded me for causing confusion between you and your sister, Mara'Belle. I hope we can put this behind us some day.
>
> Yours,
>
> JBB

"Chloe Detective number two, this is getting warmer. Something into something."

Vivid night dreams were coming frequently, and Roderick got this chilling feeling that someone was watching him. He remembered his mother telling him, don't eat too late at night or you will get scary nightmares. Roderick tried to resist eating late, except during mango season.

That night, Roderick found himself in the middle of a storm on a glass-bottom boat at sea. Fish of rainbow colors and turtles dived among the coral reef for cover. Roderick tried to stand, but the waves flung the boat and he fell on his back. Looking up, it was pitch black and only a single boat light illuminated the phosphorous on the water. The waves dashed against the boat and he cried for his mother. The screams drowned his voice and kept coming from every direction on the boat. Roderick looked out the window. The fish had disappeared and only sea-foam was churning.

It felt like forever in the dark. The sea became calm. Then he heard, "Adjust the sails. Tides low." The chilly feeling came back. There he was, a tall man in his white, sea captain's uniform, standing over him. He looked familiar, but Roderick couldn't recall where or how they met. Roderick reached to him for help.

"Are you…" Before he could finish his question, he woke out of his sleep.

Looking around, he thought about his mother, who disappeared from his dream, and the man who came to help him. Then he remembered the photograph he hid inside the Stokely Carmichael book.

"I can't believe I didn't show the picture to Chloe." Lying on the cot, he held the picture to the lamplight, searched their faces again. This time, the light made the man in the sailor's uniform look brighter. Roderick could see his eyes and a slight smile on his face. On his shirt just below the crest was a name tag. Roderick held the picture still closer to the light, careful not to burn it.

"It look like the first word is John, like John in the Bible. The one mama said had them wild dreams about the end of the world. B. Brissett. Brissett is like my name? This has got to be what the JBB stands for. A wonder if him know me?" Roderick felt that somehow the Brissett sailor-man must be somebody important.

"I want to be a sea captain like him. I want to go to school to learn sea captain work." His mind was racing like the fudge stick boats he and Chloe loved to race down Bollo's dirty water. That night, he wrote a letter to his new imaginary friend.

dear sea captain,

the other day a was digging through a old truck in my little quarters. a check say it belong to you. when you coming back for them? guess what noh, a find a picture of you with Aunt Lillian, aunt hope and my mother mara. Me find out you and me have the same last name. you know me, Captain? you so tall with good hair and fair skin like my friend Chloe father. him so light you can see the blue veins in him face. She so lucky to have a father. a don't even know my father. him leave me an mi mama when me was little. O captain, a want to be a sea captain just like you. come take me with you on the boat? why me even ask anyway, you won't want me either like my aunty, my mama, missa cupidon. aunty treat me like me drop from sky. me don't have nobody that love me. plenty day me think hard fi run away go a sea but me going to go a school first captain. me going a schooooo… zzzzzzzzzzzzzz.

Roderick fell asleep.

8

Pressed to the Wall

The Easter school term was almost over, and there was no sign that Roderick's aunt would permit him to attend school. Roderick took matters into his own hands. Without his aunty knowing his plan, Roderick got dressed in his school uniform and new brown shoes. He rolled an exercise book like a funnel, stuck it in his back pocket. He placed a pencil behind his ear, jumped through his secret window and made his way towards Perennial Primary School.

"Me not doing no yard work today. Me going to school all by myself. If I don't go, Aunty will keep me lock up like a shop boy. I will deal with the beating when me come back home. I am going to school."

Roderick walked to school after waiting for a while and a bus did not arrive. Upon entering the school compound, he noticed the children were moving swiftly to their classrooms. He loitered outside a classroom window he chose at random, listened to the teacher and the children engaged in lively debates and storytelling. Visualizing himself sitting at a desk surrounded by cheerful children, he became lost in his daydream. Roderick heard the teacher telling the class how proud she was that they came prepared with their end of term projects. They ranged from reciting poetry by Jamaican poets to telling stories about people and places of historical value to a newly independent country.

He crouched behind the huge metal window that rolled outward and hid behind it so that the teacher could not see him. Roderick listened attentively to a boy around his age recite. The boy bowed from his waist down, straightened himself, chin up, looked ahead without blinking and clasped palms across this chest:

> If We Must Die by Claude McKay.
> If we must die—let it not be like hogs
> Hunted and penned in an inglorious spot,
> While round us bark the mad and hungry dogs,
> Making their mock at our accursed lot.
> If we must die—oh, let us nobly die,
> So that our precious blood may not be shed
> In vain; then even the monsters we defy
> Shall be constrained to honor us though dead!
> Oh, Kinsmen! We must meet the common foe;
> Though far outnumbered, let us show us brave,
> And for their thousand blows deal one deathblow!
> What though before us lies the open grave?
> Like men we'll face the murderous, cowardly pack,
> Pressed to the wall, dying, but fighting back.

Roderick held on to every word the boy recited. The back of his neck became stiff with excitement. "I like how he put his right fist in the air at the end. 'Dying, but fighting back!' I want to recite like him." He smiled as the children clapped and cheered on their classmate. The applause filled the room and spilled over into the corridor. Roderick became fully immersed in the lesson. He clapped so heartily that he did not realize the children had stopped clapping. This drew attention to him. The teacher signaled for him to "Run along. Go to class!"

The children giggled. Little did the teacher and the children know Roderick had no class to go to—this was the only class he knew—outside the window.

Two days later, Roderick returned to the school. This time, he climbed over the fence to get into the schoolyard because the school had already started. Aunt Hope did not go to the market; instead, she took Nelton to the doctor because he was running a high fever, which delayed Roderick.

"What you doing scaling the fence, boy!" A powerful voice jolted him from across the fence.

"Me won't do it again, sir."

"You need to leave home earlier."

"Sorry, sir."

"Sorry is not good enough. You should be in school. What is your name, young man?"

"Me name Roderick. Roderick Brissett, sir."

"Brissett! Any relations to Felix Brissett? He used to come here, but his mother took him out some time ago. Nice fellow."

Felix Brissett? It must be the same Felix me read about in the letter. A wonder if is him.

"No sir. I don't know no Felix, sir."

"Funny, I don't recall seeing you around here before. No one calls me sir. They call me Mr. Rollins. Where is your epaulette for your khaki shirt? Where is your brown socks?" The barrage of questions made Roderick want to pee in his pants, but there was something comforting about Mr. Rollins' eyes.

Him don't look so rough though. Roderick felt the blood rush into his fingers as Mr. Rollins took him by the hand and led him to his watchman's room.

Maybe a can tell him what really going on. Him look like him will hear me out.

"Talk to me, boy. Where do you go to school because it is certainly not Perennial?"

"Mi don't go a no school. Me want to come to this school but mi aunty don't want me to go to school."

"Are you lying to me, boy?"

"No, sir… Mr. Rollins. Mi not lie to nobody, sir."

"Every child belongs in school. Come with me. I am taking you to the headmaster."

"No, sir. Please don't take me. If mi aunty find out, she going to kill mi with beating. It better mi just stay outside the window and learn what mi can learn. Mi really learning, you know." Roderick dabbed his sweaty palms on his pants, looked up at Mr. Rollins, who had covered his mouth and appeared deep in thought.

"I didn't get to go to school when I was a boy like you. That's why I had to work harder than most. Life is hard when you don't have a good education. Sit right here and don't move."

Roderick watched Mr. Rollins fetch a slice of bun and cheese and soda from a little cupboard in a corner of the room.

"I guess you must be hungry, too."

"Yes, sir. Thank you."

"You know that I still have to report this to the headmaster. Maybe, it will be the best thing for you. I am sure he can get you into the school with no problem."

"O Mister Rollins, you don't know my aunt. She is a wicked woman. Only fi her boys them get to go to school. Me have to work in the shop all day and hours a night."

"That is not good. You should be in school. You can work in the shop after school. Let's go." Mr. Rollins held Roderick by the hand and walked him straight into Headmaster Eldemire's office.

"I caught this young man scaling the fence after the late bell. I get to understand that he is not a student at this school, no school for that matter, sir."

"What is your name?"

"Roderick Brissett, sir."

"Roderick Brissett. I recall that name. I seem to remember a little boy a year ago being brought into this school to register with my dear friend, Mr. Goodman. Could that child be you?"

Roderick bowed down his head in shame and mumbled, "Yes, sir. Is me. Me same one."

Headmaster Eldemire thanked Mr. Rollins, asked him to leave and close the door behind him.

"Tell me, why did you feel the need to jump the fence? You could hurt yourself. In fact, it is against the rules of our school and you could have been in serious trouble."

"Me never know, sir. Me did just want to come inside here so me can learn something. Is two weeks now me stand up outside the street a watch di children them come inside a morning time. Is just the other day me make up my mind to come inside. Me don't want to work in the shop till me dead."

"Remember, someone already registered you to attend this school? We just have to notify your aunt that you are here. Preventing you from getting an excellent education is against the law. The government could punish her."

"Fi real, sir." Roderick's eyes widened with shock at that revelation.

"Yes. It is real."

My aunty get punish for evilness. Fi real, sir?

"Let me handle it. You can stay in Mrs. Lawes's class for the rest of the day."

"Mi cyaa stay all day, sir. Aunt Hope soon come home from the doctor and if mi not into the shop, she will kill me wid beatn. I can't take one more beating, sir."

"You won't have to endure another beating. I will see to it. Let me take care of this for you. I will walk you to class. Here is a lunch ticket. When the bell rings for lunch, you can go with the children and have lunch."

"Thank you, sir."

Roderick was worried, but happy at the same time. He got the impression that this time the headmaster would get his aunt to be reasonable and let him stay in school.

That afternoon, Mr. Eldemire drove Roderick home. Roderick thought about his first day spent inside a classroom after so many years. He thought about Mr. Eldemire and how he was handling his impossible situation.

A going home to read my new reading book Miss Lawes gave me for homework. A feel so happy. Mi cyaa wait fi tell Chloe.

Upon their arrival at the shop door, a lady was speaking with Roderick's aunt on the piazza. Mr. Eldemire told him she was from the Ministry of Education.

"So you bring down crowd on me, Mr. Brissett. You happy now?" Hope yelled out to Roderick.

I am going to get it tonight. Look at her eye them. Like she wild.

Mr. Eldemire greeted Miss Hope and the education officer. "He must be in school. This boy took himself to school all on his own. That says a lot about his interest in getting an education. It is his right, Madam."

"The two a you finish now, sir?" Hope turned both palms upwards and shrugged her shoulders.

"No need to be disrespectful. So many children are roaming the streets without guidance. We will leave now and expect him in school tomorrow."

It look like Aunty not going beat me tonight.

That night, Roderick hung his school uniform in the old wardrobe. He thought about how Mr. Rollins listened to him and told him about a boy named Felix Brissett. "A too tired right now to go back through that trunk, but one way or the other I am going to find out if Felix is the same one in the letter. A going back to school tomorrow."

9

Open Heart

Roderick spent an entire month in school without his aunty giving him grief. He did his chores to avoid annoying her. Easter holidays had come around and his friend Chloe had gone away. Stephen went to spend time with an aunt in the country on his father's side.

"Why me couldn't go spend time with Tata since me never get to go see her Christmas time? Why me have to stay with Aunty and this sick boy?" Roderick stood outside his cousins' room and watched as Nelton twisted and turned in pain. "Aunt Hope say him burning up."

Nelton's chin hung like a yellow-belly bullfrog yawning before the butterfly-kill. He had come down with a sudden illness. Petgrave's dog died from it last year. From the looks of this, Nelton was suffering.

"Me not catching this sickness at all. A hear aunty telling her customer if it turn down in him, bad things happen. Her customer say is like a plague that only ashes and green lime could cure."

Nelton turned his head from side to side like a dog with worms in its ears. The intense light from the sun made him cover his eyes. Hope told Roderick to stay home and care for him, but he was not about to hang around long enough to die like a dog, too.

"Is when this sickness going to end?" Roderick agonized. "Aunty can't stand me. I know it wouldn't bother her if I get sick too."

"Roderick!"

"Yes Aunty."

"Go bring a bowl of the soup from the stove outside and give Nelton. A have to tend to the customers them."

Walking down the hallway, Roderick could smell the rank stench of sickness that permeated the house. It was as if Nelton had soaked ten days in urine and donkey doodu.

"Me not going near that boy goh catch him sickness. Why Aunty send away Stephen, Daphne and the little girl for two whole weeks, leave me here? Nelton so spoil. I can't stand the bugger." With his right fist, he punched the palm of his left hand several times, as if looking for answers. "Going three days now and Aunty say him fever still high and him ears corner them swell up. Is what happen to him, Lawd?" Roderick ran outside to fulfill his aunty's wishes. Then he realized something like this happened to his uncle some years ago in the country.

The morning sounded much like a chorus of elephants when the field hands woke up. He rushed to the outhouse before having breakfast and take off to the field. Roderick was not always exuberant about Uncle's cock-a-doodle-do mornings. He had stretched, made a loud yawn, lumbered to the standpipe and washed his face. Uncle's kitchen was redolent with the rich aroma of Paradise Glen chocolate tea he blended with fresh cow's milk, coconut milk, nutmeg and cinnamon leaves. No one dared to miss this brew as Uncle took great pride in preparing it long before they stirred. He would serve it with warm duck bread.
This morning, in particular, thunder rolled, and lightning flashed. The rain grimaced but did not fall. The sky was as ill-omened as a starless night.

"Bring that horse, come give me so I can ride to the farm, Roderick. Yam harvest is here."

Roderick ran up the small hill; pass the water tank and a small patch of flowering banana plants where the horse rested in a little shed. He pushed in the door of the small shed and patted the horse on its hip. The horse had just dumped a fresh load of feces and Roderick could barely stand the odor.

"Let's go, Daisy."

The horse did not move. Roderick patted Daisy again, and she was as obstinate as the Cockpit Mountain.

"What wrong wid you dis mawnin, Daisy?"

Daisy neighed and stomped her right hind leg.

"Uncle waiting on you. Come noh. Cho." Roderick was getting impatient with Daisy.

"What wrong a say?" He paused. "You feel sick?"

The horse raised its head, opened his cavernous mouth, and let out a boisterous neigh. Still, she did not budge. Roderick patted the horse's nose because he knew how important Daisy was to Uncle. This time, Daisy kicked him. Roderick fell to the ground.

"That hurt, Daisy. What's wrong with you this morning? Why you kick me for?"

Roderick looked away from the horse as if he was speaking with someone.

"You know what, a better go back go tell Uncle seh Daisy look like she don't feel like goh nowhere this mawnin."

The horse made a whinny. She was not moving out today. Roderick started his descent down the stony path. He could sense something strange about the morning. The dark clouds hung over the valley like a woolen patchwork blanket. From the top of the hillock, he could see the front stoop of the house below and Uncle was lying face down on the ground.

Roderick's heart pounded like a buru drum: *Buum buum. Buum buum!*

"Help, help, help!"

He started running and he could feel the sharp stones beneath his bare feet colluding to hold him back. Roderick knew something bad happened to Uncle.

"Help, help, help!" Roderick kept yelling at the top of his lungs.

"Help, help, mama, somebody, help! Uncle drop down." His desperate scream echoed through the valley and vibrated against the water tank. He threw himself on Uncle and frantically shook him. "Wake up Uncle. Wake up!" Uncle was burning hot and Roderick became afraid. He was all alone.

"Uncle, you can hear me? You eat bitter yam. You say some of the yam can make we sick if it not fit." He shook his uncle. "Lawks, Uncle sick bad."

Boom. Boom. Thunder clapped and Roderick jolted. He knew he was in trouble this time. He realized Nelton was really sick, and it wasn't yams making him sick.

"O my God, Nelton must be have mumz like Uncle."

Roderick thought how fortunate not catching the mumps from his uncle when he was little. He was not about to get it now, not in Kingston, where there was no bush medicine woman to get him better. He was a tyro, at best.

"Why me have to help him, anyway? The boy wicked like him madda. Cho, mek him stay right there so and melt away."

Ignoring his aunt's wishes to stay with Nelton, Roderick went to his room, fetched a bunch of guineps and the reading book his teacher, Miss Lawes, gave to him. Then he climbed through the window into his secret garden. Intending to read a few chapters, he flipped through the pages but could not focus. The need to plan a way to get out of the nursing task consumed him. He examined the bunch of guineps and began an all-out conversation with them, one bite at a time.

"A wonder if Aunty will make me go to school in the morning time so I can work in the shop in the evening time like Mr. Rollins did tell me the other day? How that sound? He paused for an answer from his imaginary companion.

"Mi don't think she going to do that. Mek a think. Maybe me can ask Miss Dillon to fill in for me in the morning time. A know she want me to go a school like her children them but Aunty not reasonable. Who going to sell Miss Dillon things when she in the shop? Forget it."
He burst open a guinep skin, leaned forward and quickly sucked on the juice, careful not to get the nectar on his shirt, recalling his mother telling him it will stain his clothes.

"Hear what me going do. A going to go find Miss Daphne and ask her to come back." He bit into another guinep. "You sweet eeh!" He smiled and looked intently at the guinep. "You know what, a did hear Miss Daphne tell Aunty that she was staying with Grandma Tata. A going get up soon a morning and feed Nelton. Aunty will love that and she won't even notice when mi sneak out through the window. Mi will tek the bus go a Tata and ask Miss Daphne fi come back. Yes, that will work. Mi brain tired." Tossing the guinep seeds into the shrubs, he said, "A hope all a you make up and grow into a tall guinep tree."

He looked up and saw a green lizard crawling down the wall. Straight away, he remembered the counsel of a super slick Kingston lizard he encountered in one of his wild nightmares, seven months after the bus driver deposited on his aunt's steps.

"Strive to do good so that others can be good to you."

Back then, he was stumped by the dream and told old Suraj who explained,

"The dream is teaching you about the Daya, your compassionate ways that you must strive to extend to everyone, even those who have done you wrong."

"Now why me have to remember lizard story now? You know what; let me go help Nelton before him miserable madda come brutalize me. A have it all work out." He closed the book.

Roderick walked quickly to the backyard, cut down a brown coconut bough, with green blades, some of which were yellowing, hanging almost lifelessly over the fence, beaten by the recent rains. While stripping the leaves with his special double-blade cracked-ice handle pen knife Suraj gave him for New Year, he could hear the Petgrave's children and their friends laughing on their way home. With steady hand, he took some of the hot ashes from under the coal stove where his Aunt Hope had made gungo peas soup earlier that morning and wrapped it in a merino he pulled from the clothesline. Afterwards, he picked a handful of limes from the tree and put them in his pocket. Roderick placed the bowl of soup in the concave cushioned end of the bough, which he used like a serving tray. He wanted to stay as far as possible from Nelton.

Roderick walked guarded towards the boy's room and peeped through the half-opened door. Nelton's swollen face was like a blowfish. The corners of his mouth were scaly.

"Eh em!" Roderick cleared his throat to signal the boy that he was close by. "Get up, man. Get up. Mi bring some soup fi you lunch."

Nelton tried to open his eyes, saturated with mucus. His lips, as parched as a desert, veinal gullies that cracked open, exposed his tender pink flesh. The boy looked pitiful. Exercising great caution, Roderick pressed the door open with his foot and pushed the bough with the bowl of soup through the door, careful not to spill it.

"See your food here. Get up and drink it. Try your best don't make it burn you or me can't help you." Nelton tried to get up but was too weak. He groaned. Roderick took another step back at the sound of Nelton's groan.

"Me nah catch what you have at all, maas breddas. Me nah catch your worries." Roderick looked at him for a moment thinking. After you laugh after me so much when your mother beat and take away my things give you, a can't believe you would want me to help you now. Shaking his head at Nelton, he said, "You know you are a lucky bugger. Suraj say if you to drown yuh can't hang. Me might as well help you out you little wretch you." With that, Roderick pulled a handkerchief from his pocket, tied it around his face so Nelton would not breathe on him. Then he fed the boy the soup. It took him close to half an hour to get few spoons of soup down his throat.

Nelton squeezed his broken lips shut to show that he wanted no more of the soup. Roderick placed the bowl on the make-shift tray and put them on the floor. Afterwards, he tied the merino he had filled with warm ashes and lime around the boy's throat and his ears.

"You better pray me don't draw the cloth choke and squeeze you?" Roderick felt Nelton's heart beating fast as an akete drum: *kitim kitim kitim kitim*. He looked in Nelton's eyes; one opened, red, pus-infected eye and became squeamish at the awful sight. Nelton closed it again. Roderick could feel the vapors of heat rising from Nelton's body.

"Don't worry. You going awright. My Uncle did sick just like you one time. You will get better. Me just have to make sure me don't get sick like you. A have to take care of myself, too. Stay far."

Nelton opened his one eye again, as if to acknowledge Roderick's kindness.

Moments later, a deafening thunder ripped the curtain of the sky and the rain came tumbling down, pounding rambunctious against the windowpane. Roderick could see Nelton's chest heaving and waning.

"Listen to me good, maas breddas. Come rain or shine, me going to school when it open up in two weeks. Me hear Aunty say me will have to stay home for another week before me go mix up mix up with the children them at school. She don't want them get sick. Whatever me have to do so everybody stay well, I will be back in school."

10

Ting-a-Ling-a-Ling School Bell Ring

There was hardly a household in Olympic Gardens that was not singing the Common Entrance Examination blues, this once a year examination that tested some children's mettle for a free scholarship to attend the five-year high school of choice. Children were fretful. They had studied hard for the exam and, awaiting the results during the summer months, took the fun out of the holiday. Caught in the center of this reality, Roderick watched parents come into the shop to buy pencils and sundry school supplies.

"My son took it two times, and he only has one chance left before he turns twelve." They would pour their hearts onto the countertop. One lady holding a baby in her arm, another toddler by her side, cried because she didn't know how to help her daughter study for the test.

"Me never finish school, Miss Hope. Me never finish school. A can barely read."

These moments stayed with Roderick and made him more determined to stay in school. He was two years away from taking the exam and he had a lot of catching up to do, so much to learn. Things had quieted down a little in the shop when he heard Chloe's gate slam. The glare from the midmorning sunlight made her cheeks and long ponytails glow. Her little sailor collar blue and white dress swung gaily around her knees. The flip-flops played music like a rumba box rhythm on the pavement. Roderick busied himself stacking the shelves with matches and cigarettes as if he didn't see her, knowing his aunt gets especially fussy when Chloe comes into the shop.

"Sell me a pinda cake!"

Roderick looked up and smiled.

"You lucky. Is the last pinda cake you going to get. Here." He wrapped it in a matter of seconds and handed it to her.

"You can come over later and we study."

"Shhh. You mad. Mind my aunty hear you."

"Why you so fraidy, fraidy?"

"Mi not fraidy, fraidy. She rough me up for everything."

"Anyway, I want you to come study with me for the scholarship next year."

"What scullaship?"

"The one you take to go to high school. If you get a full scholarship, you won't have to pay school fees, Roderick."

"O is that me hear the customers them talking to Aunty about. That sound good, Chloe. But me not ready fi no scullaship. Me only interested now to make enough money to continue school. Me need more things for school. I want to work on my stone art and sell them. A have some really good ideas to paint."

"Is always money, money, money for you. You never hear me say you don't need money if you pass the scholarship?"

"You wouldn't understand. After you don't need money. Your father rich. Me don't have no father to help me."

"Sorry. I never mean to upset you."

"Is awright. Is me put miself in school. Mi just barely know anything."

"We can learn together," she said as she twisted her ponytail and flung it over her shoulder.

"Aunty say she not spending no more money on me."

"You don't need any money right now. Just come and let us practice for the exam."

"I am so far behind for this scullaship thing."

"Scho-la-ship. Say that. Scholarship."

"Schola-ship."

"You reading better these days, too."

"Well, is you give me all them books. Me trying to keep up."

"Your arithmetic is better than mine, anyway. You will be ready."

"Cho, you just want me feel good."

"Is true you are good at sums, long division and those things."

"Awright. Is true. But me don't know if me ready to take it."

"You can try more than one time. If you don't pass it the first time, you can take it again."

"Shhhhhh. Hold on. Let me check something." Roderick peeped out the door to see if his aunt was nearby. He heard her praying in her room. Every day around three, Hope would go off to read her Bible and pray. She believed it was good for her business, kept the doors open and customers coming. He pulled his head back in and leaned over the counter.

"It look like the lady from the Ministry of Education and Headmaster talk her into make me stay in school this time," Roderick whispered and reached for a tamarind ball, bit it and closed his eyes at the sourness of the candy.

"How you know?"

"I hear Aunty a talk to Miss Daphne about it but she a woman will change her mind if me get pon her nerves. We better take time talk."

"That sounds great! The longer you stay away from school, the less your chances are to take the scholarship. The headmaster will keep you back. You don't want the children to say you stay-down in class. It won't feel too good. You have to pass the exam by the time you are twelve. If you get to thirteen, you can't take it again for regular high school. You will have to go to Technical School."

"What is technical school?"

"You will learn trades like carpentry, electrical work, plumbing, cookery, accounting and those kinds of subjects."

"But that not bad subjects, Chloe. My friend Lij down the street know electrical work and him make money. Maybe that might not so bad for me."

"Let's get to the scholarship first. You can do it, mister man."

"Don't get happy yet, miss."

"I have to tell daddy you coming over to study with me. He wants you to be in school. You remember the first time he took you to meet the headmaster… you remember?"

"If me remember! Me noh must remember that. Is the first me drive in your father car. But look how long Aunty keep me out of school after that. Is me take badness and get myself in school this time."

"You are a real fighter, Roderick. I like that about you."

"Wait, a little. A have to serve this gentleman." Roderick moved over to serve the customer. His Aunty had packed a bag of groceries and instructed Roderick to give him when he came into the shop. Hope had some special customers that she took exceptional care to serve. Roderick knew this, and the man was one such.

"Here you go, sir," Roderick gave the man the package and turned quickly to chat with Chloe.

"Hey Chloe. Thank you for always looking out for me."

"No thanks needed. Is the truth. I never see a youth have to fight so hard to get an education. This is extraordinary."

"You and your big words."

"But you understand what I mean, though."

"I check so. Me amazing, right?" Roderick spun around and took a bow.

"That's right. Amazing. All you go through with your aunt! I can only shake my head."

"Every night me go to my bed, me dream about school. Me dream, dream, dream till one day me just make it happen."

"Shhh. A think she coming. Stop talk now and go over. We can meet at we spot tomorrow."

"Bye."

The idea of remaining in school was exciting, but Roderick had a genuine concern: he had no books and no epaulette for his school uniform. Things were looking bleak, but he still felt hopeful. Roderick turned to his stone art as his most viable way to make some money. He reached for his little satchel with the stones he had gathered from the garden and his many treks through Olympic Gardens.

Bugu lugu lubrum brum. The stones tumbled out onto the tile floor.

"Make all a you so loud!" He chided with the stones. "Cho."

One by one, he separated them by size and texture. Roderick knelt down with both elbows on the floor, picked a white oval stone—ran his hands over its smooth surface. He sniffed it and could still smell the rawness of the gully water that must have bathed and polished it for a hundred years. The light from the bottle torch flickered, casting ghostly shadows on the wall. A chilling feeling ran down his neck, goose pimples raised on his arms—yet he was not afraid. He took out the paintbrush and painted the ghostlike shapes that were forming on the wall—he painted them upon the stones. Then, with every brush stroke of sprightly colors, crosshatching light and dark paint, he created a round black face, two bright green and brown eyes with yellow teardrops. Roderick composed something beautiful. Nature smiled at his artistry.

The more he painted, the more the images came alive. Where the shadow was dark—he painted dark colors, and where there was light falling on the stone—he painted light. That night, he painted a dozen Stone Art. Roderick felt that this time—his stone art would turn a profit in time for him to get a trim and buy what he needed for school.

"If a can sell one every day, a must can save enough money to go to the barber, get a trim, and buy my epaulette for school." He reasoned as he organized the stones by size and patterns. When he finished, he let out a long, "Hmmmmmm. What a must call unnu?" Roderick asked permission of his subjects with pride-filled flair. That night, he named every piece of art. Some he named after the trees, the birds, the stars, or whatever he was feeling deep inside at that moment.

The next day, after he finished his chores, Roderick brought his stone art to Miss Dillon as she waited on a customer. Roderick stood quietly off to the side and watched as she carefully wrapped the yam in newspaper and put it in the young girl's satchel. As the girl turned to leave, Miss Dillon called her back, and he noticed how she gave her a little brawta, an extra piece of pumpkin, and told her it would make a nice soup.

Miss Dillon so nice eee. "Good morning, Miss Dillon."

"Good morning, Roderick." You finish cleaning up early man."

"Yes. I try to plan out my day. When I start early, I can get a little more time in the day for myself."

"I never see a little boy work so sensible. What you have there?"

"My Stone Art. I want was to ask if you can help me sell them, Miss Dillon? A need the money bad, bad. Aunt Hope say me can go back to school since she have Miss Daphne to help her. But me need the money soon, soon."

"She is going to send you back to school? No wonder rain set up." Miss Dillon grabbed the hem of her dress and swirled like a mambo dancer. "A wa a go done? She must a get religion. Thank you, Puppa Jeezas."

"Shhhh. Suppose she hear you?" Roderick laughed at her joyfulness. "You going to do it for me?"

"How me must tell you no? I will try with three first."

"You sure you don't want more?" Roderick pressed, giving them to her like they were delicate jewels.

"Let we see how this goes first. You miss the big holiday sale. If you had them ready, then you would a sell off."

Roderick was still optimistic and handed her three stone art pieces he named: Quiet Moon, Donkey Ride and Peanut Man. He observed her closely as her eyeballs rolled around. She rocked her head from side to side and smiled.

"What a way them pretty. You a get better at this thing, man."

"A going to sell them off fast. If me to stay in school, mi have to sell them off, Miss Dillon."

"Take it easy. One thing at a time."

Later that evening, Roderick took the nine pieces he had and walked to the Three Miles roundabout; the big intersection where busses heading east to west, north to south converged at a terminus. This was the perfect spot to reach people from all walks of life coming from work, going to their next shift, simply waiting at bus stops to transfer or just walk home. He placed them in a little box and set out in his ripped pants, stained cotton shirt, and sandals. Roderick had his pick of corners, so he stood by a Number 7 bus heading towards Half Way Tree via Hagley Park Road. The astute entrepreneur called out with all his might, just like Fudgie.

"Buy mi pretty pretty! Buy mi pretty pretty!"

Some folks just did a quick glance and others stopped and fingered his art. Approaching him was a woman in a linen suit and leather handbag cradled by her elbow. She stopped to admire his work.

"Which one you like, Miss?"

"My O my, they are all quite lovely. How much for this one? I can use it to hold down the papers on my desk on those windy days?"

"How much you think me should a sell it for, Miss?" She smiled. "I can't make that decision."

"Awright then, give me five shillings." Roderick eyeballed her as she went into her purse for the money.

One shilling! That's all. You mean she going to pay me that? La la. Don't fuss Roderick. If a sell all of them here for one shilling a piece me can cut mi hair and buy the epaulette. Is plenty money that.

He shifted the box and moved arranged them the stone art neatly. He positioned the larger ones closest to the customer. *Awright Roderick. Is only six big ones like these, the other one them small so them have to cost less than that. No sa. Mi a try get same fi them, too. I will figure it out. Just tend to the nice lady.*

The gracious lady picked up an art piece, rocked it in her palm ever so gently, up and down, testing the weight. She looked at him. "One shilling. Here. Keep up the good work."

"Thank you, Miss. You sure you don't want another one?"

She smiled and went on her way.

Roderick continued to call out "Buy mi pretty pretty! Buy pretty pretty." He sold two more pretty pretty. He put the money in the box.

See it there. Is not mi alone out here selling. Look the boy a sell him Evening News. Everybody a look something. It rough. Eh eh. Then is why him a look on mi so? Maybe is just mi a think something. Him a cross over this side. Roderick felt a little funny in his belly. Whenever he got a funny feeling in his belly, he paid close attention. He clutched his box and continued to call out "Buy mi pretty pretty."

"You deh pan my corner yout. Find another spot," the Evening News boy said to Roderick.

Why him want me to move from here eee? He looked at the boy's face. It had scars all over, like he lived under a house bottom. His eyes were fire red, and he smelled like five-day sweat.

"You don't own no corner," Roderick retorted.

"Yuh bright. Mi seh fi find another corner, yout!"

"For a peaceful life, a going to move. A want to sell off the stone art today." Roderick moved a few feet away and leaned against a wall. "Pretty pretty. One shilling a one."

The Evening News boy followed him. He pointed in Roderick's face, which did not sit well with him.

"I just want to sell my things like you. I need the money to help myself. What you want with me? Just leave me alone." Roderick said, moved again and called out. "One shilling a one." *Is like this boy want me to do something bad to him right now. Money can make out here.*

"A say to move from this corner boy."

"This not looking good. The boy look like trouble. A can't let him handle me like how Nelton do. I going to stand up to him today. Move me noh. Move me!"

The boy chucked Roderick in his chest. Roderick punched him in the face.

Is like Nelton follow me come out here today. What a boy provoking. He held on to his box of money and art. The two fought to the ground. Roderick was not letting up—he had him pinned to the ground and punched him repeatedly in rapid succession. "I need money to go a school. You not going to stop me this evening, yaaa bwoy. You naah stop me." Roderick was huffing and puffing as the boy took another swing at him and Roderick's box of art and coins spilled on the ground. "Me noh fraid a you. I will break some part of you."

At the heights of the squabble, a crowd formed with cheers to edge them on. The other fellows selling Evening News came to their friend's aid and shouted "Beat him up Sammy, beat him up! Tump di bwoy Sammy, tump di boy." Just then, two older gentlemen parted the crowd around the boys and stopped the fight. Roderick's shirt ripped—hardly much left to cover his lean body. The mud covered his body, having fallen where the snow cone vendor emptied water from his cart. Frantically, he scrambled to get his box, but it was nowhere to be found. Roderick wept at the loss of his art and money.

He set out on his trek back home when a little school girl, about seven, approached him. "Likkle boy, mi know who have your things."

Roderick was not sure if he trusted anyone at this point. He was too tired and upset, but he listened.
If I can get back my things, and my money, that would be nice. I better listen.

"Who have it eee. Who have it?"

"Sammy fren dem."

"Which part them live?"

"Dem no live nowhere. Dem sleep down there so."
She pointed in the direction of the gully bank.

"O mi know which part. Me and mi friend Suraj go there before."

The little girl crossed the street and disappeared into a yard behind old soldier lorries and piles of tires.

Roderick ran home, washed off, and oiled his skin with some good old coconut oil. He would be so slippery nobody could hold him down. Putting on his beret, a light bulb went off in his head and he remembered Uncle telling him how he used a slingshot to fight when he was a little boy. He grabbed his slingshot and gathered a few stones in his back pocket and went in search of Sammy and the other newspaper boys. Roderick was intent on breaking someone's hand or busting a forehead if he did not get back his art and his money. He set out, feeling like a young soldier—nothing must hold him back.

Raucous winds conspired against his gait as he whistled between the belting of car horns from impatient drivers. Derrick Morgan's tune about toughness, ringing in his head like a radio full blast, told him not to fear. Mister Tough reached the gully bank, hid behind an acacia tree that hung over into the gully. He spotted Sammy and two other boys. Quietly, he loaded his slingshot holder like a trebuchet with stone missiles, fired the first one, which landed on a jacked up car. Roderick ducked behind the tree and set off the next stone.

"Gimme my things or a going buss your head!"
He could see the boys trying desperately to see where his voice was coming from, but they could not see him.

"Shut your mout eediat!" said the smallest boy as he screwed up his face like the baddest.

"Come over here and tell me to shut up and see if a don't crack your face," army of one, Roderick, promised Twist Face.

"Me noh fraid a no boy," little Twist Face replied. In the meantime, Sammy and the other boys were edging like they wanted to run or get something to protect themselves. Roderick warned.

"Don't move. Sit down… the two a you, and make I take care a this twist up face boy." Roderick set off yet another stone that hit Sammy in his right shoulder blade.

"Whoooooooooi. You bruk mi shoulder. A going mash you up."

Roderick watched as the other boys gaped at Sammy, curled up in pain. They looked all around and tried to duck behind the shelter. Roderick smiled. Then he heard a little squeaky, girly voice.

"Awright. Awright. Hey Redyeye, give him back him things," Sammy squealed.

"Yes, Redyeye, me want all a mi money now," Roderick said and twirled his slingshot.

"Look, we don't want your drawing them," Sammy said. "Take them. We will keep the money."

Roderick twirled the slingshot in the air even faster. "Like you don't understand, say I want my money." He fired his slingshot, and it hit the buckteeth boy in the knee.

"Shitttttttttt. You bruck my foot to rahtid." He squealed like a pig in a pigsty.

"Awright, awright, see the money here. See, a put it in the box," the small boy with a big wart in the middle of his forehead said and trembled like a leaf. He started to kick the box toward Roderick.

"No. You bring the box come give mi. A not walking come over there. Bring it now."

"Don't fire no more stone," the small boy begged. "I will bring it come give you." Sweat rolled down his naked chest and arms.

"You can't trust him, Black Wart. The boy is a mad somebody," Sammy cautioned.

"Shut your mouth and make him bring it come give me, now." Roderick set up another stone in his slingshot. Black Wart breathed deeply, made the sign of the cross, picked up the box. The boys went into their pockets and each put a coin back in the box they had shared amongst themselves. Roderick made a moue with his mouth. Slowly, Black Wart walked towards Roderick. As he got closer, he put the box on the ground with his eyes fixed on Roderick and kicked it toward him.

Roderick stopped it with one foot, but kept a steady focus on any move the boys would make.

"Get out a here before we mark up your face." Sammy waved a broken soda bottle at him.

I guess is dem mark up Sammy face. It look really crusty. Roderick picked up the box, counted his money. It was all there. He walked backwards for a distance—all the while brandishing his slingshot with one arm, keeping a steady gaze on the boys.

"This stone art is good business. Next time I will know to take better care of my money." Roderick high-tailed it out of there, knowing he was closer to getting what he needed for school. This time, the wind had his back.

11

Grooming for Success

The smell of purple and white gardenias in a recycled Ovaltine can lifted Roderick's spirit. Admiring the old worn furniture he painted in bright colors and elements of nature made him feel warm inside. There was so much more space to move around now that the clutter cleared. He placed his sandals and shoes neatly in a corner. The few pieces of clothing, including his school uniform, were hanging in the wardrobe; the outside he decorated with stone art. Roderick made ample room for his paint set and books on top of three wooden milk cartons he painted in Rasta colors: red, green and yellow. The light brown walls were still bare after a good wash down with cake-soap and water.

Roderick walked over to the window and opened it as wide as the old hinges allowed. Early morning sunlight flooded the space and fresh air cooled his face.

"This is my real, real, room now," he said as the Barbary doves and pigeons hooted their good mornings. Chloe's red rooster crowed once. Roderick felt like he was in a new world.

"It's time to get a trim. So much hair pan mi head, fowl could a lay egg inna it and me wouldn't know." He laughed out loud. Then he caught himself. "Shhhhhh. You don't want anybody to catch on to this something here." The last time Roderick remembered getting a trim was Independence Day, eight months earlier on the 6th of August, when Aunt Lillian cut it for him. This time, Roderick preferred to go to a real barber, Old Jacob, who ran a thriving barbershop on De Lisser Avenue. "All me want right now is fi look good when me go a school summer term."

Counting his coins, one penny at a time, Roderick filled an old foot of socks, tied the top and put it in his side pants pocket. The sock-pouch was so heavy it pulled his pants slightly below his waist. "Me don't want Chloe fi go a school and leave me behind just because me don't have no money. That is why me glad mi Stone Art business going good. Me staying in primary school and pass the scholarship." Encouraging himself, he jumped through the window and made his way towards Jacob's barber shop.

Houses of different shapes and styles lined De Lisser Avenue: some with enclosed verandas and others with shallow steps leading to a front door. Open windows welcomed the gracious gusts of cool trade winds and vitality of folks chattering about shady government practices, hard times, naughty children and the shifting tides of Olympic Gardens. Some trees cast shadows along the pavement and Roderick tried to beat the ferocious sun at its game, teetering between its rays and random shade.

Roderick could smell delicious spicy cooking and just knew there was a pot of traditional beef soup with dumplings, dry yellow yams, turnips, scotch bonnet peppers, scallions and thyme on someone's stove. This made him long for his home in the country.

"Me don't have nobody in this world, no father, no mother to take care of me. Me have to do things myself."

A woman pushing an antiquated pram with a toddler tapped him on the shoulder. "Little boy, you are too young to be talking to yourself. Leave that to old people like me."

Roderick stared at her. He hadn't realized his thoughts were so loud.

Children played Dandy-Shandy to boisterous screams as they slipped and ducked a ball from hitting hard against their bodies, made him smile.

"You out, miss. You out!" He said to a girl who had just got clobbered with the ball. Some lost, others won, and Roderick covered his mouth to hide a snigger. A boy pushed a small child on a toy handcart made from salvaged car parts, pieces of wood and decorated to his personal whacky taste, smiled at Roderick, who returned the gesture. Roderick smiled at him, yet his heart hurt knowing how much he missed his brother and sister. There was no caring family in Kingston to play with, eat with, and have real fun.

"One day, one day, mi will live in a big house with a big family who love me. One day."

The scene brought back memories of his days in the country, making his pushcart and giving his sister a ride in it, playfully, before she tumbled down the hill and was badly hurt. That was the last time he remembered spending time with his sister because his mother got righteously irate about the accident and sent him away.

Why mama had to send me away so me don't have anybody to play with? Why? At least Esther and Shadrach get to play with them one another. This is not fair. A wonder if mama know how Aunty and her son them treat me bad. A tired fi cry now. A tired. I could just disappear. The unpleasant memory quickly left his thoughts as he approached Old Jacobs' yard.

Jacob's barber shop was one of two identical houses. Roderick had heard his aunty and Miss Dillon tell the story about how Jacob bought the house from his friend Bugzy.

The two met after Bugzy returned from serving in the Royal Airforce during World War II. Jacob lived with his wife in the house on the left and his mistress and children in the house on the right. Drinking beer and playing dominos in the back room of the barbershop went from being a Friday night special to all-nighters on the weekends.

Loud chatter and laughter spilled over the bannister as he climbed up the steps. A little mongrel dog lay idly on the step and Roderick edged his way past, careful not to disturb.

"Good afternoon, Mister Jacobs," Roderick looked past the old man, peeped to see what's going on in the shop.

"Afternoon, young man. Come this way. What you want me to do for you?"

"A want a nice trim to go back to school."

"I never seen you around here before. Where you live?"

"Is the little boy that work in Hope Flowers' shop," Bugzy chimed in.

"Oh. Miss Hope. Good woman," Mr. Jacobs acknowledged.

Good woman! My aunty is a good woman? Me don't know her at all. Roderick screamed to the gods in painful silence. *Them must have the wrong person. Not my aunty.*

Mr. Jacob patted Roderick on his mound of fluffy hair, "Nice soft curls you have here, boy. Where you get this pretty hair from?"

"What kind of question you asking the boy, Jacob?" Bugzy interjected from his corner in the shop.

"This hair don't have no Cudjoe and Maroon Nanny in there," Jacob continued as he prepared his duster brush, scissors, razor, comb and towel.

Roderick looked up at Mr. Jacob, who smiled at him. *What him mean my hair don't have no Cojo and Nanny in there? Strange man.*

"You see him eyes them, Bugzy. Look." He spun Roderick around. "The boy damn near got green eyes. So who you to Miss Hope for she don't have no white people in her family?"

"Is my aunty, sir."

"Well, she and her sister them is straight up African. So how come you so light-skinned? A can tell you is family anyway. Which one your mother?"

"Jakyee, that is not polite. Leave the little boy alone and cut his hair."

"Anybody come to my place, I have to know who them is. Ain't nothing wrong with that. Go on, who is your mother, boy?"

"Miss Mara'Belle."

"A could tell. You have a slight resemblance. Kill me dead though, him have some white man blood in him."

White man blood. I don't even know my real father or remember him. I don't even know him full name. So much wickedness happen to me, I can't remember anything about him. Who white man them talking about?

"All right, sit down over there and wait till I call you."

"Thank you, Mister Jacob."

Sitting across from him were two men who spoke loud about the government and how is time for a change for them going to change over the money. Roderick listened, trying to make sense of what they were talking about.

It look like pretty soon we goin to get new money. No more pound, shilling and pence. Seem say the govament goin take away wi old money. The one in the tam and the dark glasses don't look so happy about it at all. What goin happen to my stone art money then?

Roderick sat up tall, ears locked into the surrounding conversations.

Mama say, 'Children must be seen and not heard but me want to know about this white man Mister Jacobs talking about. A wonder if him know my father? But me can't just bright up myself and go ask him no question. Me get a little pinch in mi belly that him know something. A wish a did carry the picture with me. A could a show him. Naaah.

Shaking the thought, he turned his attention to a tall boy with a big afro wearing a white cotton t-shirt, brown and blue stripe corduroy pants and flip-flops reading an Archie Comic book. Roderick knew he had quite a wait.

The smell of white rum enmeshed everyone like mist nets around wild birds. No one could escape the stories that grew more hyperbolic after a few rounds of the national beverage. Everyone was clamoring to tell a story to liven things up, more especially, outdo each other.

Mr. Jacob cleared his throat. "Onnu hear bout the–

"Don't bother with your lying stories, Jaykee."

"You don't even know what me going to tell you."

"Yu been telling the same story from me was a likkle boy a come in here wid mi father. Now mi have six children and so-soh gray hair pan mi head," Wilmot, a short stocky man with an enormous belly and graying hair along his temples, protested.

"Is not my fault you old up yourself."

"Lawks Wilmot. Mek di man, tell him story." Bose knocked his rum glass with Rohan, captain and umpire from the Bolivar Walk Cricket club. "Go on, Jaykee."

"Wilmot don't want mi to tell mi story," Jaykee griped, draped the barber cape around his customer's neck and took a sip of the old whites.

"Go on, man. Tell your story," Bose encouraged with a big grin on his face. He pulled out a deck of cards, solicited Roderick and a boy nodding his head, ready to fall asleep.

"Come, young boy. Play along."

Jaykee cleared his throat, pursed, and licked his lips. "Well, this man married three wives: one from St. Mary, one from Portland, and one from St. Thomas. Altogether, they give him twelve children: five boys and seven girls."

Roderick covered his mouth "Twelve children? What me would do with so much children. Aunt Hope can't even take care of me and her two. It hard. How me would feed all a them. Wash all them heap a clothes and iron them? Me wouldn't want my children them to work hard like me. Them need fi play, go a school and them things there. Cho.

"Him take down with a terrible sickness and not even Obeah man could tell them what to do to make him better," Jacob continued.

"So what is the point?" Wilmot teased.

"Then wait no. Mi don't reach there so yet."

"Go on, Jaykee," Rohan cheered him on.

"Well," Jaykee continued after another whiff of the whites. "The three wives went to an Obeah man in their respective parishes and bring up some wicked duppy. Well, the St. Mary Duppy, the Portland Duppy and the St. Thomas

Duppy call a meeting and decide that them going to mix up a concoction and give him to drink. This will prevent him from littering the rest of the parish them with so much pickney since him don't take care of none of them."

Roderick perked up to zero in on the story.

Wilmot cleared his throat. "You mean the three duppy them travel that far to make mixup, mixup give him? You can't even tell a good lie."

Everyone laughed so hard they could hardly contain themselves. Bugzy weighed in. "When since duppy get so much power to make potion, give somebody?"

"You don't understand, Bugzy," Jaykee said. "Is only duppy can stop them kinda a man deh. All them do is breed up the woman them from one yard to the next without any payback fi them actions."

Roderick listened attentively as the story took yet another turn when Hector jumped up waving his finger annoyingly at Jaykee. "So who order the duppy them fi do this wicked deed, Jaykee?"

"Is why you so upset about it."

"Every time me come into your establishment, you throw word pan me."

"Me. Throw word pan you. How much pickney you have? Twelve. Right. Twelve."

"Is not me responsible fi all them dry head one. You don't see how my curls them shine, soft, and smooth." Hector ran his finger through his thinning hair and sipped his rum and Coca Cola.

"Who the cap fits, let them wear it," came Jaykee's quick retort as he beckoned to the next customer to sit in the chair.

A smile crossed Roderick's face as he remembered his mother said many times.

Who the cap fit, let them wear it. I guess this cap fit Hector this time. Him not taking Mister Jacob mouthing too well. Him think him talking bad about him. But him look like a really nice man. How come him don't take care of him children them?

Roderick walked over to the little side table and took a candy out of the jar, looked around the room at the faces of the men waiting ahead of him.

Is man like them make Aunt Hope so cross all the time. Nelton and Roderick don't have no father come around the place. Hmmm. Look like must be one a them man is them boy father. A wonder.

Old Jacob slapped the chair seat three times with his barber's towel and removed fallen hair. "Come, little boy. Sit down, let me fix you up real good."

Roderick sat in the high chair as Mr. Jacob pulled his curls apart.

"So your father live over there with Miss Hope?"

"No. A don't know him. You ever see him, Mr. Jacobs?"

"Is a long time a been over to see her. I know them two boy's father, him work for the government. She had a sailor man that used to come through there. You remember him, Bugzy?"

"Funny you ask. This little boy kind a look like him, you know. Him pale like him. Them eyes there and that little turn up lip."

Turn up lip. What him talking about. Me don't have no turn up lip. It sound like them a connect me to a sailor man. Jeezam, Chloe. It look like them man here know something about something. Roderick squirmed in the chair. His hand became clammy. His ears felt hot. He folded his arms to steady himself. Crossed his ankles, uncrossed them again. Lifted his right shoulder to his ear.

"You have to stay still, little boy," Jacob cautioned.

"You don't want the razor to cut you. This silky hair can't be hurting you at all. Is it?"

"No sir."

"What you say you name again?"

"I never tell you my name before. Me name Roderick."

"Roderick what?"

"Roderick Brissett."

"Kiss mi neck, Bugzy!" Jaykee said and picked up his scissors. "The Bible says, 'Hell hath no fury than a woman scorned.'"

"The Bible did not say that Jaykee. It is an English playwright who wrote it. I went to high school and Sunday school. Mum's the word," Bugzy replied and went back to what they were doing.

"Any of you know my father? I really want to know about him. My father left me and mi mother when I was little. I don't remember him at all."

"Now look at that, aye. I know is not your fault, Roderick. Some of these men who leave them children fi suffer with them mother only duppy can fix them."

Wilmot shook his head. "What kind a foolishness you telling the boy?"

Roderick got this feeling these men knew something about his father. Not today. *Them start to talk private to themselves. Me can't get into that. La la.*

"Is not foolishness. Man who live at plenty yard end up with nobody, not even him children and duppy don't want him." Jaykee was relentless about the ultimate demise of worthless fathers. Roderick's hair fell softly on the ground, creating little fur balls around the base of the chair.

"Listen to me, young boy," Jayke continued. "Don't fool up these young girls or you will end up alone in this world. Girls are to be treated with respect. When you become a man and have children, make sure is with one woman so you can take care of them."

Roderick shook his head. He had no response for Jaykee, but thought about what he heard.

Is so every man stay? When me grow up me going to take care of my children.

"Where you want me to put a part in your hair?"

"Part, sir?"

"Yes. One like the young boy over there. His hair is growing in now but yours will be nice and clear."

"Put it on the right side." Roderick took the hand mirror Jaykee gave to him. He looked at his face and new haircut. 'Mi look like a whole different somebody else."
For the first time, he took notice of every detail of his face. A strange feeling came over him, but he squeezed out a smile.

"Me like it, Mr. Jacob. Me like it."

"I am glad you like it, little man." Holding his shoulder high, Roderick sat still as Mr. Jacob dusted powder around the nape of his neck and along his hairline.

Chloe girl, a soon come show you mi new trim. Wait. A soon come. A have so much to tell you. Them man here bring up argument about mi father. It look like them know him. I wonder if him live around here. Perhaps him come into the shop, look at me and don't say hello to me. Roderick grinned and rubbed his palms together. He reached into his pocket, pulled out his sock with coins, and paid Mr. Jacob.

Sleep was rare these past few days as Roderick readied himself for the summer term. His aunt had stopped protesting against him attending school. Life felt a bit more comfortable.

Hu hu huhu hoooo, Hu hu huhu hoooo! came the rise and shine song of the Barbary doves that took up residence in the opening between the roof and the beams of the outhouse. Roderick had attracted families of doves that descended on the roof because he fed them every morning. Roderick jumped out of bed and rays of warm sunlight enveloped him. He made a loud whisper: "Good mawnin!" He did not wait for a reply but ran to the window he had kept half-opened all night to get some fresh air from the strange, sweltering heat.

"Hu hu huhu hoooo, Hu hu huhu hoooo," Roderick mimicked his call to the doves. "Guess who is going to school today? Meeeeeeeeeeeee. Me, Roderick Brissett. I am going to school today! It is a good day, 21 April 1969. I wrote it in my exercise book so I would not forget when the teacher ask me. She say she making sure we paying attention to important days in our life. She tell us that every day we make history and that we must write it down so nobody can interfere with it."

Chloe pushed up her window, "Morning, Roderick. Yeah. You going to school this morning for real-real-real."

"Yes. See you likkle more." Roderick closed the widow, fetched his wash rag, soap, toothbrush and a pinch of salt, threw a towel over his shoulder and ran outside.

He climbed up on the concrete edge around the standpipe, put the salt on his toothbrush and brushed his teeth—gargled, washed his face. Then he took a quick shower in the stall adjoining the outhouse. His fingertips turned purple, his teeth chattered, and his ears felt like they were falling off.

"Mi can't worry about the cold this morning at all. Aunty don't let me use the nice inside bathroom so me just have to settle mi head." Roderick could hear Mr. Petgrave's radio cracking the daybreak with Harry Belafonte's 'Jump in the line rock yuh body in time.' It was five minutes before seven—Calypso Corner—the morning wake up, shake up your body, make ready for the morning news at seven. This was how the neighbors started their day and he could see lights on in their windows. Children outside gates called out to each other to hurry and join one another or they would be late for school.

"Me don't have nobody to tell me hurry up. Me naah late though."

In no time, Roderick dressed in his school uniform. An elated schoolboy, he put his bag over his shoulder, pushed the door open. The little John Crow beaded chime he made that hung on the door handle made a melodious sound, as if to sing his praises. Roderick walked past his cousin's room, slowed to listen. They were awfully quiet.

Them must be gone already. As he approached Aunt Hope's room, he glanced at the crack in the door and it was pitch-black. Again, he listened.

Click. Click. Click.

It was the sound of the old clock every time the second hand moved. His heart beat harder than usual; his face became flushed and damp. Breathing deeply, he tiptoed past the room.

"Look like Aunty not in there. Is where she is?" When he entered the kitchen area, the smell of nutmeg and cinnamon hit him. "Mmmmm."

Daphne had prepared breakfast for him.

"Mawnin, Ms. Daphne."

"Mawnin, Master Roderick."

"Looking really good today. You happy?"

"Yes, Miss Daphne."

"Sit down and eat your breakfast."

Roderick hurried through the bowl of cornmeal porridge, poached eggs and a slice of hard dough bread plastered with Anchor Butter. He got up to clear the table when Miss Daphne tapped him on his hand and smiled.

"I will do that for you today, schoolboy."

Roderick smiled at her kindness. "Where Aunty?"

"She went to the market soon this morning."

"Where Stephen them?"

"Them gone already."

By the time he threw his bag over his shoulder, there came a knock on the gate.

"Who that?" Daphne asked.

"Is me, Lillian. Ellen and me come to see the schoolboy off this morning."

Roderick pushed past Miss Daphne and opened the gate with a flourish. Standing behind the women were Chloe, Mr. Goodman, Lij, and Miss Dillon. They all came to see him off to school. He had been sneaking out to go to school of his own volition and with many setbacks. This morning was different. Aunt Hope had given him permission. Everyone had a little something to say to him—a brief word of encouragement. Lij brought him an Oxford Dictionary. Ellen brought him a painting of the three kings of Jamaican visual art whom she admired: Barrington Watson, Albert Huie, and Karl Parboosingh.

Roderick took in the picture for a moment. "Can I hold it?"

"Yes, you can."

He held the picture with care. *Miss Ellen really want me to be a artist like them man here. She did tell me bout them a Grand Market.*

"All of this for meeeeee?" Tears ran down his face. He could not believe his friends came to see him off to school. Well, considering he told everybody. No wonder.

"Yes, all of this for you, Roderick Brissett," replied Aunt Lillian. "Go learn all you can, and don't be shy about making new friends."

"Shy Aunty? Me not shy." Roderick squinted. "Then is how me going to carry all of this?"

"I will put up the art for you in your room." Daphne moved him out of the way and picked up his gifts.

"No, no, no, Miss Daphne. I will put them in the room myself."

"You don't want to be late."

"No me won't late."

Lawd have mercy. Me don't want her to see how me fix up the room. Suppose she see the window. She will tell Aunty and she will kill me. His nose sweat. He looked over at Chloe, who pushed out her chin, a signal to go do it himself.

"Is awright Miss Daphne, I will run go put them down." Roderick dropped his bag on the floor and ran to his room.

Whoiii. That was close. Lawd have mercy.

On his return, he panted, "See me here."

"Let's go, Roderick." Mr. Goodman took Roderick's hand. "We must not be late."

"Bye everybody."

"Bye."

Goodman's 1958 Rambler motorcar awaited Roderick at the curb. He would ride in style to Perennial Primary School in Olympic Gardens with his best friend Chloe at his side. Roderick looked over at Chloe, who looked at him. She smiled. He smiled back.

"This time, me goin learn all me can so me get fi take scholarship with you, Chloe."

The morning breeze whistled softly against the car window.

12

Suraj The Wise

Today, Roderick would not mind the old man's ramblings about the war; he just wanted to see him again, to know he was all right, tell him about school and get help with his war-time homework. Roderick wanted so much to share with him he made new friends at school now that he was attending regularly. His motive set; his mission was concrete. Roderick had to find his way to the house where Sergeant Suraj lived. The only thing he knew was that the old man lived on Cling Cling Avenue, off Olympic Way, but he had never been there before. Sneaking out of his shop duty on a Saturday morning was risky business.

Maybe me can ask Nelton to watch the shop for me so me can go and come back before Aunty come from market but him is so-soh worries. Why Miss Daphne have to go away this weekend?

Last time he saw the old man, he had come into the shop to buy medicine for his terrible cold. Although Suraj was not feeling well, he still made Roderick laugh. Yet, his aunt did not like him coming around.

I can't believe Aunty chase away the big man out the place. That not mannersable. Why she believe him a put bad things in mi head. Aunty like her head take her sometime. She can't stand to see me happy. Me must just miserable like her. Me really feel good when Suraj come a the shop.

To Roderick, Maas Suraj was great company, a genuine friend and teacher. His days go by glibly with Maas Suraj in it.

"What a going to do now?" he deliberated. "I have to find Suraj. A wonder if him eat? A wonder if him awright?" These questions rolled around in his head like giant shooter marbles. There was no answer. A light soon turned on in his mind. "That's right… that's right… Chloe always go there to buy bread at the bakery. She say it not far from the little chicken farm."

One crisis at hand was to leave the shop without getting into hot water with Aunt Hope. As the thought of punishment crossed his mind, it disappeared like steam from the peanut man's whistle.

"I am goin to see him and nothing goin stop me. Aunty could a spit fire out her ears." The more he mused about it, the more distressed he became. "A better go ask Nelton to watch the shop for me. No. A better not. Nelton was always up to no good. Him is the only one at home today. Lord help me. After this boy don't know to do a thing."

Nothing else made sense. In his mind, it was the only logical thing to do. He braved the asking and confided in Nelton for the first time.

"You can watch the shop for a little while since Aunty not here, Miss Daphne leave early this morning to take her daughter to Children's Hospital and Stephen gone to football practice."

"That is whole day business, Roderick."

"It not goin take all day. I just have a matter to look after." Roderick rolled his eyes at Nelton, who by now had climbed up on the counter and sat eating a rock bun. He put his dirty feet on the counter bridge, crossed his legs and folded his arms.

"Me, you really want me to watch the shop for you, Mister Man?"

"You perch right on top there so you can see everything. Beg you to come down. It don't look good." Roderick walked over to Nelton, stretched out his hand to flip his foot off the counter bridge, but pulled back. He marched on the spot, flailing his hands through the air. Then he started tapping the counter top as Nelton grinned between bites.

This boy don't realize I got to go now. What's wrong with him? He is so spiteful. A not taking him on this morning. "I really want you to do it. If you can't do it just tell me and a won't bother you. A want to go look about Maas Suraj. Is days now a don't see him and a wonder if him awright."

"There you go again, Maas Suraj, Maas Suraj. You must really like this drunken man." Nelton swung his feet around, jumped down off the counter.

Roderick slapped the counter. "Him not no drunken man. Him stop drink rum from last Easter."

"How you know that?"

"You going to do the thing for me or you just going to ask me whole heap a question?"

"Oy bredren, take it easy. It's me have to cover up for you when mama comes back from downtown and you not here."

Roderick turned to walk away, looked back at Nelton, who was making funny faces at him. He scrunched the top of the paper bag to secure the food for Suraj. Sighed. Then he stretched his hand out to Nelton.

"A know. Just do it for me. Me never ask you to do anything for me all them time here, Nelton."

"What me get to do this for you?"

"You have to get something for this after all me do for everybody day and night?"

"How you mean. Nutt'n for nutt'n. Madness that."

"The longer we argue about this, the less time a will have to reach Maas Suraj and come back."

"All right, all right. I will do it for you. But don't blame me if things get messed up because from me born me never work in the shop."

"Cho man. You going to be awright," assured Roderick and charged through the gate. Just as he was about to hit the sidewalk, Miss Dillon called out to him.

"Where you going, boy?"

A don't think she heard me and Nelton in there or she would come in and talk me out of going. "A not going far."

"I didn't ask you that. I asked you where you going and your aunty and Daphne not here. Who going to mind the shop?"

"A going to look for Maas Suraj."

"For what?"

"To carry some lunch for him. A don't see him this long time."

"That is nice of you, but remember that Hope don't play when it comes to her business."

"Yes a know mam. A not goin stay long. Nelton goin stay in the shop."

"Mary Mother of God. Nelton! You mad or something? That boy is soh so trouble. That is not a good idea."

Roderick was not only losing time here, he was thinking that he had really made a big mistake of enlisting Nelton.

"You can help him for me?"

"A can't run my business and Hope's at the same time."

"A promise… a soon come back."
Roderick was getting antsy, but Miss Dillon was one of his chief allies. He was not about to upset her.

"Carry on, then. I will give an eye. You better hurry up and come back. Heaven help you if Hope reach home before you. Careful. You hear me!"

"Yes Miss Dillon."

With that, Roderick clutched his little paper bag with two fried dumplings, salt fish he saved from his breakfast, a ginger beer and a rock bun and his homework book.

The ground was hell hot and Roderick could feel its wrath with every stride.

"Man, a godda keep moving," he hollered at a gaggle of geese and goslings crossing the side street as if they owned it. Their noisy call told Roderick to piss off—we have the right of way. Mother goose flew up in his chest as if to slap the daylights out of him for not yielding and proceeded through an open gate.

Roderick was stunned for a moment. "What a something doh eh. Di goose them just walk straight inna di people them yard… them must be live there!"
An east wind blew across his sweaty face and hands and he could feel its natural mystic. Roderick slowed as he approached the ball ground.

"Okay. It not too far from here so. I know Chloe wouldn't confuse me." He looked up at the street signs and the houses along the way. A car coming towards him ran into a giant pothole filled with water from last night's rain. It made a big splash and wet him from head to toe.

"What wrong with them driver here? Look how him wet up mi clothes. No manners." The bag with the food got wet, but Roderick held on to it tenderly so it wouldn't rip open. He wiped his face with his hand. "A hope a soon reach where me going."

A few short blocks up the road he looked up at the street lamp and on the other side, there it was, as clear as day.

"A reach to rahtid. See it yah. Cling Cling Avenue. Me must and bound fi find him now.After me don't know which house him live into. What me going to do?"

You can't give up now, just keep walking, his inner voice cheered him on.

He stopped outside a gate where the big sign read: 'Dog Inside Keep Out.' He pressed his sweat drenched palm against the metal latch connecting two wooden frames, tipped on his toes so he could see through the peephole.

"Cho. After me noh fraid a dog," and with that Roderick pushed the gate open. He saw this big Alsatian dog, almost as tall as him. Roderick jumped back, screamed.

"AHHHHHHHH. Get away from me." Roderick continued to yell at the dog, still trying not to spill the food.

"Help. Help."

RUFFF, RUFFF, RUFF!

"O Lawd, she and six puppy. Me one. SOMEBODY help me noh." He turned to run, but the dog rushed him again. Roderick beat off the dog with the bag of food.

"WHEWWWWW."

Crack!

"Mi dumplings gone… the ginger beer, too. What me goin give Suraj now?"

"Awright Lucy. Awright. Siddung Lucy," roared a deep-voiced bearded man who emerged from the side of the house and controlled the dog. Looking around the bend, Roderick could see a few fellows laughing at him. They had stopped playing dominoes, drinking beer, and smoking in the backyard to take in the mid-morning show.

Unnu a laugh. Mi lucky the dog never tear me up. Mi still glad me save the rock bun and cheese. Roderick trembled and was about to turn and face the gate when the bearded man said,

"Relax, youth man. Who you looking for?"

"A looking for Maas Suraj."

"O' him looking for Indian," the man turned and addressed the men playing dominos.

"Indian up the street."

"Where up the street, sir?"

The bearded man called out. "Cyril. You a walk-bout, so you must know which part Indian live."

Cyril was a very short chunky man. He staggered from side to side, sipped on his beer.

Him look drunk. How him can tell me where Suraj live?

"Bottom side the fish shop," Cyril said.

"Awright. Walk wid the likkle boy here."

"Me have to spring a leak first."

Roderick giggled. *Spring a leak! You mean you want to go peepi.* He giggled again.

"Rest your foot, little man."

"Me on a hurry, Sir," Roderick replied.

"Menelek says you must sit on the step and relax for a game of six." He returned to his domino game. "What you have there, Quashie?"

Quashie, Menelek's bredren, continued the conversation that was already in progress. "Rastafari doesn't get any respect in this country. The government must atone for all the wickedness them bring down on Rasta."

"Them not going to apologize, Quashie. Is six years now since them kill off the dread them in Coral Gardens."

Quashie slaps a domino on the table—blauw! "Dis game block."

"Yes. 1963. I will never forget. I man first-born son, Tekle, came unto this cruel world that said week—the year of brutality," Menelek said and shuffled the dominoes.

"They claim man and man fighting over land given unto I and I," Quashie recounted.

Brutality? Roderick's ears perked up. *A wonder what happened 1963? My teacher say to pay attention to history. A might as well listen to the story for this man taking long in the toilet.*

"After is not Rasta did burn down the gas station. Yet, Rasta pay for it with them life. A massacre of blood, brethren. No one was indicted and not one of them go to prison for our murder, Ras," Quashie said.

You mean them murder the Rasta because them think them burn down a gas station? What a wicked set a people eee. Go on, a want to hear more. Roderick could see in the Rastaman's eyes that the hurt from this massacre was still raw, like yesterday. After all, it happened six years earlier. He attempted to say something, but he did not. Looking around the yard, he saw three black, green and red flags blowing in the wind: one from the fence, another in a tree. The third one attached to a pole that stood on a small platform with hand drums, tambourines and shakers.

The Rastaman them play drum around here it look like. Me love how drum sound.

"Education is key. Learn your history so them can't fool you. A hope you are in school, youth man."

"Yes, sir. I go to school at Perennial. Is go a going to Maas Suraj to get help with my history homework."

"Nice. What you get for homework?"

"About World War One. Suraj know plenty about it and a want him to help me."

"Sounds good. Remember to ask him about the Jamaicans who went to war."

"Jamaicans, sir?"

"O yes. A lot of Jamaicans and other people from the Caribbean helped out in the war."

"Awright. I will ask him. A need to leave now, though."

"Cyril, get the youth man a Cream Soda."

"A can't stay long. A not hungry." Menelek continued. "Emperor Haile Selassie says that 'Education develops the intellect'… you know, your mind. You understand me.'"

"Yes. My mind learning still."

"Good. Every day you tell yourself, 'Education develops the intellect.' Say it after me. Education develops the intellect."

"Educashan divlop the intellec."

"Say that every day. Say that every time you feel like giving up. Every time anyone disrespects you. You hear me?"

"Yes, sir. A hear you."

"Righteous. Let no man, woman, or child stop you from improving your life. Remember Menelek tell you that."

"Yes, Mister Menelek." Roderick looked down in reverence at the wisdom of the elder bearded man.

"Heh Ras, you talk out this game, bredren. You lose your turn three times already," Quashie pointed out to Menelek.

"Our life is in the hands of our youth. We have to grow them right so that they will be one step ahead of the wicked policemen who slaughtered Jah Jah children in Coral Gardens. It no matter which garden you live in—Coral Gardens or Olympic Gardens, them a kill the young plants before them spring up."

Roderick started a steady tremor of his right leg. He was becoming fretful that he would be late getting home.

"Cyril, Cyril!" Menelek called out to him. "Come, show the youth man where Indian live."

Cyril crawled out from the outhouse, staggering. His eyes were red as blood. "Come, likkle boy."

Roderick was unsure if he really wanted to go with Cyril, but getting to Suraj was of great importance. He turned to leave but quickly remembered his adversary, Lucy. "Beg you hold the dog for me, Mister Menelek, please."

"Ras Menelek. The dog lock up. You safe."

"Thank you, Ras Menelek. If a wasn't going to get in trouble with my aunty, I would stay and listen to your story them. I like history, anything about the past."

"You are welcome anytime. Rastaman will teach you truth and righteousness."

Roderick followed behind Cyril through the gate and onto the sidewalk. Cyril howled at the sun as he staggered from left to right, up and down, on tip toes chanting loud in slurred tones with his transistor radio held close to his ears, listening to music. "Desmond Dekker say you must take it easy, youtman. Good chune."

Roderick tried hard to keep up with the uncertainty of Cyril falling flat on his face in the middle of the street before getting to Maas Suraj.

"You need any help?"

"No. I don't need no help, yout. See the blue house up there so—it not far."

There was stillness along Cling Cling Avenue, no cars jostling for space to swerve and speed. Except for a few women washing in yards and singing to themselves, toddlers playing in the dirt, it was tranquil.

"A think we reach, Mr. Cyril. It say: 'Fresh Fish Daily' over the door."

"You can read. Who teach you to read?"

"Me teach myself. Sometimes Mr. Goodman. Him teach me. Me read every day."

"Nice. That is very nice," Cyril said, swinging the radio at a fly, missing, tumbling off balance. He steadied himself. "Awright. Next time. Walk this way down the little driveway. Him house is right there so," Cyril said, pointing to the quaint little cottage.

"Thanks Mister Cyril."

"Yu yu yu yoooo to." Cyril bumped into the chicken wire fence that surrounded a board house next door and disappeared.

Unlatching the leather strap that hooked onto a pointy piece of wood, Roderick opened the gate carefully. "Hope no bad dog not inside." Roderick went up two wide, short steps, and peeped through the opened door. He always liked to play hide and seek with Suraj—calls it lukan miti. Roderick called out to him, "Maas Suraj. Maas Suraj. A come to look for you."

Suraj did not respond—he did not move—he gave a steady gaze. The old man maintained his sitting position on the floor with his legs crossed, his hands on his knees, palms up, thumbs and first fingers touching on both hands—still. Roderick pushed the door opened—gently—ran over to the old man.

"Maas Suraj. Maas Suraj. You awright?" He waited for an answer, but one was not forthcoming.

"A bring something for you to eat." Then Roderick noticed that Suraj was reciting very softly under his breath.

A wonder who him talking to?

At that moment, he realized Suraj was just fine. So he sat on the floor a small distance from the old man.

Jeezam. Mi glad fi see him, but look how long me gone. Aunty goin break mi two foot them. A better just leave the rock bun and cheese and come back another time. He watched Suraj uncurl his feet and turned towards him.

Suraj bowed to him. "You came all the way to seek me, son."

"Yes. I did long to see you, Maas Suraj. A want was to tell you that a start school up the street. A so excited to come tell you. A make some new friends at school." Spreading his fingers on his left hand, one at a time, he lowered the tips of three towards his palm, counted: "Three friends, Maas Suraj. One name Django. The other one name Imogene and the next one name Curtis. They call themselves the Jolly Crew. Them funny you see, Maas Suraj. Them funny bad. We get together and sing under the Lignum Vitae tree lunchtime."

"Sing. You love to sing?"

"In the early part, me used to feel funny about it but them boys really good. Them help me get over it. Now me sing all the time."

"That's very good. Nice to know you are making new friends. I always wanted that for you. Tell me more about them."

"So much to tell you about them but me can't stop too long."

"I understand. Just tell me a little about them." Roderick sat up tall with his back against a wall. He crossed his legs like Suraj. He gestured with his arms.

"Django tall, tall, tall, more than all a we. Teacher call him a 'mama's boy' for him bring him lunch to school every day. Him mother give him mango, sometimes she give him an orange. Most of the time him give them away, say the juice dirty up him uniform. Him fussy like that."

"O my. Fruits are good for him."

"Teacher, teach we that, Maas Suraj. Mi never tell you, them lock up him father inna jail fi sell ganja. Him not going see him father again it look like. Him just laughy, laughy so." He hugged his knees, bowed his head and shook it. Then he sat up tall again. Bit his fingers on his right hand.

Suraj said. "Maybe, he laughs because it makes him feel better."

"A check so but sometimes him just laugh for nothing and we don't know why him laughing."

"Tell me about Curtis and your other friend."

"Imogene?"

"That's right. Imogene."

"Me tell you about Curtis first. Him bright, bright, bright. Him get all him sums right and him read nuff, nuff, nuff. Him mother and him father don't live together no more. Look like something bad happen so him live with him father now. Curtis nice though. We have plenty fun."

"And Imogene? The only girl among you boys, eh." He folded his hands behind his neck and leaned into them. Smiled. He looked off into the distance like he was thinking. Roderick's eyes opened wide. "She nice. Me like her. O Maas Suraj, she don't have no mother and father, them burn up in a fire at Back-A-Wall. She tell me is area leader order bad boy fi burn them out. Imogene don't go near fire." Roderick shook his head.

"A tell you a funny story. We was in the cooking room the other day at school and the teacher light the stove. Imogene pick up and run out the room. She put down one piece a cow bawling. The whole class buss out a laughing."

"She must not like fires, Roderick."

"She say since her mother and father burn up in the fire, she afraid she get burn up too. The teacher send her to sewing class instead. Poor Imogene."

"Makes perfect sense to change her class."

"Other than that, she is my favorite. She still funny like Django and Curtis them."

"My goodness, Roderick. You are a lucky boy. Three friends in such a short time. It must make you really happy."

"Remember, my friend from next door, Chloe, she go to that school, too. She just have a different set a friends at school. But she and me walk home sometimes and she help me with my homework."

"That is nice of her to do. You are in an excellent school, I see."

"Yes, Maas Suraj. Even when my friend them make fun of me it don't bother me anymore. Me getting used to them now, so me just laugh it off."

"Very good."

Roderick got up, tucked his shirt in his pants waist, took a deep breath and blew out hard.

"But the shop lonely when you don't come round so a glad a get into school."

"Ah, my son, loneliness is all in your mind. How have you been doing in the shop?"

"Sometimes good—sometimes bad."

"Find a balance between good and bad."

"How me must do that when all me get is batteration and bruk back work. Sometime me just feel like do something bad fi true. As true as God, Maas Suraj. If she beat me one more time a going do something bad to her. A want to go far away from she and Nelton them."

"Family cannot be washed off with water and removed, son."

"You don't understand, Maas Suraj. She brutalize me, work me like old mule, and box me down in front a people when she ready."

"You need to learn to ignore her sometimes."

"She need to stop pay me mind. A can't do anything right for her and yet me doing everything. Is time for me get out of that hell yard."

"Don't be hasty. Is there something you do to keep you calm like meditation before you go to bed at night?"

"What is that?"

"When you walked in here today, I was meditating. Even though you were trying to get my attention, I was calm and continued the exercise. It is a way to relax the mind and clear all the clutter of wrong thinking and make room for better thoughts."

"I don't think that will help me with this wicked woman. She out to murder me like the police them do to the Rasta man them."

"Which Rasta men?"

"The ones them brutalize in Coral something… me no remember, but is Coral something."

"O Coral Gardens. That was a long time ago. Poor judgment. Poor judgment on the part of the police."

"Ras Menelek say is wickedness."

"Don't burden yourself with those ills. You need to clear your mind so you can think critically and make excellent decisions. Meditation will help you."

"You going teach me?"

"When you are ready to learn—I will teach you." Roderick twisted his lips from side to side as if to zip them tight. *A cause you don't know yah Maas Suraj. There is only one way to deal with Aunt Hope—break some part of her.*
Raising his shoulders, he looked into Suraj's eyes: "A want was to ask you to help me with my project for school."

"What is it about?"

"My teacher want me to write about World War One. She say I can go to the library and look up information or I can interview somebody who know about the war. That's why I did think about you."

"That is nice of you. When is the project due?"

"In three weeks. My teacher want it to have pretty picture or anything me can find from the war that we can display on the table or put on the black board."

"Three weeks! Dedicate time after school or on the weekend to meet with me. I will be happy to help you."

"Thanks, Maas Suraj. You going to tell me them funny stories, right?"

"Funny stories you call them. They were not so funny when we were uncertain whether we would live or die."

"You can tell me any story you want. My teacher will love them." Roderick took a deep, loud breath. "Thank you. Thank you. A better run home now. A will come back another day."

"Remember, you have little time. It is raining. Good seeing you. Just keep a cool head."

"Awright then." Roderick walked out the door, smiled and skipped down the shallow steps into the lane. Someone whistled. He looked over his shoulder. Raindrops tickled his eyelids.

Is Cyril.

Roderick waved goodbye—ran, skipped, laughed and sang:

> The school boy skank is number one
> The school boy skank is number one
> Run go tell the school, this ya boy no fool

Roderick sang until his heart almost burst with joy—he felt light—he felt free. The rain must have fallen heavily near his home. The long stretch of rain drenched road was like a bright black diamond. Sidewalks had a slight glow as the sun dipped behind the clouds, casting shadows from trees and lampposts. Utility poles with electric power lines swung ominously in the wind. Two houses away, Roderick spotted Aunt Hope standing on the piazza.

What sweet nanny goat a go run him belly.

Hope was wearing a polka-dot tie-head with a plastic wrapper over it. He slowed, but the rain was beating him hard. A car sped by, splashed him with dirty water that had collected in a wide pothole.

"Why me always get splash up, splash up with dirty water? Something don't right about that. Cho man. What make him wet me up so?" He blew bubbles of water cascading down his face. As he got closer, his stomach rumbled at the sight of the long leather strap his aunty stretched from one hand to the other.

"Is what that? Me never see that one before. Aunty going to murder mi backside. Suraj tell me to keep a cool head. If I jump over the Petgrave them fence, over our backyard, through my window, she won't figure me in the house. Them wall too high and the bad dog them will tear me up. What a going do?"

Roderick saw two adults walking towards the shop, and the rumbling in his stomach subsided. The bus stopped down the street and more folks came off and walked towards the shop.

"She not going beat me make all them people see."

Building courage, he approached a fuming Aunt Hope, who grabbed him as he made his way to the gate.

"Where you coming from eee? Where you coming from?"

Roderick did not answer.

"A say… where you coming from?" He did not answer.

"John! Is you a talking to?"

John? Why she call me John? That's not my name.

She grabbed him, lashed him with the belt. He jumped up and down and pursed his lips tight. He tried to grab a hold of the belt but Hope was fast on the draw and she lashed him again. For every lash Roderick said nothing. Not only did it wear her out—it infuriated her.

"You turn man now. You don't feel it. So you not crying?" Hope raised the belt to give him one more lash and something made her pull back and cursed him instead.

"You good for nothing, boy, you."

Roderick looked over his shoulder and saw Miss Dillon shaking her head from side to side, calling out to her.

"Careful Hope. You are going to kill the child."

"Keep your mouth out of this."

"Why you don't just give him back to his mother?" Miss Dillon said and put her bundle on her head and walked down the street.

Roderick pulled away from Hope, glanced over his sore shoulder and saw Chloe staring from her veranda, tears rolling down her face.

The sky became exceptionally bright. Then it got dark. Lightning hit the ground.

Bash. Bash!

Thunder cracked and popped like bullets from a Bonanza show Roderick once peeped over the Petgrave's and watched on their television. Olympic Way was a symphony of thunder claps, dog yaps, and Roderick refused to cry. This time, he had had enough of Hope's brutalizing. There was not a sound spot on his body.

"I am getting out of this hell. I am getting out now! Hope Flowers. Wicked. Evil. Hope Flowers. You going to hell." His forehead got tight, the back of his neck stiffened. Roderick hurried to his room, murmured to himself. "I am going to break every bone in this old hog."

Refusing to feel the discomfort of the web of welts on his flesh, he packed a little burlap bag with his paint set he got from Chloe, sketch book he got from Ellen, crayons, pencil, a little cup, two merinos, a short pants, a pair of shoes he found in the trunk and the locket. The pain in his forehead was intensifying, so he tied it with a headband. Then, he put a handkerchief in his back pocket, some money he saved from his stone art. He paused for a moment. Then he turned around and picked up a small book, Animal Farm, his class was reading. Grabbed a rock bun and grater cake.

"Hoooooooooo." He breathed hard. "It hurt." Looking back at the beautiful room he had transformed into a breathable space, he sighed. "It is time for me to say goodbye to this wickedness." He climbed on the trunk and jumped through the window. There was a score to be settled before he left the yard and he walked to the back of the house, stood on a pile of stones and stoned the house. The first two landed in Hope's bedroom window.
Pashai, pashai!

There were splinters everywhere. He ran to the side of the house and continued with a barrage of stones through the boys' window. Then he ran to the front and finished the front door and windows.

"She better don't come near me or I will burst her head open with the last rock stone." Roderick spoke loud enough to be heard. He ran fast towards Pelican Parade—out of sight—on a journey to God knows where.

13

The Sprinter Hears With His Feet

The rain stopped. A gracious sun plaited silver ribbons around floating clouds like delicate ornaments against the sky. Roderick looked out at the vast expanse of powder-blue that stretched for miles ahead and appeared to touch the ground. He had been living on the streets of Kingston for most of the summer. His sustenance came from the kindness of strangers, while others chased him away. It was not unusual to see little boys roaming the streets during the summer months. Dirt poor children were not off to summer camp in the Blue Mountains. They were flying kites, riding wood framed push carts made from sundry recycled scraps. Girls made doll houses from sticks and cloth. Their dolls came alive from paper cutouts or mango seeds with hair they would comb and tie ribbons on the ends. Some pooled their pennies to cook big pots of dumplings and thick gravy from coconut oil and spices. Lemonade with lots of ice was just perfect on a hot day. Others were just looking for trouble, and those like Roderick, had lost their way. He wanted so much to connect to something better than his problems, and he screamed out to the elements.

"You out there? Yes. You. Big fluffy cloud."

A group of boys with cleats hanging over their shoulders crossed over to the other side of the road talked loudly about football practice.

"Me wish me could happy like them."

Roderick soon made room on the sidewalk for a market vendor who was approaching; his clothes tattered, and reeked of perspiration. The man carried his basket of provisions on his head and thermos in his hand. He sang about taking all his sins and griefs to Jesus. Roderick took in the man for a moment and spun away.

"If him have sin and grief, what me have? All me want is some peace so me can get through school. Now me might never go a school again. This sin and grief too much. You. Yes, you out there." He screamed at the top of his lungs and kept walking.

A shack stood lopsided on the crest of a hillet, at the corner of a small street just off the main. As he approached, he smelled old leather, shoe polish and glue as they wafted on a steady stream of wind. Roderick's feet hurt as he climbed up the slope to take a rest from walking a long way. He watched as the shoemaker fit the shoe over the last, picked up the hammer, and sharp tack. The man shook his head. The shoe was showing every sign of knowing many a hot asphalt, rugged hills, mudslides, repair after repair because money was scarce to buy a new pair. Roderick could see the wheels turning in the man's mind as if to say, I will give it one last patch, one last hope.

The man spoke clearly. "Maas Wilzo can get some more wear out of this," scrutinizing the faithful leather chestnut brown brogue when Roderick appeared at his blindside.

"What noh dead, noh dash weh, youthman."

"What you mean, sir?"

"It means if something is not dead, do not throw it away. This is good quality shoes right here so," he told Roderick as he drove the tack in the bottom of the shoe. Then he removed it from the last, blew on it to get rid of the dust, and took a worn cotton fabric. Then he wiped it in a can of shoe polish and rubbed it vigorously on the shoe until it was shiny as new.

Him care for the shoes like how me care for my one dress shoes.

"You see, little boy, if you believe that there is hope for something to live again, you do all you can to save it."

Roderick did not know how to add anything to what the shoemaker said; he just twisted his body like he had worms, shrugged his shoulders towards his ear and stared.

"Is Maas Wilzo send you for him shoes? Just on time."

Roderick shook his head, not knowing who Maas Wilzo was. He held on to the edge of the door and anchored his feet so he would not slide down the small hill.

"No. Is not him send me."

"I neva see you roun here before." Roderick had heard this statement before from other folks. He had come into town, a stranger to his own family. It was not unusual for folks to be wary of strangers, and the shoemaker was no exception. Roderick became aware of his own presence when he entered a room or walked down the street. He felt some people could smell a foreigner in his own land a mile away. The man with the leather shoes knitted his brow. It had questions all over it.

"Who fa shoes yu come fa?"

"A don't come for nobody shoes."

"So what you doing aroun here?"

"Me just a walk."

"Walk go where?"

"Me don't know. Me just a walk."

Roderick studied the man's face and wished he would offer him a seat. His feet hurt from long walks and he barely got a shut eye. At times, he would sleep in the market by a vendor's stall whom he befriended in Coronation Market or the night he slept under the shrubs at Kingston Parish Church yard. He was a nowhereian, and he knew it.
A hope him don't think me is one of them out-a-order boy who up to no good.

"You not one of them busy-body boys a walk about the place like them don't have nothing fi do?"
Same thing. A could tell that cross him mind.

"No sir. Me just a look fi find some peace."

"There is no peace on this earth until we die, young boy. So is running away you running away? The rudeboys will find you if you don't know where you are going. Where you live?"

Roderick found these questions hard to answer. The last place he wanted to talk about was Hope's shop in Olympic Gardens. The sunlight bounced off the zinc roof and glowed like a Bethlehem star. A shoemaker's shop on the hill felt safer than where he lived.

"Olympic Way. I live on Olympic Way."

"You far from your yard, son."

"Sir, mi know. Is long time me set out a walk. Mi tired."

"Life is a long journey. But running away from your problems solves nothing. There must be something wrong why you are running away. Did something bad happen to you?"

Feeling that the man was warming up to him, Roderick sat on the ground, put his little bag next to him.

Sighed. Roderick had told his story to so many people he was feeling stuck like a broken forty-five on an old Grundig record changer. His Rocksteady opus, like a leitmotif, played every time he entered a space. Roderick wanted to sing a new song. Yet he found himself compelled to tell somebody.

"So much bad things I don't know where to start. I just sad all the time."

"Be careful that you don't end up on the wrong side of the tracks or run afoul of the law."

"What you mean by?"

"Get into a lot of trouble and even go to jail." Roderick crossed his legs in a half-lotus position, took a deep breath and listened attentively as the shoemaker worked on another pair of shoes, and told his story.

"When I was a little boy, they left me alone in a whorehouse on Hanover Street in the summer of 1933. I was told that my parents drowned after flood waters swept their house away on the gully bank. Some folks told me that an old colonial cobbler rescued me and apprenticed me. I was six years old."

"Apprenticed you. What that mean?"

"Since the cobbler was very skilled at making and fixing shoes, he taught me and paid me a small pittance. I was learning and helping him out at the same time. When I became a teenager, the money was just enough to buy me cigarettes and take my girlfriend to the movies."
Roderick smiled, picked up his bag, placed it in his lap and cuddled it like a pillow. His stomach made a rumbling noise, and he squeezed it with the bag to shut it up.

A wonder if him have anything to eat. A hungry. I don't want to beg anyone for anything. I don't raise so.

"That's how you learn to do this shoemaking thing?"

"Yes, that's how I became a shoemaker. I learned how to cut and repair leather soles, dye shoes, even handbags. There was never a shoe problem I could not fix. It was in that cobbler's shop that I learned to think and solve problems for customers. Boys like you need a trade to make you think and make money so you can take care of yourself."

So how come Aunty don't pay me a little money like Shoey did get so me can buy something for myself. She just work me like old donkey. If a not apprentice what me is then?

"I see the wheels turning, youth man. What's on your mind?"

"I want to stay in school. Me like school."

"That's a good first step. Summer holidays will soon be over, and September morning you have to be back bright and early. O, I remember the good old days. I hope you find your way back to school."

Smiling, Roderick remembered the joys of being in school.

"I hope so."

"I can only point you in the right direction. I cannot mend you like an old shoe to make you look brand new. You must think your way through this crisis and cut your cloth to suit your size. Come. Sit down here so."

Roderick's stomach made a loud rumble, and he saw the expression on the shoemaker's face change to one of concern. Holding his head down to avoid looking at the shoemaker's face, he belched and a loud fart followed.

"You eat from morning?"

"Not since breakfast time, sir."

"Don't call me sir. I don't like that title. That is what I had to call the old white cobbler, when I lived and worked with him in my youth. He insisted on it. Those were different times. The name is Belnavis, but everybody calls me Shoey." He rubbed the boy on his head and went behind a curtain. A smile came across Roderick's face. "Shoey. Such a funny name but it make sense. After all, him fix shoes." Roderick could hear Shoey stirring something, the distinct sound of a metal spoon against enamelware. *Piku-piku-piku-piku.* Moments later, Shoey parted the curtain with a mug in one hand and a hard dough bread and cheese sandwich.

"Here. Eat something."

"Thank you, Shoey." Roderick lifted the cup and made one big gulp and smiled.

"How you know me love Horlicks?"

"Just drink the something. You look hungry."

"I don't get to drink the Horlicks because my aunty say it too rich fi my blood. She only give it to her two son them."

"Aye! Eat up. You need the strength. A mixed up aunty."

Roderick ate the sandwich and drank his Horlicks with delight, belched real loud and wiped his mouth with the end of his shirt.

"No. Don't wipe your mouth with your shirt. Here, use this." Shoey gave Roderick a clean rag from an enamel basin. "You did far, son. You starving."

Two Rastamen with head wraps and brooms stepped lively by and greeted Shoey.

"Hail the man."

"Hail up bredren. Look like you sell plenty broom today. Business looking good."

"Yes, I," replied the older of the two Rastas. "We just a trod through Babylon, trying to survive this rat race. Peace and love."

"Peace and love!" Shoey said and got back to work. This old 'government yard' they call Trench Town is where you find some of the most hard-working men and women. Most of the younger men are into the music because rude boy business doesn't pay."

"Me love music, Shoey. My cousin have plenty record and him play all the time. One day, I hope to be a great musician or a artist for me can draw and paint real good."

"Good. All that talent will keep you out of trouble. Police and rude boys will kill you in the streets. Stop before it's too late."

"Me not no rude boy, Shoey. My life just rough. Nobody get batter-bruise every day and live. Every day a part of my body dead off—if is not my foot—is my eye, if is not my eye, is my mouth. A have to keep walking or a going to dead."

There was a long silence between the two. Roderick listened to Shoey hammering away at old shoes. The smell of thick mustard colored glue was so strong it made him feel a little funny inside.

"I cannot understand how badly you feel every day to leave your aunty's house. It must be hard to bear. These streets are not safe, I tell you; not safe."

"I know it not safe nowadays. My Aunt Lillian yard in Waterhouse would make me feel safer. At least she wouldn't batta-bruise me like Miss Hope."

"Why she couldn't take you with her?"

"She a take care a mi cripple grandmadda."

"I still believe that a home with your strict aunt, a bed to sleep on, and a roof over your head is still the best of a dangerous situation, don't you think so?"

Is what Shoey talking about. A wonder if him would teach me how to fix shoes, too, and pay me a little something. Him look kind. But how me would go a school? "No, Shoey. It not the best." Roderick got up. Stretched. Walked to the edge of the small hill and looked over into the street. People were moving about, chattering, dogs yakking at them. Children played and screamed at each other. He put his little bag over his shoulder. It felt like it weighed a ton. He looked up and down the street and back at Shoey, who kept working and humming a tune.

"Sounds like you make up your mind, young boy. I worry for you. You say you love music. I know some young boys near to here who make wonderful music. They spend most of their day writing songs about the mean streets. Just go sit and listen to them. It will make you feel better. Maybe you will learn more than I can teach you."

"I would love to do that. Just show me where to walk. I will find them."

"Good."

"Who me must ask for?"

"You can ask for Kofi. Tell him Shoey sent you. Ask him if you can sit in on the young boys them rehearsal. If you don't see him, ask for Sister Ama. You think you can remember all that?"

"Yes, Shoey. Ask for Kofi or Sister Ama."

"Safe journey. Remember, when you finish, go home and say sorry to your aunty."

Roderick gave Shoey one last look and said nothing except in his thoughts.

Maybe Kofi will make me stay with them forever.

Roderick set out on his journey until he reached Susumba Lane. He looked up and down and crossed the lane. There came a motorcycle speeding in his direction as he tried to run across the lane.

Boom!

The motorcycle hit him in the rear end and he fell to the ground. He felt the thud of his head against the pavement. Everything went black. Through the haze, he could see folks moving towards him. The chatter grew louder and louder. His head pounded.

"Them lick him down. A one bike man lick him," someone informed the people who gathered.

"You all right, little boy?" came another.

"Him don't look like him live around here."

"Carry him go a Public Hospital, quick."

"Him head a bleed."

"Bring some sweet sugar and water. It will…"

Moments later, Roderick was fully conscious and sat up on the sidewalk. A woman was applying a cold rag with ice on his forehead. She motioned for him to hold it.

"Here, little boy, hold it on your head. It cold, but try to bear it. What's your name?"

"Roderick, mam. Ayyyye," as the pain ricocheted across his forehead.

"I know it is cold but it will take down the swelling. Where you was going?"

"A was going to see some music man dem over there, so."

"O. The Breddas."

"Yes. Shoey send me."

"All right. I will walk you go over there. You soon feel better."

"Miss, him have to go to the hospital," shouted a young man from across the street. "Somebody has to inform him family them."

"Is what wrong with you? After him not dead." He looked up at the woman, his heart rumbled, tears ran down his face.

What going happen to me? A don't want to go no hospital. Mi can't pay for hospital. If Aunty find out, it going worse for me. "Please, just take me to Mister Kofi. Him will help me." He stretched his hand for the kind lady to hold. The people who gathered cheered as he walked towards the music yard. Roderick turned around and smiled at them, pain squeezing his temples.

"Mi awright. Mi awright."

Nyabinghi drumming spilled over onto the sidewalk outside the compound. The singers were chanting Rastaman truths and rights and Roderick's heart beat loud, playing counterpoint to the rhythms. He squeezed the woman's hand, then pulled away. Roderick felt something open up inside his belly. He could feel the blood coursing through his body from the top of his head to the bottom of his feet. He turned to the woman.

"I feel like I want to just jump up and down and scream loud, loud, loud!"

She smiled. "You do just that. I am glad you feeling better already. I have to leave you here."

"Thank you, miss."

As he entered the compound, the vibration of the drums, singing, the clouds of smoke from chillum pipes made him feel even lighter than before. He sat on a small bench, looked around, then closed his eyes real tight. He could feel his brain calming down.

The man dem singing one of my Bible verse me learn in Sabbath School when me was in the country. A can't believe this.

> By the rivers of Babylon, there we sat down,
> yea, we wept, when we remembered Zion.
> For there they that carried us away captive required
> of us a song; and they that wasted us required of us
> mirth, saying, Sing us one of the songs of Zion.
> How shall we sing the Lord's song in a strange land?

The music stopped, and Roderick took a deep breath. One singer with a guitar walked over to him. "Youtman. A see you enjoy the music."

"Yes."

"I and I is Kwasi and my two brethren Manu and Cuffee are The Truths and Rights Brethren."

"The I is Roderick."

"The I see Rasta," Kwasi asked?"

"What you mean?"

"The youtman refer to oneself as The I."

"Me jus a follow what The I say."

The Ras smiled. "Nice. So what wrong with the I forehead?"

"A bike man lik I dung when I crossing to come here and just lef I fi dead it look like."

"What? Blood and fire for the wicked. How you feeling now?"

"From I hear the music, a start to feel better."

"The I will get The I some help and take The I home. Where The I live?"

A should just tell him that a live in the open, out here in the streets under the sky. If him take me back to Aunt Hope, she going to beat me bad, bad, bad for breaking her window dem. Me can still get to go a school with Chloe a morning time, study for scholarship. A will get to have fun with Curtis dem. A confuse. Twisting a string tightly around his index finger that hung from his bag, he winced at the blood that formed at the tip of his finger as if it would burst.

"A can't take no more beating, Ras Kwasi. Mi will soon dead."

"No dead business here, youthman. I will get The I home."

"A can stay here little bit and listen to the music some more?"

"Sure. We working on a stage show coming up next week."

"That sound good, Ras Kwasi." Roderick heard the jingle of the woman's bangles as she approached him. She had a white enamel mug decorated with a red hibiscus flower. She turned the handle of the mug towards him.

"A never see a Rastawoman before. You so pretty, Miss. What a way your hair tall down your shoulder dem."

"Drink up your carrot juice. Good for your eyesight." She laughed.

He stared at the Rastawoman and became lost in her beauty. She wore handcrafted wood earrings that rested on her shoulders. Her white dress flowed softly to her ankles, her leather sandals cradled her soft feet. The Rastawoman made slow, deliberate steps and sat under the sprawling branches of an almond tree behind the drummers. Then the drumming started. The chanting climbed from the earth to the sky. The Truth and Rights brethren had fired up not only the music but some Sensimilla. It was intoxicating and Roderick counted balls of smoke from the mouths of the brethren and he became calm.

The singing and chanting went into the early evening. At one time, Ras Kwasi played a guitar solo, and everyone in the yard danced. A brief shower interrupted the rehearsal and folks sheltered under a canopy. Roderick saw some Rastawomen cooking in the kitchen. The smell of spices made him feel hungry. The women served food to the musicians, and the pretty Rastawoman brought him a plate of food. She smiled with him.

"Thank you, Miss."

"You are welcome, youthman."

Roderick ate the plate of ital stew that sizzled with pepper and lots of spices. When he finished eating, he walked over to the pretty woman and handed her his empty plate. *A could stay here for the rest of the evening if dem will make me stay. A should ask her for she look kind. Don't it Roderick?* He scratched his head, picked up his bag. *She coming back. O my, she calling out to me. What a do now?*

"Come sit next to me, youth."

Walking over to her, he felt his knee buckle. He sat next to her on a wooden bench.

"What is your name?"

"Roderick."

"Roderick what?"

"Brissett."

"I went to school with some Brissetts when I lived in St. James. You any relations?"

"I don't know. I come from St. Ann."

"You kind of look a little like dem, though."

Roderick leaned his head into his left shoulder. Hugged his bag and rested his chin on it. He reached inside his bag for a small rag and wiped the sweat from his nose.

"So where are you going now with your little bag of things?"

What a must tell her. A can't tell her a don't live nowhere a just a walk. A wonder if she would keep me eee? A better think fast. The bottom of his feet tingled. He quivered inside.

"Is move a moving today to go live with my Aunt Ellen in Cherry Gardens."

"Moving? But you far from Cherry Gardens."

"A know. A just a walk till me reach there."

"Is a long way from here. You sure is move you moving?"

"True, true. See me things here." He showed her the bag. "A walking to go find her. She going to take care of me. A just want was to see the I dem and learn something. So where is Kofi?"

"Kofi inside working on some music and making plans for the concert."

"Awright then. I have to go. Aunt Ellen waiting for me to come." *A really wish dem would keep me tonight. Is awright a will just gwaan walk till a find mi way.* Roderick glanced over at Ras Kwasi, shaking his head and he could hear him whispering to the other singers.

"Troubled youth. Cherry Gardens. Uptown. Not poor man's land."

Roderick picked up his bag. "A gone."

14

Halfway Tree Park

Hours later, close to midnight, Roderick curled up on the bench at the center of the park to sleep. The stars had formed a jeweled blanket across Constant Spring and Half Way Tree Roads, even Hagley Park Road fell under the spell of its magnificence. This was the one night Public Service light company could shut the lights off because heaven declared. Roderick listened to the splash and gurgle of the water coming from a concrete water fountain that stood in the middle of the park.

"Why dem running the water in the middle of the night? Kingston don't have water to waste like that." Despite the water running, somehow, Roderick felt peaceful in the open air. *All I want now is a good night's sleep. The walking wear me out. A can hardly feel mi foot dem.*

The night was hot, his sweat was salty and flooded his eyelids. Roderick wiped his face with the shoulder of his shirt, watched intently as a woman lifted her box and placed it on her head. Blue Mountain winds wafted the woman's pungent smell. With every new gust, a smell rose and waned: lavender water, tea tree oil, rose water, tobacco, camphor oil, khus khus perfume and urine. As she got closer to him, he prayed she would not join him on the bench. Au contraire, and so it was. His thoughts brought her exactly there.

The woman stopped, making no signs of noticing him. Dressed in multiple layers of clothing with tassels of all sorts hanging around her waist, she walked gracefully in her Jesus sandals. Gently resting the box on the ground, she took her dress hem and fanned what dirt she thought was on the bench. She sat on the end of the bench in silence. The bench knew her; she knew the bench and Roderick was feeling like a stranger that night.

Easing away, ever so slightly, as if to make room and not offend her, Roderick covered his nostril and whispered a prayer; he would either have to sleep on the bench or on the ground.

The woman asked, "What you doing all alone in the park at this hour of the night because only thieves and police make their night rounds?"

Roderick thought she spoke so well she may have been an important lady long ago.

"A going to see one Aunt Ellen. You know her?"

"Ellen. No. I don't know her. Where she lives?"

"Cherry Gardens."

"You mean where the rich people live?"

"A don't quite know, Miss."

"How do you expect to find her?"

"Dem two foot here. Dem never lost me before."

"Tell me something. You sure you not running away from home this hour of the night?"

"So long as me run away from wicked people, maybe me will live to see my father again and do fun things like other children."

"That is why I out here, too. I had to find a safe place to be. I understand your suffering."

Roderick sat up on the bench. He couldn't believe a big somebody had run away, too. He stared at her; she stared back at him. They said nothing for about fifteen seconds.

Then Roderick rustled the stillness. "You really

understand? You is the first somebody say dem understand what me going through."

Clearing her throat, she bobbed her head up and down. She gazed up at the sky. Roderick followed her lead and looked up to the sky. It was as if they were both looking for something out there. Something that would make their gloom go away.

"I feel your pain, little boy. It was my story that led me to walk the streets of St. Andrew with my calico bag on my head, making the park my permanent home for the past thirteen years."

"Thirteen years? Before me born. Me don't reach there so yet. What happen make you out here?" Roderick crossed his legs on the bench, unbuttoned his shirt to cool down from the heat. Listened.

"My grandmother beat me. She blamed me for all of my misfortune. Grandma said it was all my fault. Accused me of becoming careless after my mother left me with her to go find work in England."

"Why she beat you?"

"Because of Uncle Manman, my favorite uncle."

"What happened?"

"He took my innocence, he took me away from the joys of hopscotch, dandy-shandy, Nancy Drew and Hardy Boys stories."

"I understand the rest, but I don't know what you mean by innocence. What is that?"

"When someone forces a girl or a boy to become an adult before their time."

"I still don't figure it out."

"When you get older, you will know. If I could see my mother now, I would tell her my woes," she said. "And so, I tell my stories to the silence, right here in this park."

Roderick felt a chill down his arms, and then a voltage-like electrical current squeezed each vertebrate along his spine. Tears welled up in his eyes. He propped his cheeks with both palms and looked off in space. *I want my mother, too. How long this live a street going to last? After me can't stay out a school so long. Me going drop back. Me won't know enough fi take scholarship. What me going do? Shoey say rude boy a go catch me. You out there. Yes you.*

Roderick turned around to take a quick glance at the woman who was having an all-out conversation with the wind. He came face to face with the ruin of one who buried her sorrow behind layers of clothes, sweat and tears, in a lonely park under the elements. Roderick fidgeted and rubbed his hands together to keep warm. His teeth chattered enough to get the woman's attention.

"You feeling cold?"

"Yeh, yeh, yes, Miss." Roderick felt her gentle touch as she covered him with a skirt she pulled from the box. Soon his shivering subsided. He looked up at her as she went back to mouthing something to herself. She made the sign of the cross. He rubbed his nose, put the burlap at his head like a pillow, crossed his ankles, and went to sleep.

Early morning. Half Way Tree Square stretched and yawned like a green lizard perched on rockstone, showing off its purple dewlap, ballooning in and out under its throat. The misty morning was rising from the grass to kiss low fluffy clouds rising upwards in the sky. Roderick looked around at the beautiful flowers in the park. Wreaths of periwinkle, pink, lavender and white bloomed in the moist earth amid gay bursts of yellow buttercups, attracting rollicking butterflies and long furry-legged bees. A majestic Poinciana tree in full bloom displayed orange-yellow flowers became the orchestra pit for the hummingbirds.

Sniffing the cool morning air, Roderick sat absorbed by this magical part of Kingston, watching people move fluidly between each other, up and down, crisscross, side by side, hugging, squeezing, a concerto of bodies, voices, clicking heels on sidewalks, and a mosaic of colors. Half Way Tree Square was awake.

"You want me to get you a warm cup of tea? Miss Grinnel just set out her things over there. She always brings her thermos of tea and shares with me. I will get you some, too," said the woman.

"Thank you. You want me to go get it for you, miss?"

"No. She doesn't know you, so I will go for you." The woman stood up; her bangles and ornaments of all sorts chimed with her every move, her smell rose with her. "Just watch my bags for me."

"Your bags, miss?" he said scornfully and quickly caught himself. "Yes, I will." *Watch her bag dem?* Roderick wondered what could be in her bags that anyone would want to steal, anyway. By the looks of things, her entire life story was wrapped up in those bundles.

"Is her things all the same." Then he remembered it was the skirt from the same old box that sheltered him from the cold last night. It was his joy to watch it for her and hoped he would not have to cut anyone for troubling her box. Roderick smiled. He remembered her kindness.

They drank mint tea and ate hard dough bread, and pear, taking in the sights of the early morning.

What a hustle! Traffic jam, car horns, truck horns, JOS bus horns. The newspaper man called out, "Gleaner, Gleaner!" School children shouted, skipped and laughed. Bicycle bells rang constantly. Stray dogs barked.

"And I end up here where a feel free." Roderick pinched himself out of his daydream from the realization of different freedom. The two talked for most of the morning. Roderick told her how much he loved to read and imagine being surrounded by nature. She told him how much she loved books, too. The woman reached into her bundle and took out some photographs she kept in a little cloth purse.

"Me and Mama when I was nine. Me and Naseberry my little brown dog. Pinkie, Sports Day. Netball practice. Me in the middle going to church with Aunt Ethel, Good Friday. Rosie and me in First Form at Immaculate."

"She pretty and her hair tall. Is Rosie your best friend?"

"Yes, she was my best friend in the entire world. I miss her so much."

"What happen to her?"

"When my troubles started, her parents told her to stay away from me. I was sad."

"O no. My best friend Chloe live next door to me. She nice to me since I came to live in Town. I miss her already. I know she worried about me. Me just turn friend with Curtis, Django and Imogene since me start school. I never get to tell nobody me not coming back."

"You not going back to school? Go back to school."

"But where me going to live? Me can't live with Aunt Hope no more. That's why me looking for Aunt Ellen." Tears burst from his eyes like a firehose. "If, if, if I go live with Miss Ellen, Chloe going to be sad. But I will be better off. I am her only friend in Olympic Gardens. Me and her were studying to take scholarship. She going to be sad if me don't take it with her. Miss, a don't know what to do."

"Sometimes, you just can't do anything. Be silent and listen to your heart. It will tell you what you should do."

"My heart? How my heart going to tell me what to do? Is me have to tell myself what to do, don't it?"

She smiled. "That too. You will find the answer when you are still."

"A can't tek this walking all over Kingston. Me have to find Miss Ellen today. Me and her can talk how me going to live." Roderick choked up again.

Bong. Bong. Bong. Bong. Bong. Bong. Bong. Bong. Bong. Bong. Bong. Bong.

The peeling of the Parish church bell interrupted their musings. She told him that the church bell rang at mid-day to call the people to prayer. Some people stop what they are doing and just pray about anything.

"Noon-time prayer, stronger than any Obeah," she said as she made the sign of the cross and bowed her head in reverence.

Roderick smiled at the stories she told him. "I have to go now, Miss. I must find Aunt Ellen. Although she is not my real, real aunty, she is a friend of my real, real aunties."

"I get you. I had a few of those in my time. Some good. Some bad."

"Aunt Ellen like me very much and I like her back. I have to see her today. She will help me sort out my worries. Can you show me how to reach Cherry Gardens?"

The woman took out a piece of paper and wrote the directions for Roderick. "Can you read my writing?"

"Yes, I can read much better now."

"Just follow these big roads: Waterloo, Shortwood and you must get to Cherry Gardens. You will find it before you get to the big hill. No need to be sleeping out in the street like this."

"Me never plan to sleep out in the night air. Is since me start walk, me realize how much me don't have to live with my aunty's wickedness anymore. One day it just come to me say Miss Ellen will take me and care for me. She don't have no children. I feel it in my head that when I find her, I won't have to sleep in the night air no more."

"Sounds superb, son."

She called me son.

He realized he slept on the bench with this woman, had breakfast with her, shared stories most of the morning but never got her name and she never asked him his name.

"Miss. You know, I never ask what you name."

"Maddy Maddy Mavis, Peepi Bed, Obeah Woman, Bag-a-Bundle. One teacher man calls me Persephone, for I have been to hell. Every tribe that passes through this park gives me a name. Some mock me. Some pity me. Whichever name they see fit."

"You are funny."

"Now you calling me a name you like, Funny."

"A don't mean it like that."

Roderick wanted to laugh, but pursed his lips really tight.

"No. Your real, real name."

"Not the one my mother gave me, for I lost it to Uncle Manman, in the darkness of that lonely room with the moon peeping down at me like is my fault. And so, I named myself Cherry, because he stole it from me."

"Me love Cherry. My little friend Chloe have a cherry tree in her yard and me raid it all the time." Roderick looked in her eyes at the delicate veil that masked her pain.

"Where your family is now, Miss Cherry?"

"I am my family, and everything I possess is in this box. Tonight I sleep here. Tomorrow I sleep down there." She pointed to a boulder at the center of the park. "Nobody troubles me in this park. They think I am mad. I am free under this Parish Church clock. It tells me every twelve hours that time longer than rope and one day, I will get justice."

"Justice. I know that word."

"When night comes, I love to listen to the silence; it tells me where I must rest my head. It is a good thing I listened last night, for there you were–the child of the silence. You will get all the answers to your life's questions to guide you on your journey if you listen to the silence."
She reached into her box, took out a bottle of sweet oil.

"Come. Give me your hands." His eyes popped, body stiffened. He pulled his shoulder to his ears, but warily extended his hands to her. She poured a small potion into each of his palms and proceeded to rub them gently.

"An anointing with sacred oil." She whispered, "May your life be sweet."

Roderick opened his mouth to say thanks.

She interrupted. "Hush!"

Roderick looked at her. He looked at his bag. Picked it up.

"I am going to find Miss Ellen cost it what it will."

15

Great Men Grow Strongest in Tough Towns

Roderick's head hurt and his body felt sore from the beatings and accident, but he looked towards the hills of St. Andrew and kept walking. The journey was arduous as the sun warmed the top of his head and Cherry Gardens seemed far away. Yet, he pressed on, as nothing would keep him from finding Miss Ellen. He could still smell the oil Miss Cherry rubbed on him, and he felt she was with him.

"Everything going to be all right. A glad about that."

A humming bird perched on a hedge of pink autumn sage that grew over a wall, winked at him, twittered and flew away.

"Mama, look what you send me to Town to do. Walk, walk, walk." He walked along Hope Road until he got to the corner of Waterloo Road, where he saw a woman selling fruits. He took out his last penny and told her this was all he had to buy the mango. She gave him a mango, and a rose apple. He thanked her and continued to walk. Then he turned slightly left onto Upper Waterloo Road, walked some more. His head hurt a little.

Why mi head hurting me now, eee? Roderick, you forget is a hard chop you get when the bike lick you down. Make a eat the mango, maybe a will feel little better. As he got to Shortwood Road, crossing his path was a meagre dirty-white coat dog with bald spots, where hair once grew. Its right front leg deformed. The dog joined him. Tiredness from the journey and scorching sun bearing down on his back, made him stop for a while on the sidewalk where a stately breadfruit tree indulged him shade. Well, what do you know? The little canine scratched the earth, sprayed a cloud of dust and sat in front of him.

Roderick smiled. "This dog must a know me could do with some company." He reached into his bag for the mango and bit into it. Juice flowed through his fingers, raced to his elbow. He licked the nectar, bit into the mango some more, stripped all the skin with his teeth. Then he shared a piece with the dog, who whimpered as if to say 'Yeh man.' Roderick ate until the seed was bare, threw it into the hedges along the way.

"Maybe a mango tree will grow next year." Roderick wiped his sticky hands on his pants, straightened the burlap on his arm, got on his way, dodged careless drivers speeding and honking for slower vehicles to get the dickance out of their way.

"Hey Jack," he called out and whistled at the dog. "Yes. You. You look like Jack would be a nice name for you. I am on my way to find Miss Ellen in Cherry Gardens. Don't know her address but somebody must know her. She is a very nice lady."

Jack looked up at Roderick, wagged his tail and whimpered again.

"Jack! Is what happened to all the hair on your body? O, you must have some sickness. A can bet some wicked pickney throw stone and bruk your foot why you walk hip-shotted. Kingston people strange eeh, Jack? The big people beat the pickney dem, the pickney dem beat the dog dem. Everybody a beat everybody. Me don't understand any of that. What you say?"

Roderick reached what appeared to be the end of Shortwood Road. He looked up and there was another sign that showed Oliver Road. "Did Miss Cherry ever say me to walk on Oliver Road?" Something in his gut told him to continue on Oliver Road and it soon became Shortwood Road again.

"So far, Jack, most of the people me meet since me decide fi just take a walk and get mi head straight, dem is good people. Dem want me to awright. A know Miss Cherry give me good direction."

The dog wagged its tail, and then flared his ears. Roderick was enjoying the company of a dog who only yowled and insisted on following him. He pressed on.

"Look, Jack. Look! That's Cherry Gardens Drive to the right. I bet is there Aunt Ellen live. It looks like the kind of road she would live on. A have to leave you right here so because a don't think Aunty have anywhere for you to stay. Besides, you look so sick she may have to care for you and me. That going to be too much for her." He threw his weary hands in the air.

Just then, some dogs started barking, causing a ripple effect a couple of houses in. Jack slowed, shivered, and hippity-hopped as fast as he could back down the street. Jack was gone.

"A can't wait to get a good bath, some hot food and tell Aunt Ellen all the bad things that happen to me."

Cherry Gardens Drive was a quiet road with its long stretch of smooth, black, asphalted pavement, and well-manicured grass that stretched like plush carpet runways. Palm trees grew majestically along the sidewalks and some in yards. Street lamps hung from tall utility poles, casting shadows along the road in the morning sun. Roderick could see ginormous houses siting on sprawling landscapes—some behind high walls and sturdy gates, while others opened onto the sidewalk.

What a pretty street.

The wind blew some fronds and the smell of moist earth made him close his eyes and sniff real hard. He wiped his face with his hands and the anointed oil was still sweet. Looking in the distance, thin white clouds played peek-a-boo with the Blue Mountains. It was as if the wind was sweeping the clouds across Cherry Gardens. For a while, no one but Roderick was on the street. Then voices came close behind him. He turned to see two women in colorful dresses and pretty slippers. One wore a tie head and the other a straw hat. As they passed him, he heard them talking about all the washing they had to do after the holiday party. He listened as their voices trailed in the distance.

"Perhaps dem know Aunt Ellen. Maybe a should ask dem." He ran to catch up with the women. "Miss, Miss," he called out to them. "Morning. A looking for my Aunt Ellen. She live up here."

"Morning, little boy," obliged one woman. "I don't know any Ellen. You don't have her address?"

"No, Miss."

"We can't be late getting back to work. Perhaps somebody else can help you."

"Thanks, Miss." Walking slowly, Roderick looked into people's yards. *I got to keep moving.* Peering over a stone fence, he saw a man raking leaves. "Sir, sir. Good morning. You know Miss Ellen?"

"Ellen who?"

"Just Ellen."

"What is her other name?"

"A don't remember, but she is very pretty. She is like my aunty. I have to find her today."

The man leaned on his rake, looked into Roderick's near weeping eyes, smiled. "I know a Ellen. The third house down, but I don't think she is the one you looking for."

"She pretty pretty pretty, don't it?"

"She all right." He wiped the sweat from his face.

"Look, you can try. I hope you find the right Ellen." He shook his head.

Arriving at the gate, Roderick surmised, This house looks just like Aunty kind a house. She like pink and plenty flowers. He whispered, "O Lawdy, Lawdy. Miss Cherry, a think a find her. The little palm trees around the driveway with the white paint at the bottom, is must she paint it. She loves to paint. I bet is her house this for real, real."

Confidence on his side, he walked up to the door and knocked. Two big dogs in a kennel on the side of the house huffed loud, sustained barks. A woman came to the door, short with heavy eyebrows, a fat round nose, wearing an apron and a cap, like a nurse. She was blue-black as the night with a frown on her face. She looked Roderick up and down. His smell hit her and she covered her nose. "What you want?"

"Good morning. A looking for my Aunt Ellen. She live here?"

"I am Hellene. Clear out of here right now. You and your dirty self before I call the police."

"A just looking for my Aunt Ellen. You know her?"

"What is her full name?"

"I only know she go by Ellen."

"Spell it."

"E.L.L.E.N."

"Well me spell mine H.E.L.L.E.N.E. You don't look like you related to anybody around here. Get away. Now!"

She rough like grater. Why she so mean? He heard footsteps coming behind Hellene.

"Who is that?"

"Nobody to worry about, madame. He don't belong in these parts."

"I will take it from here, Hellene. He's just a little boy." The old woman reached out her high-yellow arthritic red-nail-polished fingers, stroked his sweaty face. "Lost, little one? What you doing around here all by yourself?"

"A looking for my Aunt Ellen. She pretty pretty and kind. Is not that Ellen there. I know she live up here but a don't know which yard."

"Where do you live?"

Roderick paused. *Maybe a should give her grandma address in Waterhouse or just say Olympic Way. For if dem send me back me won't find Aunt Ellen fi take care a me, send me go a school, and dem things there. What a crosses.* Roderick had no plans to return to his Aunt Hope's home. His wanderings were over and he was finally home where he wanted to be: Cherry Gardens.

"A live in Olympic Gardens with my granny, Miss."

"Olympic Gardens?" Her eyes popped with curiosity.

Hellene interjected from behind the lady of the house's shoulder. "How can anything good come out of Olympic Gardens?"

"Not so harsh, Hellene. My children's pediatrician grew up in Olympic Gardens. What a fine doctor she became."

"That is her."

"Not her alone. I am sure there are others." Turning again to Roderick, "Does your grandmother know you came all the way up here?"

"No. She don't know. I just have to see Miss Ellen.

"You can help me find her?"

"I will have to call the police and report that you lost your way. Maybe they can help you find your way back home. Come inside and let me give you something to drink until the police get here. Hellene?"

"Yes, ma'am." Hellene knew exactly what her place was in this moment. She was there to serve and that alone.

"Have a seat, young man," the kind lady said.

"Me not stopping too long. Me better leave now. Me and police don't gree. Dem don't like sufferer. I will go back down and figure it out." He turned to leave. "Me don't want the police to find me here, for dem will beat me."

"Why would they beat you?"

"A so dem beat the boys dem around my way and where my granny live in Waterhouse and dem place there."

"They won't beat you up here. I promise you."

"Thank you, Miss."

Moments later, Hellene brought him a bowl of cornflakes and fruits while the mistress called the police. Roderick ate heartily.

"Thank you, Miss Hellene."

"No problem."

Then Roderick turned his attention to the mistress of the house, who just hung up the phone. "Your house big and pretty eee?"

"O dear. That's nothing. All the houses around here are pretty. I am sure your Aunt Ellen has a big and pretty house, too."

Roderick smiled and continued to look around, and admired the paintings and carvings that hung on the walls. *The only thing me worried about is if Aunt Ellen have to ask Aunty to let me stay with her. She not nice like that.*
There was a knock on the door. His nose tickled with sweat.

"It's the police. You called?"

The mistress opened the door. "Come in officers. This is the little boy I called about."

The officer looked at him up and down, used his baton to tug at Roderick's thin, sweaty shirt.

Lawd him scorn me.

"You have no business in this area, boy. Get out of here, now!"

Roderick trembled, hung his head.

"What you doing in decent people's neighborhood?"

"A come to look for my Aunt Ellen."

"Aunt Ellen. Really dutty boy? You look like you are up to no good. Tired of barefoot, idle sorts like you wandering through respectable people's place looking for something to thief."

"Thief. No, sir. Me not no thief. Me just want to find my aunty."

"When was the last time you took a bath, eee? When?"

Roderick could not answer. It's been a while.

"What is your name?"

Roderick shuddered, looked away, put one hand in his pocket and the bag on his shoulder. He shuffled his feet, heels in, toes out, heels in, toes out on the floor. His headache became more intense, and he held the right side where it hurt most.

"Roderick Brissett, sir."

"What is your address?"

"Waterhouse."

"Waterhouse is a big place. What street?"

"St. Kitts. The house near the big custard apple tree."

"That could be any house. You mean you don't know the number?"

"Is where my granny live but a come to see my Aunt Ellen who live up here."

He looked over at the mistress of the house whose face had puzzled all over it. She was running her hands along the back of the sofa. The woman listened to the exchange, her eyes told Roderick not to worry.

"If you knew where your grandmother lives, it could make our lives easier."

Roderick contemplated the open door and thought. *Is only one policeman so me can dash out the door. Him won't fast enough fi catch me. A can jump somebody fence and hide in the yard till him gone. After that me can go look see if me find Miss Ellen. What you say, Roderick? Sounds good. Suppose that can't work? Him might hit me with baton him have in him hand. A better try talk to him.* "Please, Mr. Policeman. If you help me look for her, we will find her quick. I know what she looks like. Please."

"You don't get it. You are asking me to knock on every door in Cherry Gardens to find your aunt. Ridiculous."

"But Mr. Policeman, suppose you was looking for a thief, don't you would find him?"

"You smart, too."

"My teacher say me smart."

"Listen, you wasting my time and the kind lady's, too."

Roderick could feel the sweat rolling down his armpits and tickling his sides. *So much noise inside my brain right now. I can't understand what anybody saying. O Lawd. A feel like a going to drop down right here. Please don't let me fall down. I can't go back to Aunt Hope. I can't. She will kill me.* His knees trembled as the policeman grabbed his arm and turned him towards the door.

"Sorry for your trouble, madam," said the policeman as he beat the baton in his palm and escorted Roderick to the squad car waiting outside.

Looking slightly over his shoulder, he saw the kind lady stretch out her hand toward him; she slipped some money in his hand and he put it in his pocket. He whispered, "Thank you, Miss."

"You are welcome. Keep this always in your heart. Great men grow strongest in tough towns."

Great men grow strongest in tough towns. Me don't want to live in no more tough town.

While riding in the back of the squad car, he was suffocating in the heat and smell of stale cigarettes. He looked back at a disappearing Cherry Gardens. Roderick cried. *Everything mash up. Look like dem going carry me go to Tata house. It don't seem like Aunt Lillian will keep me at Tata. Aunt Hope house not fit for me to live in. The area a get rough. A can't believe mama send me come a Town to suffer like this.* His head was hurting less, but his body was still sore. He leaned to his left side to ease the pressure on his hip. Raising his head, he

observed that the policeman in the passenger seat had turned
around, staring at him.

"We kill rude boys like you who don't have no
regards for the law. We hunt them down. Too much idleness
in these streets."

Roderick cringed and quickly took his eyes off the
policeman.

*Please don't kill me. Chloe would be sick every day. Jolly Crew
couldn't bear it. As for Suraj, who would go tell him? Please, please
don't kill me.* Staring out the window, Roderick saw the sign
for Waterloo Road. The squad car pulled up to the curb.

"You going to kill me here, sir?"

"What you say?"

"Is stop you stopping to kill me here?"

"I save my bullet for tougher than you. Get out and
go make something of your life. Rude boy business doesn't
pay."

Roderick took a deep breath, stepped out of the
squad car, placed his wobbly feet on the ground, burst out
bawling.

"My life hard. It really, really hard."
Sitting on the tombstone of one Ebenezer Wilhelm
Lightfoot, born 1938, died 1962, Roderick counted the years
between.

"You dead young, Ebenezer. You live a little bit and
dead off just so. Life funny, eee?"

*Roderick pulled his knees together, hugged them, looked up in
the tree that stretched like a fan over the grave that sheltered him while
he slept last night.*

A little Polly lizard ran down a branch. Roderick
chased it away. "As me was saying, Ebenezer, me a try stay

out a the cemetery but the police look like dem want to dead me off so me come lay down side a you. What a sumting eee! 'John Crow say the world no level.' Well is mi mother me hear say so plenty time when things just not fair." Roderick thought about all the people buried there.

Ever since the police let him out on the street three days ago, Roderick had been sleeping wherever he could.

"May Pen Cemetery never make me afraid at all. Anywhere is better than with that wicked woman." Hunger was getting the better of him, and he contemplated what to eat. He despised begging and was happy for the money the pleasant lady in Cherry Gardens gave him. Survival depleted most of the money she gave him.

"A wonder if the patty shop mi pass down the road yesterday open yet? It would a nice to get a patty and a coco bread. Then me can pick up and walk again and try to figure out how to get a good bath. If a could just get to bathe meself and put on some clean clothes, me would a feel like somebody."

After exiting the cemetery, he walked along Spanish Town Road to the patty shop. Upon arrival, he climbed up the shaky steps made from cement blocks at the base and a piece of plywood on top. Reaching in his pocket for his coins, he called out to the shopkeeper, "Sell me a patty and a drinks." There was just no time to fuss about the scanty paper that wrapped the patty; he jammed his hungry teeth in the crust. "Haaaaaawwwwwt." Flashing his hand to separate himself from a piece of piping hot meat that scorched his hand, he took yet another bite. Savoring every piece of the spicy patty. Roderick hit the road again.

Vendors sold from stalls, "Just like Miss Dillon." Cars, trucks, motorbikes and busses sped along Spanish Town Road, some honking loudly. Roderick felt like his eardrums would burst. "This dangerous to rockstone. Mek a stay far from the edge, yaaah. How dem higgler no afraid the bus dem run off the road. Jeezam."

He stopped to watch a group of boys play cricket on the sidewalk outside a row of tiny houses, he approached them. "Me a go get inna that." Observing the boys play for a good while, he asked the one with the ball, "Me can get to bowl the ball ?"

"Yes. You can get to bowl. Jojo, your time to bat." Is Jojo that one name.

"Thanks man," Roderick said and put his bag off to the side and caught the ball the other boy tossed to him.

They must have played for a while because Roderick noticed a lady in the yard had washed a pan of clothes, hung them on the line and she was taking them down, all dried and ready to be folded.

Dem boy don't look like dem have anything. Dem house full a hole, you can see straight through it. Lawd. Is zinc make this here house here. Rain no must wet dem. Jeezam peezam.

From time to time, a boy would leave the game and run to the side of the little house to peepi. When it was his turn, he asked, "Where is the toilet, a want to peepi?

One boy who stuttered badly, squeezed his eyes almost shut, "We we doh don't have no no toilet. We just peepi and doodu roun a back in the pit. Just draw the cover when you done."

At least me have toilet. A can't believe children live like that. Where dem bathe? Roderick could see other families in the yard cooking and eating their meals outside. Some sat on the ground, fanning flies from their dishes. After the game, the small boy asked, "So what you name?"

"Me name Roderick and mi figure you name Jojo, right?

"Yes. Me is the biggest one. Which part you live?"

"Olympic Way with mi aunty."

"Mi Grandma Myrtle know a lady who live up that way."

What a something if she know mi aunty.

The children played way into the evening. So much laughter between them.

Mi don't understand how dem don't have a lot and dem so happy. Soh so giggling dem go on with today. I never get so much joke in my life. Dem so free.

"Hey Roderick," Jojo called out to him from the doorway with a lit candle in his hand, "we going to wash up now. It a get dark. Grandma Myrtle soon call we inside for it noh nice around here a nighttime."

"Mi will walk home." He looked down at his feet.

"Grandma not going to say anything if you stay. You want to stay?"

Me would a love that. A cause Jojo don't know what me a deal with dem days here. Roderick lifted his head, Jojo waved his hands, and signaled for him to decide.

"You going to stay or what? The police say we have to be inside we house when it getting dark like now. Only dem fi deh a street. So much rude boy a kill people."

"You serious?"

"Yes. Mi serious. You can sleep for the night and leave when Grandma set out in the morning. She going on a bus ride that leave from her church on Olympic Way."

"Which church?"

"Madda Bogle church."

"Madda Bogle church! Me remember her. A don't live too far from there."

"Well is my grandma church from a long time."

At the sight of the candle, Roderick recalled wandering into Madda Bogle's church some time ago. The flickering light from white candles on the table of fruits near the altar and the smell of sweet oils. Thoughts of that day made his blood rush to his head as the people chanted and danced to the big bass drums. The warnings and Psalms Madda Bogle read made him run out of the church. She was pulling me in with a magic cord I could not see. Yet, there was something kind about her face. A would love to see her again.

"So where dem going, Jojo?"

"Castleton. You know where the river is?"

"No, me don't know it. Is a long time me no go a one river since me leave country. That would a nice for me. You and your brother dem going?"

"Grandma Myrtle can't afford to pay for all of us to go."

"You have to pay?"

"Yes."

"How much?"

"A don't know. She always bake the pudding for the church outings. So she always get to go. When money good, we go with her, but dem last few times we didn't get to go."

So we have to pay. Me have a few coins in mi pocket. Hope it will do?

"You can stay and go home with her that time. It safer."

"A can stay. A can stay. Jojo, you don't know how happy me feel right now. Awright then. Me will stay."

River. River. River to rockstone. Me, a go with him granny a morning fi real. Mi head a spin like gig. Roderick held on to his belongings and the other boys picked up their bat, ball and stumps they made from the legs of an old wooden chair. As he approached the zinc door, he turned around, looked out at the darkness falling like a curtain, no street lights, just fireflies flickering and windows coming aglow from candles and kerosene lamps.

Tonight me will sleep inside.

Although Roderick felt safer inside, falling asleep was hard for him as he watched Jojo and his brothers sleep with their mouths open, legs thrown over each other, every which way.

After all a this, what me going to do now? Maybe a can climb back through the window in my room at Aunt Hope. Try and talk to her. Tell her mi sorry fi break her window dem just like Shoey said. Tell her me will get an apprentice, hope me say it right, and pay her back. My stone art is good business, too. This way me can get to go back and finish Perennial when school reopen Christmas Term, September morning. This sound risky but a don't know what else to do. He could hear the boys' grandma in the kitchen area preparing the pudding for the trip in the morning. He eased his way and stood looking at her face, glowing by the lamplight. No one said a word for a while.

"A can sit down here, ma'am. Miss Myrtle?"

"Sure."

"Thanks, Miss Myrle."

"So what is your name, little one?"

"Roderick, miss."

"Why you not sleeping yet?"

"A don't know. A just can't fall asleep."

"You know you shouldn't be out here in the dark. It is very dangerous."

"A glad a here with you and Jojo dem. It make me feel good."

"You mean you leave your nice bed to stay here?"

"Hmm. A feel awright with you."

"Want a piece of pudding? It is still warm."

"Thank you."

"When you finish, go lie down back. We have to get up early in the morning."

Ten minutes later, Roderick was still awake and saw Miss Myrtle about to pull her curtain that separated her section from the boys.

"Me can lie down beside you?"

"If it will make you sleep, come over to this side. Don't tell me you want me to tell you a story too," Miss Myrtle teased with a big chuckle as she put on her head tie.

"Yes, please tell me a story."

"Rest your head on the pillow. Once upon a time, a tall ship set sail from Ghana, in Africa, with hundreds of little girls and boys. All the children were hungry and crying because the seaman didn't give them any food to eat. The children wanted to be back home in Ghana so they could play with their little brothers and sisters. The seaman would

190

have none of that. There was one special little girl on the ship. Her name was Serwa—it means jewel."

"What happen to her?" Roderick rubbed his eyes, peered into the dark to hear the rest of the story.

"She came up with a brilliant plan to sneak into the kitchen and get food for herself and the other starving children. Serwa believed it was the right thing to do. "

"Dem did catch her?"

"By the time she got caught, she had fed all the children. The moral of the story, don't wait to be rescued, fight for what you believe in and go after it."

"O Miss Myrtle, she was so brave."

"Yes. She was brave. She didn't wait to be liberated, but she fought for what she believed was right."

Where me hear that word liberated before? Hmm.

Soon, Roderick's eyes closed. He was fast asleep.

16

By The Wag Water River

Loose cardboard, tree barks, old tires and sundry waste materials stitched together with zinc to form the roof over their heads flailed and whistled in the brisk pre-dawn breeze. Roderick woke up to Jojo and his brothers snoring like spoons, knocking on old tin cans while Miss Myrtle packed the puddings she baked for the church trip. Quietly, he picked up his bag and followed Miss Myrtle to the door.

"You can drop me off at the church. Me don't live far from there," he said.

Miss Myrtle handed him a note. "Here, you give this to your aunty."

Police with flashlights were combing the area for rude boys and burglar suspects. A police called out to Miss Myrtle as she got into the front of the open-back Morris Minor van waiting for her outside.

"This boy with you, Myrtle."

"Yes. He's one of mine."

"Don't remember seeing him around here before."

"Everything all right, officer. Tell your wife howdy for me."

"Take care," the policeman continued to shine his flashlight in the back of the truck.

Roderick's back tensed as he listened to the policeman and Miss Myrtle. He threw his bag into the back of the pickup, climbed in, and heaved a sigh. He sat with his back against the cabin window of the truck, shaken. Roderick could barely see, as the darkness still wrapped around the

town like a blanket. The sufferers' town was asleep. As the
breeze scratched his soft skin, thoughts of daybreak splashing
in the river made him feel warm inside.

I am getting on this bus this morning so a can get a
river bath. Man, if I could just get to see Madda Bogle and
talk to her, a know she will find somewhere good for me to
stay so a can go to school. That is all I want today and
nothing going to stop me.

While unraveling the note, he looked through the
back window to see if Miss Myrtle was looking, then he read
it.

Morning Mam.

I know you were worried, but I had was to keep the
little boy with me last night because of the curfew in
the area. See, I send him back safe.
Yours Truly,

Myrtle.

He carefully folded the note and put it in his burlap.
*A cause Miss Myrtle don't know. Me not going back to that wicked
woman.* His eyes now watering from the cold air, he curled up
and dozed off.

A short while later, the pickup driver tapped on the
back window and Roderick opened his eyes. They had arrived
at the churchyard. Roderick climbed over the side wall of the
truck and he could see the round sun rising over the church.
Between the breadfruit leaves, a ribbon of light shimmered
on the wall like a cascading waterfall. Roderick walked over
and sat on a bench at the side near a small shed and looked in

awe at the dawn. A rooster crowed. Day was breaking. Church folks were coming into the yard with gigantic bags, hurrying to get on the bus to secure a good seat. Roderick knew that Miss Myrtle expected him to walk home, but he had his eyes set on sneaking onto the bus so he could get to go to the river and get a bath. There was no sign of Madda Bogle.

A waiting for the best time to squeeze myself on the bus. It look like dem back up at the door. Maybe if a go now a can still get a seat. Roderick threw his bag over his arm and moved swiftly to join a crowd forming. Dwarfed by the crowd, he saw the conductress giving directions. She stood at the top of the steps inside the bus with a notebook in her hand and checked off each person on her list as they entered.

"Praise the Lord, Brother Derrick. Sister Williams, praise the Lord. Praise the Lord, Deacon Phillips. Praise the Lord—what is your name?"

"Roderick Brissett, mam."

"Brother Brissett." Roderick could see her looking through the list.

"I don't see you on this list. When did you send in your payment for the trip?"

"I never send in no payment, mam."

"Sister Beecham."

"Sister Beecham. I have my fare right here, so." Roderick reached into his little tote and pulled out a paper bag of coins.

"See it here, Sister Bee… Bee—"

"Beecham."

"See it here. Me save every penny for the trip here."

Sister Beecham looked at him with amazement. "You saved every penny, eeh. Praise the Lord Brother Brissett. Praise the Lord. Step up. Step up higher. You may sit down anywhere you want."

Roderick moved with coolness down the aisle. The expression on Miss Myrtle's face upon seeing him was nothing short of surprised.

Quickly, he assured her, "A change mi mind. Mi going with unnu."

Miss Myrtle shook her head. "You should be my boy pickney. Gwaan go sit down."

I would give you a whipping for disobeying me. Roderick knew exactly what she meant. *The bus full. Me lucky me get a seat at the window.* As the bus rolled out the churchyard, up Olympic Way, pass houses, shacks and shops, he could see early risers making their way to work: some on bicycles, others walking, and an occasional car with headlights still on not mindful of speed limits.

Look at Madda Bogle. The last time me see her me did so fraid of her, but me don't feel fraid this morning.

Madda Bogle stood tall, took her place at the front of the bus, next to the driver, and faced the passengers.

Careful, Miss. Mind you fall down. Hold on.
Roderick smiled. Eyes wide open. He listened as Madda Bogle greeted the brethren.

"Blessed ones! Welcome. Today, we are thankful for yet another day that we have breath to praise the Lord.

"Amen." The brethren said in unison.

The bus hit a pothole and Roderick bounced up and back down. In a blur, Madda Bogle was rocking off balance.

Hold on good, Madda Bogle. Mind you fall down a say. She strong though.

"On this celebratory day, Eden Jubilee, we are taking a much needed day to relax and reflect upon God's purpose for creating humanity in his own image and placing both male and female, animals, fruit trees and everything that was good in Eden. As we return to our own Eden here on this island, by the Wag Water River, we will swim, eat, drink, laugh, and play. Above all, have sweet fellowship with the Divine. Amen."

"Amen," they shouted yet again.

Madda Bogle waved her white handkerchief in the air. "How could we not enter His gates with thanksgiving and praise? For many of you in the reach of my voice and most of us on this island, we can truly say it has been a hard road to travel and we know that there is still a mighty long way to go."

Hard road to travel fi true, true, Madda. Staring intently at Madda Bogle, Roderick sensed she must be from another place far from this earth. *O my goodness, her face shine like a morning star.* His breathing was deep and audible, the hair on his neck raised; his arms grew pimples like a plucked chicken.

As the bus made its way along Washington Boulevard towards the Constant Spring area, Roderick felt his muscles relaxing around his bag. He placed it between his legs on the floor. A sense of peace came over him. The bus stopped at a stoplight and he could smell coffee, fried salt fish and dumplings seeping through a breakfast nook. The smell competed with that of the brethren who had packed food for the trip. A man walked out with a newspaper, tapping a pack of cigarettes. Just up ahead, on the opposite side of the street, cars pulled into a gas station. Coconut and breadfruit trees in abundance hung over into the roadway, making visibility poor. The mountains were gray, and the clouds floated across them like puffs of smoke from a giant coal stove. The bus passed close to the sidewalks. Zinc rooftops covered purple, pink, brown, blue houses that peeped through giant balls of foliage, every shade of green and yellow. Roderick stretched his neck to take in a flock of birds flying towards the mountain. The more the bus swerved around tight corners towards Castleton, the sidewalks disappeared, making way for shrubs that grew wild along the roadway.

"What a way the place pretty. Is like somebody borrow mi painting set and just paint it up," he whispered to himself and smiled at the beauty of it all. The closer he got to his destination, the cooler the air. At different points on the journey, he saw a car or two wedged in on the side of the road where there was really no road. He felt like the bus would tip over into the ravine. Roderick held his stomach.

"*O Lord.*" The feeling in his stomach felt kind of nice, and he smiled.

"What a ride!"

In his big haste to get off the bus, Roderick bumped into twin girls. One covered her nose, and the other fanned her face.

"Look where you are going, boy. Him dirty eee, Arlene."

"Is the same thing me seh, Charlene."

A hard punch jolted deep in his gut. He rolled his eyes at the girls who stared at him. Roderick hissed his teeth and walked towards the shiny river. "Me just want to get a swim and cool off mi head. So much things on my brain.

Look how long me wait to get into school, now me get in, everything mash up. A wonder if the headmaster will hold me back in the same class when school open since me never quite finish last term. That not fair. Look how hard me work to reach where me is now. Me need to wash off this crosses today." He heard the twin girls laughing like turkeys as they skipped along. "The two a unnu gal pickney, gweh from me!"

The crisp smell of pine trees clashed with the rawness of the river and the arid moss that hugged the tree barks. As Roderick stood in a bed of lavender bush, the smell reminded him of his mother's drawing room, where she would display purple lavender in a frog vase on Sunday mornings. He took off his shirt, and then he rolled his pants to his ankles, used the bottom of his feet to get out of them. Bending down, he washed his clothes in a small pool of water that formed between clusters of tree branches, and laid them out to dry on the rocks. Roderick jumped in the river, buck naked. He walked towards the center of the river, arms spread outward, looking up at the sky. "You out there. Yes. You. Is me. Me Roderick." Pinching his nose, he submerged his body, head and all, in the water once. He stayed for a few seconds and repeated this two more times. When he came up the third time, the sun shone even brighter.

"Man, a feel clean. You never forget how to swim." For the next two hours, he swam, raced with some children from another group. He later learned they came all the way from Old Harbour. His stomach rumbled and he could see the women had laid out blankets on which they placed fruits and cheese sandwiches the color of the rainbow.

Miss Myrtle handed out pudding wedges and called out to him to come get something to eat.

"She not mad with me anymore it look like." He put his clothes back on; they were still a little damp, but smelled clean. Roderick ate heartily.

The botanical gardens boasted a variety of flowers, exotic humming birds and palm trees amid the placid Wag Water River. Its healing streams flowed gleefully over smooth rocks of varying colors, shapes, and sizes. Hypnotized by its beauty, Roderick took off his clothes again, jumped back in and swam some more. He gathered river stones much to his liking, crafted by time, perfect for his stone art. After a while, Roderick became tired, sat on a river boulder, took out a book to read and fell asleep.

In his dream, a woman, sitting on a rock in the middle of the river with skin black as the color of night, looked deep into his being with her dark piercing eyes. Blue-black braids grew from her crown; fell gracefully over her strong shoulders and down her back. The sunlight on her long legs made them glow like brass. She wore colorful beads of bones and feathers around her neck, wooden bracelets and a purple scarf draped with shiny gold patterns. Roderick put his palms on his face, breathed hard, wide-eyed at the sight. He smiled.

She smiled back. "I am from the continent of Africa from the Ga people of the Gold Coast. My name is Nana Abena, but here on this island, they call me Nanny of the Maroons. I lived in these hills nearly two hundred years ago. When I was a little girl, some wicked white men came to Africa and stole me, my relatives, and friends. They chained and brought us here, millions of us. The evil men compelled us to plant and harvest sugarcane to make them rich. It was a difficult time for little children. We had to work long hours in the scorching sun, digging and reaping. They did not allow children to go to school, only the plantation owners' children. If they caught you reading or if you were being taught to read, they would kill you and your teacher."

A wonder if is the same girl turn big woman Miss Myrtle did tell me about? She still alive? That is not possible.

"Killed, Nanny. Dem kill you if you learn to read?"

"Yes. That is why you need to be thankful that you are learning to read. I know you love to draw, too. That is the story you must draw on your stones. Our story."

"How you know me love to draw?"

"I watched you from the rocks as you gathered stones for your art, the way you looked at the stones, the way you rubbed the stones, the way you smiled at the stones."

Roderick jumped up from his daydream and saw a shadow riding the rippling water. He screamed, "Maroon Nanny!"

"No." The voice came back. "It's me, Madda Bogle, not Maroon Nanny. Rise up! The journey is great. Follow me."

Shaking his head, he got up, put on his clothes and walked with her.

Roderick sat next to Madda Bogle on the bus for the ride home and shared his story with this woman who had a big heart. She listened.

"Aunty is so cruel. A did have a rotten teet that pain me day and night. A beg her to send me to the dentist at the Comprehensive Clinic to take it out and you know what she say?"

"What did she say?"

"She say, 'make it stay there hurt you. Just make sure you clean up the dog doodu from the piazza before the customers dem start come in the shop.' A bawl, a bawl, a bawl when the pain lik me so." His nostrils twitched, and he pulled in the nose snort and tears that made puddles in the philtrum at the top of his lip as he recounted the horror of his exodus.

"O my. That's cruel. If she was my daughter, I would…"

"Would do what, Madda Bogle?"

"Mum's the word," Madda Bogle said softly.

Swallowing air became real hard, he said, "You don't know how me feel every day. By the time me feel a little happyish, it just gone like breeze blow away dry leaf. A bawl morning, a bawl evening, a bawl a night time. Nobody should bawl so much, maam. Nobody."

"Tears are healing. Don't worry too much. God shall wipe away all tears from your eyes; and there shall be no sorrow, nor crying, neither shall there be any more pain."

He lay his head on her breast. She hugged him and he soon fell asleep. Roderick slept for the rest of the journey and a gentle shake from Madda Bogle woke him.

"Wake up. We are here."

Roderick looked out the window. It was as if something had stabbed him deep in his chest. His heart skipped a beat, his stomach twisted in a knot. He felt his back tighten. He shook. "Here! You bring me back here, Madda?" He looked out the window realizing that Madda Bogle had redirected the driver to stop at his Aunt Hope.

"Let's go, Roderick."

Roderick held on to the back of the seat in front of him and refused to let go.

"Me not going back over there."

Madda Bogle called out to him from the last tread of the stair, reached out her hand to him. "I say come with me now. This is where you need to heal your life, right where it got hurt. Come with me lad."

He held on tighter, as if his very life depended on it. "Me not coming with you. I can't believe you a give me back to this wicked woman." He looked around in the bus and his eyes locked with Miss Myrtle's. She signaled for him to step off the bus and follow the Madda.

"You too, Miss Myrtle. All a you church people just the same? Unnu want me to go back to wickedness? Me think unnu did different. Jeezam." He saw the twin girls with mouths open like crocodiles, fast asleep.

"Come with me, beloved child of The Divine," Madda Bogle entreated.

Roderick held on with both hands. This time he watched from the top of the stairs as Madda Bogle approached the gate and knocked. He was not going back into that house. The front window parted revealing Aunt Hope's shadow against the dim light. A short while later, Hope, with curlers in her hair, came outside dragging her slippers against the ground with a long belt around her neck.

"Looking for one Hope Flowers," Madda Bogle said.

In the meantime, Roderick slowly alighted the stairs, and hid behind Madda Bogle. He peeked out as Hope approached them. Roderick shuddered but felt that maybe this time he might be safer with Madda Bogle. After all, it is not the first time someone looked out for him. It just did not work all the time.

"A know she going to punish me for breaking her windows. A just hope she don't beat me anymore. My body can't take no more, Madda Bogle."

"Is me this," replied Hope.

"May I come in?"

"Is night now and my children are in bed."

"I brought home your other child. He was with us all day. We had a wonderful time in the Lord."

"Well, you and the Lord keep him."

"The Lord has been keeping him for weeks on these dangerous streets."

"Make it quick, old woman."

"Be careful how you speak to me. Be not forgetful to entertain strangers: for thereby some have entertained angels unawares. Hebrews 13 verse 2."

"I don't reach that far in the Bible yet. I am not into no preaching tonight, mad woman."

How Aunty read her Bible every day and she don't reach there so yet. A think she just a feisty with Madda. Aunty a rude to the big woman. O my goodness.

"You call me mad? Let me get to the point. From one mad woman to the other, this little boy has been suffering at your hands for too long. It is by faith he is sojourning in your home—a home of hope and promise. Yet you chastise him after your own unholy pleasure. Children are a heritage. This country needs the children—our future generation. You got a golden opportunity to take care of one of this country's bright sons and all you do is brutalize him.

He is a very intelligent little boy. Have you ever taken the time just to talk with him?”

“Me. I don’t have time to talk to him. He is a child, and that’s that.”

“That’s the problem. You don’t have time to talk to him, but on that Great Day you will have time to talk to your maker.”

“We all have to meet our maker, ma’am.”

“From the first time I saw him last year, a trouble boy, he was looking for answers. God brought him to me today. He showed me the scars on his hands, the scar in his side. If you don’t change your ways, destruction will come upon you and your children. Repent. Repent. Don’t be stiff-necked. I warn you.”

Hope screamed and rustled her skirt like she was fanning flames. “You finish now? Fly away on the broom that brought you here.”

“Do not life up yourself in pride. The higher the monkey climbs—the more him expose. It’s a pity you do not know what is coming upon you. Mark it down in your book. Madda Bogle told you so. God not done with you yet!”

What a powerful woman Madda Bogle is eee. She know her Bible. But Aunty know her Bible, too. She bound to find something from it to preach to me when she think me not doing right.

Madda Bogle spun in a circle and the evening breeze ballooned her skirt and her scarf. The church people would say Madda Bogle spun her roll. She stooped down and made a mark on the ground with her finger. Walking backwards, she stretched out her hand like a rod towards Hope. “I personally will dispatch every ancestral duppy that crossed the Atlantic to give you a backsiding, a righteous flogging;

you will never lift a finger to this boy again. Mark my words. He will finish up primary school and pass his scholarship for high school. Come to me, boy." Madda Bogle rubbed his forehead with the big ring on her finger, placed her hand on the top of his head, spun him around three times, made the sign of the cross over his head and spoke something to herself and turned to him. "Roderick. Son. Be not afraid. God will protect you. He will restore your soul. Dry your tears. Say your prayers and go to bed." Then she rolled-her-roll three-sixty degrees twirl, three times—waved her red shawl in the wind. She left Hope's presence and went back on the bus.

Every nerve in the bottom of Roderick's feet felt like a hundred prickles from the lime tree sticking him. He gingerly retreated to the side of the fence between the gate and Chloe's wall and tried to figure out how to get past Aunt Hope, who was immobile and staring in space.

Look like Aunty she catch her fraid. My Aunty face turn color, she look like a ghost. She want to run fast from Madda Bogle. Me never see her so frighten. A wonder if something bad going catch her, Nelton and Stephen? Jeezam. Roderick hung his burlap on his shoulder, stood still and spoke under his breath with one hand over his mouth. "Me never see nothing like this in my whole life. Is true what the people dem say. Madda Bogle deal with some serious science. Miss Dillon did tell me, and me never believe her. It happen right in front a me. The spell like it catch Aunty. A wonder if she did a see things too."

A mosquito buzzed around his ears. Z*zzzzzz zzzzzz zzzzzz.* Roderick slapped at the mosquito so hard he hit his hand on the concrete all. "Cho. Miss Dillon say when the spell catch some a the people dem, all kinds of things happen:

pot boil without fire under it; man walk backwards; three headed-woman meet dem at the standpipe; rain fall on people housetop next door and not on theirs; fire walk down street like man. A used to think Miss Dillon was making fun but the way the breeze just get cold all of a sudden, it look like my Aunty who don't fraid of nobody is like this one reach her."

These omens raced through Roderick's mind and he imagined things ripping through Hope's head like a mauled wedge, chiseling out flashes of light along the sides of her eyes.

"Come inside, Master John. Now you get what you want—you bring curse on me and my family. Me wash my hand clean of you. Me have nothing to do with you in this life. You can stay here till you rotten. Just know that you are going to pay me back for the windows you broke. It's going to go like that."

John? Why she a call me John? Is the second time she call me so. A tell you Roderick she not going to let you get away with breaking her window dem. Is awright. It don't look like she going to ever beat me again. I will just sell my art and pay her back.

He slipped by Aunt Hope who was still in what appeared to be a trance. Roderick watched as she closed the gate upon the spirit that walketh by night, pulled the belt from around her neck, rolled it around her palm and shoved it in her apron pocket. They held a penetrating gaze on each other. Her eyes filled with tears.

You mean Aunty have tears. I think she never born with tears. A know she hate me but why she refuse to call me by my real name these days. Puzzle me bad. Roderick walked slowly to his quarters. He couldn't get it out of his head that Aunt Hope might just be in that dark room crying for her sins. Panning his room, he touched the dresser, the little table. Everything looked the same way as he left them. No one seemed to have come into his room, nor interfered. Too much had gone down and there was nothing to keep him there. Roderick rubbed his hand over the surface of his cot. The trunk and the memories of his last encounter kept flooding in. He hoped nobody opened it. He jiggled the lock; it was still secure.

"Me and Chloe still need to finish read dem letters in this trunk here. We need to figure out who the man in the photograph with Aunty dem. It a rock mi brain still. This JBB man and Felix. What a bangrang. Me tired." He changed into clean clothes and applied underarm cream. "A feel clean again. A can't wait to see Chloe. Is nearly the whole summer holiday a don't lay mi eyes on her. She must be fretting the whole time. What me going to tell where me was. A wonder if she still my friend when she come back from summer holiday in London? A hope we can get back to studying for the scholarship. A never get to finish up my war project last term. Suraj must wonder what happened to me. I feel this time, Aunt Hope won't bother me about school anymore. Madda Bogle says so."

Night frogs croaked outside his window. The moon looked thin yet glowed like a silver shilling. Air seeped through a crack in the window and cooled his body.

"Maybe I should catch up on my reading before I go to sleep." Thinking about the happenings of the weeks on the streets of Kingston and St. Andrew, a day by the river,

Roderick's mind was as noisy as Coronation Market on a hot summer day. Then he remembered his last talk with Suraj.

Meditate before you go to bed. Relax the mind. Make room for better thoughts.

17

Trouble On The Bridge

Roderick had a restless night.

Swept up by a heavy wind in his dream, he landed on a wide open road, the widest road he had ever seen. A street lamp swayed in the distance and fog rose up to meet it. As he hurried to get out of this strange weather, the picture with his mother, Mara'Belle, Aunt Lillian, Aunt Hope and the tall man in the sailor uniform fell out of the book, landed between the edge of a disappearing sidewalk and the street. The rain beat and pushed the picture along as the water rose. Running to retrieve the picture, he bumped his toe on a crack on the sidewalk. An electric shock ran through his big toe up his leg. He slowed to rub his foot.

Stop right there!

The picture kept moving faster now, and the rain was beating down harder. Run-hopping as quickly as he could, he stumbled into a concrete wall where the picture stopped drifting. He grabbed it.

O no. It's all messed up. Got to lay it out to dry when the sun comes up again. He looked up to see where he was. The wall extended into a bridge across a gully.

A man and a woman hugged tightly and looked at each other. Mist from the windblown leaves and twigs made it difficult for him to see their faces. Turning to figure out how far he had come, Roderick spotted a woman making her way across the bridge. "She is talking to herself. Only mad people talk to demself." The woman kept pushing back her wet hair, and it kept falling into her eyes. The wind picked up over the bridge. She stumbled. Her dress soaked from the downpour. Peeping around the beams that held the bridge together, she shook her head.

"Man, she looks serious. A wonder what she looking for?" Roderick hid behind an iron beam to see what would unfold. "O my God. Is Aunt Hope. What she doing up there on the bridge? She looking for something. How she know me out here?"

The way she marched in the rain, talking even louder to herself, Roderick gleaned that Aunt Hope was furious. Hope pointed in the couple's direction holding hands under the street lamp. She yelled at the top of her lungs and crying now.

"I KNEW IT. I KNEW IT ALL ALONG. YOU WERE KISSING HER BEHIND MY BACK. HOW COULD YOU LEAVE ME FOR THAT … THAT … THAT…"

Springing out of his sleep, the book tumbled to the ground. He picked it up and flipped the pages. There it was, just like he had placed it; the mystery picture.

"A wonder what this dream could mean. Only Uncle would understand this story here because him always a get message in a dream. If storm a come, him dream it. If the goat a go have kid, him dream it. It would be nice if me did catch him dreaming sickness so me could figure out this one. Ah well."

Mid-morning the following day, Roderick raked leaves by the side of the house. He was thinking how the summer was ending, school would begin soon and he didn't have any fun. As he bent down to remove some biscuit wrappers on the ground, he saw Nelton and three of his friends sitting on the wall between the Petgraves and the shop, whispering. Roderick eased close enough to see if he could hear what they were saying.

Dem boy up to sumting, a can tell. He stooped to pick up the leaves and trash, put them in a bag, and listened.

"So what time your mother never at the shop?"

"Saturday morning time she go to market but some Wednesday when things kind of run out she go again, early morning," Nelton informed his crew.

"What time she come back?"

"Around midday."

Roderick moved a little slower, raked again, wiped his face, took a peek at the boy who was speaking. His face was pale and freckled, with a scar under his left eye. The other boy was bulky and ate a fried dumpling that left oil over his mouth and chin. He opened his big mouth while chewing on the dumpling. "So where she keep the money?"

"In a draw under the counter."

The boys high-five each other, laughed and danced a rude boy skank.

"Listen, me will work it out so nobody will know we have anything to do with it," Nelton assured them with his arms folded, heels-in-toes-out, head leaned to one side in a pose. "I have this under control. You can bet your lucky horse on this."

Roderick's actions were swift; he filled the bag with trash and walked away as fast as he could. *I don't believe this. You mean to tell me that dem going to rob Aunty? What a wicked boy dem. A know she going to blame me for it.*

It was around two o'clock in the wee hours of the morning when Roderick woke to footsteps and whispers coming from behind the outhouse. An occasional rustle of the zinc fence that separated Mr. Mason's house in the back confirmed that something was really going wrong. Roderick lay on his cot and kept still. Loud whispers came at his back door. Then the door lock jiggled.

His heart raced. *Please don't let dem come in here.*

It got quiet again. Then the chickens got restless. Footsteps again. Roderick covered his mouth.

I can't make dem hear me breathe in here tonight. He listened for any movement down the hallway, covered his head and tried to ward off sleep. Minutes went by.

It seems like dem gone. That must thief a try come in here. How me don't hear Aunty make no sound like the time when dem try break in and she bawl out 'THIEF. THIEF. THIEF' and wake up the neighbor dem?

Around seven o'clock that morning, Roderick smelled the rich coffee brewing in the kitchen. Hearing men's voices down the hall, he sat up in bed, listened. "Who come here so early?" Peeping through the half-opened door, he saw two policemen talking with his aunt. "A wonder is what happen?" He put on his day clothes, picked up his toothbrush and salt, when Aunt Hope called out to him.

"Roderick. Roderick Brissett. Come here to me right now. That's my nephew. Him is soh so worries. Live on the street for months and just come back home."

"When Aunty calls me Roderick Brissett, something is not so right. Police. No, sir. Dem kill people." Quivering, he put down the toothbrush, threw the salt over his shoulder so that it fell on the floor behind him and walked towards his aunt and the police.

Uncle says when you throw salt behind you it gives you good luck.

"Roderick, what you know about this madness?"

"What madness Aunty?"

"You know. They broke into the shop last night and thief all me money out the draw. They even eat bun and cheese, drink out the ginger beer for Miss Gatha, and leave the empty bottle on the counter. You must know something about this."

You mean dem really break into Aunty shop? If a tell her is Nelton dem, she not going to believe me. A don't want to lie to her. Mama teach me that one lie make plenty more lies and you can't stop after that. Aunty think Nelton never do anything wrong. Me fraid a police. Dem will kill me.

"Speak up," his aunt said and pulled him to her.

"A don't know nothing Aunty. A was sleeping sound, sound, sound."

"Twice in one month and you know nothing?"

Two times? When the other one happened, me worse wasn't here that time. It is getting terrible, now it reach we. He looked at the policeman and then at his aunt. Took a deep breath. Straightened up. "No, Aunty."

"Leave this to me, Miss Hope. Listen boy, did you hear anything going on?"

If you think me going to make you kill me, you can go back to your station.

"No, sir."

"Did you hear anybody saying anything like they are going to rob your aunty?"

"Me?" Striking his chest. "No, sir. A don't hear nothing."

The look on his aunt's face told him she did not believe him. Roderick's bladder was full and about to pop. He crisscrossed his legs and flinched.

"This is a mystery," Hope said.

"This must be an inside job, Miss Flowers. There's no evidence of tampered or broken locks," the policeman observed.

"How you mean inside job? I personally — me Hope Flowers — lock up this shop every night. Except, when I have to go to the market and Wednesday night prayer meeting, I am here all the time. Nobody in this house would let anyone come in here like that."

"Tell me, Miss Flowers, does anyone have a key other than you?"

"Only my two boys and they would do nothing like this." She looked at Roderick and rolled her eyes.

"Where are your two boys?"

"Sleeping. My children would do nothing like this."

Your children would never do anything like this. Is your favorite son. Try don't pin this on me. A him an him friend dem do it.

"I need to talk to the other boys, Miss Flowers."

"Nelton and Stephen, come here dear," his aunt called out to them.

"A can go peepi now, sir."

"Yes, but come right back here. We will wait for you," the policeman said.

Upon Roderick's return, Nelton and Stephen were standing next to his aunty. Nelton held on to her dress. He looked worried while Stephen stayed cool. "The officer wants to talk with you a little to figure what happened here last night."

"What happen, mama," Stephen said, rubbing sleep out his eyes.

"It's ok Miss Flowers. I will speak with the boys. There was a robbery here at your mother's shop and you slept through it last night. Is that what happened?"

"I, we didn't hear anything, sir. Right, Stephen?" Nelton said, and leaned more into his mother's arm.

"Right," Stephen replied, still rubbing his eyes. The officer looked the boys up and down. Wrote something in his book. Looked up at them again. "I need you to tell me the truth. Your mother tells me you are the only ones with keys."

Yes. They have keys.

"Roderick, you know nothing about no robbery?" Nelton asked.

"Young man, I ask the questions around here," the policeman said with a very stern voice. "If we find out who did this, we will take you down to the station and give you a good whipping and lock you up for a very long time. You hear me? The three of you. You hear me?"

"Yes, sir," Stephen answered for all.

"Go inside, all of you," Hope said sternly.

Aunt Hope walked the policeman to the door, put her hands on her head at something the officer said.

Roderick looked into Nelton's eyes as he and Stephen walked into their room. *A don't think Nelton know that me know say is him and him friend dem do it. If him suspect me know, him better not push me. A not going to keep no secret fi him. Make him mother figure it out herself for she don't teach him right from wrong. Me not putting my mouth into this.*

It's been a week since the Christmas term started. Roderick had been feeling bad about the way he just left and didn't tell Chloe where he was going. After all, he had no clue. Ever since she returned from her trip abroad, their friendship was a little testy. She had not visited the shop that often and he could not bring himself to face Mr. Goodman.

One afternoon, Roderick met up with Chloe, who waited for him outside the art room at school. "Me have so much things to tell you, Chloe, your head going to explode."

"First things first, mister. You better have something good to tell me about how you just ran off before the school term ended. What got you so angry that you broke your aunty's windows?"

"How you know that?"

"Obviously, you don't think people in this town care about you. Everybody is not like your Aunt Hope. I find it hard to believe that Miss Hope had even a modicum of concern for your whereabouts. After all, you smashed her windows, an expense that cost her some money. In my mind, you are just a servant, and now you are a liability, a problem."

"She didn't care what happened to me."

"Strange, it unsettled Miss Hope you were gone so long. She became interested in Stephen's concern about you. I never understood the sudden shift in her attitude. I wondered if she became a better church lady; did she become a better somebody? or could it be that she just missed her little old mule?"

"I am sure she missed her old mule, Chloe."

"Anyway, before I left for summer holidays in London, your cousin Stephen and I met up and planned our strategy to find you."

"You mean that?"

"Yes. Stephen was looking for you. He was worried sick about you out there in the streets. He felt as the older cousin he should take better care of you. We both took the lead, and I made a flyer with a baby picture your mom had sent to your Aunt Hope when you were about three. You look nothing like that now, but that is all we had. We took the flyer to the Hunt's Bay Police Station, where his detective Uncle Moses works."

"You serious. The two of you did that for me?"

"Yes. Somebody had to show some leadership in such a crisis. It would not be your Aunt Hope."

"I am so sorry, but I couldn't take it anymore. I wasn't coming back."

"I understand. I don't know how you cope with all that poor treatment. When we couldn't find you, it was time for me to go to London for the rest of the summer holidays. The whole time I was in London, I was worried about you."

Roderick could see the hurt in Chloe's eyes. He reached out and clasped hands with hers. They were wet with sweat.

"Please understand me Chloe."

"I have talked to you about your temper a few times. Take it easy."

"It's not that easy. You don't get beat up every day. Why do I think you would understand?"

"Anyway, I am glad you are back. We have to study really hard to pass the scholarship."

"Great. I am thinking about starting an Art Club at school."

"Sounds good to me. I am proud of you. That's what you have to do, make things happen for yourself."

"We can work on anything: drawing, painting, sculpting, tie-die, anything like that. I am going to ask my art teacher to help us out."

"You mean Miss Fuller?"

"Yes. This way, I don't have to go home early every evening to go deal with my cousins dem."

"I am really glad you have found something you want to do that will make you happy. You need some happiness in your life, frenny. Remember, you still have to…"

"Study for the Scholarship."

"Good."

He laughed and pulled her hair. "You are good company, Chloe."

"You too."

They reached for each other's hand, held tight and skipped along the sidewalk, laughing.

"What is the song you made up the other day, Roderick?"

"Which one? Is a whole heap me make up from what day here. You mean, 'Best of Friends?'"

"Yes."

Chloe and Roderick are best of friends,
Best of friends, best of friends.
Chloe and Roderick are best of friends,
A friendship that never ends.

They skipped and sang until the sweat rolled down their faces. Their hands got clammy, but they held tight.

About two blocks away from home, the heat became intense; it was as if the sun was extremely close to the earth. Roderick sweat profusely, feeling as though he was suffocating. Turning the corner, he saw a crowd looking on in horror in the shop's direction. "You feel it too, Chloe?"

"Yes, it is hot."

Edging his way toward the crowd, he witnessed two firetrucks outside the gate. Roderick saw Miss Dillon and ran toward her, trembling. "What happen, Miss Dillon?"

"You home. Thank God."

"What happen?"

"A lot has been happening since you spending so much time at school. Your cousin Nelton and his crew have been running this place ragged."

"What you mean I don't hear Aunty say anything about it since the robbery?"

"She too ashamed. That boy is a pisser. Some days, by eleven o'clock in the morning, them come around the area. Why them not in school, only God knows. They skull school very often. I have never felt scared of little boys. I raised children of my own, but I tell you Roderick, those menaces make me afraid to sell my little food on this piazza."

"So tell me how the fire start?"

"Late morning they were back there smoking ganja. I could smell it stink, stink, stink coming through the kitchen window. Man, I only heard when something go 'boom' and in no time the fire started. The little jayse ears boy them run and leave Nelton trying to put out the fire. He got badly burned and your aunty and Stephen took him to Public Hospital."

"So where Miss Daphne?"

"She took her baby and left. I think she went to your Aunt Lillian in Waterhouse. It took the fire man them the whole afternoon to put out the blaze."

"I wonder if my things dem get burned out, Miss Dillon."

"It doesn't look like everything is gone, though. The firemen say they contained it in one section. Thank heavens. You shouldn't go in until your aunt comes back."

"Where me going to sleep now? Look over there, Miss Dillon." He pointed to a huge opening above the latticework on the door. "Thief can come in easier now. It worse going feel unsafe now. Sometimes a sit down and a consider what took up my mother's head so much that she just up and give me away to suffer like this?"

"Only time will tell, young boy. Time will tell."

"You think if I had a father around me, dem things here would happen? None a we don't have no father. Me, Nelton and Stephen. No man noh deh here to grow we." He looked over at Chloe, who was wiping her face. She waved goodbye.

"You knew my father, Miss Dillon?"

"If is the same man them say is your father, I think so."

"What him look like?"

"You look a lot like him except he was light-light-light skin. You more toffee color. Same light color eyes and wavy hair."

"For real, real, real, Miss Dillon. You know him?"

"He was a very nice man, but something happened and I don't know. I never see him around again. You fix your mouth just like him sometimes and I have to smile to myself."

"What him name?"

"Them used to just call him Captain."

"No, first name. No last name?"

"Just Captain, my dear. I stay out of people's business."

Captain. Just Captain. He reached into his pocket and took out the photograph. "Look at this picture. This man looks like Captain to you?"

Miss Dillon looked at it, looked back at Roderick and shook her head. "Boy! Where you get this picture? You best to put it away or your aunty will be very upset with you. Tired of seeing her whip you."

Roderick put the picture back in his pocket and pressed some more. "Is Captain the man in the picture, Miss Dillon?"

"I keep out of people's business, Roderick. I don't want your aunty to run me off the piazza. Try not to worry your head about these things. Everything is going to work out for you in time. Better is on its way."

"You are right, mama always say, 'Massa God is the only one last forever.'"

A cab pulled up. Miss Hope got out with Nelton clutched like her handbag. Roderick placed his hand over his mouth.

What a way dem bandage up him head and him two hand dem. Me better don't say nothing to none a dem. "Strange. Aunty don't say nothing to me, but she squeeze up her eye dem, look pan me like she believe me still know something about something. Like she want police to kill me."

The following afternoon, Roderick was on the side porch finishing up his civics homework. Spotting Nelton approaching the shop, Roderick kept working. He could sense he was bad news.

"What you doing out of your bed?"

"A can do anything I want, Mister Man."

When him style me mister man, something awful coming.

"What you want?"

"Listen here, you better don't tell mama that me have anything to do with the robbing."

"Why are you coming to me with that? Is you do the robbing? A don't business in people's business, a say. She won't believe a thing I say, anyway."

"How you mean? You better business for me going to tell her is you and your friend dem do it, Roderick Brissett."

"Me and mi friend them, Nelton? What a wicked boy."

"Mama say she bringing the police them back for she wants to get to the bottom of this."

"Well, you better be at the bottom, Mister Nelton. Mi not ramping with you this time."

"If that is how you going to handle things, well, my friend them a wait fi beat you up. It won't be pretty."

"So you a threaten me. You little stupid, liard, thiefing boy." Roderick pushed him out of the way.

"You hurt up my hand, idiot boy."

"Hush robber boy. Funny. A remember when a just come to this shop your mother beat the Bible over mi head,

"Thou shall not steal.' Who a steal now eee? Who a steal now?"

He got back to his homework, grumbled to himself. "This is a dangerous and wicked little boy. I know he will do bad things to me and nothing will come out of it. A need to just stay out of him way. It looks like him want me to get bad and do him something. What a must do, eee?" Roderick picked up his book, opened it and sharpened his pencil. "No Roderick. Don't let him make you drop out of school. Stay away from him, he is trouble own self." Roderick gave himself a good talking to.

"That's going to be one helluva mystery for Aunty and the police. I hope dem catch that little wretch and him friend dem. Me have my own mystery a go on right now. If JBB is a real somebody, then somebody must know who him belong to, if him dead or alive."

18

Worms in the Mango

Three weeks after the fire, on a warm Saturday afternoon, Roderick was still cleaning soot from windowsills and door jambs. At least the fired did not destroy his room. Fire ruined the kitchen. Roderick wanted to help Aunt Hope and Miss Daphne create a makeshift kitchen from a section of the shop. Roderick decided he would recruit his cousins, Nelton and Stephen, to help. The boys had been at loggerheads since he moved into their home.

"Maybe if I just attempt to talk to dem, they will be a little nicer to me. Aunt Hope could really do with more hands sometimes. She pressures me so much. I am going to ask dem to come help." Roderick knocked on the boys' room that was slightly ajar, poked his head in.

"Hey Stephen. Hey Nelton. I would like the two of you to join in and help me fix up the kitchen for Aunty. She doing everything by herself. We can make it look pretty so Aunty can get back to baking her black cakes and those things."

Stephen's eyes widened. " You mean you want us to help?"

"Yes. Look, man. We eating so much cold food, sometimes two, three times a week. I like tin mackerel and hard-dough bread, but I prefer it with some steamed rice or hard food. What you say, man."

"You know you right, Roderick. I love it when mama cook cow foot and rice and peas on Sundays. As for the beef soup on Saturday, hmmm good. I miss that for real. Nobody can cook it like her."

"So you going to help me set up the kitchen again?"

"I have a lot of homework to do. Can it stay till another time?"

"We need to do it like today. Nelton, what about you?"

"Me. No, Mister Man. My hands don't work."

"Really, Nelton. You just don't want to help. I don't know why I bothered to ask you."

"It's okay, Roderick. I will help," Stephen said. "So how long it's going to take?"

"Well, we can put in about an hour cleaning the tiles and painting the cupboards. Aunty would love that."

"All right. One hour."

Roderick and Stephen walked towards the kitchen area, picked up cleaning cloths, fetched a bucket of water, grabbed soap powder and a can of paint.

"What's going on Roderick?" His aunt asked as they approached the kitchen.

"Roderick recruited me to help him fix up the kitchen for you."

"What? You in charge now, Mr. Roderick," his aunt said and put her hands on her hips.

"I just want to help you make the place look a little better. That's all. I know you could do with a few more hands," Roderick replied as he tapped the box of soap powder, dispensed just the right amount into the bucket of water.

"You up to this, Stephen?" Miss Hope appeared concerned.

"Yes, mommy."

Hope didn't know what to do with herself. Roderick had taken matters in his hands to get her help.

The boys spent upwards of an hour cleaning and painting. Yet, nothing was more pressing for Roderick than to finish this assignment so he could go search for clues in letters and postcards he kept hidden in the old trunk. When he was through, he thanked Stephen, put the cleaning stuff away, and went to his quarters. He jumped through his window and into his secret garden.

A know all Chloe wants is for me to study but me want to sort out this trunk business. A want to know who is this JBB or Captain man.

The air was crisp. A golden sun was high above the clouds, the flower garden was blooming. Green shrubs looked especially cheerful except for a few yellowing and brown leaves Roderick picked off their stems. Two ground lizards were head butting at the entrance to the cellar, forming patterns in the sand. A few baby chickens, newly independent from their mother, picked grains and worms behind the fence. Rocksteady music rang from Miss Peaches' maid's quarters' next door. Roderick placed the bun and cheese on a crocus bag he had cut open to make a big mat.

"Psssst!" Chloe climbed over the fence with cherry juice her dad made from the tree in their backyard.

"You know, Chloe. Miss Dillon has me thinking even more. She didn't come straight out and tell me anything, but it is what she doesn't say."

"I am sure she wouldn't want any problems with your family. She depends on Miss Hope to keep her business going."

"You so smart. Is that I get from the little she was saying to me."

Lying on his stomach, Roderick pointed to a postcard. "What a big ship eee, Chloe! It looks like a big three-story house. A whole bunch of sailor in dem white uniform like dem having a meeting or something. What do you think?"

"It looks like they are getting ready to go on the ship."

"The typing a fade little, but a can make out the writing."

"Go on, Mr. Detective."

"Training Ship. Brooklyn Navy Yard. N.Y. They must be going to work on the ship. Look at the handwriting, Chloe. It is flashy and pretty like how Uncle writes."

"Funny, that is how my father writes, too. It looks exactly as if he wrote it."

"Read it, Chloe, because me read it already. Tell me what you figure from what it says."

Chloe, sitting lotus style on the mat, read to him:

September 19, 1963
My Hopeless Hopie,
I have done everything to get you to forgive me. I pray things get better between you and Mara. My Rodrigo is a lovely little boy. He is five now. I hope you meet him some day. Give my love to your boys. I am hopelessly in love with you. JBB

"Back-foot, Chloe. Count backwards with me."
"You are the arithmetic brains."

"62, 61, 60, 59, 58. To rockstone! Me born 19 May, 1958. Well, is so mama tell me."

"Five years. What more do you need to know? JBB is your daddy."

"We still can't be too certain. I figure him use JBB because him don't want nobody to know is who him is," Roderick surmised and clasped his hands on top of his head.

"Check out this other side of the card, girl. The stamp… I can see the date in the center of the circle, Sep 19, 2 PM with New York, N.Y around the edge of the circle."

"Must be New York him live. We can keep digging, we will come up with something," Chloe said as she took yet another look at the postcard.

Roderick and Chloe held each other's hands and started jumping up and down and around in a circle. They fell to the ground, rolled from side to side. Then, the two of them lay there just looking into each other's faces.

"This puzzle coming together one postcard at a time. JBB really loved your aunt Hope."

"She don't love nobody. Shhhhh. Careful somebody hear we, Chloe."

"You right. We are getting closer to solve this mystery right here. What a something if it check out that is your father. Hope you find him one day."

"O Gosh. A would happy happy. You know how it feel to live in the world and don't know your father? I could just hug the trunk and tell it thanks."

"I don't know how it feels, but I see all you go through. It's hard. I know it's hard."

"Sometimes a just sit down and fret. I feel lonely a night time. Nobody fi talk to." Roderick sucked in his bottom lip, cracked his knuckles, pointed his right index finger in the air. "A going to get out of this one day, Chloe. Mark my word, A going to get out of this."

"I believe you. You strong." She squeezed his hand. "I will be here with you."

"You mean it?"

"Yes. I never lie to you before. Just try to get through scholarship."

"A know that was coming. Yes. A going to take the scholarship and a going to pass it."

"YESSSSSSSSSSS."

"Shhhhhhh."

"Just put up the postcard them and let's get going on this scholarship. Here's the deal. I will help with writing compositions and you can help me with arithmetic, since you are better at compound interest and those problems."

"Sound cool with me."

"First thing I want you to work on is tenses. You speak the same way that you write. I notice when you say something like, 'Aunty ask me to clean up the backyard every afternoon,' you leave off the s at the end of ask. You need to add the s."

"Let me figure it out. You mean a must say, Aunty asks me to clean up the backyard every afternoon."

"Exactly. Another thing you always use is the word 'a' instead of 'I' when you are talking about yourself. That's how you speak, but you have to write differently for the scholarship."

"Show me what to write."

"Take, for instance, something like this: 'A like school.' The right way to say it is, 'I like school.' You are talking about yourself, what you like. When you come over Sunday, bring your Students' Companion textbook and we will work on some of these rules. Daddy will help us, too."

"A like that—"

"A—Roderick?"

"O, I like that."

Chloe clapped, and they locked pinky fingers.

"Sunday?"

"Sunday." Roderick jumped up-and-down really fast, like he was pounding yams. His face was flushed red with happiness. *Nothing not stopping me from learn fast fast fast.* He watched as Chloe climbed back over the fence. "You getting better with the climbing. Like you don't need my help no more."

"Don't watch that. Just make sure you are ready for Sunday."

"See you."

Roderick hadn't worked in the shop for days, but his aunty finished early on Wednesdays so she could go to Bible studies. Roderick watched the counter. *It peaceful eee. Me like when Aunty not here.* He opened his math textbook and his exercise book. "Simplifying complex fractions. O man, this is bursting my brain. La la. Me a go mash it up right now. Five over two third minus four over three. You got this, Roderick. You got this."

Ping. Zzzzzzzz!

Roderick shot up. "What in daylight was that?"

Approaching the shop, spinning a top, a boy hopped up onto the landing and ran to the counter.

"Jojo is you that?"

"Roderick?"

"Right. Is me, Roderick."

"Is here you live?"

"Yes, me live with my aunty."

"My Grandma Myrtle know her good good. She give me this note to give her."

Roderick unraveled the note and began to read it.

"No. Don't read it. Is for Miss Hope."

"No problem, man. Is me running this shop. Me read everything that comes through here." Roderick pushed out his chest with great pride; he was in charge today.

"All right then. So Myrtle send you?"

Jojo raised his eyebrow. "Not Myrtle, Miss Myrtle. My grand madda. She send me to Miss Hope. If grandma did hear you she would a box you inna your face. Out of order."

"Miss Myrtle," Roderick quickly acknowledged. "Let me see what she writes here." He pushed his books aside and unfurled the letter.

Howdy do Hope.

Water more than flour. Things hard this month. See a send Jojo to trust some groceries until my daughter send me some money from England later this month to pay you.'

1 lb flour

1 ½ lb brown sugar

1 tin Libby's beef

 ¼ lb salt beef

½ lb pickled mackerel

1 lb brown rice

Big gill coconut oil

Big gill red peas'

Miss Myrtle ordered food—sparingly—such were the staples. At the bottom of the note, she continued,

'Remember to drop in a piece of the fresh goat belly.'

"She is lucky with the goat belly. Mister Gifford bring it yesterday morning from the country. Is him kill the goat himself. Aunty says him do it a way that the goat don't feel no pain. You believe that?"

"How you fi kill goat and it no feel it? Well, grandma like it though."

One thing me can say about Aunty, she don't like to see the customer dem hungry.

"Let me write down how much the food cost in the book. Is me keep the credit book now."

"Don't forget to put the goat belly in the bag."

"How me must forget. Me like her plenty. Me just love how your Grandma Myrtle tell good story. She tell me how she always have this dream that won't leave her alone. She dream say somebody was a strangle her in the bottom of a big ship. She did tell you that story, too?"

"No. When she tell you?"

"The night me sleep over your house and she was a cool off the pudding dem before she wrap dem up. You did gone a your bed. Just quiet let me tell you how she tell me."
'A did hear every sound, taste the salt sea, smell dead fish, and people them raw like what.'

"Dead people in the sea, Roderick?"

"So she say." Roderick, perched on top of the counter, gave Jojo an icicle. "Cool off yourself a tell you the rest of the story."

A did just finish serving roast mountain goat meat, yam and whisky to the crew on the ship.

"Whisky, Roderick?"

"Yes, she said whisky. Make me finish the story noh."

"The Bosun, a think is so she say him name, the man that takes care of the crew, give me a little time to rest from the cooking."

"My grandma can cook real good."

"Wait noh! If you stop-stop me, a not going to bother tell you."

"A fall asleep in a corner of the ship. As plain as day, I saw a whole heap of dead body. Every last one a them strangle. The place stink, it stink, it stink so till. A jump out of mi sleep and see the Bosun about to strangle me with the rope."

"You serious?"

"Is so she tell me. That's why the old medicine man tell her to always keep dry goat belly over her bed so that the next time she have the dream, the spell would break."

"That's why she always have the goat belly over her bed in truth." Jojo stood there with his mouth wide open.

"Awright. Close your mouth now before fly full it up. That's why your grandma don't fraid of nothing. That goat belly good. A better come down off here before Aunty comes. Look, a put a little extra something in the bag. Don't let my aunty see. I work hard for it." Roderick sang one of his on the spot made up songs as he straightened the shelves.

goat belly
and guava jelly
run duppy
and good fi yu belly

"Very funny. Come check we again. Grandma going glad to know is here you live. By the way, I getting into a little singing thing with my friends them. Come join the group. A link up with some big singers at Missa B's recording studio. A write a few songs about ghetto life. The other night, Missa B gave me the mic and told me to sing one of my song."

"True true? What it name?"

"Dungle Children."

"Sing it fi me noh."

"Not now, me have to hurry up and bring the food to grandma."

"Pleaseeeeeeee."

"All right, but me have to go right after that." Jojo struck a pose and sang.

Why dungle pickney hungry so
Missa politician a wah go so?
Rain a fall and we noh have noh bed
Hungry pickney need to be fed

"That sound good, Jojo. Go and work on it."

"Fi real?"

"Yes. Fi real. You good, Jojo. You good."

"Missa B promised me to record the song and give me a chance to perform at the next stage show on Slipe Road. You going to come join we? You have a good voice, too. You can sing backup or be we roadie."

"O Jojo. That sound good. A love to sing and write songs. A don't know if I can make it because I have a big problem a trying to solve. It keep me up a nighttime."

"That sound dread."

"It dread fi true. Something don't seem so right about it. It just a wheel- and-turn-mi. But a going to solve it once and for all. Then a have art club working on. A taking extra lesson to sit for scholarship next time it comes around. On top of that, I have to do shop work sometimes. A will try but it look slim."

"Cool noh. See you when a see you."

Waving at Jojo, Roderick could not help but reflect on their poor living conditions. "This music thing is going to take me away from school again. No sah."

19

Babylon System

The mid-afternoon sun was blinding, and the wind blew the dust into a ferocious spin. Roderick was taking a much needed break from studying as he sat on the piazza with Miss Dillon. The campaigning for the upcoming general elections to choose the next Prime Minister had started only three years after the present government won the election on 21 February 1967. Flatbed trucks with men and women on loudspeakers crawled through the town that Friday, inviting the people to a meeting in the square.

> Tonight, tonight all roads lead to Bay Farm Road. Come out in your hundreds. Come out in your thousands. Hear your party leader lay out a plan for our progress in the next election.

"You hear that Miss Dillon. Dem want a election. Tell me about this election thing?"

"When you turn twenty-one years old, you get to choose who you want to be the leader of the country, someone like the headmaster at the school. So you vote for that person."

"O Miss Dillon, me have a long way to reach twenty-one."

"Yes, but you can still pay attention to what is going on in Olympic Gardens. You can help too."

"A hear dem calling into the radio station about the same thing. But why dem sound so angry?"

"Them fed up with the foolishness going on in the government. Some have it and some don't have it. We can't afford to take care of our families. Times are getting harder, not better."

"A know it is hard for some a we like my friend Jojo dem. Me, a suffer right here. That is why me going over to Lij to see if me can sell him and him parents some of the Stone Art."

"That's very good."

"A meant was to ask you, how you doing with the sale of the second set of stone art I gave you?"

"It is going to be a success. You keep up the good work. I will put all your money together and give you."

"Miss Dillon. I am so thankful to you. I need to buy paint and new brushes. It would nice to rent a room far from this miserable house where I can paint and study in peace. Aunty not bothering me that much these days, but any chance she gets, she blames me for bad things I didn't do."

"I can see why you need money for school but to get out of your aunty place, where you going to go?"

"I don't know. Somewhere. Anywhere."

"You know how much I was worried when you were gone for so long. Heaven knows I prayed day and night for you to be safe, for you to come back home. I am glad you are back and settling down."

"Thanks for your prayers. They worked."

"You see why I don't see you renting any room? You cannot afford to rent a room."

"All me can do is try. She too awful. Is me looking after myself. You know me work for her every day and she don't even give me a penny. I can't take a candy and eat it make she see."

"I never understood your aunty. Something is really off with her. She is too bitter."

"What you mean, bitter?"

"She just look vex all the time. Something bothering her and I can't put my finger on it."

"Uncle would say, Don't study her. Me not studying her anymore."

"You are something, you know, little boy."

"A going run go over Lij."

"Careful crossing the street. Look out for them careless drivers." She shook her head and whispered as he turned away. "Poor little thing. Him really get a raw deal."

"Awright, Miss Dillon. A hear you."

As he ran across the street, the heavy bag of stone art clanged like shakers. Upon reaching Lij's home, he noticed the walkway leading to Lij's front door was perfect for some pretty stone art. Roderick had not seen Lij since the strange politician big man gave him that message to deliver to him. Lij was reading while sitting on a swing on the porch.

"Maybe I can ask his mother and father if I can paint pretty-pretty on some of the gigantic stones in the walkway. Hmmm." Roderick held the bag closer to his chest.

"Good afternoon, Lij."

"Good afternoon, Roderick. How's it going?"

"Awright. A want was to stop and see you to show you my stone art. A wonder if you or your parents would buy dem from me?"

"Enterprising. I like that. Let me see them. You can spread them out on the little table."

Spreading them out, he watched as Lij pored over one of them. "You like that one?"

"Anything from nature, I. You really capture the details on the fish. Good."

"A try to make it look real. What about this one?" He handed him one with three circles in red, yellow, and green.

"Yes, I. It is simple but is some powerful colors of His Majesty. How much?"

Roderick felt a tingle in his belly. "Twenty cents."

"All right. I will buy these two," and he reached into his pocket and paid Roderick forty cents.

"Thank you, Lij. This new money gets a little tricky sometimes since we change from pound shilling and pence to dollars and cents. A try to price dem reasonable but a just doing it off my feelings. I don't know what dem things cost. At least what you give me can buy one paint brush."

"You doing all right."

Roderick put the money carefully in his pocket and fastened it with a safety pin. He closed his bag and sat next to Lij. "Your mother and father deh home?"

"No. They went to a reception to roll out a new family planning initiative my mother is proposing to the Ministry of Health."

"Okay then. I was just thinking."

"About what?"

"Dem stones in the walkway. You think your mother would allow me to paint on dem and she pay me?"

"I will ask her. If you strategize well, you can make enough money to sustain you through school."

"What you mean, strategize?"

"Play a little game with me and I will teach you what it means. Come inside with me."

"Okay then." Roderick followed, and Lij closed the door behind them. Lij took out a board game.

"You ever played Ludo before?"

"No."

"All right then. Let me tell you about this game. Follow the rules and be willing to win or lose. Now, if you lose, learn to accept the loss, not like the politicians around here that can't stand to lose. When they don't win, everyone suffers."

Roderick listened as Lij prepared the game board.

"So learn this: if you win, you must accept your win humbly. Jah don't want I and I to be swellheaded. Seen?"

"Yes Lij."

"The strategy of the game is to get home. You see those triangles in the middle? That's home. You understand?"

"Go home? If me don't have a home, how me going to go home?"

"You need a plan to get home. If you practice playing games like these, you won't need to fight and quarrel with anybody. There is always a way home. You will learn to work with other people in peace and harmony. Life will be friendlier."

"I don't have anybody to play with at home."

"You can always come over here. But you have to make the effort to become friends with your cousins."

"I can always play with my friend Chloe. She teach me Snake and Ladder. We play sometimes."

"That's a good thing. I remember being lonely as an only child."

"Who did you have to play with?"

"My parents most of the times."

"I have no parents anymore. Awright, let we play together."

"Good. Roll the dice. You must get a six to make the first move."

Roderick listened as Lij explained the game to him.

"The red corner of the Ludo board is for the blood of black people the Arabs in the tenth century enslaved and murdered. Then the Europeans colonized black people for over three hundred years. Now, the green corner is for the rich herbs and vegetables that Jah gives to I and I for the healing and nourishment of I body. The blue is Jah reflections from the sky above the life-giving waters upon the earth. Yellow is the sun that shines over the earth, lending its light to the moon, making every living thing breathe and grow. Without the sun, there would be no life. Pick your corner, Roderick."

"Me, me pick the yellow corner."

"All right. You like the sunshine. I man will go with the fire red—blood and fire for all the wicked that shed I and I blood in the streets of Back-a-Wall, Waterhouse, wherever poor people pitch them tent. Rastafari!"

"Me love to hear you say, 'Rastafari.' It sounds like a breeze a blow."

"Nice, youtman. Nice."

Half an hour later, the game got hot and Roderick was happy that he finally won a round.

"The I learn fast, my youth."

"It look so."

"Strange, it is getting extra hot in here. You want some lemonade?"

"Yes, thanks." Roderick sat there studying the game, when he heard a rattling at the front door. It was a strange sound. A light flash across the window. He pulled back and didn't want to look.

What if it is thief or police?

The dog made a scratch on the door as if someone was outside. It was dark on the porch and the light was out. The scratching sound on the door became louder. There was a loud thud. Roderick put his finger over his mouth as he saw Lij emerge from the kitchen area.

"Shhhh. Somebody outside."

"It's not my parents," Lij whispered.

Footsteps, grinding stones along the path, made Roderick quiver. He looked over at Lij, who was dialing on the phone. Roderick read Lij's lips as he whispered really low.

"The phone dead. Go under the bed in my parent's room," and pointed in that direction.

Roderick's stomach turned; he wanted to pee on himself. He squeezed himself under the bed, rested his head on the carpet, and listened.

"Police. Open up. Corporal Higginbottom here. I have a warrant. Open up!"

Don't open the door. Please don't open the door. The warm pee ran down Roderick's pants. It was getting hotter under the bed.

Lij screamed. "Babylon a goh dead I tonight!"

Boom boom boom, the banging got louder.

"Open up. Do not obstruct justice."

Maybe Lij should a run through the back door and jump the fence. Dem will shoot him. Somebody help him please or is me next.

In a matter of seconds, someone kicked the door in and Roderick could hear thumping sounds. Lij screamed for help. They were throwing Lij on the ground and hitting him with something. Then there was loud laughter. They were laughing at him.

"Dirty bwoy, you are not following area leader's orders. When big man send message come give you, respond. Have respect."

Boof. Boof. Boof. Crack.

"He says you must help the resistance. Let your father talk to the government and the money people about the plight of poor people."

"Leave my father out of this."

"O no. He is deep in it. He can't afford not to cooperate."

"I am not slinging guns for any politician."

"Shut your raaas mouth." The policemen took turns to beat Lij.

Lij screamed, "Murder, murder, murder!"

Roderick trembled, peed on himself again, but tried to stay still.

Please, can somebody just hear him and come help? Mi fraid fi come out. Police kill people. What a going to do?

"We will not murder you yet. Constable says we need to teach you a lesson."

What lesson? Roderick thought, pursed his lips, closed his eyes.

The talking died down. Roderick could hear Lij groaning.

Him not dead. A wonder if they leave yet.

Talking picked up again. He listened.

"When the right time comes, bwoy. When the right time comes."

"We not carrying you to jail tonight," another said. "Mission accomplished."

A car door slammed. Tires screeched. The engine fired, and the sound trailed toward Tower Hill. Roderick lay still in the warm pee, waiting for the coast to clear. Sweat was blinding hot in his eyes. Then he heard Lij mumble, "Help me, youtman."

It was Roderick's signal to crawl from under the bed. Like it safer now. Knees wobbling, pants wet, he walked towards the living room, gasped, there was blood everywhere. "O Lij. What dem do to you?"

"Daddy has another phone in the Study right there. Try to see if it is working and call the police. Dial 119."

"Better me call out to the neighbor dem. Why we going to call the police to finish we off?"

Folks talked outside, some screamed. A crowd gathered at the gate, chanted:

"Police brutality! Murder."

"Call the police," someone yelled from the small gathering."

"We call dem already but dem taking dem time," came the criticism of another.

A short while later, Roderick heard footsteps, and the door pushed opened. It was the Maddens. They had returned. Meanwhile, two able-bodied men were lifting Lij off the floor to take him to a car that had the engine running in the carriageway.

"Where are you taking my son?" Mr. Madden flashed his hand at those helping his son and reached for him.

"We taking him to Public Hospital. Police beat him bad," Roderick said. Roderick watched as Lij's mother acted like an efficient nurse. She stayed calm, ran to the kitchen and brought back some ice.

"Lij bleeding bad. What a wicked man dem, Roderick said."

"You saw what happened?"

"No, ma'am. I only hear for a was hiding under the bed." Roderick could see the side of Lij's temples swelling, his eyelids bleeding. *So what taking the real, real police dem so long to come?* Covering his mouth, he stayed still as Lij's mother bandaged his head. His father and the neighbor helped Lij into the car.

What a wicked thing. A wicked thing.

Two days later, Sunday-morning-going-to-church-folk, hurried to catch the bus. Putting his hand on top of his head, Roderick bawled so hard. "I going to spend the rest of my life a look for the man dem that do this to Lij." Roderick punched the door of the bus as he climbed the steps on his way to the public hospital. "Nobody should try to kill people because politician want to jook dem down for money. That don't right at all." Roderick felt every bump on the road and the bus seemed to take its time to get him to his destination.

When he finally arrived, he got off with so much anger in his heart. A heavy breeze off the ocean interrupted the garbage bins and rubbish that rolled across his path. Roderick kicked an oil can really hard. Thinking about his own near death, the tears gushed from his eyes

"Is dem things make people like me do bad things. "DUTTY. JOHN CROW. WANT. TO. KILL. GOOD. PEOPLE," he screamed, unable to feel his own body." The street went black; he was sweating, huffing, puffing. *Dem fi go a jail.*

Just up ahead, the hospital appeared to sway against the mirage along the street. He picked up a stone, flung it, and hit the back of a dump truck parked on the side of the road.

"This is not fair. It is not fair. Lij is a good somebody. Please make him get better."

At the door of to the hospital, people waited to get in, some looked sick, others fussed about something or other.

Me not in no mood to deal with dem people here. "Excuse me miss, you on the line?"

"Move and go about your business, little boy. Wait your turn."

"What a way she cross."

Finally, Roderick got to the head of the line; the guard looked him up and down. "You can't come in here, little boy."

"My uncle get beat up bad and me have to see him."

"I say, children not allowed inside here. Step aside. Better yet, get out of here."

"Why you so hard? Is my uncle."

"You need an adult to accompany you."

Roderick stepped out of the line and walked back.

Make a ask one of dem big people to make me go in with dem. Yes. I think that will work. "Sir, the guard say a can't come in without a big somebody. A can come in with you? My uncle in here and a want to go see him bad bad bad.”

“I can’t guarantee it will work.”

“Just let me walk beside you,” he begged the man, who gave him a big smile, not a word. Roderick slipped in past the guard and headed to find Lij. The corridor smelled rank. It was gloomy. Doctors and nurses in white coats and dresses paced the corridor. Upon reaching the ward, he could see many sick people lying on beds. He looked around to see if he could spot Lij. When he made his way to the other side of the ward, he saw him bandaged from head to toe. The nurse placed a basin on a little table next to him. Another nurse wrote in a chart on the window ledge.

“A can talk to him, nurse?”

“He cannot talk much, but he will hear you.”

He knit his brows, his heart raced, he sucked on his tongue and cheeks to keep his throat from drying.

“How long him going to be here, nurse?”

“It is hard to tell after over six hours on the operating table being pried open and sutured. He’s been resting for half a day.”

I don’t understand a word you just say, but a guess you know what you talking about.

“He suffered internal damage. So much trauma to his face.”

“Him foot break, nurse?”

“Yes, and his arm. I don’t know how he made it to today.”

“What you mean, made it?”

“He was as good as dead when he came in here two days ago.”

"Dead. You mean like a dead dog in the street?"

"Yes, people die and never come back when they are too sick."

"Him not going dead, though?"

"Don't worry about that. He is getting good care."

"A can go sit beside the bed now?"

"Yes." She held his hand and pulled up a chair.

"Thank you, nurse."

The room was hot. A huge fan in the corner made a clanking noise. Nurses and doctors hastened along the tiled corridor. An orderly wiped the floor and Roderick lifted his feet to make way for him to clean. Tip, tip, tip, tip. The sound of a machine was haunting.

It doesn't look like Lij is going to wake for now. The nurse says he can hear anyhow. "A bring two Archie Comics for you. When you eye dem get better, you can read dem."

"Nice," Lij said softly.

"Wicked people haffi dead, Lij. Dem haffi pay fi what dem do to you."

"Don't join Babylon's wicked system. Seek peace."

"Peace. Is war. A going to find dem, Lij. A going to find dem."

"You have school to focus on."

"If you could see my mind. A feel wicked."

"No, youtman. Come closer."

Roderick moved closer, the chair squeaked, and he became still.

"Listen to I. Blessed is the man that walketh not in the council of the ungoldly; nor standeth in the way of sinners—"

"Nor sitteth in the seat of the scornful," Roderick joined in. "So what you want me to do then?"

"Delight in Jah. Meditate day and night and anything you do must prosper. Jah Rastafari."

"The wicked people need fi delight in Jah?" Roderick huffed and folded his arms.

"Jah will bring peace if you want peace."

"How you never did get no peace from Jah. How?" He saw Lij's face change. "You feeling pain?"

"Yes. I just want you to find peace. I getting tired now."

"I guess you are right, Lij. A will think hard about this peace thing. Jah Rastafari going to help you?"

"Yes. I health comes from Jah."

Roderick went closer. He could see that Lij could not give him his usual rub on his forehead with the soft mount of his palm. There were tubes pumping medicines through his body. He sighed. Then he could hear a faint hum like a bird whistling.

No. It sounds like him not breathing too good. O, are you chanting a Nyabinghi song?"

Peace and love
Peace and love
I leave with the I
I peace I give to the I
Let not the I be troubled
Let not the I be afraid
Peace and love I Leave.

Roderick shot up, pressed his ears close to Lij's mouth. The medicines and bandages gave off a strident odor.

He swished his head. "Nice to hear you singing, Lij." He saw a tear trickle down the side of Lij's right eye that was half opened. Wiping Lij's tear with his bare hand, he whispered. "Don't leave me, Lij. I am doing very well in school this Christmas term. I want you to feel proud when I take scholarship and pass it next year. Don't leave."

Lij did not reply.

20

Slipping Into Darkness

Death News.
Lionel St. Alban Madden, also known as "Lij Tafari,"
late of Olympic Way, Kington, died on 26 February 1970 at
the Kingston Public Hospital leaving his mother Hortense St.
Clare Madden, father, Laurence Dumbarton Madden, II,
Justice of the Peace.

"Read it for yourself, boy. You read it!" Roderick
looked on in horror as Aunt poked the giant pin into the
newspaper, clipped it onto the corkboard where she put
notices for new goods and shortages.

"NO. NO. NO. Aunty." Roderick flung the bowl of
banana porridge he was having for breakfast.

"Hush. Listen. It is coming on the radio right now,
too."

> Funeral services For Lionel Lij Tafari Madden will be
> held at Gardens Free Methodist Church on
> Lyndhurst Road."

Methodist Church on Lyndhurst Road. For real. "NO. NO.
Aunty." Roderick could hear nothing but a buzzing sound
coming from the radio. It was deafening. His head pounded
like a kettledrum. Roderick screamed. Tears rolled down his
face. "He is my friend, Aunty."

"That is what happens to people who mix up, mix
up, with politics."

"Him never mix up, Aunty. He never wanted to get into politics. Lij is a decent Rastaman." Snot formed pudlles on his lips.

"That is what you think."

Roderick put his hands on top of his head, twisted from left to right.

A don't know how Aunty could talk like that. "Whoooooi, whooooooi." His weeping rattled the silence of the morning.

"Boy. Get up and put yourself together. Lij was posing like him a righteous Rasta. Wouldn't find a good job with all that schooling him get." She tightened her apron, raised the countertop, opened the shop door and walked out onto the piazza.

A can't listen to Aunty no more.

Sadness pressed into his chest. Roderick moved swiftly to the shelves and grabbed as much food as he could and stuffed it in his school bag. Without a word to Aunt Hope, he slipped through the backdoor, talking to himself. "Jojo and dem don't have nothing much but dem will be nice to me. A can stay there for the rest of the week, take the bus and go to school. A may even stay for the weekend. I have nobody to talk to in this house. Nobody who cares how me feel."

Early morning and Roderick appeared onto the sidewalk and ventured towards Shanty Town where Jojo lived. Roderick remembered Miss Dillon telling him, "We need a new government that will help poor people, get rid of the ignorance, and unite us."

Olympic Gardens getting bad, things have to change. A so confused right now. Let me change up my route this morning. A not

*going straight on Olympic Way to Spanish Town Road. Let me take
the back road. It is quiet. I can think.*

The air was cool. A motorcycle backfired. He
jumped. Then a shutter squeaked. The road got dark.

Splash.

The man who ran the fish shop threw a bucket of
fish guts in the drain on the side of the road. Roderick did a
one-leg-hopscotch out of the way and covered his nose. His
forehead tightened. The houses looked cross-eyed as school
children emerged heading to school. Lights were not on in
the bakery window, but the smell of fresh baked bread made
him hungry.

"A can't wait till the bakery open or a going to miss
Jojo before him leave for school. I better hurry up." Speed
walking and running, he made it to the big intersection,
looked up at the church with the stained windows and tall
steeple that appeared to be watching over the town. Up
ahead, Roderick saw Miss Myrtle sitting over a tub of clothes,
washing and singing. He ran up to her, grabbed her shoulder.

"Mi glad to see you."

"What breeze blow you around here so early? You
should be at school."

"My friend Lij get beat up by police and him not
coming back, him leave, Miss Myrtle."

"O my. You mean the one from Olympic Way?"

"How you know?"

"Everybody around here talking about it. It in the
newspaper."

"Miss Myrtle a had was to come here. It so bad now
round my way."

"It is bad here, too. Dem boys around here will think you are a stranger and hurt you."

"Nobody going to hurt me. Tell dem me is your grandson." He could see the smile forming on her face.

"Never mind. New government is going to make it better. Things will get better. What is that in your hand?"

"I bring some food kind for you and Jojo dem."

"You think about poor people like we, too?"

"I poor too, Miss Myrle. What Aunt Hope has is for she and my cousin dem."

"How you mean? Is for all of you."

"Because you don't know."

"Set it down on the table behind the curtain."

"I will set it down, granny."

She looks happy to get the food. A glad.

"Don't stay around here too late this evening."

"I don't fraid of no one. If I am with Jojo dem, nobody will bother me?"

Miss Myrtle smiled. "Come here."

Roderick turned back around.

"I see your heart a little heavy today. If you want, you can stay. When Jojo come from school, I will let him walk with you part way."

"I feel happy when I come here. You nice to me."

"Look, I am making some chicken foot soup for lunch. You can have some when it is ready."

A don't really like chicken foot but a will eat it because is Miss Myrtle make it. They have little, so a can't waste it. She will feel bad. "Thank you, Miss Myrle."

Sitting on a big rock, he took out his pencil and exercise book and drew. The more he drew, the better he felt.

"What you doing there?"

"A drawing. When I feel this way, I like to draw."

"That's good. When I was younger, I used to write a lot."

"What you used to write about?"

"Mostly about my feelings. Writing made me feel better. You should try writing sometimes. Get your feelings out."

"I like that, Miss Myrtle. I will try that next time."

"The more you write, the better you will get at it."

"I like to read, too, Miss Myrtle."

"Now that is very good. The reading and writing are like two best friends. They play together."

The morning rolled into the afternoon, and Roderick felt at home.

Roderick was the first to hear a knocking on the metal window of Jojo's house; he fumbled for his school bag, put it under his head and buried his face in the sheet.

Ever since the break-in at the shop and the police busting down Lij's door, this kind of knocking makes me nervous. It doesn't sound right. Roderick burst into a cold sweat, his heart began to beat like a wooden-foot man one-up-one-down on the sidewalk. It pounded louder and faster as the knocking built up. He covered his ears. Then there was a strange voice.

"Jojo, Jojo."

A wonder is who that.

The knocking continued. Someone started in a high-pitched choir boy's voice, "Is me, Jojo." The person paused. Cleared his throat and said in a deeper baritone, "Is Haulup and Drawdown out here. Missa B say to come a the schudio to record the chune tonight."

Roderick crawled on his stomach and pushed on his knees to where JoJo was snoring; one would think it was a kettle drum writing a mass choir hymn. He shook Jojo.

"Wake up, man. Wake up. Is some idiots name Haulup and Drawdown. What kind of fool-fool names that?"

Jojo jumped up at attention in ready boy scout fashion.

"Shut up! Don't make dem hear you call dem fool-fool. Easy, man." Jojo went over to the window and spoke to the two boys through the broken pane. Jojo convinced Roderick to join him and the boys, and they all snuck out into the night.

"How you so clumsy, Roderick. Careful, grandma don't hear we."

Buses were not running, so they had to walk about a mile and a half to the studio on Waltham Park Road. To Roderick, there was something peculiar about Jojo's two friends. They walked with a stylish bop to the side, almost in sync. So many thoughts ran through Roderick's mind— thoughts that these boys were perhaps up to no good. For a few chains, there was complete silence between them except for the random dogs that barked at anything that moved. The street was dark and still.

"Listen here Haulup and Drawdown," Jojo broke the silence. "A want the two of you to rope in my friend, Roderick, into this thing here with Missa B. Him can sing and him is a cool youth."

"What you mean rope een? Is every man for himself," Haulup said and pushed both hands in his pocket.

"Is how you rest so?" Drawdown scoffed at Haulup for his selfishness.

"Yes. Is the four of us now," Jojo insisted.

Roderick said nothing, but studied what was being said. Except for Chloe and the Jolly Crew at school, Roderick had no friends in his age group.

That's why I like old people better. These boys here… Cho. I don't know this music thing but will check it out.

Haulup used the stick he carried with him to beat off dogs, to knock on the wicket gate leading to the studio yard. A man wearing a black pork-pie hat, white shirt, black straight leg pants, Clarke shoes and smoking a big-head spliff opened the gate. He directed the boys to step through the wicket gate and escorted them in to meet with Missa B, who was expecting them. Inside, the studio was dark and hazy from a lot of Sensimilla. The boys choked on the smoke, but Roderick got into a coughing fit so hard that Haulup and Drawdown laughed at him. He was not happy about them mocking him, but didn't know these two rude boys well enough to act ignorant with them. What he knew best was how to act respectfully in the presence of adults. Having to balance these testy feelings in that moment was awkward for Roderick.

If it was one time ago, I would punch out a boy.

Missa B motioned for them to come into his office, where a small recording booth was off to the side.

"Hear me now, youths. We don't have all night to lay down this tune here. What the tune name?"

Jojo glanced at the other boys, turned to Missa B, "Gully Children."

"Wicked. What the group name?"

"Them two here is Haulup and Drawdown."

Roderick pushed Jojo forward because he was not about to be the spokesperson for the group.

"You serious about that? If I laugh a pop up. How about Jojo and the Clowns? Sounds better to me."

"All right then Missa B," Jojo said. "Call we Jojo and the Crew." He stepped into the sound booth and in less than an hour, they laid down lyrics to "Gully Children."

"Man, we sound good. That was a lot of fun," Roderick said, and slapped Jojo on his back.

Missa B came out to chat with the boys. He smiled and nodded his head.

Roderick pinched himself. "Jojo, it looks like Missa B happy."

Jojo shook his head in agreement.

"Here yah now, Jojo and the Crew, come back tomorrow. A going to get the band man them to put the music around the lyrics."

"Yes, Missa B. See you tomorrow," all except Roderick said in unison. They went through the wicket gate and down the street, singing.

"So when him going to pay the group?" Roderick inquired.

"Don't let that bother you. Missa B cool," Jojo tapped him on his arm.

"Cool. You must get paid for your work. I get paid when I sell my stone art."

"Missa B have him way to get money to pay we," Jojo replied and kept stepping.

"What kind of way?" Roderick paused, waiting for an answer, but none was forthcoming.

Haulup stopped walking. "Listen, Mister Roderick. Too many questions, brethren. Is we running things with Missa B. Tell him, Drawdown."

"I won't ask again." Roderick covered his mouth.

"Come on. Things are going to be good. Cool it," Jojo assured. "Make we hurry up before grandma miss we."

No one spoke for the rest of the journey home.

If dem not going to get paid, I am out. I might as well go a school, take the scholarship and sell my art.

Roderick stood outside the gate of the Gardens Free Methodist Church on Lyndhurst Road on Sunday morning, 8 March 1970. He came to pay his last respects to his dear friend Lij Tafari, beaten by political factions and died later of his injuries. Roderick wore black pants, white shirt with a bowtie he made from red, green and gold fabric he got from the sewing room at school, the Rastafari colors that honors his friend's religion. His Harris Tweed jacket was a find from the old trunk. Although the jacket swung around him a bit and the arms were too long, he felt appropriately dressed to say goodbye to his friend. Well-wishers entered the sanctuary. When Roderick got to the door, an usher asked if he was a relative.

"Close enough. He was my friend."

The usher smiled and directed him to a seat in the section reserved for family next to Lij's mom and dad. It was a small intimate gathering, mostly young people, a few Rastamen and Rastawomen. The altar where Lij's body lay in the casket, decorated with beautiful white gardenias. The smell filled the space. A woman, around 75 years old, sat elegantly at the organ in a white dress that flowed gracefully onto the floor. She wore a navy blue Victorian Topper hat with feathers on the side. The classical music and show tunes she played were comforting as mourners filed by to view Lij's body. Roderick trembled because he had never seen a dead body before, but nothing was going to stop him from honoring his friend. As he approached the casket, he looked over at Lij's parents, who wept. They bowed to acknowledge him and he them. His heart was beating hard in his chest and he sweat as he braved it to stand next to his friend's body one last time.

"You look so peaceful after all that you went through. Peace and love, my friend. Peace and love." Roderick could see the scars over Lij's eyes where they savagely beat him. He burst out in uncontrolled crying. Lij's mother went and got him, put him beside her, held his hands. Just before the Officiating Pastor ascended the pulpit, the organist played a Rocksteady medley from Lij's favorite singers, Alton, Phyllis, Hopeton, Ken. The music seeped deep into Roderick's soft place, and he relaxed. The service was somber, with inspirational readings, memories from family and friends. Roderick turned to Lij's mom and asked if he could do a tribute.

"Certainly. Are you sure you can manage without crying so hard again?"

He whispered, "I think so."

When the opportunity arose, Roderick went to the microphone. He felt like he would fall flat on his face.
I have to do this for Lij.

"Lij was my friend. He cared about me very much. He gave me books to read and taught me how to be a good person. This was our favorite Bible verse we chanted together the last time I saw him alive in the hospital.

> Psalm 1
> Blessed is the man that walketh not in the counsel of the ungodly, nor standeth in the way of sinners, nor sitteth in the seat of the scornful.

All of a sudden, Roderick heard the sound of Nyabinghi drums building sweetly beneath his chant.

> *Boom-boom, boom-boom, boom-boom.*

He looked over and some young Rastas were playing drums. It was a familiar sound of syncopated rhythms. His happiness began to surface; he smiled and continued to chant.

> But his delight is in the law of the Lord; and in his law doth he meditate day and night.

> *Boom-boom, boom-boom, boom-boom.*

> And he shall be like a tree planted by the rivers of water, that bringeth forth his fruit in his season; his leaf also shall not wither; and whatsoever he doeth shall prosper.

> *Boom-boom, boom-boom, boom-boom.*

The ungodly are not so: but are like the chaff which the wind driveth away.

Boom-boom, boom-boom, boom-boom.

Therefore, the ungodly shall not stand in the judgment, nor sinners in the congregation of the righteous.

Boom-boom, boom-boom, boom-boom.

For the Lord knoweth the way of the righteous: but the way of the ungodly shall perish.

Boom-boom, boom-boom, boom-boom.

"Peace and love, Lij. Peace and loveeeeee. Eeeeeeeee. Eeeeeeeeee." Roderick was weeping again while the congregation got to their feet, burst in ululations and clapped. The drumming rose to a crescendo as he made his way back to his seat. Lij's mom hugged and kiss his wet cheek. He looked over at Lij's dad and his face was stern as usual, but sad.

They are clapping for me? I don't check say sad people would clap.

Everything from that point on was a blur until the pallbearers carried the body back to the hearse. Lij's mom asked a friend to drive Roderick home.

Lij was a good man. He shouldn't leave like this.

21

Rocksteady Like My Dreams

Roderick sat on the ground of the piazza, putting the finishing touches on his big baigy kite. He made glue paste with boiled water and flour. After that, he cut triangular shapes from old newspaper, grease paper and pieces of brown paper bags, which he pasted onto the bamboo cross spine. Then he affixed a long string and decorated it with ribbons he got from his friend Chloe. When he felt good about his kite, he laid it out to dry. He had been working on this oversized kite for the entire weekend. Nothing pleased him more than when he hoisted his kite high in the air with its colorful tail flying in the wind. The kite made a spin, dipped, dived, spun again, almost out of his control. He was being lifted from the ground. Roderick laughed. He made hooting noises at seeing his beauty floating like a bird in the air.

"My first kite. I feel so proud. I never knew it would turn out so well." Roderick was in a whole new world with his kite when he heard a bicycle bell ring over and over. He thought maybe he wanted someone out of the way, but the ringing continued. Moments later, car horns were blowing:

Toot toot, to-toooot, toooooooot.

Grabbing the string on the kite, he turned around and saw a lady who swished her thin waist and twisted her Rocksteady hips as she strutted across Olympic Way. The ornaments on her hair sticks danced in the evening breeze. She wore a pink and white cotton halter dress that hugged her bosom and fell delicately along her thighs. The motorists kept blowing their horns. Drawn to the excitement, he pulled the kite back to earth, all the while maintaining a steady gaze. Roderick could feel his heart beating in his chest and his breath, like it would just leave his body.

Holy River Mumma! Is she? Gazing at her, he rolled the hoisting thread around the cotton reel. The woman walked past him, smiled, and entered the shop. Roderick dropped the kite on the piazza; put a stone to hold it down. Then he jumped the counter bridge to serve her.

What a good thing Aunty took me back after I went away the other day. I guess she is too tired to bother with me anymore. I still have chores though and I get to work in the shop this evening. "What can I get for you, Miss?"

"Sell me a cake of Palmolive soap and a small bottle of Dettol."

Roderick climbed up on the stool and took down the Dettol and the soap, his knees juddering, eager to put them in her hands.

"Here Miss Mona."

"How you know my name?"

He blinked his eyes and a smile rushed to his face. "Somebody pinch me and tell me." Roderick fixed his eyes on her mysterious light brown eyes that took inventory of his face.

"You have beautiful eyes," she said, "but they look lonely."

Roderick ogled even more. *What a pretty lady.* "You want anything else, Miss?"

"No, dear."

"The pin in your hair," he said, pointing to the pin that she stuck in the bun at the back of her hair.

"What about it?"

"It is so pretty. One day, I am going to make one for you." Still staring. Roderick put the goods in the brown paper bag. Somehow, he had forgotten about his kite.

Miss Hope burst into the shop. "Don't mix up with her kind, you hear me, boy? She really needs Dettol for true. She is a dirty girl that does all manner of things at night down at the Snuggle Puss."

Snuggle Puss? Where is that? Roderick knitted his brow. *Me never hear about that place before.*

"Thanks, little boy." Mona winked at him.

He could taste her voice, so sweet.

She rolled her eyes at Hope and walked tall up the street.

Why is Aunty so evil? Roderick raised the counter, retrieved his kite and got a glimpse of Mona before she turned onto De Lisser Avenue. Mona polished her nails bright red—he liked that. Ruby red lipstick lay bare, her full lips and friendly smile from her heart. As for her hair—it was neat, pressed flat in a bun that rested on her nape. The charms on her hair stick dangled with each delicate sway of her head. *Look like she really like dem pretty stick in her hair. A going to make one for her someday.* It was as if the floral of her perfume lingered, competing with the residual smell of smoke from the fire. *A going to follow her sweet perfume up the street till a find her again.* He pressed his palms on his cheeks and closed his eyes

A few weeks later, Mother's Day, Roderick decided he would go to the Snuggle Puss. He heard there was going to be a showcase that night. When he got there, he waved at Mona through the window. Mona came to the side door to meet him. She wore a bikini and bra with feather cups. She grabbed him by the arm and whispered, "What you doing here? You should be in your bed sleeping."

"You work here?"

"Yes. I dance here." She rolled her eyes.

"Like that? Where are the rest of your clothes?"

"That is why you need to go home now." She turned him around toward the gate and walked a few steps with him.

"Don't run me. I want to see what you do here."

"Little boy to rhatid." She smiled. "You can't stay here." She smiled again. "Go on home. It late."

"Me awright. Me don't fraid."

"So innocent. Think him can handle big woman business." Mona shook her head, turned away, looked over her shoulder one more time at him and returned to the club.

Roderick stood behind the column of the gate that had a little red light flashing dimly. Curiously, he watched as men filed past him without noticing he was there. Some dressed in office attire, others wore thick gold chaparrita bracelets and most of them drove fancy cars.

You mean all of dem men here come to see her dance?

One burly man with bulging eyes, already drunk, stumbled into Roderick before taking a long loud piss like he was drilling a ditch at the base of the column. In slurred tones, "Little boy, what you doing out here this time of night? Get away from here."

Roderick scampered and ran straight home. The wind blew against his soft skin and he remembered the sensation in his arm when Mona grabbed him earlier. Wanting it to last forever, he pressed the arm against his chest. Roderick went

to bed and dreamt he was walking on the boardwalk with
Mona when she pulled away and danced. He woke up in a
cold sweat.

About two weeks later, Roderick was sitting on the
wall by the gate with an exercise book and pencil. He was
writing license plate numbers and doing long division with
dem. A little kitten came up and just sat on the other end of
the wall and looked at him.

"Meow. Meow."

"Hey kitty kitty, this numbers thing is nice. I figure
dem out faster these days."

The kitten raised its head and scratched its ear. Its
green eyes glowed in the afternoon sun.

"Meow, Meow."

"Meow to you, too. You want to hear something?
The only thing nice to me more that this numbers game is
when Miss Mona comes off the bus. You ever see her? She
pretty pretty pretty. Yes."

"Booooooooooo."

The kitten ran away.

Roderick's heart like it came to his throat. He looked
around. There they were, Haulup, Drawdown and Jojo.

"Why did you frighten me so? You chased away the
kitty and could have killed me, you know. Cho. Don't ramp
like that."

"How you so soft like a girl child?" Haulup said, and
pulled Roderick by his shirt.

"I don't know any girl child that soft. Move before a
thump you in your mouth." Roderick pushed him away. The
two rough-house and wrestled to the ground while
Drawdown laughed his head off.

"Now you sound like ruffian. Yes. A so we do it inna the ghetto. Rough and tumble. See it deh," Jojo said.

"Me not in no ghetto." Roderick said as he brushed off his clothes that got soiled on the ground. After all, he had to wash his own clothes. His aunt is not very generous sometimes with the soap powder, especially when some food items are scarce. She has a way of marrying one scarce food item to another item she wants to sell fast.

"Ha. This ya town a one big ghetto," Haulup said.

"What jackass drag you come here?"

"You not very nice right now, Roderick. We come to check on you. We just wanted to see if your mama's boy troubling you again."

"Don't make that bother you. I was just here working on something. So Jojo, you still practicing your music?"

"Some lyrics for Missa B. He wants us to do an album."

"A whole album? So how much him paying you?"

"You on that again. Money is going to come. We just want to know if you coming back, right Haul and Draw?"

"Yes, we waaaaaa know." They sang like a chorus.

"Hmm. I don't know. My mind full up right now with scholarship and me waiting to see Mona."

"Mona. You mean Mona like the dam that full up of water?"

"Not the reservoir, stupid. Mona is a lady."
The boys huddled and bent over, laughing.

"A lady. Your mind full up of a lady name Mona."

"Heeeeeeeeeeeee. Bidi bidi bidi bidi bidi." They danced and laughed some more.

"I never tell you about her?" He waited for an answer, no one responded. "Yes, I told you already."

"No you never tell us," Jojo looked at the boys for confirmation.

"She is so pretty. When I see her, I can hardly breathe."

"Whoiiiii," Drawdown laughed and did a somersault.

"This is too funny."

"You are just mad because I have a pretty lady who likes me."

"Shut your mouth, no lady don't like you. You can't even buy her a handcart."

"You are just mad because nothing is happening for the three of you. You are too busy writing songs for Missa B to record and no pay."

Jojo with his hands in his pocket. "When we get rich, we will have all the ladies we want. Right now, we have to survive."

"Seriously though, Roderick, you don't know no pretty lady that working, you just lie," Drawdown insisted.

"Every afternoon, like now, I sit on the wall and wait to see her come off the bus."

"Stop," Haulup said. "Your mother never teach you not to tell lies? That's why you don't want to do the music anymore. Mona."

A bus pulled up at the stop. Roderick counted to the second when she would step onto the sidewalk.

"See her there. See her there!" Roderick sprung in the air. "I told you she would come!"

Mona came off the bus and walked past the shop. The evening breeze blew fiercely, lifted her dress, and revealed her long bronze legs. Haulup and Drawdown wore mouths and eyes wide opened like a soccer field and stared at her.

"Mona. That's her. The nice lady that I dreamt about last night."

The boys doubled over laughing again, so loud Roderick lunged at them.

"You dreaming for true," Haulup said as he folded his arms, struck a rude boy pose and clicked his ratchet knife three times.

"A big woman that Roderick. After she not going to pay you no mind. She hot though," Jojo said, flashing his right wrist like it got burnt on hot coals.

"What you mean she hot?"

"Only ghetto youth can teach you about hot girls."

"Every time she comes in the shop, she smiles and talks to me. I like her."

Drawdown pushed up against Roderick in a whisper. "What about your little friend next door? I thought you like her, too."

"She different. You better not say anything bad about her, you hear me?"

"So what the big lady say to you?" Haulup insisted.

"She talks to me about life."

"And di ting?" Haulup laughed out loud.

This made Roderick frown. "What ting?"

The two boys stopped laughing, ears perked up, sat on the wall ready to hear about Mona and the ting.

"Nobody knows her family. She lives alone in a small room on De Lisser Avenue."

"I hear she has her husband tied up in a cage and she feed him like parrot," Drawdown announced with his fist to his mouth like a roving news reporter, as serious as a heart attack.

Roderick pushed Drawdown in his chest. "Don't make fun of her. I will knock the rest of your rotten teeth out of your mouth."

"Awright, awright. Me still want to hear bout the ting —you know, the ting she talk bout."

Pointing in his face, Roderick said, "Yu see you Drawdown, yu too slack and out of order. Don't come back around here anymore."

"Take it easy, Roderick. Take it easy," Haulup jumped between the two, stretched both hands to put distance between them.

"Mona does not play with little boys. She is a big somebody," Roderick defended fiercely and sat on the wall.

"Let we play a round of marbles. Cool?" Jojo pulled out the marbles from his pocket.

"Cool" replied Roderick.

"A mean you too, Drawdown," Jojo crouched, ready to compete.

The four boys played good-humoredly for a long while when Nelton came and stood over them, making punch-in-the-eye fist grimaces at Roderick. He shoved Roderick and kicked the marbles away. Haulup and Drawdown leaped at him and pulled out their ratchet knife and icepick.

"Move fast or a going to mark your face, boy," Haulup menacingly flashed the blade left and right.

"Yes, you better leave him alone, or me, Drawdown, bore hole all over you like strainer."

Springing into action, like a praying mantis, Roderick got between the boys and blocked Nelton. "You don't know who you fooling with, you know, Nelton. These boys will do you something. Move from here."

Nelton pushed Roderick again, screamed, tried to run, but the boys surrounded him and stomped their feet. They danced around him chanting like they would never stop.

Bad boy in the ring, la, la, la, la, laaaah
Bad boy in the ring, la, la, la, la, laaaah
Bad boy in the ring, la, la, la, la, laaaah
He squeals like a pig in a sty, la laaaah.

"Stop it Haulup. You, too, Draw. Leave him alone," Roderick pleaded. The more he pleaded, the more the boys blocked Nelton in the circle and chanted. At any moment, they could fall into a trance.

"Make him go inside, boys. Pleeeeeease."

The chanting stopped. The boys let him out the circle and put up their slasher and pick. Nelton shook like a wet hen, wiped his face, looked at his hand, and ran.

"You lucky, you not bleeding and all your cream soda not running out your belly like a strainer. Just leave me alone with my friends." He yelled out to Nelton as he watched him run through the gate. "You better not tell Stephen or Aunty or I will bring them back for you next time."

Roderick took a deep breath, then he turned around quickly with a sharp rebuke. "Mad ants, mad cow and mad dog. What's wrong with you?"

"Weeeeee maaaaaaaaaaaaaaad!" Haulup bulged out his eyes like he was possessed to intimidate Roderick.

"You want the protection or not?" Jojo asked.

"I don't need your protection. Get out of here. I hate bullies like Nelton, and I certainly don't want to be friends with bullies like you. All my life I have had to deal with being treated like dog doodu. My aunty beat me for everything. Nelton gives me a hard time, but I don't want to hurt him out of spite. Just get out of here and go fix unnu self."

"Hallelujah, Pastor Roderick. It look like you get saved. I guess you don't want the protection," Haulup jeered and put his fighting tool in his pocket.

Roderick said nothing further and packed up the marbles and gave them to Jojo.

The boys hissed their teeth and left.

As Roderick turned to go into the yard, his eyes and Chloe's made four.

O gosh. She saw everything.

"You were standing there all this time?"

"Yes. You surprised," she said. "I don't know this Roderick. What on earth is going on with you? Who are these boys?"

"Mi friend dem."

"Friend dem. You keeping secrets now? Where you know them from?"

"Is a long story."

"Long story. Spare me the long story. Thank God daddy got a buyer for the house. We are moving out of this neighborhood."

"Yu going to leave me here by myself." Roderick kicked the ground and sent dust flying between them. He put his hands on his head like he lost his best friend. He tried to touch her hand, and she pushed him away.

"You are not alone anymore, Roderick."

"Is my friends in the singing group. They are recording a tune with Missa B. They are not bad boys."

"So why do they need a knife and icepick?"

"For protection. It's rough where dem live."

"Suppose them did cut up Nelton, eeh? Suppose them did cut him?" Chloe clapped her hands three times. Walked away towards her verandah. Roderick stopped her with his voice.

"They are just frightening him, Chloe."

"Frightening him? I heard him ask if you want protection. What protection you want and who is coming after you?"

"Don't worry about that."

Pulling on his hair, he twisted them in little balls like Bantu knots, sighed really loud. Edged his way closer to her. Touched her again on her arm, and she recoiled. Then she folded her arms and pouted.

"Don't touch me! I'm no fool, Roderick. Protection? Why do you need protection?"

"Yemoja!" Roderick uttered frantically, pushed his hand in his right pocked, looked swiftly over his left shoulder and then his right as if someone spoke to him.

"What's wrong with you? What is Yemoja?"

"Nothing. Nothing at all. I just remembered something Miss Livv told me."

"Who is Miss Livv?" Chloe turned to walk away, threw her hands in the air. "Never mind, I don't want to know."

Roderick reached out to Chloe, pulled her by the hand. "Just hear me out. Please."

She flashed her hands, swiftly turned her head away, and started walking. Then she turned back.

"Miss Livv is my mother's dressmaker friend. She sent me to help her pull threads and anything she wanted me to do. Her house was dark even when the sun was shining brightly outside. She kept a calabash of incense burning on a small table and a white candle that looked like it burned all the time. On the wall right above the table there was a picture of a woman. Miss Livv said the lady in the picture is an African goddess named Yemoja, who took care of the African children when they stole them and brought to St. Ann where I was born."

"Spare me the long story, mister. What does that have to do with how you are behaving badly right now?"

"Hear me out. Miss Livv told me that Yemoja will protect me from harm."

"This is crazy talk, Roderick Brissett."

"I never understood her when she told me. I only saw when she reached on top of her nightstand, picked up a little broach with a picture of Yemoja and pinned it on the inside of my shirt. She said, 'Wear it always. Yemoja protects you.' I am worried now because a think I lost the pin.'"

"You know what? You are getting really bizarre now. Don't tell me anymore."

"I say is nothing to worry about."

She stood with her hands akimbo, legs apart, shoulders erect, wagging her finger at him. "All I know, if Nelton didn't run for his life, blood would run in Olympic Gardens today, and it would be all your fault."

"Come off that now. Cho. It never happened. So when are you moving?"

"Next year June, as soon as I graduate from Perennial Primary and summer holidays start. I will spend this Christmas and Easter Terms packing a little at a time."

Roderick crossed, put his hands on his head again. Looked up to the skies. Immobile. Then he vigorously kicked the dirt, which raised a cloud of dust between them. "How you could do this to me, Chloe? How?"

"It is not my choice, it is daddy's decision. Things are getting bad around here. You were the one good boy around here. You don't see that, Roderick?"

"What am I going to do? What I must do when you are gone?"

"You have new friends to look out for you. You don't need me anymore."

"What kind of foolishness are you talking about?"

"You call it foolishness. This kind of behavior is making me sick. I can't believe you make all you going through bring you down to this level. I thought we were preparing to take the scholarship for high school. We had plans for great things, Roderick. We had plans."

They stood silently and looked into each other's eyes and the tears flowed down their faces. Roderick stretched out his hands and wiped her tears. Chloe shrugged her rejection, but then stepped closer to him, hugged him around his waist.

Roderick winced in pain. His side hurt, but he said nothing.

"What's wrong?"

"Is weeks since I get the last beating and look this sore don't heal up yet." He lifted his shirt and showed her a deep wound on his side where the belt buckle busted his flesh. Chloe jumped back from the smell.

"Come inside with me and let my father dress it for you."

"Dress it?"

"Yes. Put some medicine. Jeezam. Your aunty couldn't do that for you?"

"She doesn't care if I rotten and die. I feel it could heal a long time, but every time a scab grows on it, I hurt it up, either at school or doing yard work. That's why it can't get better."

Chloe took him by the hand, and they went into the house. This time, she had to show her father. She stopped short. Cupped his face in her hands. "Look at me Roderick. I was just thinking the other day that you are brighter than me."

"How me must brighter than you? Don't let me laugh till me bruk up."

"Look how you just buckle down and catch up with your schoolwork. We can do the same work now. You are so smart. Why do you want to throw it in the gully? Why?"

His thoughts raced. "Nobody ever told me I am smart. Nobody."

22

Just Leave It To Me

The lawn in Chloe's front yard was green and garlanded with yellow daisies, Joseph coats, carnations, a patch of bright sunflowers, ginger, orange and white angel's trumpet—you could smell them as far as two houses away. Of late, Roderick would watch Chloe care for the orchids that grew on the bark of the pear tree in the shade by the fence. Roderick walked alongside Chloe, across her lawn as she held his sweaty hand. He entered the living room. Roderick imagined Nelton lying in a pool of blood on the ground; Aunt Hope would beat the flesh off his bones before turning him over to the police to kill him. He saw the moving truck pulling out of the Goodman's driveway and Chloe waving goodbye, never to see her again. He saw Mona, but she didn't talk to him.

I can spend the rest of my life miserable or use my brain to help me out. He felt Chloe tug at his arm, disrupting his thoughts.

"Daddy. Daddy. Come quick. Look here."

"What is it, dear? Hello Roderick."

"Hello, Mr. Goodman."

"Come, let me show you, daddy."

Mr. Goodman walked over to where the children were sitting on the couch.

"Lift up your shirt and show daddy your side."

When he lifted his shirt, it exposed the draining wound. Mr. Goodman gasped at the fetid smell.

"How did this happen?"

"Aunt Hope last beating."

"But I thought she had eased off now that you are growing bigger and going to school. Did she try to put medicine on it to make it heal?"

"No," Chloe answered instead.

Mr. Goodman shook his head and went straight to the medicine cabinet and fetched cotton balls and Mercurochrome. He gently cleaned the wound and applied the medicine.

Roderick screamed at the first application, closed his eyes real tight, squirmed ever so slightly with every drop of salve applied to his wound. Chloe teared up again and placed her hands on her mouth. Mr. Goodman covered the wound with a bandage and left the room.

"You are going to be all right, my friend," Chloe assured Roderick.

"I was just thinking, Chloe. I can't afford to mash up we friendship. Is long time we are friends."

"Yes, since you came to live around here with your aunty. I remember the first time I saw you across the fence."

"I remember that day. Jojo and dem are different kinds of friends. Believe me."

"So you say. I don't like what I saw today."

"You remember when we did go down to Bollo Bay seaside down Foreshore Road?"

"If I remember? Of course. How I worried daddy would find out."

"I know, but I always wanted to go down by the sea and you carried me, anyway. The two of us sat on an old rusty scrap of a car, watching the other children race their paper boats and fudge sticks in the water. Remember?"

"O yes, and I remember how you made me play a magic trick on you with your country self."

"I remember very well. Do it again this time. I want to feel the same funny feeling again."

"Your side not burning from the medicine Daddy just put on it?"

"I won't feel it if you play the game with me one more time."

"Haha haaaa. All right. Close your fist tight, tight, tight. Eyes closed. I was talking up in my nose like patoo, remember?"

"What you talking about? Yes, I remember. Huhuhu."

Roderick closed his eyes and his fist as Chloe gripped his wrist. Then she rubbed his fist, gently, for thirty seconds.

"Now open your eyes."

If you think me going to make anything spoil up our friendship, you make a sad mistake. No Jojo, no Mona, although she nice, no Aunt Hope, nobody going to mash up this here so. Breathing deeply, he felt her press hard on his hand. Slowly, she released her grip around his wrist while simultaneously opening his fingers. She ran her middle finger from his wrist to the tip of his middle finger. "You feel it?"

"Yes, yes, yes. I feel it!" Roderick jiggled, pulled his shoulders towards his ears as the blood rushed to the tip of his finger, causing him to tingle in his palms.

"Is magic for true, Chloe!"

"My Uncle Vinny taught me when I was five."

"Chloe. Remember when it was my turn to play magic?"

"Yes. The two of us held each other's hands and walked to the edge of the water to catch up with the other children."

"O Chloe, the whole day was one big magic. I wanted it to last until we get old. We had so much fun catching ticki ticki fish and spotty goopie."

"And we put them in an old Berger paint pan we found behind the old car. You know how I am squeamish about germs, but I didn't care one bit. Just happy." Chloe smiled.

Today, in all of his physical pain and agony, Roderick could not imagine being without Chloe in his life. He had to decide whether he was going to keep bad company or buckle down and study for the scholarship.

What if I ask Mr. Goodman to take me with him to their new house? No. I don't think so. Let me think again. Yes, yes, yes. I can call Miss Ellen to move me out of here to live with her. That sounds better. She can get me into school to finish up the scholarship. But will she? How do I find her?

"You are quiet suddenly, Roderick. What's going on in your head?"

"You don't want to know. It's a big secret and I have to figure it out all by myself."

"What did we say about secrets earlier today? You forget already."

"O Chloe. This one is big and I want nothing to mess it up."

"Me mess up anything for you before?"

"O my, I never meant it that way."

Chloe pressed, "You can tell me. Maybe I can help you."

"Help me! Sounds like a good idea, but how?"

"We can go into my reading room and figure it out together before dinner is ready."

"Sounds good. Let's go."

The reading room was well lit with a desk and chair, a circular rug with pink flowers in the center, a side table with a telephone, bookshelf and a piano bench with stuffed toys on it.

"Is your little office this?"

"This is where I do my homework and spend most of my time playing with my toys. You can sit anywhere. So what do you want to talk about?"

"Shhhhh. Don't talk so loud. This town is getting terrible. My aunty treats me awful. My cousins don't play with me. I feel so by myself. It doesn't feel nice."

"I am by myself, too."

"At least you have your father. I don't have anybody. It don't nice."

"You have me. Stop the foolishness."

"Anyway, as I was saying. Is really me have to fix my troubles. Not Aunty. Nobody. I want to stay in school. I want to be happy. Been thinking if you can keep a secret, I can fix up my life."

"How so?"

He whispered, "I want to call Miss Ellen and tell her to come and pick me up so I can live with her. But I don't have a phone. I don't know her number. I don't know her address."

"That seems impossible. Then she would get in trouble for taking you away from your aunty."

"Shhhh. You are talking too loud. She is not she taking me away. I am going to take myself from all of this. I don't want to go live on the street. It is too wicked out there and the police will kill me."

"I know you were a little nuts, but I don't think that will work. Daddy would be upset if I interfere in your family business."

"I don't have any family. The boy is a free somebody. I just need a better place to live so I can finish school and get a scholarship to high school."

"That is a good reason. Guess what, I can help you look up her number in the telephone directory and then we can sneak a call to her."

"What is a telephone directory?"

"A list of phone numbers for all the folks who have telephones. Come and pray we don't get caught."

Miss Peaches' cooking smelled sweet through the house, and they needed to hurry before she called them for dinner. Chloe pulled an old directory from her bookshelf and the two searched for Miss Ellen's number.

"What is her last name, Roderick?"

"It starts with a B."

"That's not very helpful. You know how many names start with B in this big book?"

"Chloe. This is serious business for me. I will take my time and look."

"Where you say she live again?"

"Cherry Gardens."

"Mister, Cherry Gardens is a big place. What is wrong with you? The only reason I know it's in Kingston 8 is because my cousins live up that way. I guess we are looking for Ellen B in Kingston 8. What a something."

Roderick and Chloe spent quite a long time searching through the directory and thought they had it figured out.

"Ellen Birch. That's it. I remember now."

Chloe scrolled through the pages and found Birch, Ellen, showed the listing to Roderick. "I think this is her. Let's call her now."

"It's near dinner time and we are likely to get caught." She had hardly said that and picked up the telephone receiver when Miss Peaches showed up at the door.

Reading Chloe's expression on her face made the bottom of Roderick's feet tingle. "O it's all over. I knew it."

"Please Miss Peaches, don't tell Daddy anything. This is important. We are just making one call. Please," she whispered.

"Your dad is taking a nap on the couch, but I will soon call him for dinner."

Hurry up noh, Chloe, before your father wake up.

"Okay. I promise. Come Roderick."

He watched her dial the number. "It's ringing. Here. You talk to her when she answers."

"I never use a phone yet."

"Just say hello when she answers and tell her who you are. Take it from there. I will rest my ears right by the receiver and listen along with you."

"Hello. Is this Miss Ellen?" He made a big grin when she responded. "It's me. Roderick. You remember me? The boy you took shopping."

"Of course I know who you are. How did you find me?"

"I will tell you when I see you. Please, I am in a terrible situation. I need you to come and get me. I am over my friend Chloe next door."

"Which of the houses?"

"It's the house to the left of Aunty's house with the pretty flowers garden. When you come, don't go to Aunty, just come straight here."

"Come off now before Daddy wakes up," Chloe said.

"Who is that in the background? Are you safe?"

"My friend Chloe. I am safe for now. Just come. You coming?"

"Give me some time to reach your Aunt Lillian."

"Ba bye, Miss Ellen."

"Goodbye. See you soon."

He handed the phone to Chloe, and he watched as she gently hung it up. They hugged and laughed gleefully.

"I told you I know how to fix this thing. You never believed me. I am tired of this ugly life."

"The big question now. What are we going to tell Daddy? How will we explain when these two women come knocking on the door? My father won't beat me like your aunty, but he will be very cross."

"Leave it to me. I am going to tell him myself. It can't get any badder than what I have gone through already."

During dinner, Roderick shared what he had done, that it was all his idea and asked Mr. Goodman not to be cross with Chloe.

23

Between The Wheel And The Washer

Roderick sat in a corner on the sofa of the Goodman's living room thinking about the dinner Miss Peaches served up: roast chicken, steak with Gungo peas and rice, carrot juice with condensed milk. Dessert was chocolate cake with vanilla ice cream on top, in a glass cup filled to the brim.

That was the best meal I had all year.

He was happy with his friend Chloe and her dad, but waiting for Miss Ellen to knock on the door was like an eternity.

Sun was setting. He thought about how his life would change if he went to live with Ellen. There was stuff he had to do.

I love school very much and I can't wait to finish up. I still have that secret trunk to figure out about my family story. How I must move away leave Chloe? How? I can't go away and leave Maas Suraj. He doesn't have anybody. At these thoughts, Roderick rested his elbows on his thighs, covered his eyes with his palms.

The wind chimes at the front door played a peaceful melody in the breeze. Footsteps crossed the veranda. There was a knock on the door.

"Chloe, somebody at the door."

"Yes. I heard. Daddy. Somebody knocking on the door."

"Coming."

Mr. Goodman opened the door. The women wiped their feet on the welcome mat and shook Mr. Goodman's hand. He invited them in. Roderick and Chloe sat next to each other and listened.

"Right this way, ladies. Have a seat wherever you wish. Thanks for coming."

"Thanks for calling us, Mr. Goodman," replied both women.

"Call me Isaac. It was Roderick's idea, he called. I guess he called Ellen first."

"Yes, that's me he called. She is Lillian."

"Nice to meet both of you. Sorry, it's under these circumstances. Roderick and Chloe, say good evening to Ellen and Lillian."

"Good evening Miss Ellen and Miss Lillian," both said like school children when their teacher first enters the classroom. Roderick reached for Chloe's hand. He was shaking.

"How are you, Roderick?" Ellen asked.

"I am all right."

"You sure?"

"I just ate dinner." His voice was tight, almost sotto voce.

"Ladies, may I offer you something to drink?" Isaac said with palms up.

"Thank you. It's quite humid," Ellen replied.

Mr. Goodman called out to Peaches, who was clearing the dinner table, to bring some fresh Bombay mango juice she made from the tree in his backyard.

"It is not my policy to interfere in other people's affairs. However, Roderick has been a part of my life and my daughter's for quite some time. When he came to this town, he was around eight years old, reading at the sixth year old level. I have watched him blossom into an avid reader under my tutelage and self-teaching through his own curiosity and ambitions. His creativity as a visual artist is to be nurtured. But—"

"I know there's a but," Lillian said, clasping her hands in front of her face and tapping them nervously.

"He is being ill-treated by your sister, a woman who is hard to reach. I just dressed a deep sore on his body from the last flogging he got. She did not even clean and apply medicine. I can well imagine Roderick was afraid to show her. He is in a lot of pain."

O my Aunt Lillian and Miss Ellen look so sad.

"This is horrible," Ellen said.

"It is hard for me to take him because of my obligations to care for my very sick mother," Lillian said.

"Tata depends on me hand and foot. Roderick needs all the attention a growing boy deserves."

There was silence again. Then the wind chimes rustled another beautiful melody.

"Time is of the essence and something must be done, or the authorities will be the next step. At that point, it will be out of our hands," Mr. Goodman said.

"Authorities," Roderick asked softly.

"Yes. The police," Chloe whispered.

"Chloe. You knew police kill people. They will kill Aunty, too. I don't want them to kill her."

"It would be best if I live with Miss Ellen, since Aunt Lillian can't take me up at Tata."

"You should really think about it."

Lillian rested her half-full glass of mango juice on the table, turned to their intervening host. "What is your suggestion, Isaac?"

"Not my suggestion. Roderick had it all figured out himself. I am just being a go-between at this point. I want us to exhaust all the possibilities among ourselves so we can work something out in his favor."

"You hear that, Chloe?"

"Hm hm."

Roderick slouched on the couch and looked in Lillian's eyes. *Wish I could see what Aunt Lillian is thinking about now. She doesn't want me up at Tata. Miss Ellen looks concerned. I will be better off going with her.*

"I have a lot to say, but I am not a blood relative. Blood is thicker than water, a truism I learned long ago from my grandmother, Ma Lizbeth." Ellen straightened her spine, clutched her purse and crossed her ankles.

There was a long awkward stillness except for the occasional clinking sound of ice cubes in their glasses.

Lillian broke the silence. "Well, I know she has been overworking my nephew and refuses to send him to school."

All I do is work. If I never took your dad's private lesson and tried to help myself, I wouldn't be able to read my name. How come it is so hard to break free?

"Roderick is a brave boy," Mr. Goodman said. "He single-handedly put himself in school the first time. I have even facilitated some of that process, too, but Hope takes him out of school on a whim. There is no consistency."

"He cannot stay with your sister under these conditions." Ellen rubbed the top of her glass. "There is nothing logical that says he should suffer."

See it there. Miss Ellen understands that I shouldn't have to suffer so much. Roderick leaned into Chloe, cupped his fist and whispered in her ear.

"You hear her, Chloe. She is steady. She is really steady."

"Shhh. It is bad manners to whisper. Just listen."

"How are things with you, Ellen?"

"Things are fine with me, Isaac. I live alone in Cherry Gardens. Caring for Roderick could work well. It's entirely up to his family."

Family? They can't decide what happens to me. I think is my turn to do that. All this time, nobody tried to save me from the wicked woman. I saving myself now. Roderick folded his hands across his chest. Looked at Chloe, who somehow knew when his mind was running a mile-a-minute. He shuffled his bum and sat up straight, leaned his head to the left, closed his eyes.

"What's on your mind, Roderick?" Mr. Goodman asked.

Roderick did not respond until he felt Chloe bouncing him on his elbow. He looked up.

"Daddy talking to you."

"Yes, sir."

"You were deep in thought there for a minute. I was asking you what's on your mind right now."

"My mind is full up right now, Mr. Goodman. Is long time I have been thinking about finding Miss Ellen so she can keep me up there. Now I am listening to all of you and get to thinking that maybe I should just finish up the things I have to do here and then go up there."

"You can finish school where I live. Staying with me is just fine. I have plenty room for you to play." Miss Ellen opened her arms in a welcome gesture.

"You serious, Miss Ellen?"

"Of course, I am serious."

Roderick walked over to Ellen, tugged on her arm, looked up in her face. "If I go with you right now, the art club I plan to start at school won't happen again. I promise Peter and Monica to help them get their art in the exhibition. Peter more than Monica needs my help. I won't get to finish the sculpting that I am working on either."

"You are creating an art club! That is excellent." Miss Ellen gave him a fist bump. I couldn't take you away from that. As you know, I love art and would not want to get in your way."

"I am studying with Chloe for the scholarship next year. After that, I will be done with Aunty and all the bad things that happen to me in Olympic Gardens."

"Listen, love," Ellen said, "you can take the scholarship in any city. But if you really want to stay until you finish the things that mean a lot to you here, by all means, do so. Let me not cajole you into leaving here now."

Roderick paced the floor. He groaned, put his hand on his head, then he rubbed them on his pants. He tapped on the wall unit that displayed Chloe's trophies for swimming and lawn tennis championships. "Let me think this thing through good, good. I won't have Chloe around me anymore."

All the things that I found in the trunk I can't carry them with me, they are not mine. The pictures. I still have not finished reading the letters and the postcards. What about the lantern? What about my stone art? Roderick felt caught between a rock and a hard place.

The room was quiet. You could hear a pin drop. Then he looked around the room. All eyes were on him. *What about my friends at school? I have to come up with something quick.* "I feel I am doing well at school. That is all I ever wanted to do since I came to Town." The tears rolled down his face. He pressed his head in Ellen's chest and looked over at Lillian, who said nothing.

How come Aunt Lillian is so quiet?

"Listen here Roderick. I know you want to stay here, but this kind of living is not good for your mind and body. It will affect the way you learn and grow," Mr. Goodman crossed his legs and pressed his right index finger against his cheek.

"What you mean… I will stop grow?"

"Let me not burden you with these things. It is all up to you now, Roderick. Right, ladies?"

Roderick wiped his tears with the hem of his shirt. Looking over at Chloe, he parted his lips as if he wanted to say something to her.

"I am going to stay down here and finish up."

There was a gasp in the room. The tintinnabulation of the wind chimes rose as the smell of wet earth wafted in through the windows. It started raining.

"Well, ladies, you heard the youngster. Chloe, please excuse yourself and go to your room. I must have a talk with Roderick."

"Yes, Daddy."

Roderick felt a sudden dread.

I have never seen Mr. Goodman's face so serious. That's probably what Chloe means when she says her daddy can get cross with her. O gosh. No smile. Aunty is shaking her head and Miss Ellen is just staring at me. What now?

"Roderick. Come sit over here." Mr. Goodman said as he tapped the seat of an accent chair. "I have watched you make the conscious decision to show discipline with your studies. It is paying off well in your reading and overall progress in school. This makes me very proud of you. A moment ago, you made another big decision in your life not to go with Miss Ellen. I want you to know that you were born with free will. But know this: the choices you make in life come with consequences. I am not a relative of yours, neither am I your father, but I care about you. You suffer a lot and it gives me concern. Recently, you have been showing signs of deep frustration. I understand it. Your aunty beating on you is wrong. Too many parents on the island think they may do this king of harm to children. It is wrong, Roderick. It is wrong."

Roderick hugged his body. He could barely look at Mr. Goodman's face but hung on to his every word.

Harm to me. He knows she harms me. You hear that Miss Ellen and Aunt Lillian? She harms me.

"But your choice to stone your aunty's windows and run away for weeks was you exercising free will, your choice in response to her beating on you. That was not the best decision. It made us worry, and it was dangerous. Do you understand me, young man?"

"Yes, I understand you, Mr. Goodman."

"Just know that if you ever feel upset to the point of anger, I want you to come over and cool your head. If I am not here, I will instruct Miss Peaches to let you in so you can calm down or call Miss Ellen. That is my promise to you. But I will not reward bad behavior. I don't expect that from you, just like I don't expect that from Chloe. Do you understand me?"

"Yes, sir."

"I will let your aunt and Ellen take it from here."

Lillian and Ellen thanked Mr. Goodman for his good counsel and care. They walked Roderick home. The shop was still open. Four men played dominos on the piazza by the light of a single bulb that stretched from the inside of the shop and hung on a nail. Another man stood over them and watched the game. Miss Daphne walked onto the piazza with a tray of Red Strip Beers and put one next to each player. She had a smile on her face when she saw her friend Lillian.

"I was wondering where Roderick was all evening." Daphne hugged the tray flat against her chest like a breastplate. "What's going on, Lills, how goes it Ellen?"

"We are okay," Lillian said. "Just looking about this little boy. Where is Hopie?"

"She is inside there with the insurance man."

Insurance man? This time of evening. Roderick crinkled his brow.

"Hopie, is me, Lillian. Come out here, girl!"

"It's all right, you can come in. Jay and I were just finishing up here."

J? I wonder if it is the same J I am thinking of. He is tall and has pale skin like Mr. Goodman and his eyes look like puss. Hmm. He has a nice trim with a part like me. Jeezam Peezam. Could he be my father, Chloe?

"What's going on Jay? Long time don't see you?" Lillian said. "This is my friend Ellen."

Kiss mi neck. Aunt Lillian knows him, too. This must be my father. It has got to be my father. I pray so. Then he will take me out of this miserable place.

"Hello." Ellen looked him up and down. "Nice to meet you."

Lillian held Roderick's hand. "This is our nephew, our bright little nephew, Roderick."

"I know. He is getting tall. Nice seeing you, ladies. Anyway, I was just leaving." He shut his leather case, put on his hat, bowed and said goodbye.

He knows? Then how him say nothing to me. I have a feeling is my father. I just know it's him.

The man gave Ellen his business card. "If you ever have insurance needs, please call me."

Ellen inspected the card. "Jonathan deRouter. Did I pronounce it right?"

"Yes. Just call me Jay."

"Nice meeting you, Jay."

DeRouter. Well, I guess he is not my father then, but he sure has pretty eyes and pretty hair like me. Ah well. Chloe is not him. I am on to find the next clue.

Lillian and Ellen sat on a bench with soft floral cushions. "We decided Ellen will pick up Roderick every other week so he can take an art class downtown and spend a little time with her. This will ease the burden of you having to take care of him all the time.

"So who is going to help in the shop?" Roderick asked.

"Daphne will stay on full-time so you can go to school and turn out good. Right Hopie?"

"Who decides who works for me and who doesn't?" Hope flung off her head tie.

Aunt Hope got quiet. Is the first time she hearing that she would have to keep Daphne and the little girl, too. She was too angry to speak.

"Why you look so angry? It's Roderick's idea to stay with you, although you treat him so badly. He believes you are going to treat him better. If it wasn't for him, we would move him to Cherry Gardens right now. Better yet, call the authorities on the way you busted his side the last time. I can't believe you are so heartless that you didn't even care for his wound. It could have poisoned his bloodstream and killed him. Mama never raised us like that, Hopie."

What? It could kill me! Thanks for saying that, Aunt Lillian. She knows I should hate her for all the bad things she has done to me.

Roderick heard Hope grinding her teeth.

Everybody on her for me. I feel proud of myself that I made my own decision.

Hope picked up her tie-head and wrapped her hair. She folded some kitchen towels and put them in a drawer. "I couldn't tell the last time I said a hard word to this boy or lifted a hand to him. He busted my windows and ran off and for days I didn't know where he was."

"Did you try to find him? No."

"That's not a child's behavior. He's just ungrateful."

"Why didn't you let me know?" Lillian asked.

Hope covered her ears and turned her back.

Miss Ellen is quiet, she not saying a word. I wonder if she won't want me to come to her house again because she thinks I am a bad boy. You out there. Please let her still love me. Please.

Ellen cleared her throat. "Roderick doesn't have to be grateful to you for anything. He's a child in your care."

The cousins had edged their way into the company. Nelton made rude faces at everybody. "You can't tell my mother what to do!"

"Go sit down, little boy, and learn some manners," Lillian scolded, ready to give him a right hand to his big mouth. Ellen shook her head.

"Don't talk to my child like that; he has a right to defend his mother against this bull-riding."

"That's the problem; you pet this little boy and treat Roderick like hell. Stephen."

"Yes, Aunt Lillian."

"I leave you in charge of Roderick. I need you to protect him. Treat him like he is your little brother. He is your flesh and blood. Make sure he studies hard and keeps up with his homework."

"Yes, Aunty."

"I know you will graduate from high school and go off to university in the autumn. I wish you well."

"Thank you. I want the same thing for Roderick, too, Aunty."

"That's what I always liked about you. You are a caring, ambitious young man."

"Is me raise him." Hope snapped her fingers in the air with pride, like she would start dancing.

"He raised himself," Lillian lashed back.

"Ladies, ladies, ladies," Ellen pushed in. "Not now."

"I have nothing more to say. Roderick is on his own around here. I have a business to run."

I don't like when they fuss. I am going to turn in. Roderick thanked Ellen and Lillian for coming, said goodbye, and walked back to his room. He took out his school uniform and hung them on a nail on the doorjamb. He shined his brown school shoes and tucked his socks in them. Rubbing his hands over his schoolbag, he mused about the strain and joy of the evening.

"Chloe really nice to me. Look how she helped me find Miss Ellen. Staying in Olympic Gardens for now makes sense to me, since Miss Daphne is going to help out. I can really get to finish primary school."

Tapping his chest three times, he took down the sailor hat, put it on his head, looked in the mirror at his reflection.

"Roderick Brissett. Do I resemble the sailor man in the picture? No. Yes. No." He shifted the hat from side to side. Smiled. Then he put the hat back on the nail, walked over to his cot, and sat on the edge. "You are going to study hard with Chloe and pass your scholarship next year. You are going to be the best student at Perennial Primary School. Nothing will get in your way. O Miss Ellen, I am a good boy; a good boy."

24

For Honor And Art

The Perennial Primary School library was as quiet as a graveyard. There was an antique map of Jamaica with etchings of the Cockpit and Blue Mountains, vegetation, plantation houses, hunters with rifles and animals. It took up most of the back wall where the desks faced north. A map of North and South America hung on the west wall. A huge photo of Prime Minister Hugh Lawson Shearer hung on the eastern wall surrounded by photos of Mahatma Gandhi, Queen Elizabeth and Winston Churchill. Glass windows from the floor to the ceiling spread along the north side of the main room. The branches of the acorn tree, strong enough for a flock of blackbirds, swayed ever so slowly in the gentle wind. Clouds, like cotton balls floated mindlessly across the powder-blue sky. Roderick spent the entire lunchtime in the library searching books and magazines about clubs from all over the world, surrounded by rich history and a beautiful view.

"There is so much to do, so much to learn at Perennial. I want to do everything. Art Club, read every book in the library. Ooooooooo."

The bell rang. Pushing the chair under the table, he couldn't help but close his eyes one last time, open them real fast, and watch how the light from the ceiling reflected on the shiny floor, making him feel good.

He said to himself, "Hurry up or you are going to be late for class. I could live right here in this library and read anything I want. My library card not leaving my pocket."

As he came up to the circulation desk, he saw the librarian putting some cards away.

"Thanks for helping me find these books."

"You are very welcome. Take care of them." She stamped them. "I will see you soon."

"Yes, Miss. Thank you."

As customary, the students in Roderick's class formed a queue to enter the classroom. On reaching their desks, they stand quietly and wait for the teacher's directives to recite the railway stations from Kingston to Montego Bay from memory. This was homework, and Roderick worked hard on it. He could just hear Chloe in his head, "You get to Bushy Park, Roderick, before you get to Old Harbour. Try to remember that." He recited them for his teacher to much applause.

Well, the Jolly crew, Django, Curtis and Imogene, felt that Roderick just came to the school and was getting so much attention. Of course, why not? He did his homework—they often got detention for not doing theirs. Well, one day, Roderick forgot his homework on the old trunk at home. His teacher did not believe him. That's how he landed in detention. That's how Roderick, Django, Imogene and Curtis became good friends; in detention. The four clustered in a two-row, two-person-deep square: Roderick and Imogene in the front and Django and Curtis behind them. Roderick noticed that Django always had this itch to tease him, and the rest joined.

"Puss eye boy. Your eye them green like puss own. Creepy. Everybody, Roderick daddy is a puss!" Django whispered loud enough for his friends to hear.

"Puss eye under your mumma bed." Roderick yelled so loud his teacher and all the children heard him. The giggles started.

"Go to the back of the class and stand there until the class is over." His teacher pointed with the blackboard cane she used now and then to whack a student or pull them to her with the hook end. The giggles became louder, and the teacher had a tough time quieting them. On his way to the back of the classroom, Roderick stepped on Django's foot so hard he screamed.

As soon as the bell rang for the next class and they were on the landing outside, Roderick pinned Django to the ground while Imogene and Curtis edged them on. Django pushed Roderick out of his way, stood up, and wiped off his uniform. "What a way you easy to vex. Not that serious, Roderick."

Roderick pointed his finger in Django's face, "If you ever call me puss eye again, I am going to take my pencil and jook you in your eye." Then he burst out laughing.

It is this sort a foolishness made me and these three idiots become friends. He looked over at Django, whose frown turned into a smile, and the four made their way to the woodwork shop for class. Of the three, Curtis was more into woodwork because his grandfather was a contractor and builder.

After school, Roderick, Django and Curtis walked home while Imogene went to track practice. The afternoon was balmy. Children kicked small milk cartons along the sidewalk in a rambunctious soccer match. Three girls held hands, skipped and sang, "Skip to my Lou, my darling."

I always wanted to be part of the children coming home from school in the evenings. Finally. They are so happy. I feel happy, too.

"Hey Roderick, you still coming to join the Boy Scouts, right?" Django said and bumped fists with Curtis.

"I know you always wanted me to join the Boy Scouts, but when your life is not normal, these kinds of things don't happen."

"A hear you," Curtis said. "None of the three of us know what normal life is."

"For sure," Django added.

"You know what I remember," Roderick said. "The day we were in art class and we had to draw a portrait of our father or a great man in history? You remember, Django?"

"No."

"I remember, though. You just sat there and cried. I asked you what happen to you and you said your father was in prison. I was so sorry for you that day. You remember?"

"Wait, wait, wait," Django interjected. "And you, Roderick, said you didn't have a father, and we laughed so hard you cried. Remember?"

"I remember when the one Curtis told us how his life was not normal anymore since his father divorced his mother and left them. Remember?"

Roderick could see the boys were all crying again, and his tears were coming down fast. "O gosh, we are crying again!" They all burst out laughing.

"Cheer up, fellas. We can get normal again." Roderick said, kicked a stone and guffawed.

"Listen, Roderick," Curtis said. "We love the Scouts and really want you to join."

"I know who is going to be glad if I join; my old friend Suraj. He always said, 'One day you will get the courage to take the oath and learn how to become a good citizen.' I studied what he said by heart."

"You like Suraj, don't you, Roderick?" Django said.

"Yes. He is my good friend. What I really want to do is start an art club. I am going to see Miss Fuller so I can start the club next week, Wednesday."

"Next week Wednesday? That is our scout meeting day. Maybe you can start your club the following week and at least come and meet with our scout leader." Curtis grabbed a hold of the street post, leaned his head back and spun around it.

"I have to keep my word, Curtis. The others are depending on me to make this art club happen."

"Figure it out," Curtis said real loud. As he spun faster, his voice echoed in the wind.

"This is frustrating. I want to be a part of the Scouts and I know I have to do the club. You know how much I love art."

"Django chimed in. "Perhaps you can do both. Change your club day since yours don't start yet. Make it on a Monday or Tuesday."

"Phewww. Django… that is a jolly good idea. Let me see if Miss Fuller and the headmaster will give me Monday afternoons."

"Now that is what I call good thinking," Curtis said. The boys high-five. Curtis and Django turned off on Lothian Avenue, and Roderick continued to his home on Olympic Way.

"Holy mackerel! I just remember. Wednesdays is Aunt Hope's bible study. I can't tell the boys that I can't do the scout thing. They are going to say I am a spoil sport and be really upset with me this time. Django and Curtis will never understand that I don't want another beating like the one I got for messing with Aunty's bible study. O Aunt Hope, you are always in my way. Don't it?" Roderick picked up an empty milk carton, flung it in a dumpster next to the tailor shop and hissed his teeth.
"Cho!"

For two days, Roderick built his courage to go see Miss Fuller to find out if she and the headmaster would agree to Mondays after school for the art club. That Thursday, during lunch, he went to Miss Fuller who was walking around with her gradebook and pen, assigning grades to recently glazed pottery in the art room. The sharp smell of clay made him rub his palms together real fast and said, "Yes." This is what I am talking about. Curtis and Django wouldn't understand. Look at how the pottery pretty! This is where I want to be. Good day, Miss Fuller."

"Hello Roderick."

"I was thinking of starting an art club. A few of us who love to draw and paint and sculpt and them things there, need some extra time and a place to do our art. Miss, can you help us get this going?"

"O Roderick, that's very thoughtful. This is a great idea. What inspired you to do this?"

"First of all, I love to draw and paint. I figure if I get a few of my friends who like art too, that would be nice. My friend Chloe goes to the crochet club."

"That's wonderful."

Roderick walked around and ran his right hand on the edge of desks, easels and walls. He stopped by the blackboard and addressed his teacher.

"Another thing too. The other day I was in the library, and the walls have magnificent pictures. I thought to myself that we could do some of that right in this art room. I have seen nobody in here working after school."

"How do you plan to get it going?"

"Well, I would find out what time the others can make it. They are looking at Mondays after school."

"Sounds good."

"How many of you?"

"Not a lot. We just want the ones who really love art like me to come."

"Well, the rule of the school is that a club should have at least five students?"

"I think we are about three of us right now. You know big Peter, the one with the thick glasses in the classroom at the end of the corridor; he loves to draw comic strips that tell funny stories. Monica is in my class. She loves to paint."

Roderick got a piece of paper and wrote the names of the children and their classroom and gave it to the teacher.

"I know Monica loves to paint, but Peter surprises me." Miss Fuller placed the paper on her desk.

"Yes. Let him show you. He doesn't pay attention in class. All he does is draw in the back of his exercise book. That's the three of us so far. Later on, we can put up an announcement on the Notice Board in the lunchroom to invite others to join. But Miss. Please don't make too many join right now."

"I understand your need to keep it small, but we have to open it up to all the students. Apart from doing your art, what else do you have in mind? Clubs have to be fun."

"Hmmm. I was reading a lot about clubs in the library. Well, we can go on an outing to the Arawak Museum. My friend Chloe went last year, and she said when I get a chance I should go. We can put up our work right here in the art room and invite the teachers and the children to come and see what we did."

"That's an excellent idea."

"We should sell some of them and make money."

"I would have to discuss selling your art with the headmaster."

"He is a reasonable man. O Miss Fuller. You know how many nights I stay up late thinking about this. Does that mean you will help us do this?"

"Certainly. Maybe I can do some art with you, too. Since I have been teaching, I have not made time to do much personal artwork. I will run this by Mr. Eldemire and set a date to start the club."

"Remember, Mondays."

"Yes. I will remember."

"Thank you. Thank you. Thank you. I will tell Peter and Monica."

Roderick, in thinking mode, ripped a piece of paper from his exercise book and wrote a note to Peter.

> Hey Peter. Looks like we can start the art club next week Monday right after school. Let us meet in the art room with Miss Fuller. Yeah!

He folded the paper and ran to Peter's classroom at the end of the corridor. The door was open, and he knocked gently on the panel. The teacher invited him to enter. It was still. Everybody was reading, but what do you know, Peter was scribbling in the back of his book.

"Good afternoon, sir. I need to give Peter a very important message. Can you please give him this note for me?"

"Give it to him, but be quiet."

"Thank you, sir." Roderick walked over and gave Peter the note, tiptoed out of the classroom and waved his thanks to the teacher. He stood behind the door and watched as Peter read the note.

I have never seen Peter smile so widely before. He seems to be happy. I feel good that maybe now, Peter will have plenty of time to do art so he can pay attention to his other classes.

Children teased Peter a lot. He is called an oddball, but one day Roderick discovered Peter has talent. He learned that his mother is a patient at Belleview mental health hospital and he stays at home with his dad, who is always working.

Now Peter won't be lonely anymore. He has me and Monica every Monday after school to draw and laugh. Who knows, Miss Fuller might make us spend more time in the art room. But Roderick had another problem. He had to tell Django and Curtis that he cannot join the Boy Scouts. It is too risky because it clashes with his aunty's bible study. Besides, there is a fee and scout uniform involved.

The boys are going to think I am getting soft. After all, Aunty stopped beating me up. I am catching on in school. Miss Daphne is there to help. I don't think they will buy my argument at all. They are going

The second to last period of the day, Roderick met up with Curtis, Django and Imogene, the three Jolly ones. They were happy to see each other as usual. Inside his belly, Roderick was feeling jittery.

I have to tell them. I have to tell them the truth.

"Hey everybody. What you doing this evening?"

"The usual," Curtis replied. "I have to go straight home to watch my little brother. Imo going track practice, right?"

"Yes. I am going to eat my mango and then go straight to practice," she said. "Long time no get to hang out under the Lignum Vitae tree and play Ludo."

"So true," Django replied. "Everybody has so much doing these days. School work is getting tougher."

"Talk about school work getting tougher, I failed the civics test," Roderick added.

Imogene rubbed his shoulder. "O no. It was a little hard. Some questions were hard and the passage about the court was quite long."

"I knew a lot about the court because my Aunt Lillian taught me about it. I just had problems with 'Exercising the Franchise' section. Well, I can't afford to fail anything. Next year winter is my last chance to take the scholarship and pass it. I have to ease up on some of my extra activities," Roderick said.

"What extra activities?" Curtis asked.

"I have the art club to do."

"You mean you start the art club already? So what about the Boy Scouts?"

"Yes, Roderick. What about the Scouts?" Django pouted.

"Hold on. Hold on" Imogene interjected. What's with this Boy Scouts thing? I am out of the loop."

"Well, Mr. Roderick supposed to join. Let's hear his excuse now," Curtis put his hands in his pockets and leaned against the wall.

"Come on folks," Roderick said. "It's all my fault. I stretch myself too thin. I never knew how much the art club would involve. The Scouts will be too much for me at the moment. My aunt will not pay for my uniforms. Wednesday evening is her bible study, and I decided not to do anything to upset her until I finish with primary school."

"Your loss, mister," Curtis hissed his teeth and walked ahead of the group.

"Why it has to be a loss for him," Imogene said. "I am only on the track team and it takes up all my energy and time. Sometimes when I go home, I only have time for a shower and sleep. That is why I get in so much trouble with not finishing my homework. Coach plans to kick me off the team if I don't buckle down to the classwork. You see Curtis, everything in one, mister."

"She runs fast, and she thinks fast," Roderick made his comeback.

The following Monday afternoon, Roderick, Peter, and Monica got together in the art room. They spent the first half hour talking about how they wanted to run the club. They made their own rules and decided what they wanted to work on for the next couple of sessions.

"Peter, what do you want to work on first?"

"I don't work like that. I just start something that comes into my mind."

"All right then." Roderick looked at Monica, who was bobbing her head in agreement with Peter.

"Well, I want to do a painting with children playing. I don't know where they will be, but it will come to me." Monica propped up her face with her palms and rocked her head some more.

"Miss Fuller, what are you going to do first?" Peter asked.

"Well, I am responsible for your safety. I have to make sure you are safe for every minute during the club meeting. We must take attendance every time we meet."

Roderick looked Miss Fuller dead in the eye. "But what do you want to draw, paint, or sculpt?"

"O Roderick, I enjoy still life. Remember, I have other teacher responsibilities, but I will certainly make time to do some art myself. So what will you be working on, Roderick?"

"My first piece will be a hair stick for my friend Mona. She always pulls her hair back in a bun and wears a pretty stick through it. She dresses up pretty all the time, too. Well, it looks like we are all set for our art club. Yeah."

Monica and Peter joined in with their yeahs. Roderick spun slowly around on the swivel stool, imagined the art room coming alive with beautiful paintings of life in the country, the rolling hills, the valleys, cows grazing, the river clear as crystal with pretty-pretty fish swimming cheerily. He imagined Peter's cartoon drawings telling hilarious stories.

"O and Monica, she just loves to paint portraits." Roderick stopped spinning on the stool, got up, stood tall and folded his arms. He pointed his right foot outward, tilted his head to the left, wiggled his lips from side to side.

Perennial Primary School, doing my art is all right with me!"

25

Beads For Her Hair

There was something peculiar about the moon.

It was full and seemed to dominate the sky. Roderick followed its iridescent beam that bounced off the trees onto the ground like a giant flashlight along The Way. The sidewalk was wet from an early evening downpour of rain. Roderick snuck out on an adventure to see Mona at the Snuggle Puss to give her the hair stick he made for her. Its dangling John Crow beads glowed in the dark.

"Me like it. A hope she will like it, too."

It was three weeks since he established the art club and he felt it allowed him room to fulfil his promise to Mona. He didn't see any buses coming and so he walked.

"Only police and thief walk these hours of the night, Uncle would say about the farm hands who took the short-cut through his property, onto the roadway with their girlfriends to play dominos and drink beers at Maas Charlie's Coles Supper Shop back in the country."

He giggled at the memory. Once or twice he saw the lovers in the moonlight when he went to buy cigarettes for Uncle. Tonight, along The Way to go see Mona, lights were still on in some houses, showing off intricate lattice work and beautiful curtains. Saint Mary and her baby glowed through the glass window of a tiny cottage next to a bigger house in a yard. The smell of incense drifted over the fence onto the sidewalk. A couple stepped onto the sidewalk at the corner of Australia Road. They were holding hands, and the man carried a small radio with an antenna on his left shoulder. As he got closer, Roderick gathered the couple was listening to music from America, the kind his cousin Stephen played on a Saturday night. Just before he reached Balcombe Drive, Roderick saw cars filing in through the open gate, columns on either side. Trees and hedges made the yard dark, but there was a string of red lights that formed an arch at the front door. The sign read Welcome To The Snuggle Puss.

"Wow. The Snuggle Puss looks joyful tonight. Big things going on inside there. Everybody dress nicely. Men and women holding hands."

As he approached the driveway, he felt the muscles around his navel contract.

Strange. How me feel so weird? Relax. Everything is cool. Roderick walked quietly, careful not to be seen. He positioned himself under a mango tree with low hanging ripe fruits. The smell was inviting, but tonight was no time to get messy with mangoes; he wanted to smell clean. Roderick sat on a stone bench under the tree. Wanting to fulfill his promise to Mona to give her the hair stick he promised, he waited patiently to see if she would spot him and come outside. Maybe he might get a glimpse of her dancing on stage.

Buff. Baff. Rumble. Tumble. Screams.

There she was being dragged out of the club by a man who yelled. "You are a dirty little gal. After all that I do for you. You a run around with that crooked politician." Roderick hid behind the tree, his heart beat loud.

"A not doing anything like that with nobody, Screw."

"This body is mine. Me buy and pay for it. A give you everything. What more you want, Dirty gal? A going to fix this body for you nobody will want you." The man pulled out his ratchet knife and slashed her left cheek. She screamed at the pain and blood.

Jeezam. Him going to kill her. What a can do? Roderick tried to make himself more invisible.

"Don't do it, Screw. Don—"

Another slash. "Hold that!"

What a wicked man. The good good lady. Poor Mona. I am afraid to come out and help her make him see me and stab me to. She has to get help. Roderick peeped around the column to see if anyone was nearby to get their attention. Mona tried to shield her face, her handbag dropped.

"A pregnant with your baby. Don't kill we, Screw."

"My baby? Give it to the big government, man." He twisted her arms behind her back, kicked her in her belly, pushed her to the ground and spat on her, cleaned his bloody knife on her bikini top. Screw walked slowly to his car, got in, burned tires towards Tower Hill.

"Help! Help!" Mona screamed, fighting for her life.

Patrons staggered one by one to help. Roderick heard a man's voice; he listened closely, remained quiet.

"It might very well be a police job," the scrawny, gray-haired man waved his beer bottle at the patrons.

"The slasher was like a rabid dog. He sliced her as if he was preparing steak for the coal stove," came another shaken patron.

As folks walked out of the club like cockroaches, some screamed and covered their faces from the horror. Their favorite go-go dancer's near lifeless body lay on the ground, covered in blood.

"Call the police!" one frantic man yelled to the manager of the club. He took off his shirt to help stop the bleeding and cover her body from the elements. "She is losing a lot of blood. What savage would do something like this?"

All the while Roderick was still hiding, feeling helpless, but happy to know Mona was finally getting help.

What's wrong with people? I can't take this. So much blood. I never see so much blood. Is like the man butcher her like Manzie cow. "This is what Olympic Gardens is coming to. People can't get to enjoy themselves anymore. It was never like this. I will bring around my car and take her to the hospital," a patron said, shaking his head in disgust. Three men lifted her limp, bleeding body and placed her in the car. Men in fancy cars fled the scene in a hurry. Soaking wet with pee all over his pants, Roderick emerged from under the mango tree with the pretty hair stick he made for his Mona, clearly shaken. The proprietor called out to him, "Little boy, don't a tell you not to come around here no more. You saw something?"

"No, sir. Me no see nothing."

"You sure?"

"Yes, sir. Sure, sure. "He vomited all over his shirt. *After I couldn't tell me see anything. The boss man crazy. Not me. A would have to give a statement to the police. Then Screw go find out I was there and send gunman fi kill me. Uncle always says to, 'See and blind, hear and deaf.' I know better to keep my mouth shut for coward man keeps sound bone.* There was a weakness in his body, but Roderick pushed against it and fast walked home in the balmy night air, staggering like a drunken man. His breath sounded like a peanut cart whistle. Arriving at his gate, he pictured the bloody scene and vomited again. Exhausted, Roderick hurried to the standpipe, turned on the water, washed his head and body, climbed through the window into his room. Painstakingly, he reached for the hair stick in his pocket, placed it on his windowsill. Standing by the widow, his hands on top of his head, he stared intently into the starless night.

"I can't take this anymore. First Lij. Now Mona. What I must do with this wickedness? This wicked idiot town is getting too rough for me. I can't breathe in the heat. It lock up my throat. Food don't nice no more. Why? Why? Why everybody who love me get hurt? What wrong with me? Me not to have nobody to love me?"

Wrestling a puissant evil with no face, Roderick screamed his frustration into the night. There were no tears. This time, Roderick found himself in a churning cauldron of anger, with no fire underneath. "I won't tell anyone about this, but when I get big, I am going to search for that Screw. I am going to mash up that man if I see him again."

The atmosphere over the enclave where Roderick lived had changed drastically since the man viciously stabbed Mona a month earlier. Everywhere Roderick went, people whispered loudly and others were silent. For some, it became a sacred prayer at sunrise, noontime, and sundown—the life of a neighbor with child, savagely stabbed. Others had their version of the story that stuck to their walls like pin up posters of the first crime of passion in The Garden. Newspapers and radio stations carried the horror with some sympathy for the woman and unborn child, except for Miss Hope who told her customers that it was the hands of God that moved mightily in Olympic Gardens to send a message that the town needed to be purged of the mother harlot's nastiness. The Snuggle Puss of half-naked go-go dancing, sinful street girls like Mona were bringing down the good-good neighborhood lower than a breeding bang-belly pig. Slackness of all kinds was right in the midst of decent people's homes and their children exposed to this debauchery. Hope believed her ceaseless prayers and days of fasting reached high heaven. The great transaction was done. Roderick found it hard to accept that anyone would not care about Mona and the baby in her belly.

"I wonder if she is going to leave me like Lij, Miss Dillon? Mona bothered no one," he said to her a week later.

"We can only hope for the best. Don't worry your brain with these things. Grownups make poor choices sometimes, dear."

"Sometimes I can't sleep straight when night come." "Never mind. It soon go away. Just say your prayers and go to sleep."

One night, just after cleaning and closing the shop, Roderick fell asleep on his cot, worn out. He heard a baby crying, but he could not tell where the sound was coming from. The crying got louder and louder, closer and closer, but his body was in a frozen state. He could not feel his arms and feet to get up to see about the baby. Cold sweat rolled down his face and into his nostrils, tickling him, but he couldn't move. He bounced out of his nightmare, fighting the air, reaching for the baby. It was real to him. He got the sense that he was awake.

The moon and stars looked at him through the window and he felt afraid. Roderick was questioning his values as a friend. He felt he did not do enough for Mona. His feelings of worthlessness to help his friend unsettled him.

"You know what? I am going to go check on Jojo them. I am thinking like them right now. Life around here is not fit for animals and boys like us who are looking for a way out. Funny, I was really believing what Aunt Hope always told Nelton and Stephen. She never thought I needed to hear it too, but she always says: 'School first, good job with the government, a family, a few beers with the fellows and then you die peacefully in your sleep.'" Covering his mouth, he held back a big cry. "We are suffering. Just when I think things are getting normal again, I find out that nothing is normal."

The lemonade was just right in the sweltering heat. The smell of pickled mackerel bubbling in coconut milk and lots of pimento and garlic made Roderick, Jojo, and the boys hungrier than ever. He had stopped by to see his friends to clear his head. Sitting on a log at the side of the house, he counted thirty days until school ends for Christmas holidays. He was not about to ruin everything he had worked for over the school term, but too many bad things were happening in his world. Roderick crouched. He listened as the boys talked about juggling school and the music business.

"Just checking in to see how you are doing with the music thing, Jojo."

Jojo turned to him. "I can't believe this. I thought you just forget about we."

"No. I just had to concentrate on my lessons. It is hard to focus when so many bad things are happening around you. I have big dreams like you, too, Jojo. They are just different."

"Sometimes at night, all we can hear around here are gunshots. We can't go outside. So we sit down in here and make up songs and sing. Hoping that one day, somebody will discover we and give we a whole heap a money so we can get out of this. Maybe we could live around where you live, it better than here so."

"Yes man is true," Haulup added. "Nice lawn and garden. Your aunty's house is large, even your little friend next door's house."

"Drawdown wants to say something here." He stood up, pulled up his pants above his waist, made his silly face."Is not music me did always want to do, you know."

"What you really want to do?" Roderick asked.

"I want to be a doctor like the one that worked on my grandmother's gout at Comprehensive."

"But we don't have no doctor around them parts here." Haulup pulled him to sit.

Roderick thought about what the boys were saying. "Everybody has a dream, but it's how to reach it."

"Look!" Jojo brought them back to reality. "We really need money. That is the only way we can get this music thing going and get out of the ghetto."

"I want out of my condition some days but I just want to finish primary school, take scholarship and go to high school. It seems to get tougher every day."

"Man, you don't need to finish school. Nothing in school for boys like us. All we need is money."

"I don't think the music thing is going to help me," Roderick said.

"Missa B said him know the right person to help us. We going to the man house little later, come. This is our chance."

"Hey Roderick, don't think so hard, man. We have the answer," Jojo said as he pulled a merino over his head.

"How you know me thinking?"

"A see it in your face. You gone leave us five miles down Spanish Town Road."

"Very funny. You wouldn't understand. Listen, I am only following you to go see this man. I am not looking for any money."

Roderick and the fellows walked for miles to meet with the mystery man Jojo claimed would give them the money to pay Missa B to finish the engineering work on the record. They reached a vast compound that opened onto the street. It had no gate. Jojo lead the way while Roderick, Haulup, and Drawdown followed slightly behind. It was dark. Roderick noticed Jojo turned many corners, behind shacks and outhouses. They had to bend down to walk under clothes hanging on lines, fluttering, drying in the night breeze. It felt like they took an eternity to get to a baby-blue shack with a black door and one window to the right. Two quick steps led to the door. Roderick watched as Jojo knocked. A dog barked from within, then a raspy voice like a hoarse Fire Baptist preacher said, "A coming."

Clack. Clack. Clack. Clack.

Roderick heard four locks pulled, and the door opened, but he saw no one. He whispered, "Jojo, the door open."

Upon entering, Roderick saw a tall man with his back slightly turned, cleaning his gun.

"Come inside yout."

"Is me Haulup and the rest a them."

"I know is you," said the man.

"A bring another soldier for you. Him name Roderick, Haulup pointed in Roderick's direction."

"Roderick you say?"

"Yes, sir."

The big tall man turned around and gave a menacing grin, exposing his two upper gold-capped front teeth. "You bring me another soldier. Him clean?"

"Yes. Him good, man. Him good."

"First things first, him have to get rid of that name, Roderick. Too long." He ran the gun along the side of Roderick's face. "You look like a Lead. Yes, lead like the belly of a bullet. That's a good name for you. You think you can do this kinda work?"

"Yes, I can do this work." Roderick answered with no thought. He was not only out of his zone, but he was being initiated into a world that may be the antidote for his pain. *What kind of work he wants me to do? I thought he was going to give us the money to pay Missa B to record the music.* Studying the man's face brought on a strange feeling in his gut that unsettled him. It was as if he had seen him before. A foreboding brute, the man teased Roderick with the Smith and Wesson, cocking the trigger. Roderick was shaking in his pants, but a gun would take care of a lot of his troubles. For a moment, he remembered Suraj telling him that one day he would become an outstanding soldier. He told him stories about being on the battlefield with sharp bayonets and rifles, not a little ratchet knife like the one Haulup carried.

"You not ready for the lead, yet," the man cautioned, as if eavesdropping on Roderick's thoughts. He reached in his pants pocket for an Opaki ratchet knife. "Look at this beauty! Pure carbon steel. Sharp like razor. Punctures the flesh deep on contact. Hit the right spot and the chances of survival are slim. My people ship them straight to me from Germany." He lunged at Roderick with the blade and laughed. "Hold this!"

Roderick dodged the knife like a Kung Fu fighter.

"Impressive, young boy. Impressive. That's right, you do the stabbing. You don't get stabbed. When your mind is strong and ready, my soldier will teach you how to use it. Right Haulup?"

"Yes, I will teach him good."

This is getting really scary Roderick wiped his sweaty palms on his trousers but feigned toughness and street smarts.

He gave me a ratchet knife. I am in deep doodu. This is not what I agreed to do. Maas Suraj taught me that using knives and sharp objects require training. We should use them responsibly. Safety first. Knives are not used to carve people. Roderick felt sick to his stomach, like he would vomit. *I better not vomit in this man's house. His voice sounds familiar. I heard it so many times before.* Something clicked in his brain. His shoulders tightened. *Jeezam no. Could it be him?. The wicked man at the Snuggle Puss.* He searched his memory for more clues.

What am I doing here? This is no place for me. He shook inside. *Does he know I am having terrible memories? Yemoja protect me? If the man figure out I was there the night of Mona's stabbing, he would kill me on the spot. Uncle told me one time that dead man tells no tales.*

The man had a gun, and Roderick had a knife. It would be all over for him in one shot. They had to get out of there. Roderick looked over at his friends with a nervous twitch on his face. "You ready?"

"I am in charge around here, soldier. I ask all the questions," the man said, a swift reprimanded for a wannabe rude boy.

Drawdown said, "Sorry," and pulled on Roderick's shirt for him not to speak anymore.

The man bent down to pick up a big head spliff and his gait confirmed to Roderick that he was the same man who did the stabbing. Every organ in his body felt like they were shuffling around like a deck of cards. His bladder was tightening. Any moment he would wet his pants.

"You see this bad boy here?" The man brandished his gun. "It fixes any rude boy who falls out of line with me. You understand?"

Roderick did not answer.

"I say if you understand!"

"Yes, big man."

"No. Not big man. The man name is Screw Driver. That's right, Screw drives this town. Tell him Jojo."

NO. NO. NO. You stabbed Mona. For all I know she must be dead.

Screw handed Jojo some money. "Give this to Mr. B to finish the engineering on the tune for me. See youtman, I take care of all my soldiers. You can get anything you need, just don't cross me."

"Yes, Screw Driver." Speaking his name made Roderick cringe.

"All right soldiers. Gwaan through. A have a little job for you to settle when you finish the tune."

"No problem, Screw Driver," the boys said with great enthusiasm. Facing Screw Driver, the boys backed up out of his presence with respect, as if he were royalty. Once fully out the door, they turned and walked down the lane.

"We get it! Screw come through for we again." Jojo jumped in the night air.

"Again. Is not the first time?" Roderick inquired. "What kind of job he wants us to settle?" Roderick continued, with a slight tremor in his voice.

No one answered his question. They walked silently into the night to Missa B's studio.

"I guess I am talking to myself. If this is how we are going to make money, I am out." Roderick looked at Jojo, who looked away. Still, there was silence.

I am going to waste that Screw for messing up Mona so badly. Won't say anything to the boys. Just have to get out of their company and go far away.

The inter-school's art competition was coming up and Roderick was spending more time in the art room after school. Every year, children from all over the island came together to show their best work to a host of judges. This was Roderick's first time, and he wanted to win.

"This sculpting of my Mona will be the best in the competition."

Just a few days before the competition, the Jolly Crew walked into the art room. They looked worried.

I wonder if something happened to one of them.

"What's going, Roderick?" Imogene pushed him on the shoulder.

"Nothing. Why all of you look so dreary?" Roderick said, wringing the cloth he was using to clean his work area.

"We are concerned about you, Roderick. You've gone into yourself; you don't have time to hang with us anymore. Remember the Jolly crew? Yes. We same one." Imogene folded her arms.

"I have been working hard on this competition coming up."

"We know that, but you usually find time to play dominos or just talk crap," Curtis said.

"I want to win this competition. I must put her in the museum, my Mona."

Turning to him, Django said, "So what motivated you to do this sculpting?"

"Is a long story."

"I figured it was a long story."

If they only knew the agonizing pain was that I met my Mona's stabber, face-to-face, and that I almost got into a deal with him and my sufferer friend to make money. This is a painful secret.

Curtis pulled up a stool next to Roderick and just stared at him, working.

"Is like you losing your courage," Django said.

"I thought we had something special." Imogene pressed her palm on his shoulder. "You know you can talk to me anytime, even when these two coconut heads are off gallivanting."

"It is not like you to miss our domino sessions," Django said. "Dominos is serious business. We swore we would never break up the special time we share. That's why we came to make sure you get the help you need."

"That's right," Curtis said. "We figure that something is wrong and you are not telling us."

"My mother say, 'Is not everything good to eat, good to talk about.'" Roderick dipped the cloth in the water and smoothed out Mona's left cheek. "I have to get back to work. Not much time before the competition."

"Wish you luck. We will come cheer you on, anyway."

Roderick could tell Django wasn't buying his story. There was more to it.

Imogene put her hands on her hips. "You don't get to keep secrets in this group, mister."

"That's what Django and I learn in Boy Scouts. It is the very reason we encouraged you to join, but you didn't. We stick together. Scouts stick together."

"I might not be a Scout, but I stick with my friends," Roderick said as he stroked the face of the sculpture.

Imogene sighed and turned to the boys. "Let's go. If Roderick has a decision to make, we have to believe his mind is strong enough to do the right thing."

"We help each other when we are in trouble. Remember that," Curtis said and made an about turn while the others followed behind him through the door.

Turning on his stool, Roderick reached for a fudge stick, went back to carving the intricate details of the eyes and lashes, hoping to make it look real. The hair stick with beads in the back of her head was a source of pride. The tactile nature of sculpting became his meditation, a poetic synergy of clay, water, and passion. A chilling feeling ran through his veins. Ever so gently, he cupped the wet clay sculpture in both palms, kissed it; tears welled up in his eyes.

"Sorry Mona. I did not help you that night. The whole thing scared me."

26

Tata Uprising

Flash flood warnings and the skies over Kingston were threatening. The meteorologist reported high tide along the seaboard. Roderick wanted desperately to visit his grandmother, Tata, in Waterhouse before the rains started. Lately, mean people like imps jeering at him in his room haunted his night's rest.

"I really need to go visit grandma. She does not have a clue what I am going through. Everything is spinning out of control." He got up, tried on the shoes that he found in the trunk. He wiggled his toes inside and it felt like some shoey made it just for him. "It fits me now. It fits me. It looks like I grew into it."

Roderick went to see Aunt Hope, who was making a cup of tea in the kitchen area.

"Aunty. I am going to go look for Grandma Tata. I haven't seen her this long time."

"You asking me or you telling me?"

"I am asking you."

She smiled. "Carry Nelton with you. He hasn't seen her in a while."

"He will not want to come with me."

"Or you don't want him to come with you."

"No Aunty. He can come."

"Never mind. Next time. Go on and tell her a say howdy do. Come here. Let me give you something to carry and give her."

Thank goodness she is not stringing that miserable boy onto me. He looked on as his aunty put together a little parcel of things for Tata.

"Here. Take care. When you coming back?"

"Sunday. I have plenty of homework to do."

Is the second time I see my aunty smile with me since the first week I came to Kingston. She must be going to heaven tonight. I can't believe it.

Roderick ran across the street to get on a bus that was approaching. Paying the conductress, he noticed that she only had one good arm, and the other cut off at the elbow where she held the bus ticket holder.

I bet is her wicked husband cut off her hand. She is beautiful. At least she didn't allow it to stop her from making money.

For the duration of the trip, he stared at the conductress from time to time, as she skillfully pulled tickets and collected fares.

Is two months now since the man stab up Mona. I hope she is still alive. What a wicked act. Is man like that police must kill not little sufferer boys like Jojo and me. I can't wait till Christmas comes again to get a break and sell some stone art.

The hand rails by the steps afforded him stability as he got up in the moving bus to get off at the next stop.

"Goodbye, Miss." Roderick smiled at conductress, who nodded and smiled at him. He ran up the street to Tata's house, burst through the front door that was opened to let in fresh air.

"Evening Tata." Roderick rushed into her arms and almost toppled her over in the wheelchair.

"Boy, you growing big now. You nearly bounce me down. Look at you!" She hugged him tighter. Roderick could smell the sweet white powder she dusted all over her ebony body. Her hair was silvery soft and smelled like coconut oil. Tata sipped on a drink of white rum and milk.

"I am glad to see you, Tata. It's a long time since I wanted to come spend time with you but I had little time to spare."

"What you have to do so?"

"You don't know?"

"Know what?"

"Aunt Lillian didn't tell you? Aunt Hope been so hard on me most of the times. I worked every day in the shop up to recently, hardly any schooling. Is just of late I am going regularly. When she is ready, she beat beat me up."

"That girl Hope was always ugly in her ways, but for Lillian not to tell me anything is outrageous."

"She must be forgot, Tata."

"Forgot something like that. Is not so I raised these girls. I raised them to be thoughtful."

"O Tata. Many days I wish Lillian would take me to her house, but she didn't have any space. She said she has to take care of you."

"This is my house. Every brick. Every piece of lumber. I decide who comes and who goes. I will find out why Lillian makes decisions for me. She will hear from me."

"I don't want any trouble, Tata."

"No trouble dear. You are all my offspring. What is mine is yours, too."

"My mother didn't want me. Aunt Hope doesn't love me. I lived on the street for most of the summer holiday, sleeping under bus stops, in the park, cemetery, market, all about Tata."

Tata gasped. "Lord, take the case and give mi di pillow. What you saying to me, child?"

Roderick could see her pupils dilating. She poured some more of the white rum and milk into her glass and became contemplative.

Tata gone into herself. I hope is not me cause it.

"No child of mine ever lived on the street. None of them. Lillian allowed that to happen to you."

"More than once, she said she couldn't keep me."

"Hogwash. You deserve to have a roof over your head, like all of my children. I gave every one of them a start in life, including that ungrateful Hope. That shop she has there; I helped her buy that piece of property so she could build the house and then convert."

"Sorry to make you bring up those things. I didn't mean to upset you."

"Right is right. Lillian lives here for free. Yes, she helps take care of me, but I have other people who help me out, too, so she can live her life." Tata pulled Roderick closer to her breast and wiped the tears swelling in his eyes. "You are a good boy. I am not as strong as I was ten years ago." She reached into her bosom and took out a little thread bag with money—counted coins and gave to Roderick. "Here, you take this and whenever you feel like coming to see me, just get on the bus and come just like you did today. I love you, Roderick."

"I love you, too, Tata." Roderick felt a special love emanating from Tata; a love that he had not experienced since he arrived in Kingston.

"I will talk to Lillian when she comes back. This house is a welcome haven for children all the time. I don't know what got into Lillian to keep me in the dark."

Tata says she likes children in her house. So why Lillian never took me in. Strange.

"You remember Miss Dillon?"

"Yes. That girl was a talented dancer. We used to go to teenage dance party back in the day."

Miss Dillon… dance. O Tata!" Roderick widened his eyes. "I know Miss Dillon likes you very much. She loves to tell me, 'In your grandma's heyday, her house was full of children from all over the neighborhood, coming in and out from morning until night.' She said even her children, too."

"O yes. Dillon knew me from the labor movement in the 1930s. Back then, children had to have manners. I didn't tolerate any rudeness and disobedience from anyone. I hope you are behaving yourself."

"Yes, Tata. But sometimes I get ignorant when Aunty beat beat me up."

"You have a little temper there." She pulled on his left ear.

"A little. Tata, I will not lie to you. That's why I wanted to come see you. Miss Dillon always tells me you give good advice to young people. The other day she made me laugh so hard. She said when her son Josey wanted to name his baby Hibiscus, you remember that, Tata?"

"If I remember. I tell him you don't name your child Hibiscus because the flower is pretty. You name the child pretty if you want to wake up every day and call her: 'Pretty, come here Pretty!' So what kind of advice you want from old Tata? Come sit right here so."

He pulled up a hassock and sat on it.

"Take all the time you want, but I have some young area leaders coming for advice this evening."

Taking a deep breath, he began. "I was thinking. Is a lot of things happen to me of late. Politician killed my friend Lij. It was on the radio. Did you hear about it?"

"I know his father very well. He used to patronize me at my bar in the early days. Awful thing."

"That thing hurt me, you see, Tata. It hurt me. Then just the other day, bad man stab up my friend, Mona. Sometimes I don't know how I feel. Other times, I just want to do bad things. You know, I saw the man that stabbed Mona. I got into a little situation the other day and he was going to give me and my friends money to do a little business."

"Hulo Hulo! Careful, darling. Careful. Sorry about Mona and your other friend. It is very sad and I don't want to lose you."

"But the man that hurt her, he doesn't know that I know he did it."

"Do your other friends know you know it's him?"

"They don't know anything."

"Good. What your right hand knows, don't let your left hand know."

"I used to hear Aunt Hope say that."

"I taught her well. Now, back to you. Just stay away from this man. Tell your friends you will not be part of the business. Finish school and help your grandma's community. If you take money from these types of people, you will owe them for the rest of your life. You may even lose your life. Stay clear. You hear me."

"Yes, Tata. He gave me a ratchet knife."

"Good Lord."

"He said he will tell me what to do with it next time. All I think about day and night is to beat him up bad for what he did to Mona."

Tata covered his mouth. "Steady yourself. Steady yourself. Violence is not the answer. You must first learn how to take care of yourself and then take care of your community and young women like Mona. There is always work to do. Do not allow your mind to be idle, rubbish will pile up in it. Let us pick this up tomorrow. I hear a knocking on the door. Come in, it's open."

Miss Dillon was right, Tata always doing something for the community.

"Good evening, Mother Flowers," came voices loud and soft, squeaky and deep as young people filed into the living room. Roderick set his eyes on everyone who walked in while Mother Flowers gave a nod to her guests, reclined in her wheelchair, her eyes dim from cataracts. She took a sip of old king rum, rubbed her knees, and cleared her throat. There was a hush.

I can't tell if it was the rum, or just her way of calling the meeting to order. Twelve young people I counted, some in school uniforms, some in work clothes, and others just regular people from the neighborhood.

A pleasant breeze came through the front door as everyone settled in. Roderick had a front-row seat.

What a way everyone is orderly. Is true Miss Dillon was telling me that Tata is a superb organizer, a magician. She knew how to keep a cool head when the workers were upset. I really need to hear how she is going to help the young people this evening.

"Talk to me, young leader."

"We are trying to get permission to have our political meetings here every third Friday. We need money to finance a community center and get some jungle gyms, a big stage for concerts, a real park for Waterhouse, Mother Flowers. The politics mashing up our business left and right."

"Politics is everywhere, it is in everything. Look, every one of you here related, you are family. It doesn't matter which party your family joins, you need a park, right?"

"Yes, Mother Flowers."

"How you proposing to make that happen?"

"That is why we came to you, Mother Flowers."

This group is serious. They are not looking to get wicked money. They want to work for it. O my gosh, Jojo could even get to sing on the stage. Roderick's face was relaxing, and he felt at home.

"Listen, young people, sometimes you will lose even your best friend in community work. During the uprising, a lot of my friends and I had a falling out, but I kept working towards the goal. The governor called a state of emergency. Everything locked down. All of Kingston was dark. That's how I remembered the uprising." She took another sip of the king-rum. "It wasn't any hooligans. It was people fighting for what was right."

"You not sending us to fight and kill people, Grandma?"

"Why would I do that? O, this is my grandson. I wanted him to listen in tonight so he can start thinking about what is really important in life. Say hello to the folks, Roderick."

"Hello everybody."

"Hello," came right back like thunder.

"I want you all to think seriously about this project. Why you are doing it? Who you are doing it for and when you want it done? With a clear plan and everybody working together, it will happen."

Roderick noticed that everyone had stopped speaking. They were thinking. Some were writing in notebooks. He thought about what Tata asked.

"We need to answer these questions that Tata is asking us. You can't expect her to come up with the ideas for us."

Did I just say us?

"You are right, Roderick," Tata said. Talking cannot build this park. You have to do like we did in the old days, when the community church had to be built. Everybody came together with bricks, mortar, steel and their two hands. That is what we need to put down in those notebooks you all writing in. Volunteer. Delegate. Build. In no time, you have a park for the children.

This is expert advice. Sounds better than that music thing. It can help people. Tata set a great example for all of us. "What you saying, Tata, is that everyone here has some purpose. We all can help out," Roderick said as he wrote in his notebook.

"I leave that up to you to figure out." So what is your next move, young leader?"

"We are putting together a proposal for the different government ministers responsible for land, education, recreation and those things," the spokesman stated, as he took his thumb and clicked his pen a few times.

"Good start. So what you want from me?"

"We know you know everybody, all the movers and shakers."

"If I laugh a drop out of mi wheelchair! The movers and shakers I know can hardly shake these days. Them bones tired. You need to reach out to the younger generation, young men like my grandson. He has a good brain in his head."

How grandma just making mi head swell up so!

The meeting was going well until two men walked in. One was tall with big shoulders and wore a pin-striped suit and black and white shoes. His hair was black and cut close to his scalp. The other was short and wore shiny-narrow foot pants, crepe sole shoes and a baseball cap. He had shifty eyes.

"Good night, Corporal Higginbottom here," the tall man said.

"Night O." Mother Flowers said. She didn't look up but stirred the brew in her glass with her finger.

"This is my partner, Bull."

"Like Bulldog? Who the hell name them pickney, Bull? What is your real name, boy?"

"Bull, and them call me Bulldog, mam."

"Get the backside out of my house until your mother can give you a better name! Why she gives you a dog name? If she was my daughter, I would clobber her tonight, she wet-up herself."

There was not a dry eye in the room. Everyone laughed so hard, tears rolled like the Rio Cobre swelling up over Flat Bridge. Roderick could see the blood coming to the surface of Bulldog's face. His forehead was tight. The other man stood erect.

It look like him is the Bulldog in the area. Well, Grandma is not afraid of any Bulldog. I am getting a weird feeling about these two. Roderick covered his mouth as if to keep his thoughts in.

Everybody just got quiet.

"We can talk now, Mother Flowers," the big guy said.

"Go ahead. Make it quick."

"We just came to say that we are all for building the park for the children, but these young people going about it in the wrong way."

Higginbottom. Why does that name sound familiar to me? Roderick searched his head. The same weird feeling hit him in the stomach again.

It looks like Grandma knows they are not up to any good. A ruckus in her house will never happen. Rumor had it she kept a Smith and Wesson from her days working in the bar downtown. She knows how to use it.

"The children have a good plan, so you better listen and work with them. We all need the park. All a we hungry so we better get along."

Higginbottom weighed in. "We need to bulldoze the abandoned shacks that harbor rats and stray cats. All that land can expand the scheme."

Grandma Tata sat up straight, put her glass down. "Is not shack, man. That is poor people's homes. Why you want to bulldoze them? You have any place to put the people?"

"You are the same people," said Higginbottom, "who talking about progress and you don't realize that you have to make room for progress."

"Which people are you talking about? That is what's wrong with this two-party system—each side opposing simply because they can. Listen to me and listen good. If you want anything done, forget this two-party, tribal business. We get nothing done fighting against each other. You want the playground and the center or not? Well, cut out this foolishness and get to work. Next time, better come with a good plan in place. I adjourn this meeting."

A foreboding thunder roared African jungle fierce.

"Young people, hurry and get home to your families before the rain comes down hard. You know how that water moves fast on these roads and the gully-bank can overflow in no time. Be safe and tell everyone I say howdy-do."

Everyone thanked Mother Flowers, said goodbye and hurried out.

"Close the curtain there, Roderick," Tata directed him as she unlatched the clasps of her wheelchair. "Rain set up. Look like the rain is going to catch Lillian out there."

"I hope she all right, Tata. What a meeting tonight. I feel they are going to get things done."

"They are smart. Just those two jokers. I know about them. Create a lot of problems in the area. I hear they burn down people's houses and those things. I don't want them in my house again."

"I have a funny feeling I buck up the big one before. Something about him makes me feel funny. Anyway, good night, Tata."

"Go wash up. Some crackers on the kitchen counter. Put a piece of cheese and jam on it and get some lemonade out of the fridge. You prefer some Horlicks?"

"Horlicks? Me like Horlicks bad bad. Before a wash up, a have something to show you, Tata." He took out the mystery photograph and showed it to her. "You know these people in the picture?"

"Boy, my eyes are not too good in the night but I will try. This is an old one." She took the picture and looked closely. She smiled and smiled. Shook her head. Smiled some more.

"Why are you smiling so much?"

"That John. That John. So handsome. He was something else. Nice fellow, but him mash up a lot of things."

"What him mash up, Tata?"

"This happened long before you were born. He came between them two girls, your mother and your Aunt Hope."

"Is he related to me?"

"Why you ask. You don't remember seeing him at all. Your mother didn't tell you?" Grandma Tata returned the photograph to him.

"Tell me what, Grandma."

"John is your father. That's what he is to you, your father. When you were little, he had to go back to America to serve in the Navy."

"I knew it. I knew it." Roderick threw the picture in the air. Put his hands on his head. He walked around in circles. "Why didn't he take me to America? Why?"

"Your mother would not let him take you after he asked your Aunt Hope to marry him."

"Married? That's why Aunty does not like me. Why mama sent me to her in the first place?"

"Your guess is as good as mine. Do not worry your little head."

"I don't know if I would be better off with him in America or with mama after this." Sobbing, he pushed his hands inside his shirt, hugged himself, and then shivered vigorously.

"But I suffered at Aunt Hope. You think he would have made me suffer so?"

"Come to me, sweet child," she said and wiped his tears. "Better must come one day. Get your Horlicks."

"I don't want anything to eat."

"Listen boy, gas will take up your stomach. You must eat something. Come help me fix it for you."

"Thank you, Tata. I don't feel like eating. I am going to sit over here and listen to the rain falling and write in my book. Jojo's Grandma Myrtle told me that when I want to feel better, I must write."

"All right then. Don't stay up too late. I am getting tired now."

"Goodnight, Tata."

Roderick walked to the window, looked out at the rain falling on the vegetable garden. The backyard was awash with the shimmery moonlight while the chickens cuddled under the shed. There was so much to process tonight and Roderick held it together. No more in the darkness of secrets and lies. He imagined what his life would have been like if his father and mother were still together. Nothing was more comforting than being with Tata. He sat on a chair, took out his notebook, and wrote.

> I feel so much better now that I talked to Grandma Tata. I am just going to concentrate on school. As for all those wicked people I met, the one Screw, the police will take care of him for me. The wicked politicians who killed my friend Lij, police will fix them for me, too. One day, I will help to make this

evil go away. One day, I will remember Lij and Mona with my art. The young people and I who came here tonight will build that park for the children. One day."

Roderick closed the book, went to the kitchen and made himself a mug of Horlicks. Then he took a nice long shower and went into the guest room. Putting on his pajamas, he reminisced about the day, the wisdom of his Tata, and the new people he met. Roderick crawled under the sheet and covered his head. He could hear Tata snoring in the other room. She was out like a lightbulb.

27

Blackbirds Nine Night

Dear Chloe:

Death. What a wicked something. It is all around me. Nothing, nobody in this whole wide world taught me about death. Nobody. O Chloe, I forget was to ask how you are doing? I hope you are fine. I am fine, just feel sad a lot today. As Grandma Tata would say, "I am between a wheel and a washer. I don't feel equal today." That's why I decide to write you.

I am sitting on her veranda next to a big column and some hibiscus hedging. Nobody can see me, but I can see everybody. The house is on a quiet street. It's three weeks now I am over here since she take sick. Last week she just took down worse. Now she is gone. She went with all her love. Right in the middle of the Christmas holiday. Only old Suraj still here who loves me. O Chloe, nothing good don't leave in Olympic Gardens for me, nothing, no one. Lij gone. Now Grandma Tata is gone. Poor Mona, she got so mashed up that she must be gone, too. I dream all the while that they come back. I never know if they did just gone for a little bit. Nobody don't tell me nothing.

Noone asks me how I feel. My heart can't take it anymore. It looks like I can't stop dead from taking away the people them that love me. Is like dead spirit peepi on Olympic Gardens. Mi heart can't take it.

Nine days since Tata closed her eyes. The ice truck just drop off plenty blocks of ice for her send-off party tonight. Miss Dillon told me that back in the day, Tata used to throw the best parties. I can see Tata's friends and her family coming in and out of the gate. Some of my cousins that I have never met before from England, Canada, America, all over the place moving through here. Their talking sounds nice, you see, foreign accent and all. Some of them bringing in suitcases. Looks like they are going to sleep here tonight.

Please don't correct my grammar, Chloe. This is the best way to tell yu how a feel.

Tata was really special. Look all these people who come to remember her tonight. She is like a Governor General. My Grandma, Tabitha Louise Heaven-Flowers, born on 21 November 1890 in the parish of Westmoreland. She died in her comfortable bed, my favorite bed with big pillows and teddy bears, the Bible on the nightstand, right here on St. Kitts Road in Waterhouse, 7 December 1970. She just turned eighty years old last month. My granny, my Tata.

This letter is going on for too long. I have to go help out inside and take a little nap before the place fills up with people. Maybe tonight, I will get to see Tata's spirit come through the door before her funeral tomorrow. O Chloe. I would be so happy.

One more thing. I hope you sitting down when you are reading this part. Guess what? Guess what? The sailor man in the picture? Yes. Him same one. Well, Tata told me just before she died, he is my father. Yes. John B. Brissett, Mr. JBB. Is my father. I don't know if he is dead or alive, though. That explains why Aunt Hope called me John two times. She so full up with him in her heart.

Write and tell me how you like your new bicycle. I can't wait to see you so I can get a ride off it. Miss you, Chloe

Goodman. Roderick misses you very much. I wish you were here. Just tired of crying. God knows.

Your friend,

Roderick

Roderick wrote his thoughts in his book. Closed it. "Maybe one day I will get to mail this letter to Chloe. I feel better." Roderick sensed that this was no ordinary dead-yard. He could feel a ruffling in his chest, a kind of happiness as everyone pulled together to cook, mix drinks and set up a long table for the feast that would start at midnight. Walking over to Ellen, he handed her records so she could play Tata's favorites on the old record changer: Count Basie, Duke Ellington, Sam Cooke, Elvis Presley, Marvin Gaye, Brook Benton, Percy Sledge. Domino competition and Ludo games were loud. Roderick could hear his mother, Mara'Belle and Hope talking loudly amidst the sizzling of fish frying, and pots and pans clanging. It was getting hot and Roderick turned to Miss Ellen. "Can I bring you something to drink?"

"Yes. Bring me a glass of sorrel."

"All right, I soon come," he said and walked toward the kitchen. It was really hot in the kitchen, yet Roderick felt an abnormal chill rush deep under his skin. Lillian was mixing the rum punch and he could smell the sharp edge of the brew.

What makes them stop talk soon as I come in the kitchen? Eh.

"May I get a glass a sorrel for Miss Ellen, please?"

No one responded. Mara'Belle just picked up a glass, put ice into it and reached for the sorrel. Not a word. The tension stuck to the kitchen cupboards like a hundred croaking lizards until Hope broke the silence. She turned to Mara'Belle, looked her dead in the eyes.

"Tell me something, Mara'Belle, why you never write me since you make strange man drop off Roderick at my doorstep?" Hope said with her hands akimbo.

"Is not time for that now, Hopie. It is a long, long story."

Long story. Mi love story. Take time pour the sorrel Aunty, I want to hear everything. Roderick listened to every word.

"Longer than the letter you sent with him. I guess each page was for each of the years."

"You know that life was difficult after his father left." Father? What father?

Roderick's ears perked up, and he was no longer in a hurry to get the sorrel. *Let me hear her side now about my father. I was waiting for the right time to let them know I know.*

"I couldn't care less why his father left. You got married and had two more pickney. The new man could well father the boy."

"Yes. But it is different when it is not your own child."

"What you mean. Cupidon couldn't take care of Roderick, too?"

Go on, tell me more, mama.

"It's not that easy, Hopie. I wasn't working for a long time."

"You leave your good good work at the hotel say you find religion. Look, Mama still carried on with all of us after Papa died."

"Those were different times, Hopie, and you know it."

"Different times, my foot."

"Yes, different times. John left me and Roderick with nothing."

John. She admits is John him name. Grandma told me the truth. Now me hearing it from them. Kiss mi neck. He looked on as Mara'Belle's hands trembled around the glass of ice.

"What is fi yuh can't un-fi yuh. If he was yours, he would have stayed with you and Roderick," Hope said, and took a sip of her drink.

"What you mean by that? I think you bury that old hatchet long time."

"How me must bury it when me have to look in the boy's face morning, noon, and night? For all I know, you sent this boy to torment my soul. John was never in love with you from the very beginning. He was in love with me. You couldn't keep your filthy paws off him and your dress at your ankles."

Mama's chest a go up and down, up and down like she was going burst open. Please don't throw the glass hit Aunty. Please. Is true. Is really true. Like this John mash up them something. Roderick gulped down every word.

Hope and Mara'Belle just gave into their long, rotting feelings. Somewhere in Hope's mind, she wanted him to hear this. His mother shook her head and gestured for Hope to stop talking.

"Not now, sis."

"Oh yes, Mara'Belle, this is just as good a time as any."

"Have some reverence for the dead. We are all grieving."

"Mama never stopped you from your loose ways. She always made you do what you wanted to do, anyway. She knew about John and me. She liked him for you because she never stopped you from fooling around with him behind my back."

Story come to bump, Chloe. Puppa Jeezas.

"Not now, Hopie…not now, please," Mara'Belle pleaded.

"Oh yes. Now! What happen—you don't want your husband to hear because you tricked him into believing you are a respectable lady? I should have sent Roderick back to you long ago. I am always sorry for you when you are in distress—songbird. It is the good Lord in me that makes me keep him this long."

"Don't make I laugh in here tonight," Lillian mocked without looking at them.

All this time, Aunt Lillian just kept her mouth shut. There she goes, posing for the slam. She is good at it. It's coming but she not even looking at them.

"The ancestral spirits know I have words for both Mara'Belle and Hope, more caustic than boric acid. Them two woman here have more secrets than Rahab but are unwilling to atone out of spite. Come Roderick," Lillian said and edged him out of the way.

Hope lunged at Mara'Belle and punched her in the face. Lillian turned and grabbed Hope and pushed her against the wall. The women wrestled.

Roderick called out, "Stop it—stop it!" He looked at his mother and Aunt Hope.

"What a mess." Roderick shook his head at Lillian, incredulously, who resumed squeezing the lime into the bowl of rum punch as if nothing happened.

"Want something, Roderick?"

"Beg you take the glass of ice from mama and pour some sorrel for Aunt Ellen. Please give me a Coca Cola, Aunt Lillian."

"I will get it for you." She reached into the icebox, handed him the soda and poured the sorrel. "Go on back outside."

Roderick stood there in wonder for a moment. Then he broke the silence. "You all right Mama?"

"Yes, son."

"Yes, son, my big toe," Hope yelled.

"Yes, is her son," Lillian griped.

"Nobody not talking to you, Miss Goodie-Goodie."

"You really don't want to start with me, Hope Flowers. You have more skeletons in your closet than the pharaohs had mummies."

"Shut your damn mouth, Lillian. You are always acting like you are Saint Avila. After you are not better than anybody."

"This is too much mixup-mixup." Turning around to leave, Roderick stumbled into Ellen.

"Tabitha Flowers' girls! Have you no shame or respect for the dead? There is a child in your midst and the house is filling up with people. Control yourself. Come with me Roderick." She reached for his hand and the glass of sorrel.

"This is family business." Hope pointed menacingly at Ellen.

"She does more for this family than any Flowers so kiss off you dirty John Crow." Lillian rolled her eyes and poured herself a drink. You could hear a pin drop.

"My heart is full right now," Mara'Belle choked on her words. "When this is all over, I am taking my son back with me."

"Over my dead body," Hope retorted.

Roderick pulled away from Ellen. "You never wanted me, Aunt Hope. You treated me like a dog. I scrubbed your shop. Swept your yard. Washed the boy's clothes. You barely wanted to send me to school. I had to fight and fight to stay in school."

Mara'Belle squeezed her hands over her mouth. "You mean that is how you treated my son, Hopie?"

"Your son," Roderick said. Eyeing everyone in the kitchen, he heaved and spoke with a voice he never heard before, deep and stern. "You gave me away to this wicked woman. I suffered. I bawled day and night. Where were you? What were you, Mama? You never even wrote to me. You kept my sister and brother from me. Nobody wanted me. What is this now? I am no one's Christmas present. Don't want any of you. I want to be free from all of you. Come to think of it, I would be better off putting up a zinc house on the gully-bank like Jojo them because I know how to wash, cook, clean, go to school and take care of myself." His face washed with sweat, but there were no tears. His breathing was swift, like he was pumping air in a bicycle tire.

"Don't talk like that; I am here for you now."
Mara'Belle moved towards Roderick to hug him but he
stiffened his body.

"You. Won't. Have. To. Rescue. Me. Where were you
when I had to walk on the hot road without shoes?
Sometimes rain soaked me because I didn't have bus fare.
Police could have killed me when I slept out in the elements.
Eeeee. Where were you when Aunt Hope brutalized me? I
only want one thing. One thing. To take scholarship and earn
a free place to high school. When I am done, the whole of
you can forget about me. Sorry I came into this world to
bother all of you. Sorry."

Slamming the bottle of soda on the kitchen counter,
he backed into the doorway. The silence was deafening from
where Roderick stood. No one said another word until Ellen
spoke.

"Don't be sorry. You are here for a purpose."

"Why Tata had to go? See heaven, why it wasn't me
gone so all you wouldn't have to suffer to keep me? "

"Listen everybody," Ellen said, touching him gently
on his shoulder. He rejected her touch. "This is hurting the
child. Clean up your mess, but not in his presence. The guests
are waiting."

One by one, the sisters agonizingly resumed their
duties to serve the many guests who came to celebrate their
mother. The crowd was getting feet deep and so Ellen and
Lillian moved the furniture closer to the walls and created a
clear path from the front porch to the backyard. The music
was loud, and some folks played drums, knocked old Dutch
pot covers like cymbals, scraped graters, anything they could
find to make music and sing Dinki Mini songs.

"I don't know how they can have fun with all their evil." Roderick was astonished "Tata would not put up with their out-of-orderness."

Glancing across the room, he saw his mother sitting alone with her hands cupping her cheeks. *She looks sad like me, but I am not sorry for her. How can she stomach herself after she gave me away? I really need to get an answer from her how. She needs to tell me about my father.* With firm countenance, he got up from his chair, walked over to where his mother, Mara'Belle, was sitting. Resting his hand on her thigh, he looked in her eyes; she put her palm on the back of his hand.

"Mama, you all right?"

"After all this, I don't know what to tell you, son."

"Tell me. Why you sent me away?"

"Is a long story. The music is so loud, I have to scream so you can hear."

"Tell me anyway. I can hear you well."

"I made a big mistake. I can see that now."

"What mistake did you make?"

"I was feeling a lot of shame."

"Shame for what? Me?"

"How my life turned out. I didn't feel like I knew how to love you the way a mother should."

"Is that why you gave me away? You felt shame to love me. I don't understand. This one baffles me. I remember it was me and you alone for a long time before Esther was born. We used to do fun things. Did you stop loving me when Esther born?"

"Not that easy to explain. I don't know. Sometimes adults don't think things through."

Rubbing his palms together, biting his bottom lip, he pulled his shoulders to his ears. "Mama. Just tell me the truth. What happened between you and my father?"

"It's a long story."

"You feel shame because of my father, too? Grandma Tata told me about him before she died. I want to hear your side of the story."

"She told you?"

"Yes. So where is my real father? Is he dead?"

"Your father lives in America."

"America? North or South?"

Mara'Belle smiled. "You keeping up with your geography, I see."

"Yes, mama. I study with my friend Chloe. I love school. It is my peaceful place on this earth. So tell me, North or South?"

"North America."

"Is my father the one they call 'Captain,' too?"

"Yes. They call most of the sailors that used to come through town captain."

"I was going through an old trunk and found a lot of clothes, postcards and letters he signed, 'JBB.'"

"Letters?"

"Yes. Letters he wrote to Aunt Hope."

"O God no!" She tried to cover his mouth so no one would hear, but he brushed her hand away.

"Yes. He signs his name, JBB. What that stands for?"

"John B. Brissett."

"Brissett like me?"

"Yes. He is your father. Sorry you had to find out this way. You were small when he left."

"It is all right now. Do you know how I can find him?"

"I am not so sure anymore. He used to write and then he stopped. I kept some old letters. I brought them for you."

Old letters. I guess he loves to write. Let's see if he signed these JBB like the ones he wrote to Aunt Hope? "Why you never post them to me?"

"Foolish. I was foolish, son. I just didn't want to cause any confusion."

"Confusion? My whole life is confusion."

Mara'Belle handed him a little straw bag. "Don't open it out here until you are ready to go inside to bed."

"Why I shouldn't open it?"

"I just don't want anybody to see what is in there. Some things you have to learn to keep to yourself."

"We don't have secrets between us. You have only lied to me all evening. I don't want to hear anymore."

From the corner of the room, he heard the singing grow louder as folks came in and out of the gathering to celebrate and pay their respect. There was no shortage of white rum and liquor of all sorts, or mannish water soup. All and sundry types of roasted meats: fish, beef, pork, duck, chicken. The house smelled like a well-fortified restaurant. No one went hungry. The pair stopped speaking for a while and Roderick started nodding his head back and forth.

"It's getting late. Time to get some shuteye, son. I think you should come back to the country with me."

"Country?"

"Yes. You can get into a good primary school and take the scholarship next year."

Roderick's ears got hot. He could feel his blood rushing to his head, he flared his nostrils. The music stopped.

"I. AM. NOT. GOING. TO. NO. COUNTRY."

Roderick sensed all eyes looking at him, screaming at his mother. He sprung up from the chair. "Back? Not me. Forward. That's me, Mama. Forward."

"You will do what I say, and that is final. There is no need for you to stay here and suffer."

"I can't suffer more than I suffered already."

"You don't have a choice in this matter. When I was a child, whatever my mother said I should do, I had to do it. You don't get to dictate your terms here."

"You are right. Back then, I had no choice."

"Go to my room, now!"

"Your room!"

Why does she want me to sleep in her room? After I don't know her.

"I sleep in the room with Miss Ellen. Goodnight, Miss Mara." Roderick reached for the little bag she gave him. He took in the folks staring at him, and Mara'Belle with her hand akimbo, lost.

"You are really John Brissett's son."

"John Brissett's son! I heard that before."

The music started up again to loud chatter while Roderick made his way to the small room where Ellen had stored her overnight bag. He slammed the door, placed the bag on a small vanity, and sat on the stool. The music was now a dull hum and although he felt sleepy, his head hurt a little. Roderick opened the parcel his mother brought for him.

"Country? She wants to take me back to the country. Only six more months and I will finish primary school."

Some chew sticks tumbled out the bag onto his lap. There were two merinos, cloth bag with exercise books, Bible, photographs of Esther and Shadrach.

"Them grow big eee. Why Miss Mara never let me grow with them? Look Brown Dog, la la, even him grow big too."

Also inside the bag was a little bundle of small envelopes. He zeroed in with laser eyeballs. "Noooo. Is the same way the letter them me find in the trunk looked with the string around it." Pulling them apart, he peered to see the date on one of them: August 11, 1962. Roderick opened it. His face flushed, and he felt hot again, then the goose pimples ran down his spine and along his arms.

"I can't believe this is happening to me tonight."

My beloved Rodrigo,

You should be reading well by now. There is no need for me to write little notes at the bottom of your mother's letters for her to read to you. I know how you loved to read. It was our favorite time together. I miss going down by the beach with you on Sunday mornings to eat fried sprat fish and dukunu with chocolate tea. I remember the first time I threw you in the water and you thought you were drowning. Missing my time with you and hope to see you soon. Please write and tell me all the fun things you are doing.
Love always,
Dad.

"Dad. I have a dad, too."

The door opened, he looked up. Ellen entered. The music barged in with her and faded as quickly as she closed the door. He studied her face.

"Why are you not sleeping yet?"

"Surprised to see me in here?"

"Yes, and no? I am happy you are here. What are you reading there?"

"My mother brought me some letters that my father wrote me from North America."

"Really? That's very nice. So you have been reading them."

"Yes. Aunty, it bothers my head why my mother never mailed them to me. All this time, I thought I didn't have a real father, one who cared. Look here, Aunty, my father always wanted me. Why didn't my mother send me to live with him in North America? Why did she send me to Aunt Hope?"

"That's a question only Mara'Belle can answer."

"I am not asking her any more questions. She never really answered them. Miss Ellen, she failed the exam. She failed."

"You have been through a lot this evening. Don't think about it too much. Try to get some sleep. We have a long day tomorrow at the burial."

Bowing his head in his right hand, Roderick took a deep breath, swayed his head slowly from side to side. "I just don't understand, Aunty. I have to fix this myself."

"Shhhhh. Don't let duppy get your last word."

"You think Tata turn duppy yet, Miss Ellen? I hope she frightens all of them tonight."

28

When Ashes Cold

The rain came down clear as crystal, unsettling the rich brown earth, making slushy puddles of mud around his ankles, devouring his new dress shoes. Roderick was claustrophobic under a wide black nylon umbrella he shared with Miss Ellen, fighting gusts of wind and rain at the edge of Tata's grave.

"Aunt Ellen says this is the last time I am going to see you, Grandma Tata, once you go down into the ground. All I want to do today is to say goodbye to my Tata. You are my number one beautiful somebody in my life. Now you are gone. You say I am not too young to get involved in community development. Well, Tata, from today, I am going to develop me first."

"I am the resurrection, and the life: he that believeth in me, though he were dead, yet shall he live," came the comforting voice of Reverend McBath.

"Resurrect like Jesus, Miss Ellen?"

"Shhh."

"Well, I want to see her face when she comes back to life."

"Shhh. Listen."

Reverend continued: "Sleep on beloved Sister Flowers. Sleep and take your rest."

Roderick saw Mara'Belle's knees buckle, and she dropped to the ground with her face in the mud, screaming,

"Whoiiiiiiiiiieeeeee!"

Roderick stooped in the rain to help his mother, but Hope yanked him up by his wet shirt.

"She messed up so many people's lives; she may as well bury her damn self in the mud. Leave her. She needs to bawl."

The venomous sting shot from Hope's mouth as she raised her hand to heaven, "Praise the Lord!"

"Why Aunty? Why?" He yanked his body away from her, slipping and sliding in the mud. Roderick shook his head. *What a cruel woman.*

A few of the brethren from Mama Flower's church pulled Mara'Belle from the mud that covered the front of her dress. Roderick could not imagine a brawl like this at his beloved grandma's funeral.

"Ashes to ashes. Dust to dust. Until we meet again on the banks of the glorious river, Miss Flowers." Reverend McBath closed the prayer book.

Tears rolled down Roderick's cheeks. He clutched onto Ellen, shaking.

"Tata gone. Tata gone fi true."

On his way home in the car, Roderick could cut the silence in two with a machete—it was so thick. No one spoke. In the muteness, he relived moments of his grandma's funeral inside the big Anglican Church at the foot of Tower Hill Road. Ellen and Lillian outfitted two rows of mahogany benches from the altar to just about two feet from the front entrance. They covered the single aisle in the center with a scarlet rug. Stained glass windows on both walls with the praying hands in the center interceded for poor people. Jesus, with his arms spread opened on the cross on the back wall behind the pulpit–relived his sufferings every Sunday and today was no exception. Mother Flowers' coffin took center-stage, draped with a velvet white covering with rainbow colors of beautiful flowers from God's garden. It was as if the entire town packed the church. Standing room only. Well-wishers on the outside peered through the doors and windows, listening and singing along. All of Olympic Gardens came to Mama Flowers's funeral, well, so it seemed. Folks from all walks of life gathered. They all knew Mama Flowers' love. No wonder Roderick smiled so much at the magnitude of the crowd and the ceremony. This was unlike anything he had ever experienced.

Mara'Belle, slated to sing her mother's favorite hymn by Frances Jane "Fanny" Crosby, "When Jesus Comes to Reward His Servants," but the songbird was too fragile to hold a note except to weep. She walked slowly towards the casket, often drifting to the right as if she downed a bottle of Ginger Wine. Every move she made revealed her curves in her black laced hobble dress that flared at the knees. Sheer stockings with a seam that ran up the back of her long thighs, accentuated the muscles from climbing many a country hill. Her red stiletto heeled peep-toe shoes, black laced gloves and a black pillbox hat with delicate feathers and netting veil made her the classic mourner.

I never see Miss Mara like this before. She looks pretty in her black dress. She can't stop crying. Poor Miss Mara, her voice shaky.

"Mama. Mama. I don't want to be selfish, but why you leave us now? You came on this earth to do good and you did a fine job being good to everybody. When I was a little girl, you used to make Jackass corn cookie and you would make fun of me because it was so tough to bite and chew. I still have trouble with the Jackass corn. You taught me how to share, how to be the best Mara'Belle that I could be. You taught me who I was, that confident girl looking back at me in the vanity mirror. I tried to pass it on to my daughter. O mama. So many people came to say goodbye to you today. Everybody is here. The children from Perennial School sang the "Ave Maria" beautifully. They came because you treated them well. I did not treat my son Roderick like you treated them. I just didn't know how. So much I wanted to tell you, but I was afraid that you were so ashamed of me. Please forgive me, mama. Forgive me. But I am married now; serving the Lord, baptized in the Seventh Day Baptist Church. I know God forgives sins, but I know if you ask Him for me, he will listen to you."

A blabbering delivery truck horn jolted Roderick from this memory.

"O my, she is so sad!" He raised his eyebrows, looked over at his two aunts and Miss Ellen. Still, no one spoke. Roderick closed his eyes as the car cruised along Penwood Road. He had a sense of where he was and so he relaxed.

The mood was somber. Roderick preferred a soda from the cooler while Lillian served hot soup to the immediate family who gathered. About fifteen minutes later, Mara'Belle, having gained her composure, emerged from Tata's room in red pedal pusher pants, peasant-style white cotton blouse and leather slippers. She patted Roderick on his head and sat across from him on a hassock covered with embroidered linen. It was an awkward moment as mother and son did not share a word. He knew the will was to be read by Mr. Gladstone Waldemar, the son of one of Mother Flowers' customers of many years, a young man who grew up in her hands. Roderick listened attentively to the young barrister.

"As you all know, your mother and grandmother, Tabitha Louise "Tata" Heaven Flowers, was of sound mind up until her passing. She leaves the house here at St. Kitts Road to Lillian, her wedding band to Flora, her fine dining cutlery to Clofield, the five acres of land in Ocho Rios to Roderick, her Bible, and one hundred dollars for Hope and her boys.

"WHAT? Grandma Tata left Five acres of land for me in Ocho Rios? She gave me land. A boy without a home. I can build my own house someday. I will get Uncle to farm the land so I can make money to continue my education."

Lillian jumped up really fast. "What a wicked woman. How could she give this child five acres of land? What got into her?"

"Yes. That's the only thing I can agree with you on," Hope said, shaking her head in amazement. "Mr. Waldemar, are you reading that right, sir?"

"Yes. He points to it. It is right here."

"This boy did not earn it." Lillian twisted her hands and bit down on her lips. "I am going for a walk. This is making me sick."

How Aunt Lillian just change coat so? She was really upset. I thought she loved me. She was mad at me. Mad with Tata. This is sickening. "Tata told me she gave all of you a start in life. Now, she is giving me a start in life and you are upset about that. What a selfish lot you all are." Roderick clasped praying hands upon his lips, looked up to the ceiling, "You out there. Yes. You."

"Quiet!" Lillian shrieked. "This is so unfair."

"No. Let him deal with his feelings," said Mr.
Waldemar, who continued to read the will. "Twin girls,
Princess and Sarah, will get fifty percent of the insurance
money and share that equally with each other and the other
fifty percent to be shared equally among the other siblings;
and a gold pendant from Captain John Brissett to Felix."

There was a hush after the reading of the will.

"Captain John Brissett. Felix," Roderick turned to
Mr. Waldemar: "If my father is John Brissett, then why didn't
he leave the pendant for me? Why, Felix?"

Dead silence again, and then Lillian spoke. "Explain
to the young man, Hope. Explain to him, Lillian said."

Hope started a tremulous tap on the floor with her
foot. "Roderick Brissett. John Brissett's son. I don't know
where to start."

"Just start. You know the story." Lillian knocked on
her glass.

"Sorry. Sorry for all the pain I put you through. But
it's your mother who came between me and Felix's father.
She went and got you."

Mara'Belle sprung up. "Tell the truth, Hope. Tell the
truth. He was mine to begin with. It was you who butt in.
You were there when it started. Go find the real father for
your son. John is not his father and you know it. You were
always trying to make me look bad. You hated school. All you
wanted to do was chase after the sailor men. Mama did
everything to get you to stay in school. That's why you think
Roderick didn't deserve school."

"That is a lot of hogwash you've practiced over the
years, just waiting for this moment." Hope got up in

Mara'Belle's face. "Tell the boy you and I were doing the same bad things. Tell him."

"Stop it!" Ellen interrupted the quarrel. She stood up, threw her scarf over her shoulder. "We can't do this in front of the children. They are already confused and hurting. This is only salting their wounds."

Roderick stood up, folded his arms, leaned on the wall and looked into every face in the room.

"So Mama, you sent me away. Aunt Hope, you sent Felix away. The two of you never wanted your boy children. Why you didn't send us to our father in America? I am done with all of you."

"Listen here, Roderick," Hope said after a puff on her cigarette. "I don't pretend to be perfect like your mother. I loved your father but couldn't bring myself to tell you about him. You found all you could in that trunk. Although you were wrong to nose around in my business, it was as much your business, too. I am not sorry I took you into my house. Only sorry things turned out so bad. At least you are in school now. You can stay with me until something better comes up and you finish your schooling." She took two puffs, dusted the ashes on a saucer.

"You didn't need to offer to keep me. Although it is going to take me longer to get to school on the bus, I am going to pack my things and go live with Miss Ellen tomorrow."

"I like how you fix up around the back room. It is really pretty. You can stay there as long as you want. The little garden around the side, you know by now it meant so much to me and your father. That's over with now. I want to see my Maker one of these days. Man means nothing to me anymore."

"You mean to tell me you knew I fixed up the room and the garden all this time, Aunty?"

"Yes. I wanted you to enjoy something that I couldn't give to you."

"Enjoy, Aunty? Me? I am really surprised to hear this now. Miss Daphne and her little girl can stay in that room. I don't know what you are going to tell your Maker and Tata on that day."

"Don't worry about that. Me and my Maker have that sorted out a long time ago. I am not sure about Tata, as you can see she left me and my other boys almost nothing. She is still bitter, even in her grave. I don't know about her resurrection."

"Don't say that, Aunty. Tata is coming back. She was a good woman. My grandmother is coming back for me." Looking over his shoulder, he could see Mr. Waldemar packing his briefcase.

"Well, folks, my work is done. If you need my help with any legal matters, here is my number." He placed his business card on the center table. "Little man, everything is going to be all right. You have a good head on your shoulders. You are so smart. Be strong."

"Smart. You hear that. I am smart."

"Are you feeling all right, Roderick?" Miss Ellen rubbed his hand.

"Not too all right. Everything I am hearing now gives me a little more pain in my belly."

"Are you hungry?"

"No, it just started hurting when I was coming from the cemetery."

"Let me get you something to eat. You don't want gas to fill up your stomach. It will hurt more."

"Thank you, Miss Ellen."

Hearing Mara'Belle take an audible deep breath, Roderick closed his eyes.

Miss Mara couldn't even offer me something to eat. Miss Ellen had to do it. I don't know. I don't know about my mother. She is a real stranger to me.

He took the bully beef sandwich Miss Ellen made for him, ate it and made a robust belch.

"I told you it was gas."

"You right, Miss Ellen." He hugged her tiny waist and kissed her face.

"Grandma gone, Miss Ellen. She gone."

"We don't come here to stay forever, dear. Grandma lived a noble life. Everyone loved her."

Counting on his fingers, he said, "Grandma and Lij. It is like Mona is dead, too. She will never be the same. Only you in here love me. Who takes care of little boys' hearts like mine? Tell me who, Miss Ellen?"

"That is a tough question. All I know is that I will be here for you whenever you need me."

"I don't even know how to reach your yard. I walked miles and miles to find you, but couldn't find you."

"You did that? When?"

"The other day when I couldn't take it anymore. I wanted to come tell you what I was going through."

"I will write my address and my two phone numbers. This way, you will have it all the time. You are coming with me tomorrow. Yes?"

"That is what I said and meant every word. I don't have a mother. She and her sister never cared much about me. I don't believe a word they said today."

"Don't talk like that. I know you are sad right now, but it's not the time to be rude to adults."

"I am not ruuding. I don't know how I am still alive."

"You have a strong mind. Did you hear what Mr. Waldemar said? You will live until you are as old as Miss Tata."

He smiled. "You really believe that, Miss Ellen. All me hear them pass two days, I made my mind up. It doesn't matter if anybody thinks my idea sounds stupid or not. I am going to study hard and pass that scholarship next year. It is my last chance to take it before I turn twelve next May. I will save money from my stone art business and figure out a way to earn off the land. One day, I can purchase a plane ticket to see my father in America. Yes, Miss Ellen. I am going to America. I am not afraid of anything anymore."

29

As Perennial As The Blue Mountains

It's been two weeks since the Flowers buried Roderick's grandma. He spent as much time as he could prepping for the scholarship. He heard that students who passed scholarships and go to high school usually get good government jobs and make money. For months, that is all he could think about, scholarship and making money.

Roderick was called to the headmaster's office for the second time since he started Perennial. He was to meet him at the beginning of the first period in the office; the children called it the Throne Room because he sat in a big chair like those in a palace. The first time he was called to the Throne Room was after he had missed so many days when he ran away from home. It wasn't a great encounter and Roderick did not know why he was being summoned today.

It was eighty-five degrees and climbing. The sun had taken up breathing space in every corner of the building, in the hallways, and on the playfield. Morning prayers had just ended and students were returning to their classrooms in single file along the corridor. Roderick spotted the headmaster at the head of the line and he knew it was uniform inspection day. He straightened his epaulet and made sure it fastened properly to his shoulders. His brown shoes were shiny, his khaki pants and shirt were clean, and he smelled like he had a good shower that morning. Roderick liked to dab a little cologne on his collar, but supposedly, the headmaster did not like them wearing cologne or strong perfume at school because it triggered the allergies of others.

Well, today I think I went a little overboard on the rub-rub. O gosh. I hope somebody didn't tell him. Come on Roderick. He is going to smell it and you will be dead meat. "Choops. At least I don't have to worry about my hair. He likes when we comb our hair properly. I will get a pass just for that. Thank goodness I can go to the barbershop more often."

His hands sweat, his nose tickled as water popped one pore at a time. *Listen Roderick, your only concern right now is to pass the scholarship. Stick to the plan. Don't worry about what may happen in the Throne Room. Grandma Tata is with you.*

"Good morning, Mr. Eldemire," Roderick said when the headmaster got to him.

"Step aside, young man."

He pulled me out of the line; everybody is looking at me now. Where is the Jolly Crew to just create a little ruption so he can forget about me? Miss Chloe she is goodie-goodie, she never gets in trouble. At least she is always in my corner. O well.

After the headmaster finished inspecting the students, some went with the Home Economics teacher to wash their dirty uniforms and the rest went to class. Roderick waited in the headmaster's for him to get off the phone.

Hurry up. Give me my punishment. Let me get back to class. I want to hear what I got for my composition. Still struggling with English grammar and can't miss class. Huumm.

He pouted, folded his arms and tensed his face.
Squeak.

The glass door opened. Roderick looked up at the towering Mr. Eldemire standing there. "Come in, young man. Sit there."

"Am I in trouble, sir?"

"Why do you think you are in trouble?"

"I don't know. I was just fretting."

"Not today. I called you in to let you know how proud I am of your hard work."

"Proud, sir!" Roderick scrunched his forehead, looked steadfastly at the headmaster who kept pacing the area in front of his desk.

"When you came to this school two years ago, you were way behind. I have watched you stay late for extra lessons, create an art club, mount an art exhibit, enter the inter-school's art competition, help your teachers and still travel a long way to your new home in Cherry Gardens. I know you had some tough times, but so many students here have it much worse than you." He took out a sheet of paper.

That's my paper. What is he doing with it?

"I have here in my hand your composition. Miss Lawes wanted me to read it because she is so proud of how far you have come with your writing."

"I passed it, sir? I am not that good at grammar. It is still hard for me."

"You did exceptionally well. I am amazed at the way you handled the topic, "Zinc Fence Boy." Is this about a real person?"

"Yes. It is about a real boy I met when I ran away from home. His name is Joseph, but we call him Jojo."

"Why did you choose to write about him?"

"It was easy for me to write about him because I know him and his problem so well. I didn't have to burst my head to make up a story. I wanted to write about him because he is very poor, but he has dreams of becoming a big singer. He hopes to afford enough to get out of the ghetto, sir.

Sometimes I sit down and worry that he might get mixed up in badness and lose his way.”

“You are so young to be that thoughtful. Anyway, don’t worry too much about Jojo. He will make it out all right.”

“I hope so, sir. I really hope so. It doesn’t look very promising. Maybe one day, I can help boys like Jojo to stay out of trouble and make it out of the ghetto.”

“That’s commendable. In the meantime, practice and think positively so you can take the scholarship in three weeks. You will know if you are successful at some time the summer. I see this is your only opportunity, so make it worth your greatest effort. Writing as well as you do, I am confident you will succeed in the examination. Here, I want you to wear this Library Captain badge.” The headmaster pinned it onto Roderick’s shirt. “You have earned the respect of your peers and teachers, especially our Librarian, Mrs. Rhone. She would like you to help her stack the book shelves and help a student in Class One who is struggling with reading.”

“Me? Library Captain, sir!”

Stack the bookshelves. Help someone to read. Meeeeeeeeeee?

“Yes. One more thing.”

“What is that, sir?”

“This letter came from the Cultural Office. Read it.” The headmaster gave Roderick the letter and smiled.

“Congratulations, Roderick Brissett. Your sculpture, ‘Girl in My Dream’ won first prize in the inter-school’s art competition.’ I won, sir. I won!” Roderick sprung up, spun around, ran fast on the spot, waved the letter. “I won!”

"Make the best of the rest of the school year. Now run along to class. Here is a note for Miss Lawes saying I held you in my office."

"Mr. Eldemire, thank you." Roderick ran through the door, down the corridor. "We won! We won! Mona, we won!"

Five months later and Roderick and children all over the island who took the scholarship in January waited anxiously for the results. The trades blew over the Blue Mountains carrying the fresh smell of the giant Eucalyptus tree that grew in all its majesty behind the tool shed. The brilliant yellow sun rose ceremoniously, as promised. Red-breasted hummingbirds hopped from tree to tree, twittering their one-love lyrical descants. The helper had set the breakfast table on the deck overlooking the swimming pool. Ackee and salt fish, fried dumplings, hot cocoa with coconut milk, berries, Otaheite apples, pineapples and ripe bananas made for a very delicious early morning experience. Being with Miss Ellen was Roderick's dream come true. He would not spend the time alone because Miss Ellen invited Chloe and her dad to breakfast that morning.

"What a year it has been eee, Chloe? All I want today is to get my hands on the newspaper to see if the Ministry of Education published my name. I want to see if I passed a scholarship for high school."

"Roderick. That is not a bad thing to want today."

"I was worried about the writing section."

"O come on, Roderick Brissett. All those compositions you got all As in the past year. What you talking about? When it came to arithmetic, you were always better than me. I knew it. Dad knew it, too."

"I am so tired from all the studying we did, morning, noon and night. I hardly got much sleep."

"Well, better we do it now when we are young." Chloe twisted her pigtails. Thanks for being my friend Roderick. At least I had somebody to hang out with sometimes."

"O Chloe. Is me must thank you. All the things I went through, you were my friend in it."

"We sound so mushy mushy."

They laughed so loud it startled the dog from his cool out spot.

"I made up my mind to move up here with Miss Ellen after the funeral so I could get some peace of mind to study for the scholarship. Although it was a long trip back and forth to school, it was worth it. At least it was only for six months."

"We don't know if we pass the scholarship yet."

"Listen, Chloe. I passed. I know I passed. My name is in that newspaper, you hear me? Miss Ellen and your father are coming now. Good morning."

"Good morning," Miss Ellen and Mr. Goodman said, one after the other. Mr. Goodman pulled out Miss Ellen's chair so she could sit, then he sat.

"I just enjoy being here these past few months, although I run in and out for school. Now I get to settle down and see how everything is so pretty up here, Miss Ellen. The pool, the garden, the breakfast. I have never seen anything so beautiful first thing in the morning. It is just like the colors in my paint set." Roderick said with a smile.

She smiled. "I am glad you like it here. I try to make myself comfortable so I can do my art."

"He's right, Miss Ellen. It is perfect here," Chloe said. "Right, Daddy?"

"Yes. It is perfect here."

"Today is a big day for you children and all those who braved it to take the scholarship." Ellen picked up her cup of tea and sipped.

"Whether or not you passed the Common Entrance Examinations, you were already winners," Mr. Goodman assured.

Roderick looked at Chloe. Frowned. "Passed the common entrance or not? Mr. Goodman is not serious. I have to pass. Deep inside of me, I know I worked double, triple hard to pass. I know I pass." He reached for a slice of hard dough bread and plastered it with Ackee and salt fish.

With a glint in his eyes, Mr. Goodman said, "I admire your confidence, young scholar."

"I agree with you, Isaac. They have both worked very hard," Ellen continued as she savored every bite.

Roderick felt Chloe's hand reach under the table and pinch him on his thigh. He shot up. "We pass, Chloe." They laughed.

"We better!" Chloe said with a smirk on her face.

Looking over at Mr. Goodman and Miss Ellen, Roderick sensed they were enjoying a little private chat because they smiled so widely, but he could not hear.

"Although I only spent two years at Perennial school, I got a lot of help from you and Mr. Goodman."

No one spoke for a while except for the birds chirping and the lawn mower running next door.

So much food. O God! So much!

"You all right, Chloe?"

"Yes. I was just thinking that this was my second time taking the scholarship. The first time I was ten, and I got a half scholarship. Daddy said I should try again since I had two more tries. Remember that, Daddy?"

"O yes. I remember. Do you feel you were better prepared this time?"

"Yes, Daddy," Chloe finished her porridge, took a deep breath.

After breakfast, Roderick walked over to Mr. Goodman, who was sitting in a chaise chair at the pool reading the newspaper. "Can we look for our names now, sir?"

Mr. Goodman said yes, smiled and pulled out the scholarship section and gave it to him.

"Thank you, sir. Come Chloe, let's look for our names." Roderick spread the newspaper on the deck and began the fretful search for their names.

"Well, B comes before G, lady," Roderick felt the need to compete ever so slightly.

"I know that. You chose Ardenne and Calabar."

They struggled through the oversized pages of the newspaper.

"It would appear as though there are more children whose last name starts with B." He ran his fingers along the page.

"You are moving too slow. Roll over, mister." Chloe used both hands to move swiftly through the alphabet. "Brissett. See Brissett here. Roderick A. Brissett! You pass full scholarship for Ardenne High School!"

"Mi pass! Mi pass fi true! Let me see. Let me see."

They jumped up so frantically they slipped on the

paper and ripped it. They hugged each other, danced around until they were giddy.

Peeping over to see if the adults were looking, he saw Mr. Goodman looking over his section of the newspaper and Miss Ellen cleaning her glasses. Mr. Goodman and Ellen clapped heartily, as if it was their first time knowing the results.

"All right, children. We have one more," Ellen reminded them.

"The G them plenty too," Roderick pointed out.

"For real." Chloe sat up, crossed her legs, and leaned towards the paper on the ground. "Gager, Garcia, Gayle, Geller, Gooden, Goodman… Chloe A. Goodman. Holy Childhood High School. Government Scholarship! Yes. Yes. Yes. Yes!" Chloe screamed her head off.

Cheering her on, Roderick said, "Although you had two tries, getting a top scholarship makes me proud of you, girl."

"You think you are glad? Is me glad that you pass. Now you don't have to take so many buses to high school. You are much closer living here."

"I won't have to wake up so early and go out in the dark to get to school on time. That was the toughest part, but I got used to it."

The children observed Mr. Goodman and Ellen, who got up, walked over and hugged them.

"We are proud of you both." Mr. Goodman's admiration was palpable.

"Definitely pleased with the hard work you both put in." Ellen's voice gushed with sincerity and pride as she embraced the children.

"O Miss Ellen, I am glad that I came to stay here with you. I am even happier you said yes."

Chloe streamed rivers of tears. "Well, well, huh, huh, Beverly Hills is not far from here. We can visit one another regularly."

Roderick turned to Mr. Goodman. "I still don't believe this, sir. I don't know what to say."

"You don't have to say anything. From the beginning, the discipline you displayed for your studies was commendable. Once you got those books in your hands, you never stopped reading and asking questions. You went through a lot. Now, you deserve to have a better life."

Stretching his hands towards Chloe, Roderick held hers, looked in her eyes. "Don't cry." His stomach tightened. "You are a real, real friend," Roderick searched her wet face for that usual smile he got when she was happy. "I have not forgotten my other friends, though. Django, Curtis and Imogene have one more year. Jojo and the boys have a little way to go. Hope they are doing fine. They want to do the music thing so badly, I worry about them."

"Everybody will be fine. One day you will go back and see them," Chloe comforted him.

"What about Maas Suraj? I didn't get to tell him I was moving away."

"But you didn't know. Stop worrying your head."

The two families spent the next hour talking and laughing about life. It was time to say their goodbyes. A slight drizzle popped in to say hello and no one seemed to care. They stood around in it.

"Bye Miss Ellen. Bye Roderick." Chloe waved. "I will call you on the telephone tomorrow, Roderick."

"Yes. Call me. Ba bye, Chloe." Roderick tumbled a cartwheel.

"Keep up the good work. You and your dad are welcome to visit anytime," Ellen said as she bent down to prune a few Josephs' Coat plants by the door.

"Thank you, Miss Ellen."

Ellen reached out her hand to shake Mr. Goodman's hand. He did not shake her hand; instead, he bowed graciously and kissed the delicate rising of her coco-tanned knuckles.

The children giggled.

"We have two wonderful children to raise," a smiling Mr. Goodman proposed with certainty.

Ellen placed her right hand on her chest, looked over her glasses and tested lightheartedly.

"We?"

Roderick smiled, looked at Chloe, who splayed her palms by her slightly raised shoulders, all wide-eyed. He was at a loss for words to express his joy except to say, "All this for me!"

The fact that he had successfully earned a scholarship and the rough times were fading beyond the Kingston skyline was a lot to process.

"Now I get to go to high school!"

He swung around the post on the deck, yelled out to the birds and the butterflies that played hopscotch in the hedges. The Blue Mountains gave a nod to his strength and courage. A steady wind blew over the mountains, echoing the cries of Maroon children whipped for learning to read. Roderick felt like fire was in his bosom. He took off his shirt and dived into the pool, submerging his body three times. He wiped his face, spread his arms wide, pulled them in and curled them across his chest as if he had gathered all the morning air. He breathed deeply. He looked up and out at the horizon, as a double rainbow wrapped itself around the clouds. He could taste its beauty like cotton candy melting syrupy sweet inside his daydream. Roderick thought about his life in Olympic Gardens, the pain from overwork, the beatings and the friendship he felt with Chloe. Now freedom shone like a sun dance on top of the enduring Blue Mountains. For life became stones on which to paint his sorrows and sketch his rainbow dreams.

"This is sweet."

ACKNOWLEDGMENTS

Thanks to all who read *No Life in Olympic Gardens*, the first in this literacy fiction series and those who attended the *Performance Book Signing Experiences*, you have been the catalysts for continuing the journey with Roderick Brissett in this next novel, *Long Walk to Cherry Gardens*;

To Faith P. Nelson, book publishing consultant and coach, thank you.

To Chris Eboch whose content editing encouraged me to improve my knowledge of plot development and make the book more accessible to children, thank you. You are now an Honorary Jamaican Language reader.

To Pamela De Mont-Sims who I can call upon for those hard to find histories about Jamaican culture, thank you.

To my sister Sandra Bonner-James for beta reading at several stages of the writing process and for giving me sound advice about language usage, I am indebted.

To my sister Antonette-Bonner Wiggan, my go to for all things Jamaican, our childhood memories, you name it, she has answers, thank you.

To my brother Dwight who makes sure I drink enough water to keep me hydrated and tells me to get some rest, thank you.

To my sister Evadney who calls just to say, "I love you," please know that love is the reason I write, thank you.

To Jennifer Ubiwa who believed in this project from the very beginning, thank you, my friend.

To Devon "Bobsled" Harris for encouraging me during the writing process to tell an authentic story he recognizes and to *Keep on Pushing*, thank you.

To my dear friends, Dorret, Sadie and Marcia on whom I call with questions about aspects of Jamaican political life not easily found in books, thank you.

Heartfelt thanks to the Sisal Publishing team for your guidance and support from pre-production, production and post-production; so much had to be done to get the print book into the hands of readers and e-book on e-reader devices, thank you.

To my daughter, Keisha and granddaughter, Jamaya, I am forever grateful for your support that makes me know every day that together we can achieve greatness, thank you.

Literacy Gateway Institute is an educational solutions business that trains parents to become co-teachers, develops and implements learning systems, literacy curricula and wellness tools to improve student performance in content area and standardized tests. The institute facilitates results-driven interaction between educational institutions and the communities they serve.

literacygatewayinstitute.com

www.ingramcontent.com/pod-product-compliance
Lightning Source LLC
Chambersburg PA
CBHW051159190726
48288CB00006B/1716